HOW TO DEFEAT
A HERO

The Henchman's Survival Guide, Book 2

By J Bennett

ACKNOWLEDG-MENTS

Thank you to my critique crew, Hummingbird, Vine, The Fat Tubist, and Wild Infinity

Cover by Sinisa Poznanovic

LIST OF ACRONYMS

- FIG - Fame Is the Game
- TAW -- Tech Always Wins
- NBD -- No Big Deal
- BGR -- Betrayal Gets Ratings
- RoS -- Ratings or Swiped
- VRIR -- Virtual Reality Is Reality
- PIC -- Pain Is Currency
- RAE -- Ratings Are Everything
- HALC -- Hustle a Little Currency
- RTS -- Ride the Storm

CHAPTER 1

We are a city of great deeds, great sacrifices, and great heroes. There's no place like Big Little City. ~ Mayor Grimbal Wisenberg, 14th Re-dedication of The Hero Statue

~

There are plenty of brill opportunities to wreak havoc upon Big Little City, which is why it's so disappointing that we're on our way to kidnap the mayor.

How unoriginal.

I'd expected something better on my first mission as a henchman for The Professor.

Let's just be clear about this. Every two-cent vil who wants to grab a little fame has taken a shot at nabbing Mayor Grimbal Wisenberg. I'm guessing Wisenberg orders his window replacements in bulk.

Leo's a canny producer. During our henchman tryouts, he revealed a knack for throwing well-considered and thoroughly unhappy surprises at us. So why did he devise such a cringey launch of The Professor's semi-reality show?

Course, I can't show my disappointment. The cams are rolling as the rental van trundles us to our devious destination. That means my face is frozen into an expression of intent seriousness. Squished between Sequoia and Mermaid in the back row, I close my eyes and remind myself to think of them by the new henchman handles. Sequoia is Nitrogen and Mermaid is Arsenic. It'd be just the perfect launch to my henchman career if I blurted out the nicknames I made up for them during tryouts. A streetlight washes over us, glinting on the lab goggles pulled over our eyes. When we pass the light, darkness descends again, halted only by the glowing LEDs in each of our bowties.

I glance out the window as we approach Iconic Square, home to the governor's mansion. Traffic is light. A tourist trolley rumbles past, only half-filled. It's been two weeks since Shadow's last attack left five tourists and two police officers dead. Our tourist revenue still hasn't recovered from the rampage.

Shadow. Even the thought of that unhinged vil makes me shiver. He's the whole reason I had to turn to this henchman gig in the first place. I push the image of his glowing red eyes out of my mind. I need to focus on the mission and the part I'm supposed to play. Cue about a thousand butterflies in my stomach.

Some lameitude K-pop song hums over the van's speakers. It's obvi that The Professor didn't pay the extra fee to either choose his own music or request silence. It's also a big ego slap that we're rolling to our first mission in a rental van owned by the city. Our particular ride includes an image of Shine, the city's most glam sidekick, splashed across the side hawking toothpaste.

Irony of ironies.

The rental van and the shrill K-pop are more reminders that our show is on the tightest of budgets. PAGS doesn't mess around anymore. The media conglomerate gives you just enough funds to cobble together a few eps, and if the audience doesn't heart you, they'll swipe your show out of existence. This is true even for the big comeback of The Professor, one of the town's very first and most famous vils. These days, he's got to prove himself and grab eyes just like every other newbie sponsored vil or cape.

We pass the huge statue of The Hero bathed in soft lights in the center of the Square. The synthetic marble statue of a female hero embracing a small child looks suspiciously like Beacon.

What if our town's most popular cape shows up tonight and tries to stop us? Even without all the expensive modifications in her suit, her combat skills are legendary. Also, she has a particular bone to pick with us considering we have something that belongs to her.

Why does my fitted lab coat suddenly feel so tight?

The van rolls into a dark alley a block away from the mayor's mansion. The City Council conveniently overlooks the need to add adequate lighting to alleys throughout Iconic Square and the rest of Biggie LC.

As soon as the van stops, Mermaid heaves open the van's door and leaps into the night, her body fluid as water. The cam drone latched to the outside of the van rises up in the air, drinking in our gallant exits. I begin to squirm my way over the seat toward the door, but Gold beats me to it from the front row. He flashes me a devious smile as his shoulder bumps me back. He jumps out into a crouch and looks around before quickly scuttling against the wall next to Mermaid.

That lens grabbing bastard! Gold is all charm and betrayal wrapped in a toothy grin. We're supposed to be a team, but no one wants to end up on the cutting room floor when Leo's done polishing this latest ep. FIG–

Fame Is the Game, at least here in Biggie LC.

Biting my cheek, I finally make my way out of the van. The lasso on my hip snags a seatbelt nub and I have to yank it loose as I stumble into the night.

Great moment, Iron, I think to myself, using my new henchman name.

I'm a little soothed to see that Sequoia also manages to blow his van exit. Course, he has an excuse. It's not exactly easy to leap from a small van when you're roughly the size of a moose. The ripped sleeves of his green lab coat and glowing red bowtie make him look particularly menacing. If only he didn't give me a sheepish smile as he shoves himself through the seats and lands on the sidewalk. That little expression is a dead giveaway that under all those hard muscles he's a huge softy.

Mind your face, I mouth silently to him. It's something that Tickles the Elf emphasizes all the time on his blog, *The Henchman's Survival Guide.*

Sure, 90% of what we do won't make it into the ep, but you never know which frame or reaction Leo will use. This gig isn't a stepping stone toward future greatness for me; it's a paycheck, but I still need to stay relevant enough so Leo doesn't get any ideas about killing off my character in some heart-wrenching plot to gush The Professor's ratings.

Speaking of the boss, it's his turn to make a grand exit. He wobbles unsteadily, playing heavily on his "bum" leg. And then he's out of the van, leaning against his cane, looking around. The Professor is a sight to behold. His bowtie swirls in shifting colors and the ragged edges of his burned lab coat flap against his thin frame. Wires along the hem of his coat spit bright sparks.

This is not The Professor of the old days. Sure, his frizzy silver hair is the same and his deep laugh is iconic as ever, but he's gotten a gritty makeover. Even his voice has taken on gristle as he whispers to us.

"Elements, you know the plan. Wisenberg is an ally of Beacon's and all the other heroes in this town. I want him in my lab."

I nod stoically. Gold steps forward. "We won't let you down, Professor," he says, his voice about three octaves lower than usual. Typical lens grabber move.

The five of us turn, and Mermaid leads the way as we slink down the alley onto a small backroad that will take us right to the mayor's mansion. Her long legs eat up the distance and I keep my eyes on her swinging blonde ponytail. As we walk, I unlatch the lasso from the belt beneath my lab coat. Truth is, even after two weeks of practice with my signature weap, I'm still the definition of sadpocalypse. I'd begged Leo to let me use something different—a stun laz gun like what Gold grips at his side would be hardy—but Leo rebuffed me.

It's my own fault. I'd sloppily used a lasso in my iconic move to join the Professor's henchman squad two weeks ago, and now Leo claims that viewers associate me with the weap.

When we reach the mayor's house, a city cam drone spots us, pulling out of its lazy auto circuit and zooming down for a closer look. I feel like gulping. The low-paid city employee currently humaning the bank of cams operated by the City Council will immediately know what's going down and will place a call.

If this were a normal town, that call would go straight to the police department. Not in Big Little City. Instead, the watcher will tip off some hero who needs a ratings boost. We've probably got 20 mins at the most to get this kidnapping done before some cape crashes our party.

"Nitrogen, do your magic," Mermaid says.

"It's not magic, it's science," Sequoia hisses back. I can see the tension in his shoulders, but his hands are sure as he pulls a variety of small vials from the intricate belt strapped around his waist. Opening up a collapsible dish, he begins to pour. All of this—the belt and the vials—was Sequoia's idea, and Leo was canny enough to recognize the genius of it. Sequoia may look like a brute on the outside but he's the smartest among us. Positioning him as the group brain was the perfect complement to his real-life personality and it goes against the grain of expectations.

"Hurry," Gold hisses. He makes a show of glancing around nervously, the golden beads in his dreadlocks winking with the movement. Good idea. I've been watching Sequoia quickly stir his solution. That's not going to get me lens time. I look around too and swing my lasso loosely back and forth as if I'm ready for a fight

"K," Sequoia sighs under his breath. He moves forward to apply the solution to the door, but Mermaid grabs the dish from him and splashes its contents across the scan pad.

"Hey!" Sequoia hisses. His solution quickly burns through the security pad. Sequoia makes to push the door open, but Mermaid slams through with a massive kick that Leo will def put in the ep. I'm half-disgusted, half-jealous with Mermaid's superior fame instincts. She takes off inside the house and Gold shoves past Sequoia to follow her.

"Lens grabbers," I whisper to Sequoia and shrug.

Gold and Mermaid want to play that game? Then we're going to have to play too. Sequoia bounds into the house and I follow. Mermaid and Gold have already triggered the motion sensor lights so my goggles automatically switch off from night vision mode.

Sequoia and I run down a plushly carpeted hallway filled with portraits of previous mayors. I glance at the first portrait in the row and recognize Luna Renaldo. She was the original mayor of Biggie LC after PAGS turned this place into the very first semi-reality town. Rumor is she was forced into retirement after a kidnapping-related back injury led to a very strong appetite for Mellows. Being the mayor has its perks, but it also means you live with a bullseye on your chest.

By the time Sequoia and I make it to the mayor's bedroom door, Gold and Mermaid have already taken out his two robo guards. I have to admit I'm a little relieved. My fighting skills are decent, but I'm about 50/50 on successfully lassoing Sequoia, even when he stands 10 meters away from me and doesn't move.

Gold shoulders through the mayor's bedroom door and we spill into the room.

Mayor Grimbal Wisenberg shoots up from his bed, revealing a stylish pair of silken blue pajamas. His jet black hair is perfectly combed and oiled, and I can't help but notice the sheen of powder on his face.

The mayor's got cams all over this place, along with motion detectors, and the fighting outside his door couldn't have been quiet. It's obvi he knew we were coming, but he turns in a perfect performance of surprise. His mouth drops open in a round O and he sputters, "What... what is the meaning of this?"

"My hypothesis is that your capture is imminent,"

The Professor says behind us. We henchmen peel away to let him step forward, though I notice Gold only takes half a step back so that he's almost shoulder-to-shoulder with our boss. That's guaranteed to get him in the shot.

"The Professor!" Wisenberg gasps dramatically. "Where are my guards? GUARDS!"

"You will find that they are otherwise occupied," The Professor says. He nods toward Sequoia who takes a step forward holding a newly concocted vial in his hand. I move in behind swinging my lasso lightly. I hope my expression is menacing. I also dearly hope Sequoia's formula works to knock out the mayor so I can just tie the rope around him instead of trying to lasso him.

"I would like to formally extend an invitation to tour of my lab," The Professor says. His voice is deep and liquid, every word perfectly articulated for the cams. He is in his element. Though this caper is clearly beneath him, he's playing his role with all his gusto.

"No. Never! You won't get away with this," Wisenberg cries. He scrambles from the bed and puffs out his chest. "I'm not going anywhere with you!"

"I'm afraid the lab tour is mandatory as is participation in my experiments," The Professor says. He gives Sequoia another nod. The big henchman takes one step toward the bed and then the bedroom door splinters open.

We all spin around and I have to force my mouth closed. It's too early for capes to arrive from the City Council tip. But tell that to the three muscled figures standing in the doorway, each wrapped in glinting carbon fiber suits. The twisted, toothy masks on their faces are even scarier in person than on the eps my roommate swoons over.

"Mayor Wisenberg, might we be of a little assistance?" asks Argon, leader of the Dragon Riders.

The Professor is flummoxed for just a sec and then recovers. There's only ever one play when capes show up. For the first time tonight, I'm in sync with my fellow henchmen as we all turn to face our adversaries. My hands are so sweaty I worry about dropping my pitiful lasso.

"Get em!" The Professor growls.

And then, on my first henchman mission, all hell breaks loose.

CHAPTER 2

Sure, the suits have some useful features, but what really gives us our power is the heart beneath. ~ Argon, The Dragon Riders, interview with Reena Masterson

~

Four henchmen versus three Dragon Riders. You'd think we'd have a decent chance, especially because Mermaid and Sequoia are both canny fighters. You'd be wrong.

TAW – Tech Always Wins.

The Dragon Riders are the top trending cape team in town which means their sponsors are pouring dollars into costume upgrades and advanced weaps. As Candor leaps toward me, his anti-grav boots propelling him halfway across the mayor's bedroom, this point really hits home. I scramble out of the way as his feet cut through the space previously occupied by my head. He lands solidly. Holographic fire ripples down his green-and-purple helmet.

"I've always preferred brawn over brains," he says and waits. I realize it's my turn to throw down a witty retort.

"Well, I've always preferred, uh... my lasso!" I manage.

His lips pucker in confusion. Witty rejoinders are not my strong suit. Sadly, neither is my lasso. I swing it and toss it at him. We both watch the loop rise and then slap down on the floor just in front of Candor's bulky boots.

He snickers. That stings.

His amusement doesn't last for long. I lunge at him and greet his face with my elbow. Here's the difficulty, though–TAW.

TAW, TAW, TAW.

My blow was strong enough to loosen teeth and turn his nose into a blood gusher... that is if he weren't wearing a super-strong, carbon fiber mask. As it is, his head snaps back and he releases an un-gallant profanity as he stumbles. I grab onto his helmet, jerk his head low, and slam my knee into his abdomen three times in quick succession. I may have zero skill at lassoing but my three years of mixed martial arts training do come in handy.

Time for my finishing move. I hit Candor with a swift jab to the groin. Well, it *would* be a finishing move to any male not wearing what accounts to full body armor. As it is, Candor shoves me away with an irritated grunt. He straightens up and thrusts his palm at me. I hear a faint whine and notice his gloved hand glows with energy. *Dragon's Howl,* I think and a feel a tiny moment of pride for remembering the name of his concussive weap.

Then it hits me and I'm airborne.

I fly through an artful wicker closet door and slam into something solid. Pain ratchets through my shoulder and I look up, dazed, at a woman who wears a silken black negligee and stockings.

"Have you come to play?" she asks and gives me a saucy wink.

This is right about the time I notice the small whip

clutched in her hand as well as her cat ears, striped markings on her face, and large, emerald cat eyes. So the rumors are true. Mayor Wisenberg is a robo rubber. Seems like he's got a bit of a feline fetish as well.

I sit up and groan.

"You seem to be in physical distress," the sexbot says and her whiskers tremble. "Would you like me to contact the authorities?"

"Nope, I'm hardy," I mutter. "Just got hit with a Dragon's Howl. NBD."

I push myself to my knees inside the mayor's closet. Colorful pant legs and embroidered suit jackets dangle around me.

"You're not doing well in this fight," Bob informs me. The scruffy face of my Totem shines on a holoscreen emanating from the thin silver Band on my wrist.

"Didn't I put you in sleep mode?" I grumble. The room outside the shattered closet door has taken on an odd tilting motion.

"I can automatically override that setting when a major life event is occurring," Bob explains. "Would you like me to record your defeat for future posting when your Iron Stream goes live?"

"Thanks for the generous offer, but no." I slowly put my feet underneath me. Nothing seems broken, but that might be a temporary state of affairs as Candor stomps toward me.

"It doesn't take a scientist to know a life of crime doesn't pay," he says as he grabs the lapels of my red lab coat and lifts me up. No doubt his costume is giving him serious strength assistance.

"Neither does contracting herpes," I mumble.

J Bennett

Beneath the decorative dragon teeth lining his mask, his real teeth grind. "THAT is a vicious rumor!" he hollers and slams me into the wall for emphasis.

"Oh my, this level of violence is not appropriate," says the sexbot from the closet.

"And who are you?" Candor asks.

"My name is Kitty," she replies brightly. "I am just a normal member of the cleaning staff." Her tail swishes gently behind her.

Over Candor's shoulder, I watch my fellow henchmen struggle against the other two Dragon Riders.

"Get The Professor out!" Mermaid hollers as she gracefully dodges Beyren's sloppy punches. She executes a fancy roll across the mayor's bed, grabbing the comforter as she lands on the other side.

Sequoia and Gold are across the room, double-teaming Argon, who seems like the only Dragon Rider with any real fighting skills beneath his modded costume. He grips chakrams in both hands, each alight with holographic flames.

Sequoia peels away from the fight and rushes toward The Professor, who has been ranting from a safe distance near the door. Sequoia slings our skinny boss over his shoulder like a rag doll. It's not the gentlest of moves but we're all doomed if our villain gets captured.

Can't have a very good vil show with the boss rotting behind bars.

Just as Sequoia turns toward the bedroom door, a figure steps into the entryway blocking it. Candor's hand is tightening on my throat so it might be a hallucination, but I swear this newest visitor resolves into a skinny man wearing a black outfit patterned with

16

white diamonds.

And the cape. Of course the cape. There's only one shigit hero in this town who actually wears a real cape.

"Buddha's eye jelly," I mutter.

Candor looks over his shoulder and his eyebrows fold down into the open wedges of his mask's eyeholes.

"Who's that?" he asks.

"Freeter," I gasp out.

Candor releases another expletive. No sponsored hero wants an unsigned wannabe crimping on his fight. That's a more common problem than you might think here in Biggie LC. Almost everyone in this town plays the Fame Game. If you aren't sponsored then you're striving to be sponsored. That often entails grabbing lens time on sponsored shows any way you can to try and raise your profile.

There's also another reason to despise freeters. They screw things up.

Still pinning me to the wall, Candor yells over his shoulder, "Hey, this is our fight. Tail it!"

"I shall go where justice requires," the freeter replies.

"Huh?" Candor sputters.

"He... always... talks... like... that," I wheeze. It just so happens that this freeter and I have a history. It started with his failed attempt to prevent a bank robbery last month when I was just an innocent patron trying to keep her dollars. He also came to my unnecessary rescue when I was sorta being robbed by a previous coworker. So far, I've been more than unimpressed with his heroic aptitude. The only points he gets in my book are for his dogged determination in the face of a supremely ridic costume, lackluster fighting skills, and zero budget for helpful suit mods and weaps.

"Professor, your dastardly plans shall be thwarted!" the freeter hollers. Whatever inane cliché he's readying for his next verbal volley is shoved back down his throat when Sequoia tucks his head and barrels right into the freeter. The move reminds me of that brutal game they used to play in the olden days, football. The freeter bounces helplessly off Sequoia's massive shoulder and lands on his back.

This is a typical outcome for him.

As I use my quickly dwindling consciousness to appraise my situation, a part of me is glad that Sequoia is making a clean getaway with The Professor. A bigger part of me would really, really like to be able to breathe again.

"Perhaps you should use your safe word," Kitty offers. She still stands inside the closet next to me.

Candor seems indecisive with this new turn of events. His eyes bounce between me, the dazed freeter jamming the doorway, and the retreating villain. It's the opening I need to make my last desperate move.

"Kitty, spank him," I gasp. The sexbot is probs programmed to respond only to the mayor's commands, but if Wisenberg perhaps prefers additional company, he might have opened her command structure.

Kitty smiles and marches out of the closet. "Oh my, you are naughty," she giggles. She playfully smacks Candor on the ass with her little whip. "Down boy!" she says in a husky voice.

"Hey!" he snaps turning his head toward her. It's not much but I'll take it. I kick his shin as hard as I can from a position of no leverage. I feel the impact through my boot and Candor's grip loosens. I drop to the floor gasping in ragged breaths.

Get up. Fight, I think desperately to myself, but all I can do is lift my head and look up at Candor. Beneath the fierce dragon teeth lining his helmet, I see a smirk on his lips. "The Professor might have gotten away, but you won't escape the cleansing fire of justice."

I know what that means. Candor has decided to stop playing with me. He must think he's generated enough fighting footage, and he did get off those two half-decent lines. It'll be enough for his producer to edit a nice little scene for the team's next ep.

Now it's time for him to end our fight, which he could have easily done all along with a Dragon's Fire shot, which is just a fancy stun laz shooter built into his costume. All the Dragon Riders have them. After I'm incapacitated, Candor will dangle me from his sky skimmer, and we'll go for a ride of shame ending at the front door of the Big Little City police station.

That will be the humiliating conclusion to my brief and disastrous career as a henchman.

Candor raises his arm. I tense and prepare to try and dodge the shot.

A blur of movement catches my eye. Gorgeous and fast as a lightning bolt, Mermaid descends upon my foe. Unlike me, she doesn't waste her time throwing punches or kicks into Candor's impenetrable suit. Instead, she drops low and swipes his legs out from under him in a brutal sweep.

Candor slams onto his back, hard enough that I hear his breath punch out of his lungs. I'm yanked to my feet. Mermaid holds me up as I totter.

"T... thanks," I manage. Over her shoulder, I see Breyden hacking at the comforter twisted around his legs with his shimmering heat sword. Smoke billows from the melting fibers. Mayor Wisenberg is nowhere to be found. He probably scampered off to his safe room as soon as the Dragon Riders showed.

He's gone. Our mission is a failure.

"Let's go," Mermaid hollers.

Candor is already regaining his breath. He holds out a shaky arm and the Dragon's Fire ripples just past my shoulder, close enough to make me flinch.

"Should we grab one of the Riders?" Gold asks. He's lingering by the door. His foe, Argon is sprawled on the floor, twitching. It's so not fair that Gold got to choose a gold-plated stun laz pistol as his weap.

Mermaid ponders his questions then decides. "No. Too bulky. We won't move quickly with them."

"They'll have trackers in their costumes, too," I add. Gold and Mermaid aren't from Biggie LC, so they might not know these things.

"Get to the meetup!" Mermaid says to Gold. She looks at me. "You hardy?"

I gather my lasso and nod. Mermaid gives Candor a heavy kick to the chest, knocking him down to the floor again and then races for the door. I make to follow her, then pause. I glance back and a small idea sprouts in my mind. We may not be able to carry a Dragon Rider, but that doesn't mean we have to leave without a trophy.

"Kitty, follow me and make sure you keep up," I say.

The sexbot smiles. "Certainly. I like playing tag."

"I bet you do," I mutter. I look up at the cam drone buzzing overhead and give it a small, devious smile. We may have failed miserably at our first mission, but at least the audience will get a good laugh at the mayor's

How to Defeat a Hero

expense. Serves him right for not locking out Kitty's command structure.

I rush across the bedroom. My entire body throbs in pain, and my neck is already swelling so that it feels like I'm breathing through a straw. I hop over the groaning freeter who still lies in front of the door's entrance.

"Fighting crime isn't a good look for you," I tell him. It's a half-decent line. Too bad I wasted it on a freeter.

"Justice... will prevail," he stammers.

"Not today," I laugh and run out of the mansion with the sexbot close on my heels.

CHAPTER 3

Falling into that solar furnace may have scorched my skin and mangled my body, but it also burned the need for vengeance into my soul! ~ The Professor, S10, E1

~

"This result is utterly, UTTERLY unacceptable!" The Professor barks. Our boss paces in front of us, hands clenched behind his back. His face is tight with anger and he's not just playing for the cams. He is truly raging. "You were supposed to be the best of the best, but you have failed me in such a simple, little request."

Down in The Professor's secret lair, we four henchmen stand on the practice mats at attention to accept his criticism. I keep my expression appropriately chagrined, eyes forward, and try not to focus on how much it hurts to swallow. At least my shoulder feels better. Gold recognized the dislocation right away and popped it back into place. With his background, I'm not surprised he knows his way around minor combat injuries.

"We were supposed to be magnificent. As marvelous as a supernova shockwave rippling across ebony space," The Professor says, shaking his head. His spikey silver hair wafts with the movement. I notice his limp seems markedly improved.

I cut a glance toward Sequoia. My friend's pale, freckled face is slowly turning the shade of a tomato.

The Professor is a personal hero for him, which means this verbal lashing has extra sting. On my other side, Kitty's face is puckered into an unhappy pout. Her tail swishes as she, too, receives this pummeling.

When Kitty and I straggled to the pre-determined rendezvous spot after the caper, Sequoia looked up her model number and figured out how to turn off her GPS tracking. None of us knew how to power down the homing chip in her hand, so now her left arm ends with an empty stump. I'm sure we can find an after-market replacement hand. Plus, there's still plenty a robo can do with one hand and I'm not talking sexy good time stuff. If Kitty is like most high-end sexbots, she also possesses an advanced suite of housekeeping and cleaning programs.

"Professor," Gold murmurs softly. The youngest member of our henchman group hangs his head in an exaggeratedly sheepish manner, but now turns his face up and thoughtfully purses his metallic gold lips. "The Dragon Riders pounced on us within mins of us breaking into the mayor's place. That can't be a coincidence."

"We were set up," Mermaid adds more bluntly.

I nod. I've come to the same conclusion. The next part of the equation is obvi. Someone tipped off the Dragon Riders, someone who knew all about our caper. That list is pretty damn short. I resist the urge to throw accusing glances at my fellow henchmen.

Could be Gold. I know from experience he wouldn't flinch from stabbing us all in the back, metaphorically of course, as long as he could step on our bleeding corpses to grab a better opportunity. BGR – Betrayal Gets Ratings. Still, I don't think it was him. He's conniving but also canny. It's too early to make his move. He needs to build his Persona first, and for that, this show must be a success.

If I had any Loons in my bank account (which is currently at a negative balance), I'd put my crypto-currency on Mermaid as the traitor. According to rumors, the tall and beautiful blonde has been working the semi-reality market for years, hopping from show to show, even appearing on *Z Town.* You don't survive long in *Z Town* with rainbows and kittens. Personally, I wouldn't trust Mermaid to care for a robo pet.

Maybe she's already made a deal with some other producer or sponsor. The Professor's name still carries a lot of weight in this town, and he'd be a big bag for any up-and-coming cape if she could deliver him. Then again, she did save my ass tonight. We wouldn't have made it out of the mayor's mansion without her. And she wasn't exactly making life easy for the Dragon Riders as she handed out beat-downs like personal favors.

"It was shining luck we made it out at all," Sequoia says.

"The only shining luck is that we have Arsenic on our team," Gold replies, tossing a short nod to Mermaid. He's been trying to work a love angle on her for two weeks but she's not having any of it.

"I don't want to hear excuses," snaps a new voice. We turn toward the elevator door, which has just opened. Leo steps out, Goggs perch on his forehead, pushing back his wavy brown hair.

Speaking of absolutely pointless love angles...

I immediately feel my cheeks flush. *You're such a drooling lobotomy,* I think to myself. Sure, Leo is hella handsome in a clean-cut way you don't often see in this town filled with flaunting peacocks. Sure, there's something intriguing about his unflappability. But he's a producer. The head producer of The Professor's show to be exact.

Producers are scum.

Their job is to stick forks in our souls and twist just to amuse a bored audience. Leo has already proven himself to be a brilliant manipulator. He pushed us through a brutal obstacle course during our henchman tryouts and then sniffed out my growing friendship with Sequoia and set us against each other in a winner-take-all combat bout. My entire face hurts just thinking about the huge, freckled fist that put me down. That ep launched last week, and I made a point not to watch it.

Leo is bad news. He is soulless with a wry smile on the side. So, I bite my lip and ignore my quickening pulse as he marches toward us and stands next to The Professor. Instead of laying into us, he waits. I can't help but glance at the small mole under his left eye. The blemish captivates me. He could so easily have it removed but he keeps it, almost like a statement.

"That mission was a disaster," he says quietly, "not because the Dragon Riders showed up unexpectedly, but because you couldn't work together, not for ten minutes."

His amber eyes are weapons, and he cuts us with his disquieting glare. "We created a plan. Everyone had a role, but you were too focused on striving for lens time instead of working as a team. Perhaps if you had, you might've been able to adapt to new circumstances and still succeed."

I look down at my black boots, keeping my chagrined expression in place until I realize that with Leo in the frame this scene won't make the next ep. No viewer wants to see a producer on the screen. It ruins the kay-fabe–that weird little mental trick audiences pull on themselves so that they believe what they know isn't real. Our whole town–all of this cape and vil parody–runs on self-delusion. We pretend it's all real and the audience is happy to play along.

"The Dragon Riders knew we were there," Mermaid says and juts out her hip. She is also clearly aware that this scene won't be used.

"So what?" The Professor snaps. "A minor surprise, something well-trained henchmen should easily be able to overcome."

When he speaks, Leo's voice is soft, but it seems to hold thunder at bay. "I know some of you dream of spinning off, headlining your own show. You mug for lens time at the expense of your villain and, more importantly, at the expense of our storyline and the quality of our show."

He pauses to let his words sink in. "That behavior has to stop or this show is doomed."

I swallow and wince at the pain. Next to me, Kitty processes the fact that he is displeased and lowers her head in shame.

"We are balanced on a knife's edge," Leo continues. "The Professor may have been a big name in the past, but he's got to prove himself just like every new show. Our budget is almost non-existent and so is the patience of our sponsor. We need to deliver ratings, and we need to do it fast or we're over."

His words are a sharp slap. I knew our show was underfunded and lifting huge expectations, but I didn't realize the situation was so dire. Are we really in danger of getting swiped? Sequoia's expression is so crushed I worry he may cry.

"What about Iron's little extra credit assignment?" Gold asks. "That'll shake things up."

Leo nods. "When that ep comes out tomorrow, it'll boost our ratings, but we can't depend on one desperate gambit that happened to pay off."

Desperate gambit that happened to pay off? Anger flickers inside of me, mostly because Leo is right. My one big triumph *was* a despo move, and it only worked because I deceived someone who might have been a friend. I shove away the guilt that sprouts in my gut. *It was the only way to make it on this show,* I remind myself. *I had to do it.*

"The honeymoon is over," Leo is saying. "If we don't deliver good, exciting eps with successful missions, start packing your bags."

The Professor's frown digs deep trenches into his face. He must be under a lot of pressure, too. After all, it's his name in the title of the series.

"In seven days I have to deliver a new episode," Leo says. He takes a moment to gaze at each of us. "That's enough time for one more mission. One more chance to prove this team can get the job done."

Leo turns his back and walks toward a side door that leads to his office. The cam drones pull out of their auto-drifts. I don't even have to adjust my expression; it's already set in the appropriate depressed look.

My mind reels. I'd assumed that with The Professor's name and reputation we'd have a little more leeway, a little more goodwill. But no, we live by RoS just like every other show.

Ratings or Swiped.

That's the hard justice of the Fame Game.

"So, my elements, it seems we need to learn to work together," The Professor says. He paces again. His anger is palpable in each hard strike of the cane. "Perhaps I can assist you all in this worthy endeavor."

A small smile curls on his lips. It's never a good thing when a villain smiles.

***

Ten mins later, the cam drones hover around us on the other side of the lair as we scrub a huge tub of scientific beakers that Sequoia used to practice his concoctions for our heist. This part of the lair includes tables, an ancient chalkboard, and shelves stuffed with random pieces of tech and vials filled with glowing compounds.

Sequoia is at the start of our little cleaning train. He dunks a beaker in a sudsy solution then hands it to me. I stick a little brush down the tube and wiggle it around before handing it off to Gold, who dunks it in another cleansing solution. Mermaid is our caboose, drying the beaker and setting it in a long rack to dry. I could have easily programmed Kitty to do this work for us, but of course that's not the point. The sexbot hums softly to herself as she sweeps the other side of the gym.

"How's the shoulder?" Sequoia asks me.

"Hardy," I murmur and hold out my hand to accept the new beaker. I keep my arm close to my body; my shoulder aches every time I reach out. Fortunately, Sequoia has long arms and places the beaker right into my hand each time.

"That whole speech was a rat's fart," Gold complains as I pass my beaker to him. He's rolled up the sleeves of his lab coat to reveal coffee-colored arms and dunks the beaker without looking or swishing it in the solution as The Professor demonstrated. "Maybe, *maybe* some of us were trying to, you know, amp up the energy of the heist, but that's only because the whole plan was dregs to begin with. Kidnap the mayor? How many times has that been done?"

He looks to Mermaid. "You were iconic, by the way." He subvocalizes a command and his Band illuminates a holographic image of a T-Rex giving two thumbs up with its tiny arms. He wears a glitzy Hawk model Band, but I've noticed a few flakes on the edge of the strap. My guess is it's probs a knockoff—all show, just like its owner.

Mermaid ignores him. Her face is closed, her hands moving automatically. Even with this simple chore, her tall, powerful body moves with uncommon grace. She jerks her head to toss a long strand of sunshine hair out of her face. I wonder what thoughts swirl inside her cunning mind. Is she planning her next betrayal?

Gold frowns. Looks like his romance angle is turning into an unrequited love storyline. He tries again. "Iron was looking a little brittle there. She wouldn't have made it out without you." He flashes me a grin.

"I had... the situation under control," I lie. I hate Gold's smarmy grin, the way he's glamming even during our dour punishment. And also that he's right. Mermaid did save my ass, and I'm still wondering why. My best guess is also the simplest. It made her look good. She was hardy. I was weak. The Professor will see that, and so will all the viewers. She also earned major teamwork points, but if that was her goal how can she be the betrayer?

Who is the mole? If someone in our organization is

feeding info to another producer or sponsor, our next mission is already doomed. Next time we might not even be lucky enough to escape with our freedom and a sexbot.

If we don't fig who it is, our show is dead as steering wheels.

"Iron," Sequoia says softly. I blink and realize he's holding a dripping beaker in front of me. Suddenly I'm looking at my friend in a whole new light. *Could it be?* No, not Sequoia. We've been allies since almost the beginning of the henchman tryouts. Trusting someone is always a risky proposition, and it can be doubly dangerous in a semi-reality town where everyone's looking to get ahead. But I've never regretted my decision to unmask myself to Sequoia and reveal my true identity.

I take the beaker from his hand and shove my little brush inside. Sequoia's real name is Chauncy-Steward-Rine, and he's from Chicago. He has lots of money and a wicked right hook. He's also kind and sensitive and so city soft that I worry about him living in a cut-throat town like Biggie LC.

Big hearts make easy targets.

Unless he's been playing me this whole time. I look at him, at those powerful shoulders and that mop of curly orange hair on his head. He's rolled up the sleeves of his green lab coat, showcasing a constellation of pale brown freckles up and down his arms. He smiles at me. "Wanna practice after we finish cleaning up?"

I sigh and return his smile. We've come this far together, and I've only just gotten Sequoia to stop apologizing for knocking my lights out in our matchup during the final tryout. I can't start doubting him now.

"Sure. Just go easy on the shoulder," I say.

"Arsenic, how about we sneak in a practice sesh?" Gold suggests to Mermaid. "There's so much I can learn from you."

She glances at her Band, a sleek silver Falcon model. (My guess is it's not a fake.) "Maybe another time. I've got to go feed our 'special guest.'" She tosses her towel to Gold, and he catches it against his chest. He frowns as he watches her walk away, whether because his wooing is falling flat or because feeding our "guest" is a prime opportunity for ep time, I'm not sure.

"I'll practice with you," Kitty pipes up. "I especially like to grapple." She bats her eyelashes.

Gold grins at her. "Well, at least someone around here appreciates me."

***

It's late into the night when I leave the lair. Fortunately, I don't have far to travel home. It just so happens that my villainous boss is also my landlord. I take the secret elevator up to the sitting room of the mansion, quickly stuffing my tinted goggles, bowtie, and lab coat into my bag before the doors ding open. I manage to shove my lasso into the top of the bag as I slip past the potted plants and quickly push the trick bookshelf back into place. Someone just walking through would never know a secret elevator to a basement lair even existed.

After The Professor's show was swiped nine years ago, he converted this mansion into a set of two apartments on the second floor and two penthouses on the top floor. I've since learned from his son, Matthew, that he never really needed the rent money. Personally, I think the old man was lonely. He missed being adored and despised in equal parts by the world. It's the whole reason he fought so hard to finally get this relaunch.

I drag myself to the stairs. Usually, I walk up them as they churn, but today I just allow them to carry me up to the second floor. It's easy to spot my butter-yellow door, right across the hall from the gray door of my neighbor's apartment. That neighbor is Leo.

Yep, it's awkward as a turtle-squid hybrid. I try not to glance at the gray door. Try not to imagine him inside, editing footage of me in his office. Try not to wonder what he thinks of me behind those inscrutable amber eyes.

I try. I fail.

Just as I turn to my own door, my simple Swan Band vibrates with an incoming message. I glance down and my heart twists. It's from Alby.

"Open message," I subvocalize and hold my breath. My Band produces a holo-screen that washes up my forearm. On screen, a short vid plays. I watch as a gray cartoon cloud slowly churns across the sun. A single ray of sunshine spikes through, lighting up a small patch of grass below. A little red flower unfurls its petals.

That's it, the end of the vid. No text, no recorded words from my brother, but the message speaks volumes. It's been months since Alby's reached out to me for anything except to plead for money.

I choke in a short breath. This is small—just a silly little cartoon—but it's also huge. The sunshine, the flower. Alby's feeling good, possibly even hopeful. The expensive therapy program I bought for him two weeks ago must be working. *Maybe he's finally getting better,* I think. The thought scares me a little because now I'm the one feeling hope.

No matter what, I've got to keep making the

monthly payments for his therapy software. That won't be a problem when I get my first paycheck from the show in a few days. *As long as the show survives.* Suddenly, I'm not feeling so hopeful anymore. I take one more step forward. My Band syncs with the yellow door, and it swishes open. All I want to do is drag myself to my room, collapse into bed, and play Alby's message about a thousand times. Unfortunately, something stands in the way of that goal.

That something wears a glowing white skirt covered in zippers, a lime green bodice cinched tight for optimal cleavage swell, and matching lime green heels. This week, Lysee's hair is a pile of platinum ringlets swept up and fastened to the crown of her head.

"Oh, darling," she cries upon seeing me stagger inside. "Are you badly beaten? Was Candor as tall as he seems on his Stream? What was his breath like on a scale of 1 to 10?" She giggles. "That must have been AMAZE to be so close to him when he was choking you."

"Yes, amaze," I grumble. "I take it the news is out?"

"Course!" Lysee laughs like I'm a dolt. "It's everywhere. The Dragon Riders already released clips on their Streams, and Rena Masterson did a promo for a segment on the fight tomorrow morning." My roommate lowers her voice to the husky tones of our town's most famous reporter. "Is this new incarnation of The Professor a failed experiment?"

I sigh. Leo won't be happy about any of this, especially since my addition to the team was supposed to be the big twist of tomorrow's ep.

Lysee looks at me expectantly, and I notice her eyelashes are also lime green. My roommate and I tried out for The Professor's show together and swore each other to utter secrecy if either of us should make the cut. It's actually a relief that I don't have to hide my henchman identity from her.

"Things didn't exactly go as expected," I tell her.

"Poor thing," Lysee murmurs. "But what about Candor's breath? Didn't you just love it when he said, 'It doesn't take a scientist to know that a life of crime doesn't pay.' He's so clever. You really need to work on your lines."

"I bet his producer came up with those lines for him," I snap and slump onto the couch. It's obvi my roommate isn't going to let me escape. She carries a lime green purse on her shoulder, which means she's on her way out, probably to a club to try and catch the eye of anyone who looks like they might secretly be a vil, a cape, or a producer. The town's three nightclubs are also regular targets for vil attacks, which could lead to ep time for the terrified, scantily clad patrons. I idly wonder how full the clubs are after Shadow's recent horrific attack. It's almost brave of Lysee to put herself at risk when he's still on the loose.

Lysee totters over to the couch and collapses next to me. "I'm glad you escaped," she says sincerely. "It looked like a close one." A gentle citrus aroma wafts from her smooth, pale skin.

"Yeah, it was," I admit. "We've got some kinks to work out." *Like finding out who's leaking our missions to the capes.*

"About that, see, I was thinking..." Lysee leans into me, grabbing my hand. I can practically feel her endless currents of energy running through me. "Your show needs a big twist. So, what if I accidentally stumble into the secret lair, right? And then I try to tail it, but you nab me and hold me hostage. Oh no!" She throws an arm across her eyes. "And all the other henchmen are like, 'What do we do with this gorg girl?' They all want to end me, but you step up and say, 'No, let's brainwash her.' So, The Professor builds this machine thingy with a metal headband with wires sticking out of it. And I'm screaming and crying. No, no, NOOOOOOO!" Lysee thrashes her head from side to side, her silver hair bouncing over her eyes. "But eventually the machine works. I get brainwashed. I am soooo loyal now. Obsessed with The Professor and the mission, and he makes me a henchman too, and we are best friends because you protected me."

Lysee smiles, big and bright. Her Band shoots up a holographic image of three teddy bears applauding. "It's such a canny storyline, right? And maybe my clothes can get torn, you know, with all the struggling. You should just run it by The Professor or by Leo with your endorsement." She lays her head on my shoulder and looks up at me with her big eyes, tinted green this week. "After all, I helped you become a henchman. You printed your lab coat on *my* 3D printer and used my goggles and my lasso, and I'm soooooo happy for you, but those were *my* things, so really this is such a small favor in comparison."

I force my aching head to nod. Lysee has been pitching me these brill ideas for the past two weeks, desperate to get on The Professor's show. If I wasn't so exhausted, I'd probs feel a little guilty over the irony that I'm living Lysee's dream. She's spent the last five years of her life plotting and flouncing, despo to grab eyeballs, get sponsored, and develop into a Persona, capital P. She wants the adoration and praise, the glittering fame, and a Stream following in the eight digits. She's as striver as they come, and here I am, the room-mate who despises everything semi-reality, grabbing a spot on a show.

"I'll bring it up to Leo," I tell her truthfully but don't mention the part where he'll give me a curt "no" just like he has to all her previous suggestions.

Lysee offers me a dazzling smile. I try to duck away, but she grabs my face and gives me a kiss on the lips. It doesn't matter how many times I tell her I'm not poly-amorous; I think she's still hoping I'll come around.

"Wonderful and waterfalls!" she sings, bouncing up from the couch. She glances at her Band as her hunky and well-behaved Totem, a shirtless genie named Fer-dinand, sends her a message.

"Oh, I'm late!" she squeaks. "My friends are already at the club. Ta, my darling. Wish for a big, messy hos-tage situ at the club for me." She sails out the door, zip-per-covered skirt bouncing with her steps.

As soon as the door slides shut, it's everything I can do not to immediately fall back onto the couch and fuse into its soft material. Instead, I haul myself up and force my legs to carry me to the bathroom and then to the kitchen, where I blindly grab a nutra-pack. I slink to my bedroom, crashing onto the thin mattress like my body was made of rocks.

I peel the wrapper off the food bar and take a bite. I can't fig if this is supposed to be banana-apple fla-vored or the pineapple-raspberry mix. At least it fills my stomach and, thanks to gov subsidies, hardly costs a thing. Nutra-packs are designed by the gov to provide the ideal amount of calories and nutrients for a full meal, and that's all I really need right now.

"Thanks, Sage Anders," I mutter, though I'm pretty sure she and past presidents only subsidize the nutra-packs to prevent widespread protests.

My body is despo for sleep. I only have six hours until I need to leave for class, and yet my mind still buzzes from all that's happened today. We have to find the mole. If our next mission falls apart our show could get swiped.

No job means no paycheck. My universal basic income barely covers my rent, and this is the cheapest place in town, on account of it being in the same building as a villainous lair. If our show goes the way of the glaciers, I won't have enough money to cover material cartridges for Lysee's 3D printer and the boxes of tasteless nutra-packs I live on. There's no way I could afford the extra food I send my mom or Alby's therapy program. I glance down at my Band, at his message sitting in our private Stream chat.

There's one other thing I need this paycheck for. My college tuition. That degree is the only thing I really care about. Once I finished this semester, I'll only have one more year to go until I earn my bachelor's degree in public policy. Then comes grad school to get my master's, which is my ticket out of this lobotomy town. With a master's degree, I'll be able to try and join a think tank where I could work with super-smart people to come with ideas and policies to help our fractured society.

This country needs all the help it can get. Automation has taken so many jobs, stolen so much pride and purpose from people. Towns are dying and shops are shuttered while factories churn with endless robotic parts moving in beautiful harmony without a human in sight.

It's no surprise that so many of us breathers have retreated into virtual reality worlds where adventure and meaning still lurk. Others spend their copious time swimming the Streams, building weightless friendships with Personas (capital P), watching shows pumped out from PAGS's ten media sectors, including over a dozen cape and vil shows that come from Biggie LC here in Sector 8.

So many in my gen have retreated from society, going Hikikomori. Others burn through life as quickly and brutally as possible with the help of Throttle and alcohol. Many just simply slip away into VRIR– Virtual Reality Is Reality.

Like Alby.

My brother, my Twinly One, is deeply damaged and I'm the one who broke him. I can never make that better, but maybe I can fix this world, even just a little. It's a silly, naïve dream, but it's the only shot at redemption that I have.

All of that—the degrees, the think tank—depends on me staying in school, and that requires money. The Professor's show must go on, and I need to find a way to make that happen.

And then it hits me.

Buddha's belly button! I don't know who the mole is, but I know someone who does.

I sit up in bed as thoughts swirl through my mind. This is going to be tricky. I'm the very last person he wants to talk to, but I've got to try. I swing my legs around and stand up, all my exhaustion evaporating as my pulse speeds up.

Time to pay The Professor's "special guest" a surprise visit.

CHAPTER 4

*When you dedicate your life to helping others, you see
the good in people. I put my trust in someone, and that
wasn't a good idea.* ~ Shine, Interview with J Bennett

~

As I move through The Professor's lair, the automatic lights flicker on showcasing the empty training
area and silent lab. Even The Professor has finally retreated to his penthouse upstairs. I open a door at the
back of the main training area and walk down a small
hallway, past empty rooms. My best friend, Matthew
told me that his place used to be filled with half-made
inventions and scuttling media assistants back in the
early days of his father's show. At the end of the hallway, I face three black doors.

"Turn off Band," I subvocalize.

My Band produces a holo-screen that washes across
my forearm. Bob's scruffy face appears. "You sure you
want to do that?" he asks. "It looks like you're doing
something nefarious. That could be good for your Iron
Stream when it goes live."

"Turn off," I say again.

Bob sighs and burps a little. "My command structure requires me to ask one more time. You wanna turn
off your Band?"

"Off!" I hiss and think up a nice and colorful curse for

The Compendium, the company that makes the Stream software that powers all Bands. Finally, the holo-screen disappears, and the soft glow emanating from my Band extinguishes.

I suck in a deep breath and step up to the retinal scanner next to the door furthest to the left. This sloppy plan of mine can go wrong in so many ways. Leo and The Professor will receive a notification as soon as I enter the room. My hope is that both are asleep and won't notice my unauthorized visit until morning.

The door to the room whooshes open and the lights turn on.

A figure lying on a small bed at the back of the cell snaps awake. He tries to jump to his feet, but the shackles clamped to his wrists and ankles have retracted at my entrance, and they whip him back onto the bed. His costume flashes gold in the light.

"Sorry, I didn't mean to startle you," I say as the door closes behind me.

Shine, the world's most beloved sidekick, assesses me as he gains his bearings. "An illicit nighttime visit," he muses. "Have you recognized the error of your ways and decided to free me?" He flashes the famous smile that melts teen hearts. "Or were you just unable to help yourself?"

In his blog, *The Henchman's Survival Guide,* Tickles the Elf is very clear about the dangers of henchmen falling for captured capes. Apparently, this is a common occurrence. There's absolutely no risk of that happening in this case. Adan, the man behind the mask, may be as hot as a summer day in Riyadh, but his ego is just as sweltering. In fact, that arrogant smile of his makes me feel a little less guilty for capturing him in the first place.

"You're wasting good lines," I tell him as I turn toward the door. Perched above it, a small cam records our prisoner night and day, partly for security purposes but also to gather useful b-roll for what I assume will be future prison cell montages. I reach for it, standing on my tip toes, and just barely manage to swat the power button with my fingertip, turning off the cam.

Next to the cam, a round, black device emits a continuous jamming signal. Shine's Wyvern model Band includes a state-of-the-art locking mechanism. We wouldn't be able to pry it from his wrist unless we hacked off his arm. The jammer ensures that he can't get any messages out or that any tracking devices embedded in his costume can't report his location.

I leave the jammer on.

When I turn around to face our prisoner once again, I see that he's stretched out on the bed, hands folded behind his head. In this small, bland room with its simple bed and dry flush toilet in the corner, Shine is a brilliant splash of gold and orange hues. His helmet gleams. I know The Professor would give just about anything to be able to wrench it off Shine's head, but it uses the same locking technology as his Band.

I take a deep breath. "I need your help."

Shine chuckles. "I'm not exactly in the mood to grant favors, especially to you. Though these shackles are awfully itchy. Perhaps you'd care to loosen them?"

"I'm not letting you escape," I tell him flatly.

"Escape? Who said anything about escape? I've grown rather fond of this place. Helps me work on my meditation."

See, these are good lines. Witty and endearing. Lines

that will make tween hearts throb for poor, gallant Shine, trapped deep in The Professor's lair. I ignore a twinge of jealousy at his superior media savvy.

"There are no cams running. Stop flaunting," I tell him.

In response, Shine closes his eyes.

"You knew where The Professor's mansion was. You knew there was a secret elevator in the sitting room," I accuse. I'd found him trying to figure out the key code just before I captured him. "Someone fed you that information. Who was it?" My voice climbs in desperation. "Who is the mole?"

Shine stares at me, his bright green eyes as sharp as ever behind his mask. "Your neck is bruised," he says. "Looks painful."

"It is."

"Show me your Band."

I hold it up so he can see that its lights are dark. "It's off. Not recording."

He gazes up at the ceiling. "You should have sparred with me when I offered, Alice. I could have taught you a thing or two about fighting." He uses my real name on purpose, reminding me that he holds my true identity in his hands.

"I was good enough to beat you," I point out.

"Through treachery," he replies.

"I'm a henchman, not a hero." The words feel dirty as I speak them. Adan is right. I did trick him. I used our friendship–if that's what it is–against him to grab this henchman spot.

"So you'll excuse me if I'm not exactly inclined to further your career," he says. He turns his back to me. "Now run along. I can't sleep with the lights on."

A part of me appreciates his bravado but most of me is pissed by it. I stare at the curve of his back, at those well-defined shoulders and that perfect ass.

Well, two can play at this game.

I lean against the door of his cell. "You missed a chem test last week. Ollie is worried about you. A few of the girls in class are equally distressed." I click my tongue sadly. "Oh, and I almost forgot, the midterm is next week. Pret-ty important."

Shine doesn't respond. It was a poor gambit. I slide to the floor and prop my back against the wall next to the door. "Why does a famous sidekick need a college degree anyway?" I ask. It's a question I've pondered a lot over the last two weeks.

"It's a good way to meet women," he says, his voice muffled by his pillow.

"I think it gives you a chance to feel normal," I say. "You live your whole life in this heroic fantasy. Flashy costume. Risky missions..."

"Adoring fans," he adds.

"Mobs of fans who don't even know a true thing about you," I clarify. "It's exciting. Brills and thrills. But it's not real."

"Wow, those are some deep thoughts," Shine says. "Let me guess, you're a psychology major."

"The whole world loves you, but they don't even know who you are," I say.

"Neither do you." Bitterness laces his voice.

I pull my legs up to my chest and rest my chin on my knees. I'm not really sure what I'm doing, but at least we're talking. That note of anger in his voice is the first real emotion he's shown since his capture.

"I know that you're driven," I say softly. "And you're

smart. You've got amaze lens instincts. I bet Beacon saw you as a threat. That's why you came here by yourself. You were trying to spin off. You just needed a big score. Bagging The Professor would have impressed sponsors, shown them you can stand on your own."

Shine is silent. I lean my head back against the wall and listen to the mild throb in my shoulder. My eyes are heavy with exhaustion, and my mind feels loose, like a hem unraveling.

"Beacon never keeps her sidekicks for more than a few years," I say. We both know Shine's been working with her for almost four. "She's always looking to upgrade. Switch things up. Re-energize her viewers to gush her ratings. You were trying to spin off before she retired you."

Only one of Beacon's sidekicks has ever managed to successfully spin off. Bright was her longest-serving sidekick. They worked together for five years, and there was something truly special about their relationship. They had a bond that seemed to go beyond just the storylines. Bright was smart and beautiful and savvy enough to save her earnings. She spun off in a spectacular fashion, betraying Beacon and transforming herself into the villain, Cleopatra.

Rumor has it, Beacon tried everything to squash Cleopatra's career. She sank her sponsors, pulled all the strings she could with the City Council to block Cleopatra's show. But Cleopatra self-funded her entire first year. She bribed new City Council members and grabbed a spot on PAGS's platform. Eventually, her show thrived, though Lysee tells me Beacon never forgot, never forgave that betrayal.

"Beacon will pull you up, turn you into a Persona,

capital P," I say, "but if you glow too brightly, she'll snuff you out."

Without turning around, Shine says, "Beacon is brilliant. She's the only hero who's stayed relevant since this town was created. You remember that train fight with The Professor?"

I nod and realize Shine can't see me. "Who doesn't," I tell him. "That fight made her career." That was fourteen years ago. The Professor was the most famous vil in town and Beacon was just one of a dozen small personas trying to grab viewers.

"She wasn't supposed to be on that train," Shine says. "The City Council President had picked Clarion to stop The Professor."

I frown. Clarion? I hardly remember that macho cape with his red tights and cheesy laugh. He was glam for two or three seasons but now he's gone as the glaciers.

"Beacon discovered the identity of one of The Professor's henchmen," Shine continues. "She seduced him, and when the time came, she got on that train at its third stop. Clarion was waiting at the fifth stop." Shine laughs. "The City Council President was furious, but ratings are ratings. After Beacon's ep aired, she was too popular to swipe."

I've never heard this story before, which is saying something. Biggie LC is a small town, and a good quarter of its citizens have their hands in the local vil and cape scene one way or another. Rumors fly faster than a Dragon Rider's sky skimmer.

"Why are you telling me this?" I ask.

"I just want you to know that Beacon gets her way." His voice is soft, ringed with ice. "She will find me, and when she does, your little show is over."

I heave in a breath.

"Do you know what her Aura Arcs feel like?" Shine continues. "Course you don't. She used them on me once, during the sidekick tryouts." He clicks his tongue. "You can feel the power right before that wave of energy hits you. It's not pleasant."

I don't have to know what Beacon's Aura Arcs feel like. I've seen the rippling, concussive wave spread from those golden orbs knock down henchmen like bowling pins. The truth is I've been expecting Beacon to kick down the front door of The Professor's lair at any moment, her famous Light Blade, Aurora, in hand.

I try to match Shine's breezy manner. "She's sure taking her sweet time."

"She'll come."

"We're releasing your capture ep tomorrow," I tell him. "I'm sure in her next ep, Beacon will rage and cry big tears for you. It'll give her a nice ratings boost. In fact, I bet she'll string this storyline out for as long as she can. Fans will be despo to tune in as she searches for you and vows vengeance." I shrug. "And, of course, she's got Shadow to worry about too. You might be here a while." I pause to let that sink in and then add lightly, "The Professor is making good progress on his singularity pod."

We both know that as soon as my vil finishes the machine, he'll set up some grand, public demonstration with Shine strapped into it as his guinea pig. It will be yet another humiliation for Shine and possibly the final nail in the coffin of his career.

Shine turns on the bed to face me. This move is complicated by the short tethers of his retracted bonds. His mask doesn't cover his mouth, so I can see his perfect white teeth as he smiles at me. It's not a happy expression. "You're learning the game fast," he says, "but I think I liked you better when you were ranting about the evils of semi-reality. You were pompous as hell, but at least you stood for something."

He's right and I hate him for that. I did stand for something once, and now I'm betraying my own convictions with every second I wear this scarlet lab coat.

"You've been wearing that mask for two weeks straight. Can't imagine how your pores are holding up," I sneer in reply.

Adan sucks a pained breath between his teeth.

I stretch out my legs and look around the cell. It's so small. So gray. When his tethers are lengthened, Shine can walk around, do some push-ups and air squats, but not much else. Maybe he has some games or old eps downloaded on his Band that can while away the time. It must be hard though, knowing that he'll soon be humiliated by the launch of our next ep, that he's a hapless pawn in our storyline until he gets rescued or we arrange a contractual death for his character. That's a common outcome when capes and sidekicks get captured and can't save their brands.

"How much was it worth?" Shine asks.

I shake away my thoughts and notice that he now sits upright on the bed. "How much is what worth? The identity of the mole? I don't have any dollars."

"No. How much was the test worth?"

"The test?"

"The chem test. How many points?"

It takes my brain a moment to shift. "Why do you care about the chem test?" I ask.

"I told you, for the girls," he says but looks away.

"100 points," I tell him.

"Damn," he sighs. "I was keeping a solid B in that class."

"You can recover if you ace the midterm," I say and then realize how lobotomy that sounds. He won't be taking the midterm either, not unless Beacon rescues him.

"Sorry," I say shortly.

Adan is quiet for a moment, then his green eyes find mine. "You haven't told them who I am," he says. "My true identity. If The Professor knew, he would've already used it against me."

I move to cross my arms, but my shoulder throbs angrily. "You know my identity too. It'd be mutually assured destruction."

Adan shakes his head. "Your identity isn't worth a handful of dollars. Yeah, you'd lose this gig if I gave you up, but you could sell my name to The Professor, to any vil for a fortune. But you haven't."

He's right. Shine is one of the biggest Personas in town. Tween girls across the world practice kissing his hologram every night. Unmasking him would be a rating bonanza to any vil in town, and it would also end his career. Once his face was known, he wouldn't survive a single hour without every vil and two-bit wannabe striver combing through his personal Stream and running him out of town while likely beating him to a bloody pulp in the process.

All my money woes could be answered with a whispered name, but it would also mean ruining Adan's life. I've battled with myself every day, but I just can't do it. Adan may be arrogant and as annoying as a hoload at the bottom of your soup bowl, but there's also something good inside of him. I've seen glimmers of it. Sometimes he can almost seem heroic.

"Are you sure there are no other cams in here? You aren't recording on your Band?" Adan asks suddenly.

"No, I swear." I don't know how much my word means to him, but it must be enough because he nods his head. He's quiet a moment and then nods again as if making a decision.

"I'll give you the info you want," he says and bites his lower lip. "But I need you to do me a favor."

"What kind of favor?" I push myself to my feet as my pulse quickens. Adan seems nervous. His shoulders are tight beneath his suit. I wish I could see his face under his mask.

"It's, um, personal. Alice, this has to be an agreement just between you and me." His eyes are pleading now. "You can't tell The Professor or any of your henchmen buddies or anyone."

I don't like the sound of this one bit. It's got trap written all over it and then underlined several times for good measure.

"Tell me what it is," I say.

Adan looks at me. The silence is long. Tense. And then, softly he begins to speak. When he finishes explaining his request, he glances away. I wonder if he's blushing beneath his mask.

"Yes," I hear myself say. "I'll do it." Such a small, ridiculous favor for such valuable info. "Now, spill."

He takes a deep breath, and I lean forward as a thousand needles tumble down my spine.

"I wasn't trying to spin off from Beacon because she's going to retire me," Adan says. "I need to spin off because the City Council is trying to swipe her show."

CHAPTER 5

Gorgon, they say your heart is stone, but I see the truth. ~ Rip Cord, S1 E13

~

I pound on the door to Leo's apartment. If he were a normal person, I could just ping him through his Band. But Leo is not a normal person. He actually paid serious currency to make his Stream private, which means I have to knock on his door like we're all living in the 20th century.

Eventually, the door swishes open. When I see Leo's scruffy jaw and mussed hair, I remember how late it is... or early, to be exact. Leo blinks at me, but the sleep is already vanishing from his eyes as if he's used to snapping awake on a moment's notice.

"What is it?" His voice is calm, but I hear the underlying tension, the readiness for the sudden crash of an emergency.

I storm into his apartment. Leo backs up, not exactly inviting me in, but wisely moving out of the way. The place is utterly ridic. The man doesn't even own a kitchen table or a couch. Things like a coffee table, side tables, and lamps are obvi out of the question. The only decoration in the room is a single photo on the wall–not even a holographic photo or vid in a frame. It's a static image and not a very good one at that. In the blurry shot, two brown-skinned children wearing robes look beseechingly into the cam.

I wonder if the photo comes from some Sector 3 show he worked on. The Sector 3 Media Region is dedicated to children's programming. Parents from all over the country pack their bags and drag their offspring to Sec 3, despo to turn their kids into stars.

"Why don't you have a couch?" I ask. "Everyone needs a couch."

"Haven't gotten around to printing the parts," he says. He's lived here for over a month.

"People have nowhere to sit," I say.

"And?" He raises an eyebrow. None of this—me barging in and carving circles into the floor with my pacing—seems to faze him. I wonder what it would take to make him mad.

Leo glances at his Band and frowns. "You made an unauthorized visit to our prisoner." He looks at me, those amber eyes probing. "Though, I suppose if you were the mole you wouldn't have come to me. And I hope you'd cover your tracks better."

"They're setting us up," I blurt out.

"Who?"

And then, right at this moment, I realize Leo isn't wearing a shirt. His body is well-defined but not bulging with fake muscles that only come from synthesized protein packs. My eyes travel down his chest, and I spot two more moles, one under his collarbone and the other sitting just above the seam of his gray pajama bottoms on his left side.

"Who?" Leo asks again.

I drag my eyes up to his face as shame blossoms hot across my chest. "PAGS," I sputter. "PAGS is setting us up."

Leo crosses his arms over his chest. "PAGS is a multi-national conglomeration with media markets all over the world and over 16,000 unique media properties. I doubt they care what we do."

"Tatianna Wentworth cares what we do," I say.

That, at least, gives him pause. "Tatianna Wentworth is the president of the City Council," he says after a moment. "She cares about all the sponsored shows that run in Big Little City."

"I spoke to Shine."

"I gathered."

"And..." I stop, not sure how much to tell him. Does he need to know that Beacon has been self-funding her show for the last two years? That she doesn't get any help from the City Council anymore and has to create all her own missions? For some drooling reason, I feel protective of this secret, of Beacon's reputation.

"You have a special relationship with Shine," Leo says. It's not really a question. I doubt Leo has ever asked a question he doesn't already know most of the answer to. I wonder what his cams caught on the day I captured Shine; what his eyes saw in our interaction.

"I hardly know him," I murmur.

"But you got him to talk?"

"I can be persuasive."

Leo knows I'm holding back but he just nods, letting my lie stand on its whisper-thin legs.

"It's Tatianna Wentworth," I say, moving our convo back on track. "She told Shine where to find The Professor's lair. She was helping him to spin off."

The ten members of the City Council report directly to PAGS and serve as the primary sponsors of all the vil, cape, and Persona shows in Biggie LC. They greenlight new shows and swipe the ones going gutter, as well as allocate funds that pay for costumes, weaps, and production crews.

"She set us up," I emphasize.

Leo turns and gazes out the window at the graying sky. Dawn approaches. "She sponsors The Dragon Riders," he says. "I suppose that's the reason she directed us to kidnap the mayor."

"What?" I snap. "That was her idea?"

Leo nods. Rumors have always circulated that sponsors take a hand in guiding plotlines and coordinating between shows, but I never thought they issued direct instructions. "But you're the head producer!" I say. "You and The Professor choose our missions."

Leo turns back to me and the expression on his face says I should know better by now. "Sponsors control the purse strings. That means they have a long reach. When they tell you to kidnap the mayor, you kidnap the mayor."

My mind whirls with the implications of what he's saying. My feet keep moving. I guess it's a good thing Leo doesn't have a cute little rug on the floor. I'd be wearing holes in it.

"But why?" I stammer. "We've only put out three eps. Why would Tatianna Wentworth try to ruin us before we've even had a chance to find our feet?"

Leo pulls a hand through his hair, trying to smooth the cowlicks that make him look a little young, a little vulnerable. "Sometimes they create shows with the intention of destroying them. They use a new Persona to rile up the storylines for their bigger Personas."

I feel myself nodding. Just last year, a cape named

Rip Cord parachuted right into a love triangle between Seed of the Elementals and Gorgon of the Dark League. Those two ended up in an iconic fight and Rip Cord was "killed" trying to stop them. It gushed the ratings for the Elementals and the Dark League for months.

"But this is The Professor," I manage.

"He's got a lot of nostalgic value but his brand of villainy is..." Leo pauses, trying to summon the right word, "faded." He tilts his head slightly as if he's thinking out loud. "Tatianna Wentworth brought him out of retirement, hired me to do a nice reintroduction, but they only wanted to use him to get a big win for one of her more established Personas."

"Shine," I say.

"And when that failed, she tipped off the Dragon Riders. That team's trending up right now. Defeating The Professor would be a good boost to get them into the top viewership leagues," Leo says.

"Well, what are we going to do about it?" I demand.

Leo must hear the growing desperation in my voice, but it only makes his lips quirk in a small smile. "What is there to do, Alice? This happens all the time. When a sponsor wants you to go, you're out."

Not Beacon, I think to myself.

"We're going to get another gutter mission," I hear myself say as the full implication of our situation downloads. "And Tatianna will probs tip off another of her up-and-coming capes."

"Sometimes that's how the game works," Leo says.

I realize something. Leo isn't mad. Leo isn't even surprised. He looks... resigned.

"You don't give one damn about any of this, do you?" I say. My shock is shifting inside of me, turning dark and molten. "You're just giving up on the show, on The Professor!" My voice is rising. I'm losing it. Because Leo is giving up on me, too and I practically sold my soul to get this far.

"Alice..." his voice is soft.

I wave my hands around the room, ignoring the swell of pain in my shoulder. "Where's your couch, Leo? Where's your kitchen table and your chairs? Where's your service robo and your fake plants and a little robo dog sleeping in the corner? Where are the holo-vids on the walls or the holo-windows showing some stupid landscape, like the rainforest or the surface of the moon?" The words pour out of me, hot and wounded. "You never meant to stay here. As soon as you get the notice that our show is swiped, all you'll have to do is throw your 3D printer and that stupid pic into your old suitcase and leave town."

I walk up to the picture hanging on the wall and squint at it. The children have such large eyes in their small, thin faces.

"Is this from Sec 3?" I ask him, accusations and acid in my words. "You throwing despo kids into competition shows, watching them struggle to win, to survive?"

I made the long trip to Sector 3 once to participate in a semi-reality show. I smiled for the cams. My brother, Alby and I set out on a grand adventure, and I was certain we'd win the comp and fix all our problems with the prize money.

Instead, I ruined his life.

"That picture was taken in Tanzania," Leo says softly.

"What?" I croak. Tanzania is a hell hole, filled with

parched villages, starving kids, and cruel warlords, each more violent than the next. Much of the African continent has been in a constant cycle of chaos and war for decades, battered by crumbling infrastructure and unending corruption. They say you can't grow a weed for a thousand miles thanks to the nearly permanent droughts.

I look at the picture again. The children seem even skinnier. Now their eyes seem afraid.

"Why were you in Tanzania?" I finally ask.

"It was clever, poaching the mayor's robo on the mission," Leo says. "It'll add humor to the next ep."

I sigh. Leo has his own secrets, and something tells me those secrets are wounds that still bleed inside of him. If he weren't a producer, I might feel sorry for him. Instead, I feel sorry for myself and for our show.

"I saw an opportunity," I say and turn toward the door. It swishes open as I approach.

"You have a talent for seeing opportunities and taking them," Leo says behind me. I glance over my shoulder. The rising sun sprinkles golden highlights into his messy brown hair.

"What were you doing in Tanzania?" I ask.

"Go to bed, Alice," he says as the door closes behind me.

CHAPTER 6

I trust that the Supreme Court will make the right decision in the Castillo v PAGS case. While life is sacrosanct, we cannot smoother a business in red tape. If the viewers don't like what they see, they'll vote with their eyes.
~ President Sage Anders, Press Conference

~

"Wakey wakey, self-esteem is shaky!" Bob sings in a voice as pleasant as a saw trying to cut through metal. My entire body resists regaining consciousness. My slumber had been deep and empty, just the way I like it.

"Go away," I groan to my sallow-skinned Totem.

"You've got class in an hour and, seeing as you have negative $26 in your account, my guess is you're walking," Bob answers. His shimmering butterfly wings flutter on his back.

"Uhhhhh." With a strength and courage that rivals anything Beacon has ever managed in her career, I drag myself out of bed and throw mildly acceptable clothing onto my body. I've worn this t-shirt and burgundy skirt combo before–practically a felony in Lysee's mind–but I've never been able to hang onto the whiplash fad cycle. Anyway, I don't have enough dollars for material cartridges to print myself new clothes even if I wanted to.

I drag a brush through my long, straight brown hair

and then pile it into a sloppy bun on my head. A glance in the mirror shows me tired brown eyes, a neck mottled in bruises, and boobs that are still too small. I consider switching to a turtleneck, but it would be too much work, so I just walk out of my room and head toward the bathroom.

A figure sits primly on the edge of my couch. His black hair hangs in intricate ringlets along his forehead and he wears an expensive, emerald green coat patterned with black lightning bolts down the back. The black fingernail polish is newly lacquered, and he's chosen to double up on the black eyeliner and black lipstick today.

"Morning," I mutter to Matthew.

"Afternoon," my best friend replies. His blue eyes gaze at me with the ever-present disappointment I've come to expect. "You look like someone mistook you for a punching bag."

"Wasn't a mistake," I admit. "We had a little run-in with the Dragon Riders last night. My lasso skills are still wanting."

"Oh my. Oh my!" a stilted voice chirps from across the room. "Do you need medical aid?"

"No, Betts, I'm fine," I reassure Matthew's service robo as I make it to the bathroom. I glance at Betty and see that Matthew has added bright, luminescent tattoos to her silicon skin. She now sports a variety of equations down her arms and a splendid dragon across her upper chest. The unicorn horn is still firmly affixed to her forehead.

"Forty-one people have died as a direct result of participation in semi-reality shows over the past ten years," Matthew says.

I try not to roll my eyes as I splash cold water on my face. Matthew's current dream is to win one of the numerous trivia shows they produce over in Media Sector Two. He's been training for months and now seems to delight in weaponizing his trivia knowledge.

I scrub my face with a pump of Lysee's super expensive facewash made from synthesized botanicals that used to grow in the rainforest. My own generic facewash has been empty for over a week.

"Add fancy facewash to the roommate reimbursement list," I tell Bob.

"That list is getting pretty long," my Totem informs me.

I know. I don't even want to look at it, but I'll square everything with Lysee as soon as I get my first paycheck.

"Eighteen percent of all medical center visits in the United States are directly related to participation in a semi-reality show," Matthew continues.

After washing my face, I lean against the bathroom door and perform the elaborate routine of squeezing out a tiny bit of toothpaste from my nearly empty tube. "There won't be nearly as many semi-reality deaths soon," I assure Matthew. "Castillo v PAGS is going to change that."

"Assuming Castillo wins," Matthew says delicately.

"Of course Castillo will win." My voice is sharp even to my own ears. Castillo *has* to win. The Supreme Court has been deliberating on the case for weeks, trying to decide if PAGS can be held liable for creating dangerous conditions that led to the death of Yolina Castillo in season nine of *Z Town.* The answer is obvi. The show's producers hid a rusty chainsaw in some far-flung corner of the town. They claim it was meant to be used by survivors to build shelters or kill the robo zombies, but Ashlan Cooper decided it was a whole lot easier to just behead Yolina Castillo instead and win the game.

The case isn't just about Yolina Castillo though. It's about whether PAGS can be held legally responsible for any of the deaths and injuries its shows promote. When Castillo wins, producers won't be able to put chainsaws into the hands of desperate, half-mad contestants or give children incorrect maps and let them wander through the desert until they both collapse.

A memory flashes in my mind. *The hot, grilling sun. Alby's flushed face begging me to keep going.*

I realize my toothbrush is sticking out of the side of my mouth, dribbling foamy toothpaste down my chin. I shove away the memories of that punishing sun and change the subject. "How's the brain training going?"

Matthew's been a trivia sponge for months, and I've watched his progress with a mixture of pride and concern. His mind is an endless pit of knowledge, but there's almost something manic about this quest. We've gone on this dizzying ride before. Matthew has a tendency to grab a goal and squeeze until it dies in his arms.

"I've had some trouble concentrating lately," he says, and when I turn toward him I see that he's staring at me.

My toothbrush pauses in the air. "Wait, you blaming that on me?"

"Course not." He gives me a big, fake smile.

I groan and turn to spit into the sink. This is how things have been between me and Matthew for the past few weeks, ever since I begged him to get me into his dad's henchmen tryouts. Matthew is one of the warmest, kindest, and most generous people I know, but there's also something fragile about him, like he carries around a permanent crack in his soul. Even a small push or fall and his whole being is at risk of shattering. I was able to drag him out of that tailspin into darkness once but I'm not sure I could do it again.

"This is just a gig," I tell Matthew for the billionth time. "I still hate semi-reality."

Matthew looks away but I know he feels betrayed. He and I initially bonded over how much we both despised the Fame Game and all the strivers who vamp around town. Matthew has good reason to resent the system. When his father, Gerald, signed on to become The Professor for the show's first run 16 years ago, Matthew was his first hire.

The Professor was famous for building doom machines and planning heists with his adorable son, Energy at his side. But the show warped Matthew, twisted truth and lies and hammered that crack inside of him. He's never forgiven his father, and I'm starting to wonder if he'll forgive me for putting on my scarlet lab coat each night.

When I finish up in the bathroom and emerge into the living room, I notice Matthew rocking slightly on the couch. My stomach twists. It's something he does when he's stressed. Doesn't even notice it.

I make a mental note to check his apartment for drugs tonight before my henchman shift starts. I need to spend more time with Matthew. I need to make him understand that I'm still the same person I was before I joined The Professor's show.

"Uh, you are planning to go to class, right?" Bob asks.

I glance at the time. *Buddha's banana nut bread!* I rush to the kitchen, grab a nutra-pack, and race for the door.

"It might just start out as a gig," Matthew says, "but soon you'll forget who's the character and who's the reality. Trust me."

"I do," I say softly, "but I'm not going to change. I'm still me."

"You're already changing," my friend says sadly, as if to himself.

I grit my teeth. I want to stay and argue, to make him understand but I don't have time.

"I gotta go," I mutter.

"Ta," Matthew says sarcastically.

"Have a very wonderful day," Betty adds sweetly behind him.

As soon as the door to my apartment slides closed behind me, my eyes leap to Leo's gray door across the hall. All my anger from yesterday crashes onto my psyche.

Oh right, our show is being shipwrecked by Tatianna Wentworth, the most powerful sponsor on the City Council, and there's nothing we can do about it.

I rush down the hallway toward the stairs, and my brain churns with the vast problem in front of me. As soon as things settle down, I'll focus on helping Matthew. For now, though, I need to figure out a way to save The Professor's show and my paycheck!

***

The first class of the day is chemistry. I honestly don't know why I waited until my junior year to take this general-ed class. But here I am.

I head into the small room, always expecting to smell the faint scent of chemicals. That's lobotomy, of course. We've never touched real chems in this class. Instead, we pour holographic carbonic acid into holographic beakers and heat it over holographic Bunsen burners.

As always, Ollie waves me over to our shared table as if I don't sit there every time.

"Ta, Alice," he says, his head jerking in three precise nods while his blue eyes dart away from mine. He's a skinny kid and his body practically hums with coiled energy. His eyes dart everywhere while his fingers endlessly tap the tabletop. Today, he wears bright green suspenders over a black shirt and loose black breeches. Precise black stripes cut through his blond hair. Bright green sneakers complete the same look the leader of *Eat Your Noodles* was wearing in their new music vid, "Mom, Make Me Noodles."

That K-pop band has been gushing their Stream score lately, at least according to Lysee who has watched "Mom, Make Me Noodles" at least a hundred times this past week.

Poor Ollie. While my great social crime is to care little about fashion, Ollie dooms himself in the opposite way. He's a copier, meticulously trying to fit in, but being far too obvi about it. I guess that's why we're at the weirdos table. Not that I mind. Ollie's interesting and refreshingly honest, not to mention brills at chemistry.

"Adan has not yet arrived," Ollie announces as if the empty chair next to me wasn't speaking loud and clear. "This will be his fourth absence. I messaged his Stream again last week to tell him about the test. He has not acknowledged any of my messages."

"Wow, strange," I murmur and lay my forehead onto

my folded arms.

"Have you attempted to message him? Perhaps he is very ill. Alternatively, I have wondered if perhaps he was injured in the Toury Massacre."

My hands tighten into fists. Toury Massacre is what they're calling Shadow's little murder escapade two weeks ago.

"Law enforcement officials have not yet apprehended Shadow," Ollie continues, oblivious to my groan of disapproval. "The Big Little City police have opted not to request assistance from additional law enforcement agencies or federal agencies. Mayor Wisenberg promised to catch him by the end of the week, but that was two weeks ago. Did you see the latest news clips today? He presented the Medal of Valor to the Dragon Riders for protecting him against a failed kidnapping plot last night."

"What?" I squawk, pushing myself upright. "Those shigits got Medals of Valor?" A few students glance over at me. "Good for them," I manage through clamped teeth.

"Alice, you have additional injuries." Ollie states.

"MMA practice," I say. It's the same lie I used last week and the week before to explain the bruises and bumps from combat practice at the lair.

"You must be more careful," Ollie chides me. "You aren't overriding the safeties on the combat robos again, are you?"

"Nope. This was just practice with the other students," I say, which is sort of true if you replace the word "practice" with "no holds bar battle" and the word "students" with "an arrogant Dragon Rider who probs has herpes."

"Well, you need to work with less accomplished students," Ollie says.

I chuckle. "Great idea." Ollie never holds back his opinion, and I appreciate that even when the truth hurts as much as the bruises around my neck.

"Two minutes until class starts," the teaching assistant calls from the back of the room.

I close my eyes, hoping to snatch a tiny nap, but to my annoyance I realize I'm not tired anymore. My brain is on alert and I know why.

"What do you think Shadow is doing?" I blurt out. If anyone has a decent guess, it'd be Ollie. He's more than a little obsessed with capes and vils and spends his free time meticulously updating his in-depth wikis on them.

"Preparing for something bigger," Ollie answers at once. "That would fit his past behavior. Every appearance is an escalation of his prior crimes."

That's exactly what I don't want to hear.

"How can he get away with it?" I ask. After the Toury Massacre, everyone believes he's a lunatic freeter causing chaos for some unknown reason, but I've started to develop a different suspicion, something dark and terrifying. How has Shadow been able to elude the thousands of cams throughout the city as well as the massive search operation conducted by our officers?

"He's been good for ratings, hasn't he?" I ask.

Ollie nods vigorously. "Yes, oh yes. All the heroic shows have markedly improved ratings, and Reena Masterson recently broadcast a special devoted entirely to Shadow that is performing extremely well."

I open my mouth to speak, then stop. The words burn on my tongue, the suspicion made of acid. "What if he isn't a freeter?" I whisper. "What if he's been sponsored this whole time?"

Ollie doesn't even pause before answering. "Shadow can't be signed. The town rules don't allow for the murder of civilians. He also carries unlawful weapons. No producer could legally develop his storylines and no sponsor on the City Council would approve it. Also, he does not have a show or even his own Stream."

"Maybe... maybe it's not about having his own show. Maybe he's a tool to increase the ratings of other shows. And what if he doesn't tell his sponsors what he's doing?" I say. "He just does it, and the ratings are so good that they just... let him get away with it."

Beacon didn't ask permission before she faced The Professor on the BLC Express, I remind myself.

Ollie shakes his head emphatically. "He is breaking the law. They must apprehend him."

The lights dim and my Band vibrates as it shifts into forced sleep mode. Class is starting, but my thoughts keep churning. Ollie thinks that the laws of our town are unbreakable, but I know better. Great ratings can bend any rule, even break them.

That's why producers are always looking for ways to up the potential for conflict and violence on their shows. PIC – Pain Is Currency.

I blink and try to focus on the holo-screen in front of me. The class program boots up and our instructor, Professor Hersherwitz appears on screen. Professor Hersherwitz is a cartoon blue unicorn wearing a lab coat, bowtie, and rimless glasses. He grins at us with his square horse teeth. We have no lesson or lab today. Instead, Professor Hersherwitz spends the lecture reviewing all the material on next week's midterm.

After each practice section, a bubbling beaker pours out questions for short practice quizzes. Ollie quickly completes them for our table.

Thank Buddha for him. I know I should help, but as Professor Hersherwitz drones on, tossing out bad chemistry puns and amusingly antiquated slang, I can barely keep my eyes open. These long nights in the lair are not doing my internal body clock any favors.

Finally, the lecture ends. Before he signs off, Professor Hersherwitz says. "I hypothesize that if you study for one hour each night, the result will be a good grade on your midterm!" The blue unicorn fades from the screen and the lights brighten in the room. I lean back in my chair with a sigh.

"Midterms are next week," the teaching assistant reminds us. He walks down the aisles, skinny as a wraith, blue hair dangling in his eyes. "My office hours are noon to three each day if you have questions."

Poor guy. He probs has a master's degree in teaching, but I doubt anyone pings him during office hours, much less actually stops by. Professor Hersherwitz has already pointed out six different practice modules available on this class Stream. Software trumps breathers yet again.

As my Band hums to life, I tell Bob, "Add chem practice modules to my to-do list." I'll go through them this weekend after our next heist, assuming I'm not rotting in the city jail or strapped to a bed in the med clinic.

Ollie's fingers drum, drum, drum on the table. "Would you... would you like to study for the midterm?" he asks softly. "Together. Not separately."

I can't help but smile. "You already know all this stuff. You don't need to study."

He shrugs three times in quick succession. "Yes. But you do."

I laugh. "Sure," I hear myself say. "My schedule is a little, um, chaotic this week, but how about I ping you when I get some time?"

Ollie perks up and nods. "Okay. Yes. Ping me. When you have time. Ping me."

The other students stream out of the room while a single city-owned cam drone hums above. My social stratification class is in 20 mins. All I want to do is collapse into bed for a few more hours or a few more days, but that's not on the agenda. As soon as my second class is over, I have a mission to complete. Adan held up his end of our bargain. Now it's time I do the same, even if it could land me right in Beacon's crosshairs.

CHAPTER 7

*Shine, wherever you are, do not give in. Do not give
up. I will find you, and if the worst shall happen, I
will avenge you!* ~ Beacon, Stream Video

~

Twenty mins after social stratification class, I find
myself walking down a pretty street with some pleasant name, like Ivy Grove or Tulip Path. I'm just a kilometer and a half outside Iconic Square. This is prime
real estate, and the cute little homes I pass show off
cute porches and well-manicured lawns. These houses
are old, part of the original town of Pana before PAGS
took it over, changed its name, and started paying
people to dress up in costumes. Most of the homes have
been heavily remodeled, their roofs remade with solar
tiles, the windows wired to broadcast holographic
landscapes.

My steps sound loud on the sidewalk but I'm sure
it's just my imagination. A rental car zips by me, the
faces of The Dark League members plastered on its side.
Lizard's tongue lashes around the entire car and Scream
has her jaws agape. As the car passes, I keep my eyes
down on my Band pretending to swim my Stream. Bob
has offered up some sort of talent show out of Media
Sector 4. On the holo-screen that washes across my
forearm, a woman in a pair of hover boots dances awk-

wardly in the air while the judges tsk.

Every so often, I glance up trying to spot the glint of a lens. My ears strain for the purr of a cam drone hovering nearby. The City Council owns a whole fleet of cam drones that it dispatches around the city to pick up images of everyday life. Producers for sponsored vils and capes can access the images and use them as canned footage for their eps or to get additional angles when big fights go down.

I try to look as boring as possible. Nothing to see here. Just a normal girl walking down a normal street. Zero ratings potential.

City cams aren't the only risk I face. I'm also on guard against the sudden appearance of a stickup guy, (which doesn't have to be a guy, of course). The City Council keeps a small group of hoodlums on the payroll to harass and rob townies. These lowlifes give the capes someone to fight and help them pad their eps if the action is lagging. Most of the stickup guys stay close to Iconic Square, but you never know when one will pop up out of nowhere and wave a laz pistol in your face. That happened to me just two weeks ago when my old coworker, DeAngelo tried to rob me. A nice little throat punch encouraged him to back off, and we were working out our differences when that drooling freeter in the white diamond costume showed up

I smile. One benny of being utterly broke is that I don't have anything for anyone else to steal.

"We're here," Bob says, his unshaven face interrupting the talent show on screen. "It's just one street over." He burps, and I wonder again why I paid actual money for his crass personality filter all those years ago. I supposed some dark, tangled part of me invites the abuse.

No time to deep dive into my twisted psyche. I've got a lobotomy mission to set into motion. I give the street one more visual sweep. All clear. Pulling in a quick breath, I veer off the sidewalk and slip between two houses. I hop a small fence and dash through a yard. I steer around a garden set on a wheeled platform that can be pulled inside during dust storms. Tender green shoots rise hopefully from the soil, some already holding out dainty leaves to the sun. Nearby, a dog starts yapping excitedly.

Real or robo? I can't see the dog, but since its sharp cries don't stop, I assume it's real. Good. A lot of robo pets include security software that alerts their owners if they perceive something suspicious. Gives a new meaning to the concept of a guard dog.

I hop over one more fence and find myself in a pristine yard. The verdant grass is perfectly cropped. What a waste. Californians would froth at the mouth if they knew someone was dumping water on grass. Then they would capture, filter, and reuse their froth because that's how precious H2O is out on the coast.

A cobbled path runs through the yard to the back door of a charming blue house. It looks like an original of Pana, restored with care, love, and lots of dollars. A wide patio includes plush benches, a bar, barbeque, fire pit, and in-ground spa. The large shed in the corner of the yard probably holds a lawn care service unit.

As I follow the path to the back door of the house, my heartbeat grows fast. Here's where things get dangerous. I slip the small bag I've been carrying off my shoulder, unzip it, and pull out the chunky piece of metal nestled within.

Adan's Wyvern model Band feels heavy in my hand.

That might have something to do with all the diamonds encrusted around its visual interface or just the
incredible risk it represents. Beacon isn't dim. She'll be
synced to the GPS tracker in Adan's Band. The moment I
turn this thing on, the clock starts ticking.

And that could be the least of my worries. *What
if Adan betrays me?* I've been pondering this all day. I
watched him program his Band in his cell before he
handed it over to me, but he could have slipped a sub-
vocalized command past me. It would have been so
easy for him to set a message to automatically send as
soon as his Band comes online. He could tell Beacon
where The Professor's hideout is or even my true identity.

My only defense is his word. Adan promised he
wouldn't try anything. It's a flimsy shield at best.
Standing in front of the door, I waver. I should leave.
Right now. I'll tell Adan I did what he asked. He'll never
know, not until he gets out, and by then he'll probs have
more worries than whether or not I completed this
ridic task for him.

I turn my back to the door but stop. I remember the
way he looked at me when he finally explained his request. The pleading in his voice. The worry that lined
his handsome face.

And then there's the fact that I gave him my word.

I close my eyes. Before I chicken out, I trace the
sequence Adan showed me along the inner side of his
Band. The golden-plated Band immediately hums to
life. A holo-screen projects out from the center of the
Band and a gorgeous azure bird unfolds her wings.

"I have so many updates for you," the bird says
in a pleasant voice. "Over 300 pings, 1800 new pics,

vids, hologram uploads from your friends, and you've missed several important tests and homework assignments. Your Stream Score has dropped 13 points due to lack of activity, and…" the Totem stops, finally registering that the face staring back at her is most definitely not Adan.

"Well, this is concerning," she says. "Unless you have a good reason for being in possession of this Band, I shall have to alert the authorities."

"Quiet," I hiss at her. "Pause all program updates, notices, and recommendations. Don't even think of calling the cops. Go into hibernation. Passcode: Striped Puffin."

The bird fluffs her feathers indignantly but then disappears. The codeword worked. I let out a relieved breath, but this is only the beginning. I step up to the door. Its shining brass knob is all for show. The locking software in the door recognizes Adan's Band and the door slides open. Lights flicker on inside.

"Buddha's orbital sockets," I whisper as I step inside. The place is perfect. Sun streams through huge windows in the kitchen landing on quartz countertops and one of those fully self-cooking stoves. Bronze pots and pans hang decoratively above the stove from hooks in the wall.

I move through the kitchen into the living room and rock to a stop. An Anders 3500 3D Printer takes up an entire corner of the room. It is a truly beautiful piece of machinery. The thing is massive, built within an expandable workstation. With enough materials cartridges, Adan can print just about anything he ever wants. That's probably where he gets all the fancy, chipped-up shirts he wears to the gym. I've heard that the 3500 can even print nano-tech.

I tear my gaze away from the 3D. I don't have time to stand around gawking. Not with Adan's Band humming along in my hand like a ticking time bomb. And yet... I can't help but turn in a full circle, taking in all the glam of the room. Fancy lamps stand on opposite sides of the room framing a massive, coffee-colored couch. A bookshelf rises up in the corner filled with real, physical books. I touch a globe sitting on the shelf and it lights up, a holo-screen projecting a live satellite overlay.

This home is luxury to the max, and yet something seems off about it. I frown, trying to think what it could be. Something moves into the open doorway on the other side of the room. My heart just about knocks itself out of my ribcage.

Beacon!

She's here already! Adan somehow found a way to forewarn her. She's going to pummel my spleen and twist my nerve fibers into decorative knots until I tell her everything, including the password to my childhood diary.

The figure rolls through the doorway and I dance back out of the way of a strike. My leg bumps a side table and I shift around it.

"Oh my, oh my, a guest," my adversary chirps. "How wonderful! Would you like a cookies n' cream protein shake?"

I blink. The figure rolls into the light, revealing rounded curves and a wide smile on a flat face. It's a matronly service robo that looks kind of like a snowman. *Hmmm*, I would have pegged Adan's taste as leaning toward a gorg female service robo; one of those models that can be used for "a variety of purposes" as the marketing always puts it.

"I must apologize. Adan isn't currently home," the robo says. "My name is Martha and I am at your service. Are you hungry? I can prepare a kale and walnut salad. That's one of Adan's favorites."

"No, no, I won't be staying long," I stammer. "I'm just here to, uh, check on his..."

"Oh, Sweetheart. Yes, of course. He always worries about her." The robo gives an approximation of a chuckle. "Of course I've been caring for her. All her vitals are normal and her waste excretion is—"

"That's, that's good. Adan just wanted me to be sure," I say and then glance down at the fancy side table I bumped. *Blight!* On the table, a crystalline peacock figurine lays on its side. That thing is probs worth more than a real kidney on the open market.

I pick up the figurine and set it back on its feet. A piece of its colorful tail has chipped off. Well, clearly that's Adan's fault for foolishly filling his living room with expensive and breakable things. As I pull my hand back, I brush a holo-frame on the table.

It brightens to life and plays a recorded holo-vid. Within the sterling silver frame, two girls run toward me. One is a gawky teen still growing into her long limbs, the other a girl no older than ten with a black waterfall of hair streaming over her shoulders as she runs. A man rushes behind them, grabbing both around the waist with strong arms. He spins them around in a circle, and the girls erupt into squeals and giggles.

The man lets the teen go, but swings the younger girl around and behind him so that she sits on his back. The cam zooms in. I can see the clear resemblance in all three faces. The teen is smiling, and she looks at the man, who must be her older brother, with clear adoration. The man is Adan. In the vid, his hair is longer than it is now, and the star pattern on his jeans was a fad two years ago. He skips out of the frame, his youngest sister on his back. There's no volume but I'm pretty sure he neighs.

Even after the vid ends, I stare at the darkened holo-frame. Adan has sisters. I try to shrug this new info away. He's still arrogant as the sun and as ferocious a striver as anyone in this town. A new thought hits me. *What if his sisters are worried about him?* Maybe he usually talks to them every day and now they don't know where he is or what's happened to him. They almost certainly don't know that he's Shine. A cape isn't legally allowed to tell even his closest family members such valuable information.

In the early days of Biggie LC, when the non-disclosure agreements weren't as tightly written as they are today, several capes and vils lost their shows when conniving siblings or even spouses sold them out for a hefty payday. Stone Crusher, the original leader of the Dark League, went this way after he forgot his three-year anniversary. His wife took that oversight a mite personally.

"Would you like to see Sweetheart?" Martha asks behind me.

"Uh, yeah. Yes," I mutter and turn away from the side table and all the uncomfortable realizations the holo-frame contains.

Martha beckons me down a short hallway and toward a door at the end. As soon as the door swishes open, a cry rings through the air that is both supremely musical and supremely pissed. I move past the service robo and step into the room.

A huge, ornate cage hangs from the ceiling, taking up a good quarter of the room. The creature inside is absolutely stunning and clearly knows it. Rich shades of indigo paint her wing feathers. Silver feathers pattern her chest and rise proudly from her thick crown. The symmetry of her coloring is a clear sign of genetic breeding.

The cockatoo must be worth a fortune.

Right now, that fortune hops angrily around a scattering of fake branches in her cage. She stretches her wings and jumps to the front of her cage, wrapping curved talons around the bars. I almost step back.

"Sweetheart has not been happy," Martha says behind me. "She's missed Adan's attention. They play many games together each day. Perhaps you would play a game with her?"

"Today!" Sweetheart cries in a fluty voice. "Love You. Love You." Her voice is glorious, something that must have taken generations to genetically perfect.

"I'm not here to play games," I tell Martha. "Have you been feeding her properly and changing her water?"

"Yes, of course," Martha says. I have no doubt about it. A service robo doesn't forget her programmed commands. Adan just wanted me to ask. "How are the food supplies?"

"We have enough for exactly six more days, but the apples have all gone bad. Adan gives apple pieces to Sweetheart when she sings."

This additional evidence that Adan may secretly be a decent person only increases my discomfort. "You have permission to order additional food," I tell the robo, "as well as any toys she needs and an ongoing supply of fresh apples. Password African Gray." Adan's Band vibrates in my hand.

"Command acknowledged," Martha responds. "I will duplicate the previous order for food and toys."

"You have permission to continue this order each time the food runs low until Adan returns," I tell her.

"Command acknowledged."

I idly wonder what else I can command Martha to do. Probably not much. If Adan was smart, he would have locked me out of all non-bird related commands. I turn back to the cage. The special absorbent paper at the bottom of it looks at capacity. A shame that Martha can't clean the cage. Technically she can, of course, but apparently Adan doesn't trust his service robo to interact directly with Sweetheart.

Today's top-of-the-line service robos, like Martha, have gotten incredibly good at modulating the pressure they use when handling different objects, but there are always stories of lesser models accidentally strangling dogs on walks or painfully twisting their master's limbs during "extracurricular activities." It's been a fad for some time for rich people to insist on handling their young children and pets on their own. Some of the Captains of Industry have even been known to hire human workers to care for their kids, just like in the old days.

Sweetheart lets out another beautiful and angry call. I glance at Adan's Band again. Has Beacon traced its GPS signal? Is she already on her way? I unlatch the cage and swing open the big door. Sweetheart launches out, and I watch in awe as she glides down to a nearby decorative tree in the corner of the room. She's practically got the wingspan of a personal flier.

"Seize the day," she says. "Seize the day. Ta."

I grab up the soggy paper in the cage and nearly gag at the smell. I guess there are some things the geneticists haven't perfected yet.

"Here, throw this away," I tell Martha, shoving the damp papers into her arms. "And you know what? Go ahead and make me that cookies n' cream protein shake." Might as well reward myself for this lobotomy risk I'm taking.

I find the closet Adan described in the back of the room. Of course, it's a cave-like wonder, roughly the size of my bedroom. Inside, the shelves are stacked with bird supplies.

"Damn, Sweetheart, you're as spoiled as a child actor," I mutter. I can't even remember the last time I've eaten a real apple. Just as I lean over to grab new absorbent floor pads for the cage, I feel a soft puff of air overhead followed by the feeling of very non-soft talons landing on my head.

"Really?" I grumble. The bird shifts to settle her weight. "I thought you were supposed to seize the day, not my head." Sweetheart responds by twisting around, pulling my hair and pricking my scalp. She sings a soft song, the trilling notes haunting and beautiful.

"Yeah, yeah, nice genetic upgrade," I mutter. "Stop showing off." It doesn't take long to lay down the fresh papers but I feel every second ticking away. The bird isn't dim. As soon as I'm smoothing the clean papers at the bottom of her cage, she scrambles off my hair and flaps up to a bar jutting from a wall near the ceiling.

"I understand," I tell her. "I wouldn't want to go back

in this thing either." To his credit, Adan has turned the cage into a bird paradise filled with fake branches, rope swings, colorful toys, puzzles, and some weird mechanical thing that probably gives her bird massages.

But, at the end of the day, it's still a cage.

Kind of like Biggie LC, I think morosely. Sure, I *could* leave town, but with no Loons to my name, where could I go except back to the desolate stretch of parched land where my mom and brother live?

The weight of Adan's Band brings me back to the present. Beacon must be on her way already. How much longer do I have? Ten mins? Five? Is she striding across the porch right now? I push down my panic and hustle to the closet. As Adan carefully instructed, I find the red bag filled with square treats. They look like blocks of various seeds glued together by honey. I put one treat on a branch in the cage.

I hope against hope that the bird goes straight in for the treat. Instead, Sweetheart stares daggers at me from her perch.

She won't go into the cage without the song, Adan told me.

Buddha's nose hairs!

"Sweetheart, Sweetheart," I sing,
Voice so pure and feathers so bright
I must leave you now to continue the fight.
But don't sing a sad song, pretty girl
I'll be home soon, my darling pearl

Like magic or just professional training, the bird opens her wings and floats down, landing on my outstretched arm. Then she sings back the melody of the song with an incredible range of notes. The sound is truly enchanting. Too bad Sweetheart ends the song with an angry caw when I move her into the cage. I wiggle my arm, probably harder than Adan would like to get her to jump off. Then I slam the cage door just in case she tries to bolt.

"Here you go, dear," Martha says behind me, holding out a cup filled with a black-and-white speckled drink. The cup is real glass, not the cheap, over-recycled plastic I usually print.

"Thank you!" I take the drink from her. "Now, delete all memory files from the past half hour including all audio and visual files, but maintain accepted commands. Afterward, shut down for one hour and then reboot. Password African Gray." I hold my breath. Here is yet another trap Adan could have laid for me. If Martha doesn't accept this command, Beacon will be able to extract all her memory files. It would be as easy as getting dirty in a dust storm to run a facial match protocol, which will lead her right to my personal Stream. From there, a hop over to the city's database will give her my address in less than a nanosecond.

"Command accepted," Martha says. "Erasing files. Shutting down." She tilts forward as her face goes slack.

"Good girl and thanks for the drink," I say, giving her a friendly pat as I power walk into the living room. Time to tail it, except… a tantalizing thought stops me. I bet Adan has his extra suits hidden somewhere in this house. That's precious tech. He's got the best gear in town: lightweight, strong, flexible, and full of smart upgrades like impact cushioning mini-thrusters in his boots, limb accelerators, and gloves coated in a special polymer that let him climb the sides of buildings.

If I could find his costumes, maybe even some extra weaps, it would be a game-changer. I take one step back toward the hallway and then stop myself. He's probably hidden his things somewhere that would take me hours to find. If he was smart, he'd also put them in a safe with biometric locks.

No, I can't take the risk and let Beacon find me here.

I drag my eyes off the closed doors in the hallway and jog through the living room. I glance at the holo-frame, now empty and quiet on the end table. Then it comes to me. I know why this room, this entire house feels so wrong.

It doesn't have a personality. It's like Adan pulled this decor right out of some interior designer's Stream collage. Everything feels for show. There's nothing real about him at all in this place except for the back room where Sweetheart sits in her cage.

I don't have time to dwell on this. Grabbing a sip from the glass, *mmmm, cookies n' cream,* I dash out of the house. The back door slides shut and locks. I fumble to power off Adan's Band. As soon as the glow fades from the visual interface, I shove it into my bag while relief loosens the knots in my stomach. I scramble back over the fence, setting off the neighbor's stupid dog again.

Back on the side street, I force myself not to run.

Look normal. Just a girl walking down the street. Maybe I'll seem like another striver, hoping to get robbed by a stickup guy so a cape will valiantly rescue me. Just as I reach the corner of the street, I hear the soft whine of an electric motorcycle. And then, *whoosh,* it flies by, glittering gold. A slim figure bends over the handlebars. I recognize that golden helmet, the scarlet chest plate stamped with the iconic lighthouse pattern, all that blonde hair streaming in the wind from beneath the helmet. Three cam drones follow in tight formation around the rider.

It's her.

Beacon.

I stop on the sidewalk and stare after her in utter awe. In the three years I've lived in Biggie LC, this is the first time I've ever set eyes on her. I'm not even breathing, though she's gone, racing toward Adan's home where she won't find anything except a powered down service robo and a loud, pissed cockatoo.

I take another appreciative sip of my cookies n' cream protein shake and continue my stroll back to The Professor's lair.

CHAPTER 8

*The semi-reality life is a rollercoaster. If it isn't,
something's wrong and you're probs about to get swiped.*
~ Tickles the Elf, The Henchman's Survival Guide

~

Mermaid is so damn fast. I duck one swing and suddenly my legs are flying out from under me. I hit the mat, roll away from a nasty foot stomp, but then feel the pressure of her bo staff grind into the vertebrae at the top of my neck.

"You're thinking too much," she says. "You've got to feel the moves. Let your body react."

I'm pretty sure she came out of the womb with a triple black belt. I gingerly turn as she lifts the staff. My shoulder throbs, but it seems to be working fine. Across the main room of the lair, Sequoia gives me a sympathetic look. He's taken more than a few turns against Mermaid during these nightly training sessions but I don't see his ass on the mat nearly so much.

"Well done, Arsenic," Kitty says. The newest member of our gang wears a pink, buttoned-up lab coat and pink science goggles dotted with rhinestones. A broom leans against her ample bosom.

"You too, Iron," Kitty says to me.

"Yeah, it took her a full eight secs to beat me this time," I groan as I sit up on the mat.

"Well, it's truly the effort that counts," Kitty responds and giggles flirtatiously. Oh, right, I almost forgot she's a sexbot.

"You are improving," Mermaid says.

"I just need to improve faster," I grumble.

Mermaid nods and offers her hand. She wears a white tank top with teasing wedges cut out. One wedge along her side reveals the shimmering blue scale tattoos that inspired my secret nickname for her. The truth is, I'm not sure what to think of my fellow henchman. She's intimidating as hell–equal parts gorg and lethal. Her long legs stretch for kilometers, but they're lean and muscular enough to crush the air out of a grown man. Her tank top shows off a slim waist and generous boobs. I can't see her eyes beneath her tinted goggles, but at our henchmen tryouts she wore masks with eye-hole cutouts. I know her eyes are green as emeralds and fringed with long lashes. She's got a face that practically begs to be splashed across holo-ads for toothpaste or acne cream or vacations to New Hawaii.

She also possesses the skill set of a trained assassin. If the rumors are true, she's put them to good use on several other semi-reality shows. I take her hand and she pulls me to my feet. It's a nice gesture, but I can't make the mistake of considering her a friend.

She's too cunning. Too crafty.

"Thanks," I mutter.

"Your ep comes out tonight, right?" She knows it does.

"Yep."

"You ready for it? You'll get new fans, but a lot of people won't heart the woman who brought down Shine."

"I'll deal." Truth is, I haven't thought much about the ep today. I don't plan on watching how Leo cut and edited my betrayal of Adan's friendship. Plus, all the Stream followers in the world won't matter if our show goes belly up. Nothing I can do about that right now, so I focus on what I can control.

I scrounge around for my bo staff and find it near the edge of the mat.

"I want to go again," I say.

I may not trust Mermaid as far as I can throw her but she's a damn good training partner. She doesn't hold back, and she doesn't show a drop of mercy. Over the last two weeks, my combat skills have markedly improved under her unrelenting tutelage.

"You sure?" She raises an eyebrow.

In response, I pull my staff in close to my body and shift my weight to the balls of my feet.

"I can spar with you, Iron," Sequoia calls. He's in the laboratory part of the main room where he's been scratching notes on the ancient chalkboard for the past hour, working on some component for The Professor's secret singularity pod. Even Sequoia won't tell me how it's supposed to work. All I know is that when it's ready, our "special guest" is going to get the first ride.

"Keep doing what you're doing," I say quickly to Sequoia. "It's important."

My friend gives me a searching look and then quickly turns his gaze back to the board. *Buddha's back hair.* I should have been more diplomatic, but the truth is Sequoia's no good at sparring with me. He holds back and lets me get in too many hits.

I think it has something to do with the lingering guilt he feels for knocking a few of my circuits loose when Leo matched us against each other during the henchmen tryouts. I've forgiven him for that brutal match about a thousand and one times, but I'm not sure he's forgiven himself. That's all well and good–Sequoia's one of the most decent human beings I know–but that doesn't help me one whit to get better.

"I'll spar with you, cowboy," Kitty says to Sequoia. She makes a very suggestive gesture with her broomstick.

"Any chance you can turn off her sex drive?" I ask my friend.

I watch the back of his freckled neck turn an amusing shade of red. "Um, no, it's part of her... um, core personality profile. Well, I mean, we could, but then we'd have to wipe out her entire programming and upload a new personality, and Leo said we didn't have the budget, so..."

"I get it," I say, waving away the rambling explanation. "Kitty, keep the sexy going, I guess."

"Aye, aye!" She gives me a salute. Her whiskers tremble.

I glance at my friend again. "How about I graciously allow Arsenic to beat my ass for a few more mins, and then you can help me suck slightly less on the lasso?" I offer.

Sequoia smiles. He never seems to mind performing the role of my slowly moving lasso target.

"Ohhh, she wants to tie you up. Better say yes to that," Gold drawls as he saunters from the secret elevator, late to practice as usual. I wonder what trouble he's brewing in his spare time.

Gold shrugs off a stylish red jacket, letting it drop to the floor. "Be a robo and hang that up, will ya, sweetheart," he says to Kitty. Beneath the coat he wears garish, neon yellow workout pants and a tight orange tank with gold slashes across it. He looks to Sequoia. "Hey big tree, want to go a few rounds? Let's see if I can knock you down."

Gold knows all my nicknames.

I give Gold a little shake of my head to let him know exactly what I think of his line. He shrugs. Cam drones buzz over our heads in lazy, automated loops. They record all our practice sessions, but unless one of us shatters a femur, none of this footage will likely make it onto the ep. Gold uses this time to practice new quips and fine-tune his character.

"Alright, what are we doing?" He claps his hands together. "Arsenic, maybe when you're done embarrassing Iron, you can teach me a few holds?" His gold-dyed eyebrows dance above his goggles.

Before Mermaid can answer, The Professor's office door opens. He and Leo have been huddled in there for at least a half-hour. We all perk up. Gold puffs out his chest and Mermaid pulls out her ponytail, causing a curtain of blonde and blue hair to tumble down her shoulders.

Now that our vil is in the scene, our odds of getting some ep time just shot up.

The Professor's face is a storm cloud of anger. His thin lips pucker and the tip of his beakish nose is red. Even his wild silver hair seems to be standing a little more on end. He stalks across the room, banging his cane with every step for emphasis. He's so angry, he's hardly remembering to limp.

I glance at Leo, searching his face for clues, but of course I'd have an easier time finding glaciers in the

Arctic. His expression is completely unreadable, and he stays back, standing just outside The Professor's office so as not to be in our frame. When he slips his heavily modified Goggs over his eyes, it's almost like he disappears, his consciousness transferring to the cam drones that pull from their automatic loops.

A wallop of fear hits my stomach. What if they found out about my extracurricular visit to Adan's home this afternoon? I tried to be so careful about ducking away from all the cams, but Leo's a sneaky bastard. If Leo or The Professor figured out that I know Shine's true identity and didn't tell them, they'd probs strap me into the singularity pod until I told them everything, including the name of my robo goldfish when I was five. Then they'd swipe me off the show so fast I'd spin like one of those old-timey tops.

The Professor makes his way over to the laboratory side of the main room and stands imperiously as we gather in front of him.

"My elements," he booms, "last night you failed me, but a good scientist doesn't give up after one disappointing experiment. They try again, and fortunately for you, I am willing to give you another chance to prove yourselves."

Conscious of the cams, I cross my arms over my chest, then see Mermaid has already adopted the same posture. I drop my arms and nod to The Professor. I've got to play this breezy. Either they know my secret or they don't. No sense in broadcasting my guilt.

"For too long, Big Little City has laughed at my genius," The Professor booms. "The City Council has refused to fund my leading-edge research. Shield University denied my request to use its labs, and BLC Bank rejected my dearly needed loan requests. They never understood, so it's time to make them understand."

Even as he rants, The Professor is clearly off his game. Gerald, the man behind the Persona, relishes these classic monologues. Usually, he throws his arms around and his voice bounces from strangled whisper to bellowing anger. Today, his voice is loud but flat and his arms dangle at his sides.

I tune back in as he finishes listing off his grievances. "And so, my elements, in order to complete my singularity pod, I need funds for the last specialized components. In three days' time…" he pauses to take a breath, but it somehow seems to deflate him. "… In three days' time, we rob BLC Bank."

Stunned silence.

Rob the bank?

No big-time vil would lower themselves to performing such a basic, uncreative heist. Only the smallest vils hit the bank, scrounging for something to save their dying careers. Robbing the bank is humiliation. Worse, it's desperate.

I feel a wave of embarrassment wash through me on behalf of Gerald, followed by a spark of anger that quickly kindles. This must be the next move by Tatiana Wentworth to drown our show.

Sequoia recovers first. "Yes, Professor," he says roughly.

"Yes, Professor," Gold follows quickly, trying and failing to hold his signature smirk in place.

"Yes, Professor," I force myself to say.

"Yes, Professor," Kitty sings and licks her lips suggestively.

Mermaid is silent. She stares past The Professor at

Leo. If she had the ability to shoot lasers out of her eyeballs, I'm sure he'd be a smoldering corpse on the ground.

To his credit, Gerald squares his bony shoulders and narrows his eyes. "Do any of you have a problem with my decision?"

We shake our heads, none of us willing to point out that this mission is ratings suicide.

"Good," our boss says. "Then let us plan. We have little time to spare."

***

Two hours later, silence reigns across the lair. The chalkboard is now filled with a scribbled list of supplies, equations, and the beginnings of our bank robbery plan. In one corner, a little chalk stick figure holds a bunch of other unhappy stick figures in a big lasso.

I stare at the board and sigh. The other henchmen left as soon as they were released. Sequoia invited me over to his place to watch The Professor's latest ep, but I made up some lame-o excuse about hating to see myself on cam. Mermaid and Gold tailed it too, probably to sulk or worse... start planning their next moves after our show is swiped.

It's not over yet, I remind myself as I sling my bag over my shoulder and head to a back door in the lair. We managed to slip away from the Dragon Riders at the mayor's mansion and tonight's ep will surely generate buzz. Maybe it will be enough to convince Tatiana Wentworth that our show is worth keeping around. After all, RAE – Ratings Are Everything.

I walk down the hallway and turn into the small kitchen. Technically, it's Sequoia's turn to feed our prisoner, but he let me take over his shift even though it's a highly valued commodity among us henchmen. The chance to taunt Shine, if one is canny enough with their words and threats, always ups the chances of grabbing a little extra lens time. Sequoia had raised his eyebrows at my request but hadn't asked questions. He really is a good friend.

In the small kitchenette, I prepare the tray. Our special guest doesn't get anything fancy for his meals, just water in a biodegradable cardboard cup and a nutra-pack. I'm about to grab a rando bar as usual, when I stop. I remember that silver holo-frame at Adan's house, the two girls laughing as their big brother swung them around. Adan is a person. And obviously not a half-bad one at that. His career will be battered when our ep launches, maybe ruined forever if Beacon doesn't rescue him soon, and it's all my fault.

I take down the variety box of nutra-packs and rifle through it. Near the bottom, I find what I'm looking for. Cookies n' cream flavor. I put it on the tray. As I walk down the hallway, I stumble and the bar tips off the tray. Grumbling, I lean down to pick it up. A cam sits in the corner of the hallway. Quickly, I swipe Adan's Band from my bag and hold it under the tray while I pick up the bar and toss it back on.

Adan sits on his bunk when the door to his cell whooshes open. We're both aware of the cam recording in the room.

"Ah, I see you're still here," I say in a casual tone. "Has your stay with us been satisfactory?"

"I'd prefer better company," he says in a bored voice even as his eyes search my face.

"I'm so sorry to hear that," I reply. "I'll be certain to let management know. We do wish to make your time with us as comfortable as possible. In fact, our chef whipped up this meal just for you."

Leo has instructed us to set the tray down near the door. When we leave, Shine's wrist and ankle tethers extend, giving him range to roam throughout the room. We're never supposed to approach him or get anywhere near arm's reach. According to Tickles, many henchmen make this mistake and earn a one-way ticket to getting choked out with shackle tethers.

Ignoring Leo's rules and one of the primary directives of *The Henchman's Survival Guide,* I march right up to Shine and shove the tray into his lap. His hand touches mine, then feels the Band, which he shoves under his leg, using the tray as a cover.

I dance back, out of reach and sneer at him. "Beacon isn't coming to save you, my little pearl."

Shine nods and I see a small smile touch his lips.

I should go, but Leo will be suspicious if I don't vamp for the cam a little more.

"And our singularity pod is almost ready," I tease Shine. "I'm not exactly sure how it works, but I can't wait to find out."

Shine tilts up his chin, slipping back into his role. "If I get crushed in that singularity pod, at least I'll die knowing I made the world a better place. What about you?"

I scramble to think of a good line. "If I die knowing I made you and a few other capes suffer, that's good enough for me," I manage. Not exactly a brills comeback.

Shine raises an eyebrow.

"Enjoy the meal," I sputter and turn to the door.

"My compliments to the chef," Shine says and laughs

as I stomp out.

Okay, so no points for lines, but at least I got Adan his Band back. Favor complete. That's one weight off my shoulders. Now, if I can only figure out how to turn our sadpocalypse mission into a success.

Just as I pass The Professor's private office, the door slides open.

"Iron," my boss says in that deep, chilling voice of his, "join me for a moment. I've something to discuss with you."

He knows. The thought crashes through my brain. *He knows and he's going to swipe me.* It's everything I can do not to gulp as I take halting steps into The Professor's office.

CHAPTER 9

We have all the confidence in the world in NASA. There's way too much money on the line for them to screw up a fourth time. Not to mention how many Stream followers they'd lose if we go out in a huge ball of flames. ~ Phoenix Shuttle Commander Thane-Ambrose Garcia, Live Q&A on NASA Stream

~

As I slink into my boss's office, I expect to see The Professor. But it's his alter ego, Gerald, who greets me from behind a massive desk. He still wears The Professor's costume–the singed lab coat and pulsating, multi-colored bowtie—but the worn expression on his face gives away the fact that my landlord sits across from me, not the zany character he plays across the Streams.

"No cams, Leo," Gerald says, waving a dismissive hand. A small cam drone that has approached the doorway behind me retreats back into the main gym just before the door slides shut.

I've never been in Gerald's office before, not even on the secret tour of the lair Matthew gave me several years ago. According to Matthew, his father spent hours every day in this small room after his show was swiped, meandering through crinkled blueprints of his solar furnace or using the old Pod in the corner to watch eps of his show.

Today, the office is cluttered and dank, obviously re-decorated for the new show. A massive chart of the periodic table hangs on the wall, each square filled with a glowing holographic image of an element. Old, yellowed scientific textbooks, like the kind students used half a century ago, line a rusted shelf on the side of the room. Old parts fill another shelving unit and physical blueprints of The Professor's singularity pod lie across his wide desk. On top of the blueprints sits an elegant white plate filled with the discarded crusts of a grilled cheese sandwich.

"Have a seat." Gerald motions to an old chair on the other side of his desk. I plop down and it squeaks with my weight. I'm pretty sure it's been here since his original show. I tuck my hands into my lap unsure of what expression to show. There are no cams in the room, but it's starting to feel more and more automatic to "mind my face."

I force my eyes to meet Gerald's gaze and try to project a mix of polite inquisitiveness and breezy confidence. Deep lines dig into Gerald's forehead and heavy crescents curve around each side of his mouth. His sharp, beaky nose and watery blue eyes are so familiar. He gave those features to his son. Matthew has always looked more fragile, more breakable than his loud, energetic father, but right now, Gerald is more vulnerable than I've ever seen him.

"I believe congratulations are in order," Gerald says. He tents his hands over his desk, his right elbow almost hitting the rim of the plate.

I think my spine actually trembles. *He knows.* He's going to play this out. Tease and taunt me before firing me. But then why send the cams away?

When I don't say anything, Gerald continues. "Tonight's ep was excellent. The viewers are, what do the kids say? Gushing." Gerald gives me a wan smile that doesn't look proud or happy. "I have you to thank for that. Shine's capture will reverberate throughout the city. It will reinforce my reputation and begin to build yours as well."

"I didn't see the ep," I blurt out. Is he toying with me? Lifting me up only to swat me down?

"No?" Gerald frowns. "See that you do. And I suppose your Iron Persona Stream is live. Be sure to attend to that regularly. Your fans, no doubt wish to hear from you."

"K…" I mumble. Leo, or more likely, one of his virtual production assistants set it up last week and gave me access. He's already posted a few pics to the Stream and some short clips of my performance during the henchmen tryouts, but I'll be expected to add updates and interact with fans. I can't help but grimace. Constant Stream engagement isn't just a requirement of my job, it's a survival skill for any persona (lowercase p) hoping to stay relevant to viewers. But all I see is more work, more fakery, more Fame Game flattery.

I grab the sides of the chair with my sweaty palms. "Is that all?"

"Iron, I… I mean, Alice. There is something else. Something delicate." Gerald clears his throat. "I, well, I suppose this is somewhat unorthodox due to our villain-henchman relationship…"

I strain to follow along. *He must know I helped Shine. He's going to swipe me after all.*

"I just… I just would very much appreciate it if…" Gerald pauses, as if he's teetering on the edge of a cliff, unsure if he should take the plunge. "...if you can provide an update on my son."

Plunge taken.

I stare at him as all my thoughts lurch and shift. Then it downloads. *He's not swiping me. He's asking about Matthew.*

"Oh, uh, yes, of course," I say.

"I don't wish to invade his privacy, of course," Gerard says quickly. "I only wish to ensure that his health is good. Mental and physical."

Gerard's eyes shy away from mine. His fingers twitch. It's heartbreaking. Silently, I curse Matthew for his stubbornness, for the resentment he carries against his father like some badge of pride.

"Well, to be honest, I haven't had as much time to spend with him recently, due to the new job," I admit. I lean back in the chair, wondering if I should voice my worries. Matthew's been anxious lately. I remember how he rocked on the couch this afternoon. He's beginning to spiral, but he would never want me to tell his father. Do I owe it to him to keep my mouth shut, or does Gerald deserve to know that another storm threatens on the horizon?

"He's... he's... fine," I manage. "I mean, fine by Matthew standards. He's training for a trivia show."

Gerald nods. "Yes, he told... I'd heard that. Is he any good?"

"Yeah. He's stuffed more facts into his brain than most robos could hold on their chips." The small smile on Gerald's face encourages me. "Let's see," I say, searching for safe topics. "He's been painting his fingernails black. He eats too many protein packs, and Betty has a new dragon tattoo on her chest."

Gerald nods, happily accepting these small crumbs.

What I don't say is, *Matthew feels isolated. He still blames you for his panic attacks and for pushing his mom away by obsessing over the show. He thinks you broke his mind by turning him into a mini-villain as a kid before he understood your show was just semi-reality. He thought it was real.*

"I cannot tell you how much I truly appreciate your insight," Gerald says. Even though he wears the costume of The Professor, I can't see any of that bombastic vil in the old man sitting on the other side of the desk. I see a father struggling to understand his son the only way he can, through someone else.

Without thinking, I lean across the desk. "I'll always look out for Matthew," I vow. "He's got a sadness inside of him, but he's an incredibly loving and wonderful person."

Matthew is the only person in this whole town I would trust with my life. He's the one I would call if I needed help; the one who would come to my rescue even if it didn't serve his own objectives. He is selfless, at least when it comes to his friends.

When it comes to his father...

"I fear I have torn his soul in a way that seems irreparable," Gerard says. His smile seems heavy. Now those blue eyes finally come up and meet mine. "I apologize. That is not a burden you deserve on your shoulders."

"I hope he forgives you someday," I say impulsively. "He's only hurting himself with all this resentment."

Gerald stands up and turns away from me. "I thank you for the kind thoughts," he says in a voice dragged through gravel. "And I thank you for the friendship you show my son."

"Always," I say and I stand up too. When he doesn't say anything more, I murmur, "I should go."

"Alice, you have done me a great favor today."

His words burn because I haven't done him any favors today. I know Shine's true identity. I could release it in a single utterance and give The Professor one of the greatest ratings gifts of all time. And yet, I stay silent.

"I shall give you a favor in return, but I beg you to keep it to yourself," Gerald says. "It is best that your fellow henchmen not know."

"Sure," I manage.

Gerald folds his hands on the desk and looks down at his knuckles. I look at his hands too, at the knotted veins so blue beneath the thin layer of his skin.

"The bank robbery is a rudimentary heist, isn't it?" he says. "So beneath the dignity of The Professor." I keep my eyes on his hands and gaze at the stretch of pale liver spots. "I want you to know that it was not devised by myself or Leo. We were directed by the City Council."

By Tatianna Wentworth, I think. I widen my eyes to force an expression of surprise, hold it for two full secs, and then shift my face into what I really feel, frustration. "It doesn't matter," I tell him. "Sure, bank heists have been done before, but we just need to find a way to make it interesting."

Gerald is already shaking his head. "You don't understand, my dear," he says, all the power and purpose dried up from his voice. "We have received very particular instructions this time. The Elementals, what's left of them, will make a *surprise* appearance with two trainees in tow. We have been expressly instructed that we shall knock out Gust and Rain, but alas, the new trainees will capture me."

"What?" I gasp. No need to feign shock now.

Gerald smiles down at his hands. "I have been instructed to lose. To give myself up. It is the proverbial end of the road."

"But...but..." I sputter helplessly. "But why?"

"Politics, my dear. Leo received a tip that the City Council was pulling strings to damage our show. He called a few of his contacts and discovered that one particular sponsor had quite an ambition to spin off Shine. We meddled in that plan and she is not pleased."

Tatianna Wentworth! Blight her! I feel flames of rage kindle to life inside the pit of my stomach. I wish a sandstorm would tear the skin right off her body! Then a new thought occurs.

"This is my fault!" I gasp. "I captured Shine!"

"You did and it was brilliant." Gerald finally looks up at me. "To see him trussed up in his own Torch Whip! What a scene that was."

"I ruined your show." My legs don't feel strong enough to hold me and I drop back into the chair.

"It was Shine's intention to capture me, which would have ended the show anyway." Gerald reaches over and I feel his hand—thin but strong—cover mine. "We were never meant to succeed."

My throat closes up as a shower of realizations soak through me. The City Council wants to get rid of Beacon. One way to weaken her is to spin off her popular sidekick. But how? What vil is a big enough catch to propel Shine to his own show? Tatianna Wentworth must have known Gerald was hankering to get back in front of a cam, and he possessed waves of nostalgia to keep him afloat for at least a couple of eps.

It was all a setup from the very beginning. Our show was over before it ever began.

"It's... not fair," I choke out.

"No. It isn't."

We stay there, his hand resting over mine, for several secs, and then he pulls his hand away and self-consciously adjusts his bowtie.

"I just thought you should know," Gerald says gruffly, "so that you can make plans. Grab as much lens time as you can on this last heist. It may help you if you should ever seek employment on another show in the future."

"I don't want to be on another show," I bite out bitterly.

"You have a strong screen presence, my dear," Gerald says, collecting a little of his old voice back. "Just work on the pith of your lines and I am confident you'll find work again."

But what about you? I think. Gerald fought for seven years for this chance at a comeback. What will he do now? Go back to watching reruns of his show in this forgotten, dusty office while this house slowly falls apart around us? The thought makes my heart ache. I force myself to my feet. My brain pounds with this poisonous news. I turn to go once again.

"Alice, please keep this to yourself. The others..."

I nod, understanding immediately what he means. If Gold and Mermaid knew this was our last heist, they would go off script, grab as much lens time as possible, and maybe even switch sides to try and glom onto another storyline. Our last mission would be even more of a raging disaster than it's already meant to be.

On shaky legs, I wobble out of The Professor's office.

The door shuts behind me, and I lean against the wall to catch my breath. I close my eyes as flames rage impotently inside of me. I feel so angry, so frustrated, but mostly I feel helpless. A hot tear slips down my cheek. I wipe it away as my ears catch a distinctive hum. I look up and see a cam drone floating across the gym, its lens trained on me. I grimace and turn away, hot waves of shame flooding through me.

"Don't you *dare* put this in the ep," I hiss, knowing the cam will pick up my voice and that Leo will hear it from his editing station in his apartment.

***

As soon as I walk through the door of my apartment and it slides shut, a wave of weariness crashes over me. My stomach gurgles, but I have no energy to even drag myself to the kitchen. I glance at my Band. It's almost midnight. My Totem, Bob, has sent me several angry messages demanding to be taken out of sleep mode. I ignore them. My eyelids are like anchors. My brain swirls with all that I have learned, but I push those serrated thoughts away. I can't think about how our show is doomed. I won't.

"Ta," says a soft voice from the couch.

I jerk, startled. The living room is dim and quiet. I hadn't even noticed Lysee curled on the couch. Something feels wrong. It takes me a moment to figure out what it is. Her Pod is off. That never happens. As long as Lysee is awake, the Pod is on, splashing our wall with constant updates on new K-pop songs, Persona Stream updates, and pings from her friends, while cape and vil eps play on a side screen.

I move into the room and come around to the couch. Lysee wears a simple pair of lacey pink pajamas. Not a zipper or bow in sight. Her hair hangs down her back, like a shining silver waterfall, and only the lightest touches of makeup enhance her pretty, heart-shaped face. I'm not used to seeing her without bright lipsticks and glittering stick-on jewels. She looks ethereal and gorgeous and it scares me a little.

"Is everything k?" I ask.

She smiles. "Oh yes. Everything is hallowed. The Professor's ep was brills. You got great lens."

"I haven't watched it."

She laughs and looks toward the wall. Her gaze is far away, like she can see out some invisible window. "It's funny where the path of the universe takes you, isn't it?" she says eventually. "You. Me. All the twists and turns."

"Yes, definitely," I lie, not understanding a word. Someone's obvi been swimming in the deep end of the self-help Streams.

"I am at peace," Lysee says.

"That's, uh, that's great," I manage. "You want a nutra-pack?"

She shakes her head.

I sit on the couch, uncertain, while my mind spins with all my own problems. "You sure everything's hardy?" I ask again.

Lysee puts a hand on my knee. "Yes. I know my purpose."

"Alright then. Good talk." I stand up.

Tomorrow.

Tomorrow I'll figure out what's going on with my roomie. It's probs just a new serenity path or something. I move to my room, each step weighed down with a hundred pounds of worry. Lysee twists on the couch.

"It's our duty to follow our destiny," she says. Her wide, green-tinted eyes are heavy with sentiment.

"Go for your destiny, Lysee," I tell her, half-heartedly.

She smiles again. "That means so much, coming from you."

I approach my bedroom door and it slides open as it syncs with my Band.

"Alice," Lysee's voice calls behind me. "I love you."

"Love you, too," I reply automatically and then enter my room. I've been meaning to decorate this place, I swear, but the only accessory I need right now is the bed in the middle of the room. I don't so much lie down as crumple onto the soft mattress.

I close my eyes, but blissful sleep doesn't come.

Our show is as good as swiped, I think. There goes my one chance to pay for college. *Maybe there's a job in town.* Except I already literally asked at every shop and restaurant just a few weeks ago. No one is hiring, and I don't have any skills to HaLC–Hustle a Little Currency, or beg for microtips in exchange for showing off some sort of interesting talent or skill on my Stream.

A new thought hits me, and this one, at least, makes me smile. If we're going gutter with this doomed bank heist, the least I can do is tip off my roomie. Lysee works as a bank teller specifically for the lens grabbing opps the position offers. She loves nothing more than to be threatened by vils and gallantly rescued by capes, all while the cams roll. Maybe she and I can even come up with a little side story where she strangles me with my own lasso or something. If I'm going the way the glaciers, I might as well give my friend a little of the lens time she craves in the process.

I'll throw the offer to her tomorrow when my head isn't throbbing with exhaustion. For now, I drag myself up into a sitting position. "Unmute," I say to my Band.

My glum Totem appears on the holo-screen projected onto my forearm from my Band.

"Bout time," Bob says. "You look like you got run over by a herd of elephants, and then they backed up a couple of times."

"There are no more elephant herds," I tell him. "Least not in the wild."

"Whatever. I gotta lot of responses pouring in from The Professor's latest ep." he says.

"Not right now."

"Fine. Your loss." He shrugs, and his unshaven jowls quiver. The rainbow-hued butterfly wings on his back flap once. Every day I regret loading him with a sarcastic and cranky personality, and yet I can never quite convince myself to change it. Of all the people in my life, sometimes Bob feels the most refreshing.

I stare at him and realize that I don't know what I want. Something easy. Something hopeful.

Then I know.

"Show me the Phoenix," I tell my Totem.

"Coming up." Bob burps and the screen on my Band morphs into the endless black blanket of space. A glowing strand of light shows the long arc of the ship's trajectory as it nears the big red planet where decades of robo-built structures await the brave and fragile 200 humans on the ship. After the first colony ship floundered from a hull breach less than halfway to the planet and the last two ships burned in the Martian atmosphere during failed landings, there was talk of scrapping the entire enterprise. For ten years no new colony ships made the attempt. One of the few things Sage Anders did right when she was elected was to work with a few top Captains of Industry to fund this fourth and likely last try.

"Enhance," I say, and the video zooms in so I can see a silver icon of the ship. I lay on my pillows, shoulder throbbing, neck sore, but smiling as I watch the beacon of a ship sail through black space. Two hundred brave, stupid souls are trying to do something meaningful, trying to push the story of humanity farther than it's ever gone before.

This is real, I think drowsily as my eyes sink shut and sleep takes me.

CHAPTER 10

I have been known to manage a few surprises
when my back is up against the wall. ~ Iron,
Interview with J Bennett

~

I dream of the desert.

The sun hammers me, soaking into my skin, turning my blood into fire. The sand grabs my legs, dragging me down with each step. I hear voices in the wind. My father's soft murmur, the lullabies my mother used to sing. I will not make it out of the desert. I already know this. My blood will burn away. My bones will dry and splinter.

But I keep walking. I must.

Someone walks beside me. It must be Alby. He and I fought the desert together, until I fell. I look over, but it is not Alby.

Beacon walks at my shoulder, the sun glinting off her metallic gold-and-scarlet costume. The lighthouse icon glows on her chest, and her violet eyes are steady as they meet mine. She doesn't say anything, but somehow I know we are going to make it. We will cross the desert. The audience will be pleased.

I wake up to sunlight. It streams through the window of my bedroom, nudging my eyes open. Usually when I dream of the desert, I seize awake with a pounding heart and sweat-soaked PJs. But this morning I feel at peace.

The dream lingers, and it's almost as if Beacon is still at my side, confident and protective. Ironic, considering the real Beacon would kick my ass and drag me to jail if she got the chance.

"Finally," Bob says, appearing on the holo-screen of my Band. "You've got a lot of work to do. Your fans are savage to hear from you. So are your shades."

"I thought I put you in sleep mode," I groan.

"You took me out last night, but then you got all sappy over watching the Phoenix instead of attending to your fans." He projects a holo-vid of a weeping panda scooping ice cream into its mouth from a huge container.

"Fans?" I mumble, wiping the grit out of my eyes.

"And shades. You're the top trending Persona on the hate chart in the entire sector right now."

Shades? Why would I have anti-fans?

"Your Iron Stream is at 132,349 followers since The Professor's ep aired last night. They're still pouring in. You've also got 16 interview requests lined up, and Reena Masterson wants you to call her."

"Reena Masterson?" My voice is a squeak. Our town's most iconic reporter wants to talk to me? I feel adrift in a strange, swirling sea. And then it starts to download. The Professor's show. The new episode where I captured Shine; where I marched him down to the lair and The Professor formally invited me to become his fourth henchman.

"Shocking, but it seems like you've somehow managed to become a Persona," Bob says. "And a well and truly hated one at that."

I sit up in bed, pushing away the tangle of sheets and

blankets.

A Persona. Capital P.

A Persona is followed. A Persona is known. A Persona is the thing everyone in this town dreams of being.

It rocks me. Scares me. Disgusts me.

For a moment, I feel my life spinning away from me, my fingers too slow to grasp it as it rushes down an unfamiliar path. This is the thing I never wanted. I used to mock the strivers and now I'm one of them. My stomach is fluttery and queasy at the same time.

"... and you've got two new messages on your normie Alice Stream," Bob is saying.

My focus snaps to that. Something normal, from my real life. "Show me that," I tell him.

The holo-screen on my forearm shifts, glowing white for a moment, and then Alby's eyes are staring back into mine. My heart squeezes painfully as I look into my brother's round, pale face, into those brown eyes that match my own but settle deep in puffy pockets of sleep depravation.

Is something wrong? Did Mom get sick? Has Alby had a mental setback or does he only want more money for some pointless upgrade in his VR game?

"Heya, Twinly Two," Alby says. He squints. I realize he's outside. This, all by itself is a shock. Alby doesn't go outside. Not unless he absolutely has to. "So, that drooling program you put into Tayla says I can't play *Tears of Doom* for another two hours," he grumbles. I close my eyes, thankful again that I spent my last Loons on that super expensive therapy program that I interfaced with Tayla, his gorgeous Totem.

Alby continues, "Tayla says I need to interact with the real world. It's utter lobotomy, but..." here he shrugs and glances over his shoulder with a clear look of longing. He's probably gazing at his trailer and the pair of Goggs inside that will let him jump back into the game, *Tears of Doom,* that he's currently obsessed with. "But we've been doing some conflict resolution work, and it's actually been helping me advance in the game. You know, strengthening my headspace. I'm so close to going pro, Alice. A few more months, really." He looks down. "Anyway, since I'm on a break, I thought I'd help Mom with some of her plants or whatever."

The cam shifts, and suddenly my mom fills the screen, a gentle smile on her tanned face. "Hello, Alice. I hope peace and generosity find you on this day," she says. Dirt cakes her hands, and I see several large pots in front of her, each one holding a tangle of delicate green shoots. Mom insists on growing her food the dirt way, despite the heat waves and dust storms and bouts on intense rain. It'd be so much cheaper for her to use her UBI to buy monthly supplies of nutra-packs like me, but she spends it on "real food" like rice and vegetables. Course, "real food" is expensive, especially because it seems like there's a super drought in some part of the country every year. UBI dollars don't go very far. It's one of the reasons I feel the need to give Mom and Alby any extra money I can spare.

The cam flips back to Alby. I notice that his dark hair, still long and shaggy, looks washed. So does his shirt. He even looks a little thinner. His face and body don't seem so swollen and unhealthy.

"Tomatoes are starting to grow," he says. "See." The cam flips once again, and now I'm looking at a tiny green nodule sitting on a thick stalk. "Anyway, Tayla says I can spend an extra hour in the game if I reach out to family more. So there you go. I've been meaning to start watching the cape and vil shows coming out of Biggie LC to see if I can tell who you are, but you know, with my training, I don't have much time. I hope it's going iconic. And..." The screen shifts to my brother. "Stay safe, Twinly Two."

"And be kind," my mother's voice says somewhere out of the shot.

The video ends. I stare at it in shock.

Alby made a video. For me. And he didn't ask for money. He didn't babble about some emergency. And he was outside.

This is big. Huge. Supernova. The therapy program must be working. One of the best things about the program is that it's compatible with Alby's game, *Tears of Doom.* Tayla can actually enter the game and put him through therapeutic sessions while he plays. She can also turn off the game even outside of the government's legally mandated five hours of power down for every 19 hours of play.

"It's working," I say out loud, and something wonderful and dangerous blooms in my soul.

Hope.

"Hey, hey!" Bob barks at me. "Back on task here. We're going to have to seriously elevate your social media game for your Iron Stream after this hot debut. More pics. More vids. Daily vid diaries. That sort of thing. Let's start with maybe brushing your teeth."

Then a thought hits me like a sledgehammer and all my hope crumbles to dust. That sledgehammer has a name.

Tatianna Wentworth.

Standing in my bedroom, a drooling smile on my

face, I suddenly remember that our show is going to get swiped in three days when we try to rob the bank. All this fame will be gone in an instant, and so will the paychecks I need to cover the hefty subscription fee for Alby's therapy program. That money also goes toward buying rice, bread, oatmeal, and other staples for my mom while she lovingly grows clusters of tomatoes and carrots that could never hope to feed her.

I blink into the sunlight as my thoughts swirl and congeal into a single word.

No.

I can't let Alby down, which means I can't just stand by and let our show go gutter.

No.

No.

NO!

Within the mess of anger, hopelessness, and fear for Alby, something tugs at my brain. My dream hasn't totally evaporated. I see Beacon again, those red lips smiling at me, that streaming golden hair.

The City Council is trying to swipe Beacon's show, too, I realize. We actually have something in common. Though not *that* much in common. Beacon actually has the money to fight back. She can afford to hire her own producer and save her slot on the PAGS programming platform.

I stand up. As I move toward the window, I catch my reflection in the mirror. Tangled brown hair falls around my shoulders and my t-shirt is rumpled from sleep. Not exactly a fierce henchman.

I remember what Adan told me about Beacon's big breakthrough. Like me, she took a crazy chance. She ignored her sponsors and producers and snuck onto that train to face The Professor. She grabbed such powerful ratings that the City Council fell all over themselves to promote her.

It was risky but it paid off.

I watch myself smile in the mirror. "Thank you, Beacon," I whisper.

I glance at my Band. Still a little over three hours until my first class starts. Bob has pulled up the second message on my Alice Stream. It's a ping from Ollie offering to study for the chem midterm. I definitely need to do that, but I've got something more important to handle first.

Humming "Mom, Make Me Noodles," I wash my face, comb my hair, and then twist it into a braid. I tie a white bow at the bottom of the braid and don my henchman costume–red lab coat, flashing white bowtie, and the cracked gray-and-green goggles.

Now I'm glad I never managed the energy or the dollars to actually decorate my room. My blank wall is the perfect background for my first official vid on my Iron Stream.

"Bob, record on my mark," I tell my Totem.

"Wait, you're actually recording a vid... voluntarily?" He looks stricken and his rainbow wings flutter in agitation. "Can Totems have heart attacks?"

"Just do it," I say. I turn my wrist so that the cam embedded in my Band gets my full face. A holo-screen projecting up from the Band shows me what the cam sees —a calm and confident henchman. I count down from five. When I reach one, the recording light brightens.

I smile. "I'm glad so many of you enjoyed my little scuffle with Shine," I say. "We're so excited to have him as our special guest. I just wanted to let all my fans know that The Professor is planning something big." I take a breath and force my smile even wider, almost gloating. "So get ready. School is in session." I finish with a short laugh and then stop the recording.

Sure, it wasn't the most shining vid ever, but it *was* a statement.

"Want to record a few more tries?" Bob asks.

"Nope, post it to my Iron Stream."

"You're supposed to get Leo's permission before you put anything on your henchman Stream," he says.

"I've got admin access."

"That's so you can respond to comments."

"Post it," I tell him.

"Yes, ma'am." He salutes, his double chin quivering. I feel exhilarated. True, the vid didn't say much, but it was my secret pledge that I'm not letting go of our show without a fight. I just promised the world a daring escapade, and now I've got to deliver.

I quickly send out private messages to my fellow henchmen.

***

When I get home from my classes, I only have 15 mins to prepare for the special meeting I've called. I glance at my Band. My Iron Stream numbers continue to tick up. It seems like half the world wants to buy me a drink and the other half wants to murder me. My Stream is gushing with the tormented rage of tween girls, boys, and nonbinaries. Bob has started filling a folder with all the gossip stories about me and Shine. Separate folders hold fan comments, marriage proposals, and death threats. I don't know how to process this lobotomy new world I'm in, but fortunately, I don't have the time to ponder it too deeply.

I notice two messages in my private chat channel from Leo. No doubt he wants to compliment me on the brills teaser vid I posted this morning. Being the humble employee I am, I decide not to indulge my ego by reading his messages.

I swing into my apartment and almost collide with Betty.

"Ay!" she cries, spinning in a slow, jerky circle. "I'm walking here!"

"Jersey accent," I say.

"I wanted to give her a little 'tude," Matthew says from the couch. I immediately look him over. His black hair is a little flat, and the bottom button on his silver jacket is unfastened. Not good. When he's on the happy mental health train, Matthew is agonizingly fastidious.

"Your dad says hi," I tell him as I toss my bag in my bedroom.

"I'll send him a heart emoji."

Betty turns and clips our couch.

"What's wrong with Betty?" I ask.

Matthew shrugs. "Drinking problem."

"Robos don't drink." I study Betty. She's such an old model that she never walked quite normally, but there's a distinctive jerk in her gait that seems to be pulling her off kilter.

"Her wiring is probs loose again," I say. "You can bring her into a shop, get her tightened up." The robo's over a decade old. Circuits and chips are bound to sputter out.

"I think she's fine."

I plop down on the couch next to Matthew, reach over, and push his bangs out of his eyes. Usually, he gels them to the side, but today they fall limply over his forehead.

"She's not fine, Matthew," I say softly. "She's breaking down, but she just needs a little help and then she'll be good as new."

Matthew turns his face away. "Maybe I like her a little broken."

"Just not too broken."

There's so much more to say. So much more I need to do for him, but a part of me feels resentful. Why does he have to go crumbling to pieces when I've got so much else on my plate?

"I'm having some people over soon," I say. "It's kind of a private thing."

"I saw the ep last night," he says. "The way you nabbed Shine, that was clever. And low."

His words sting because they're true.

"I saw an opportunity."

Matthew stands up. "And you took it."

"Let's talk soon," I tell him. "I've got some, um, stuff to do over the next couple of days and then midterms, but after that, we'll have an all-night dance party."

All-night dance parties are this thing we made up where one of us chooses a truly terrbs song and the other has to make up a dance to it on the spot. We do this back and forth until we're both too exhausted to go another round. Then we usually end up talking the rest of the night or watching a rando vil or cape show and adding snarky commentary the whole way through. Lysee is always up to join us for the lobotomy dancing, but she usually huffs to her room when we start mocking her fav shows.

"Yeah, sure," Matthew says in a way that clearly implies he holds out no hope for me. "Come on, Betts."

"Coming through, coming through," Betty says as she saunters to the door on her wobbling steps.

"Your dad really cares about you," I tell Matthew as he moves through the open doorway. He stops. I can't see his face, only the hunch of his thin shoulders beneath his flashing silver jacket.

"I know," he says morosely and then the door slides shut behind him.

I drop back down to the couch and consider the million and a half ways that convo could have gone better. I need to find a way to spend more time with Matthew. I should also let Lysee know that he's going dark. All her giddy happiness can usually cheer him up. Course, my roommate was cartwheeling across a different universe last night. I should probs check on her too, to figure out what that was all about. I pull up her Stream on my Band and see that she checked in at the bank for work. I open my mouth to vocalize a quick "hope you're doing okay" message when I get a ping from Sequoia. My Lysee wellness check will have to wait. I give Bob permission to open the door to my apartment.

When Sequoia walks in, he seems to fill up the whole place. He stops uncertainly near the couch and gives me a shy smile.

"Thanks for coming," I tell him.

"Course." He looks around. "Cozy," he says. "So, um, what did you want to talk about?"

"Wait here. I'll explain soon." I pop up off the couch rush into my room to quickly throw on my henchman uniform. I grab my goggles, but I perch them on my forehead instead of pulling them over my eyes.

Just as I return to the living room, Mermaid pings me. I take a deep breath and send the signal to the door.

As it glides open, Sequoia quickly pulls his goggles over his eyes, but I leave mine alone.

Mermaid slips quickly into the apartment. She wears her goggles, but a long black coat hides her costume. As soon as she sees me, she frowns.

"It's drooling to unmask, even in front of your teammates," she says.

"I know, but we've got bigger problems," I say.

"Is Gold coming?" Sequoia asks.

"I don't know," I admit. "He didn't respond to my message."

Mermaid stays near the door. She hasn't unbuttoned her coat. "What are you hatching?"

I hesitate. Can I really trust her? *No, but I have no choice.* I have to be bold, like Beacon.

"There's something I need to tell you. Both of you," I begin. "This bank heist, it's—" My Band pings. I sigh and give the command.

Gold saunters inside my apartment in full costume. "Stellar ep last night," he says. "You got the whole country raging. I think they despise you more than Sage Anders." He shakes his head with reluctant admiration. "All those death threats. I'm big enough to admit I'm jel."

"I didn't know if you were coming," I say.

"I like to be a little unpredictable," he says and drops onto the couch as if he owned the place. "But I couldn't have you all scheming without me." He peers up at me and his eyebrows dance above his goggles in surprise. "Whoa, unmasked. I guess we've got to trust you now."

I ignore him and look around the room.

"Why are we here?" Mermaid demands. She looks like she's secs from stomping out the door.

"We're here because our show is about to get swiped," I say.

That gets their attention.

CHAPTER 11

Your fellow henchmen are your teammates. They can become like family. That don't mean you should trust them. They want lens time just as much as you do. ~ Tickles the Elf, The Henchman's Survival Guide

~

"Blight!" Gold hollers as soon as I finish explaining everything about our perilous situation. He follows this outcry with some of the dirtiest, crassest, and most creative cursing I've ever heard. "... should 3D print Tatianna Wentworth's ovaries into a hat and make her wear it around Iconic Square," he continues.

"You're sure of this?" Mermaid asks me. Her expression is grim, but she doesn't seem too surprised that our show was created to fail. If the rumors are true, she's been running the semi-reality circuit for a long time. She's probs seen more than her fair share of dirty tricks. Likely, pulled a few of her own, too.

"We were set up at the mayor's house. That much is clear," Sequoia says.

"My info is solid," I tell them. "I got it directly from The Professor." I feel guilty betraying his trust but it's all for a good cause. I've got to get the others to believe me if we have any hope of preventing disaster on our next mission.

"I didn't realize your relationship with him was so

cozy," Mermaid says and lifts an eyebrow.

"Why doesn't The Professor fight it?" Sequoia asks. My friend's face is pale. Well, paler than usual, and it's taken on a slight green tinge. He leans heavily against a wall. He rejected his father's mandate to step into the family business in order to try out for The Professor's show. He's been mum on the exact consequences of this decision, but I imagine he won't be very welcome at the next family reunion.

"He doesn't think he has a choice," I admit.

Gold's head snaps up. "And you think we do?"

"There's always a choice," I say.

Gold smiles and nods. "I hear you. We've got to go supernova during the heist. Something that will grab eyes. Enough that we can spin off without The Professor."

"All of us?" Mermaid asks dubiously.

"Of course. We can make our own group." Gold bites his lower lip, worrying at his gold lipstick and then snaps his fingers. "What if we made up a team of other outcast henchmen? Who's that vil that just got swiped? He wore that huge battery pack that shot electric volts."

"Turbo," Sequoia says.

"Yeah, Turbo. He had those two henchmen who ran around charging him up. Maybe we reach out to them."

"We can't spin off, not after just four eps," Mermaid snaps.

"We're not going to spin off," I say, "because we aren't getting swiped."

"You just said—" Sequoia starts, but his words die when he glances at my face.

I take a deep, deep breath and move to the center

of my small living room. *Courage is for the desperate,* Tickles wrote on last night's blog. Well, desperation has a new name.

"Alice," I say. "That's my name. Alice Hannover. This is where I live."

"You live above The Professor's lair?" Gold asks at the same time Mermaid says, "Don't tell us your name, you shigit."

I glance around the room, trying to meet each of their gazes through their goggles. "Our show is about to go gutter," I say, choosing my words carefully. "In three days it won't matter if you know my name or where I live. All of us, we'll have nothing."

"Not nothing," Gold mutters, "but it'll be a long climb back up."

"The only way we survive is by doing something big," I continue, ignoring him. "Something so bold, so lobotomy that the sponsors will have to notice us." I pause. No cams are rolling, but this is the most important performance of my life. "Leo was right. Our last mission was a disaster. Not just because the Dragon Riders surprised us, but because we were trying to grab lens instead of fulfilling the mission. That can't happen again." I raise my voice. "If we want to survive. If we want to pull off something iconic, then we're going to have to work together. We're going to have to trust each other. We're going to have to be an actual team!"

I look around the room as my heart skips a beat in my chest. Mermaid crosses her arms over her chest. Gold presses his lips in a skeptical expression.

"Chauncy-Steward-Rine Briggs," Sequoia says and pulls off his goggles. His eyes are a pale blue, almost gray.

"Aw hell," Gold says. He fidgets and then yanks his goggles off. "Darius. Not telling you my last name." His eyes are the color of honey, just a few shades lighter than his skin.

"You're all lobotomy," Mermaid says. "We don't need names to trust each other. We just need the right incentive."

I knew she would be the most difficult to persuade.

"Are you willing to at least hear me out?" I ask her.

She doesn't uncross her arms. She still stands close to the door. But she says, "I haven't left... yet."

True. But will she agree to help or is she just keeping her options open? Mermaid is the best fighter and the most strategic thinker of all of us. We need her on board to have any chance of success.

"Alright, everyone. Goggles back on," I tell them. "Henchmen codenames only. I'm going to record the rest of the meeting."

"This just gets more and more drooling," Gold laughs, tugging his goggles over his eyes.

"Should we really be recording a scheme against Tatianna Wentworth?" Sequoia asks doubtfully.

"If our new mission is a success, Leo's going to want these planning vids to splice into the ep," I explain.

"Could be a trap," Mermaid says. "Maybe we aren't getting swiped at all and you just want to show The Professor and Leo that we're willing to go against their orders."

No surprise that a schemer expects betrayal at every turn. "I just gave you my name, my face, and my address," I tell her. "I'm at your mercy. If I double-cross you, just unmask me."

Her lips purse. I try to imagine the machinations

running through her brain. Then she uncrosses her arms, walks purposefully across the room, and sits on the couch next to Gold.

"Alright, let's start conspiring then," she says. "That'll make for some drama at least."

My hands shake a little as I set up Lysee's personal cam drone to auto record. I sync it to my Band and station it to hover in a corner of the room.

"Nitrogen, move a little to your left and come closer to the couch," I tell him as I back up, watching the screen input on my Band. "K, we're all in the shot. Here we go."

I hit record and explain the situation again—everything about being set up and my conviction that this next mission will be our last. This time I keep out Tatianna Wentworth's name and lay the blame on shadowy interests in the town. The others play up their shocked reactions. Gold leaps off the couch, raises a fist, and releases an avalanche of Stream-appropriate curses.

Mermaid rises from the couch as well and glares out the window, standing at the edge of the frame I marked out before I started recording.

"So what are we going to do?" Sequoia eventually asks, setting me up perfectly.

"Simple," I say with a grin, "we choose our own adventure."

"A different mission?" Gold feigns uncertainty. "But The Professor won't like that!"

"We don't have a choice," I tell him. I do my old trick of letting my gaze settle on each henchman. In my mind, I imagine the music Leo will add to this scene for our future ep. The sound will begin to swell with power and purpose right about now. "We're desperate," I tell the team. "There's power in that."

"We've got to pull off something good," Mermaid says.

"We've got to pull off something utterly enthralling," I correct. "It has to be something no one's done before. Like nothing the civvies in Biggie LC have ever seen!" I pound my fist into my hand. My heart is racing as the fake energy infects me. The others nod along.

"I assume you have something in mind?" Mermaid says, turning back to the group. The light from the window turns her hair into spun gold.

"Oh yeah." I pause dramatically. *Great pauses are the whipped cream on the tension pie,* Tickles the Elf likes to say.

After one more breath, I announce my big plan. "We shoot something up into the sky, like some huge cloud or something, that hovers over Biggie LC and blocks out the sun." I wave my hands overhead to illustrate. "It will cast everything into darkness."

I smile smugly. I'd actually gotten the idea from a recent convo with my brother, Alby. I look around at my silent teammates and continue enthusiastically. "The entire town runs on solar power. With no sunlight, there'll be no streetlights, no 3D printers, no drone deliveries. Even Bands will stop working without an external charge. All the other vil and cape shows will go down. Their cams won't work. Everyone will be in the dark... except us!"

I imagine a crescendo of music, then a dramatic silence in its wake as the cam pans to the surprised and rapt faces of my fellow henchmen. Except, when I glance around, I notice that my teammates are anything but rapt.

Mermaid is already shaking her head. "No way we can pull that off in three days. How exactly are we supposed to—" here she tents her fingers into air quotes, "—shoot some huge cloud or something into the sky?"

"Well, I haven't exactly worked out all the kinks yet," I manage. "I thought maybe Nitrogen would be able to..." I glance at Sequoia, begging for a lifeline.

"You're talking about interfering with the entire environment of the town," he says slowly, an apology clear in his voice. "I don't see how we could create an effect that would maintain a fixed position. And then we'd have to design a way to reverse the effect."

"But... but," I stammer, "... people do stuff with the environment all the time. The U.N. is spraying seawater into clouds to lower the earth's temp."

"Those are climate scientists," Sequoia says. "They have highly specialized training."

"Not to mention legal permission from the U.N. and thoroughly tested equipment," Mermaid adds.

"And, besides, every town has solar battery reserves that can last for weeks," Gold says. "We'd have to sabotage those, too."

My soul is a balloon and my teammates just jabbed it with a hundred needles.

"Well, fine, you guys come up with something," I huff.

"It was a creative idea," Sequoia offers.

"No, it was sadpocalypse," Gold says and then rubs his hands together. "Let's see, let's see." He begins pacing. I bet he reads *The Henchman's Survival Guide.* Tickles always says that movement grabs eyes and lens time.

"Let's steal a page from Shadow's playbook and start

blowing up buildings all over town," he says. "That'd get attention."

"No!" I snap. Shadow's grease-covered face and glowing red eyes seep into my mind. I feel again the terror of the night he stepped into the restaurant where I worked. When I close my eyes, I see the holo-clock bobbing above his wrist, counting down from ten minutes...

"That's... that's not The Professor's way," I manage. "We shouldn't do anything that puts people in serious danger."

"We'd give them some kind of warning," Gold says with a shrug.

"What's our goal?" Mermaid asks. "What does The Professor want?"

"Well, that depends," Sequoia says. He moves closer to the couch. "His arch-nemesis is Beacon, of course, so anything he can do to defeat or punish her is always on the top of his list. But then he also wants to build and test new equipment."

"We don't have time to build a new machine or weap," I say.

"But we can twist Beacon's tits," Gold replies, a smile growing on his face. "Her pretty boy is sitting in a cell in the lair. We dim Shine's lights and she'll come running."

A bolt of panic shoots through me. Sequoia speaks up, "But The Professor and I are already building the singularity pod. We need Shine for that."

"What's the point if The Professor gets nabbed before you finish it?" Gold snaps back. "I say we use him now."

I open my mouth to speak up. We can't put Adan... I

mean, Shine in real danger. Before I can form a coherent sentence, Mermaid steps in.

"Money. That's what this bank heist was all about. The Professor wants money for supplies and equipment."

"... and paychecks," Gold mutters.

"We kidnap someone," I say. "Someone we can ransom."

Gold throws up his hands. "We just tried to kidnap someone!"

I ignore him. "What about the new police chief? What's his name?"

"Everyone and their service robo has kidnapped the police chief," Gold says.

"Uh... Reena Masterson?" I mumble.

"She gets kidnapped once a month!" Gold groans.

"Well, everyone with any fame in this town has already been kidnapped," I snap back. "We could grab the school lunch lady. You wanna do that?"

"Then we take someone from outside of town," Sequoia says.

Shocked silence falls across the room. My mouth actually drops open.

Gold recovers first. "Dinosaur farts. We can't pull off a heist outside of Biggie LC."

"All semi-reality activities have to stay within the borders of the specified semi-reality town," I tell him. I may have skimmed most of the fine print of the resident contract when I moved to Biggie LC, but even I picked up on that part. It's kind of the rule.

"We went out of town to run the obstacle course," Gold argues back. "That was half a state away."

"The Professor must have gotten special permission

from the City Council for that," I tell him. "They'd never give us a green light for something like this."

"You said we had to do something big," Sequoia says simply.

"This is different," I sputter. "Crimes committed outside of town are... crimes. We wouldn't just lose our show and our jobs. We could get arrested, carted off to a drooly camp." I know I'm breaking the fourth wall. None of this talk about our show, town rules, and City Council permission can go in a future ep, but right now that doesn't matter. We've moved into a whole new realm of lobotomy.

"They're only crimes if we get caught," Gold says quietly.

All the excitement is draining out of me, replaced by a growing sense of dread.

"Did you have someone in mind?" Mermaid asks, staring intently at Sequoia.

He swallows, then nods. "Not only that, but I can get us access."

The four of us are quiet, each contemplating this new reality.

"We need to all agree," Mermaid says. She puts her hands on her hips. With the sun from the window shining behind her, she almost looks heroic. "We share the risks and the rewards."

This is a precipice. I know I need to back away, plug my ears, and break up this meeting at once. But if I do that, our show is over and so are my financial prospects. I remember how impossible it was to find any other work in town. I actually shiver at the memory of the terrbs platypus rap song I'd written in an attempt to garner pity tips from my tiny group of followers.

The money I'll earn from this show is the only thing keeping me in school and on my way to my degree. That degree is my ticket out of town. My mind tumbles down the familiar path of my greatest fear. If I lose this paycheck I'll have to slink back home to Quincy and become just another subsister, hidden in a repurposed cargo container in a dusty square of land that even GPS doesn't bother pinpointing.

In the end, though, even this horrific prospect isn't enough to convince me to jeopardize my freedom.

Something else does.

Not something. Someone.

Alby.

I look down at my Band. In the corner of my Alice Stream, I see a tiny thumbnail of his video message. I remember how the sunlight played across his face, how he looked less bloated and exhausted. He's getting better. The therapy program is pulling him back from the poisonous tendrils of the virtual reality world where he hides.

And my paycheck from this show is the only way I can afford the subscription to his therapy program. I need to help Alby. I need to put all the pieces of him back together. Because I'm the one who broke him.

"I'm in," I hear myself say. The words sound far away, drifting over the precipice into a new, perilous place. I look around at the others. No one has left the apartment. Without words, they've all decided too.

Gold looks at Sequoia. "Who is it? Who we going after?"

Sequoia waits a beat, playing it up for the cam, for all the ears that will be aching to hear. "We're going to kidnap Ash Anders, the Mayor of Chicago."

Buddha's spleen polyps! My gasp isn't a staged reaction.

Gold laughs. "Ash Anders!"

"This is going to be dangerous," Mermaid says. Her face is grim but determined.

"Ash Anders!" Gold hoots again. "We're going to kidnap the president's son!"

CHAPTER 12

Fav hero? I don't watch semi-reality shows. My fav heroes
are the police officers who protect our city every day. ~
Mayor Ash Anders, Chicago Times Interview

~

Three days later, we henchmen assemble in the lair
to set out on our doomed bank heist. The Professor
limps purposefully out of his office, head held high. He
stops before us, and after a moment of silence, hollers,
"Big Little City will tremble with fear tonight!"

He raises both hands in the air as his bowtie flickers
from black to an inky green hue. "Every citizen will
jump at their own shadow. Each creak in the night will
send shivers down their spines. We will be an acidic
compound, corroding their courage until this entire
town buckles."

He grounds out those last words. Sparks sputter
from the wires hanging from the hem of his lab coat and
his silver hair sticks every which way. In spite of what
he believes will be our inevitable failure, The Professor is giving viewers a show. Despite all the fear eating
through my guts, I feel more than a little nostalgic.

"WHOO!" Gold shouts, pumping his fist, grabbing
for the lens as usual. He's been buzzing around the lair
with a mad energy since he arrived. Mermaids beats her
chest with her fist. Kitty claps, slapping her one hand

against her thigh. I force my hands to clap. Sequoia looks like he's just trying not to pass out. I feel the way he looks, dread twisting up every single part of me.

So much can go wrong tonight, and if it does... I force a reassuring smile on my face and give Sequoia a little nod of confidence.

"Onward!" The Professor shouts and limps toward the elevator. The others follow, but Leo catches my eye and beckons me over with a short nod. He stands near the back of the lair, outside the frame of the scene. His enhanced Goggs sit on his forehead, pushing back his wavy brown hair. Those Goggs let him control the four cam drones that will be capturing every part of our heist tonight while he sits in his editing studio.

We'll give you quite the ep, no matter what, I think. What I say out loud is, "I've got to go. We're on a strict timeline."

"You look nervous." His amber eyes seem to cut right through me.

"Robbing a bank is scary work. I might trip," I reply.

"You and the others have been acting strange all week."

"Really?" I put a hand on my hip with fake casualness. I hate how aware I am of his body, so close to mine. He wears a white t-shirt today with two green lines slashed across. That's about as decorative as he gets, and I appreciate the simplicity of his wardrobe. Living in Biggie LC, I've discovered that there's often an inverse relationship between outward and inward complexity.

"Nitrogen hasn't been spending extra hours in the lair," Leo continues. "Arsenic doesn't practice on her own anymore. You all seem..." He searches for the word. "... united."

"Isn't that what you wanted?" I glance back at the elevator. The others are already gone. Only Sequoia waits for me.

"When things that I want happen I get suspicious," Leo answers. "You're planning something."

The shirt looks good on him. So do those faded jeans he wears all the time. He doesn't recycle his clothes much. I like that about him. I like a lot of things about him. I just wish he weren't half so canny.

I give him a smile. "Just keep those cams rolling."

I expect another dry rejoinder. Leo's good at those. But instead, he says, "Don't do anything reckless."

I have to laugh at that. "You're a producer. Your purpose in life is to get me to do reckless things."

Something flickers in his eyes and his lips press together. If I didn't know better, I'd almost think he cares. The thought makes me uncomfortable because though I like almost everything about Leo, there's one thing I don't like.

One big thing.

Leo is a producer. His loyalty isn't to me, only to ratings. *And he's already given up on our show,* I remind myself. If it were up to him, we'd just lay down and let Tatianna Wentworth swipe us into oblivion.

That's how much Leo cares.

"Iron," Sequoia calls.

"I've got to go," I tell Leo. "Stay sharp. It's going to be an interesting night."

Leo opens his mouth to speak, but I turn around and jog to the elevator. Only when I break away from his gaze do I feel like I can breathe again.

Topside, we trundle into a car Gold hired. Beacon's

face is plastered on the side of it, along with her famous phrase: **I am the beacon in the night!**

Coincidence, or just Gold's sense of humor?

We're quiet on the ride over, but my brain bubbles with endless questions. Did we think of every possibility? We've gone over our plan a thousand times, walked through it step by step, but it still feels weak. So many things have to go right. If even one of us makes a mistake...

Our glowing bowties light up the darkness as some inane K-pop song plays through the speakers. This moment reminds me of our last heist, except Gold and Mermaid aren't glamming for the lens. The mood in the car is tense. We all know what's on the line.

Getting caught committing a crime outside of Biggie LC will earn us a ticket directly to a rehabilitation camp. I shudder. Sage Anders loves to tout how humane and progressive the rehabilitation camps are. I guess when compared to human cages, solitary confinement, and murdering your own citizens as we did in the not-too-distant past, anything looks like a step up.

The gov is all too happy to broadcast vids of rehab camp inmates playing baseball, immersed in positive feedback VR worlds, and receiving education and job training, but everyone knows the truth about the drooly camps. The guards and counselors are only supposed to use psychoactives on the inmates to balance mood disorders, but when all the rehab camps were privatized ten years ago, the new owners realized it was a lot easier and cheaper to babysit inmates made docile by drugs.

In a fit of macabre fascination two days ago, I dug up dozens of stories on the news Streams of inmates marching into rehabilitation camps and not remembering the next five years of their lives. Interviews with ex-guards reveal that some camps slap skin patches onto inmates laced with high doses of Mellows. The inmates turn into drooling zombies. No one comes out of the drooly camps the same. Their minds are warped, their brains spongy from the drugs. No wonder the re-offend rate is so low. When someone can barely remember their own name, it's hard to be a criminal mastermind.

No surprise that many drooly camp inmates graduate right into a gov care facility for the disabled – also privatized. The Captains of Industry who own those companies are swimming in currency made on human suffering.

My fear begins to shift into anger, and this, at least, makes me feel a little better about our heist. After all, Ash Anders is part of the problem. Just because he talks a big game about protecting our rights doesn't mean he's any better than his mother, though there are plenty of rumors floating around that he despises her. In the end, all politicians are the same. Power first. People last.

I blink and realize that we're almost to Iconic Square. The Professor sits beside me staring broodingly out the window. I wonder what he's thinking. He believes this is his last mission, that he'll end the night in disgrace. All his work to revive his show, to become relevant once again is set to be snatched away by some younger, more popular cape.

What a bitter pill. Good thing Tatianna Wentworth isn't getting what she wants. *Not today, bitch.*

Our car turns toward the bank... and then drives

past it. The Professor is so lost in his thoughts he doesn't notice for a moment. Then his head jerks up and swivels.

"We missed it," he says.

The car turns down an alleyway, its headlights shining on Mermaid's sleek, black car.

I take a deep breath. "No, Professor, we didn't."

*

The drive to Chicago takes a little over three hours, with one pit stop sheepishly requested by Sequoia. At roughly two hours and 50 minutes, The Professor is still not on board with our plan.

During the first hour, the car boomed with his voice raised to its highest angry teacher level as he lectured us on the consequences of committing a crime outside of Biggie LC, as if we weren't well aware of the risks. The second hour included bitter accusations of mutiny followed by demands that we turn the car around immediately.

We all try to reason with our boss. Gold offers shining promises of the potential glory. Mermaid explains the painstaking preparations we've made, all the potentialities we've addressed. It's only as we cross into the city and I see the looming skyscrapers in the distance that I understand what I should have said all along.

I know what The Professor needs to hear.

He sits next to me, chin up, arms crossed over his chest, lips pressed tightly together.

"Tatianna Wentworth is setting you up," I remind him. "They're using everything you've built, The Professor's entire history, to deliver a little nostalgia so they can give some up-and-coming cape a little boost for a week."

He grunts. It's a soft sound, but I know I have his attention. Bands of light scurry through the car, projected by holo-ads along the road. Everything outside glitters with light and life, but I ignore it all, focusing on the imperious man next to me.

"You've fought for seven years for this remake," I say, "and now they're trying to cheat you. The City Council wants to swipe your show, make you a laughingstock. They want to grind you into irrelevance."

The Professor actually flinches at those last words. I've thought a lot about a convo we had a few weeks ago. When I'd asked him why he spent so much time trying to claw back a show, especially when he didn't need the dollars, he'd said, *I suppose, my dear, I can't abide irrelevance.*

He fears being cast off the screens, left to fade away into a blur of half-forgotten memories. Gerald, the man behind The Professor, needs the fans and the shades. It's about being seen, having value. Having a purpose.

"If we heist the bank, it's all over," I say. I'm speaking to Gerald now, not The Professor. "The show. All your plans. Your legacy."

Even as I speak, I'm well aware of the cam drone, perched quietly on the dashboard, its lens focused on me. Leo can't use anything I've said—no breaking the fourth wall and acknowledging we're a show allowed—so I give him something powerful he can use.

"BLC Bank is no place for The Professor," I tell my boss. "It's too small for the greatest villain Big Little City has ever known."

My heart clobbers in my chest. Sweat sprouts across my upper lip. I just have to find the right words. In the row of seats in front of us, the others are quiet. No one tries to jump in or grab my lens time.

"It's time to show the world who we are," I stage whisper to my boss. "It's time to make a big move no one suspects. This is how we fight back against the system. Think of it as a grand experiment. The risks are huge..."

"But so are the rewards," The Professor says.

I have him. Mermaid leans around her seat and gives me a nod.

"Very well," The Professor says quietly. Shadows hide his face, but I see him raise his head, jut out his chin. "Very well," he repeats, louder. I feel a swell of pride, but I don't have time to dwell on this victory. We're nearing our target and Mermaid begins speaking rapidly, filling The Professor in on his role in the proceedings.

We had a backup plan if The Professor refused to cooperate, but it wasn't pretty. His support will make things much easier, which is to say not quite as impossible as they look now.

While Mermaid lays out the plan, I collapse against my seat and gaze out the window. I try not to let my awe show. Of course, I've seen pics and vids of the big cities—Chicago, New York, San Francisco, Atlanta—but I've never actually been to one. The streets are huge, filled with humming cars and cargo trucks stopping and turning in beautiful, automated harmony.

Holograms swish to life on the sides of buildings and models reach out from the flat surfaces to beckon customers or show off some new lux item. Overhead, I hear the buzz of personal fliers, and on the sidewalks a few people zoom by on rollers, most with Goggs strapped to their faces. Pop-up food stands dominate nearly every corner, selling old classics, hot dogs, pizza, and gourmet synthetic protein burgers.

Everything is so big. So bright. So busy. No wonder the empty plains of rural Illinois seemed alien to Sequoia. He's lived his whole life in this rushing, glittering dream.

"Do you have your own flier?" I ask him. His big shoulders spill out from each side of the seat in front of me. He's been quiet during The Professor's rants. I wonder what it feels like, returning to the city he turned his back on.

"My dad owns three fliers," he says. After a short pause, he adds, "My sister and I were allowed to use the oldest one, sometimes."

"Damn," Gold whispers. He's trying not to gawk at everything, but I see his eyes glued to the window. This is obvi his first time in a real city, too.

"What's it like?" I ask, trying to imagine how it would feel to lift off the ground, to surge through the air and feel the engine and pulsating air jets just behind me while the outstretched wings held me aloft.

Sequoia shrugs. A band of light moves across his face as he turns his head toward me, and I see a soft smile bloom and disappear on his lips. "For me? It was normal."

Our car turns, and up ahead the grand Chicago City Library looms. The building is intimately familiar to me though I've never seen it before this moment. How many times have I walked through its doors and scurried down its hallways in the VR simulation we used to practice this heist?

And yet, here, in real life, it seems so much bigger, so

much more beautiful than the VR version. The building is awash in light, a colorful holo-screen announcing the charity auction to fund a teenage VR addiction clinic in the city. I glance down at my Band to check the time and feel a minor shock at the blank screen.

Right, we'd locked down our Bands before leaving the limits of Biggie LC. I'll eventually need to turn my Band back on, but no sense in geo-tagging myself at the scene of our upcoming very real crime until absolutely necessary. It's bad enough that Mermaid's car has already passed hundreds of cams on the way here.

We'll deal with that when we need to, I remind myself.

Just before we reach the library, Mermaid's car turns onto a quieter side street and pulls into a drop-off zone in front of a squat building. Most of the lights in the building are dark but a few windows shine bright, showcasing late-night workers.

I crane my neck, wondering at those squares of light and the people sitting behind them. What kind of work are they doing? Most white-collar jobs have been wiped out in successive waves of automation but a few must survive here in the city. "The great accountant extinction," my Grandma Rosario used to joke.

I shake these thoughts out of my head. *Focus,* I snap to myself.

The car idles. "Alright, time to suit up," Mermaid says.

Sequoia goes first. The rest of us shuffle out of the car and stand in the warm night air while Mermaid's car shakes with Sequoia's movements.

"He'd better only be changing in there," Gold jokes but no one laughs.

A few mins later, Sequoia emerges, now wearing a

sleek, dark-blue suit with softly glowing white piping around the color and cuffs. He smiles sheepishly, while Gold whistles and encourages him to do a full turn "for the ladies."

I'm up. I swing into Mermaid's car and pull my duffle from under the seat. The next few mins involve me shimmying out of my lab coat, goggles, and under-clothes and tugging on a slinky red dress. The dress is tight over my hips and loose in the chest. Made pre-cisely for Lysee's perfect proportions, the dress strug-gles to stretch to my dimensions. I doubt my room-mate will even notice this dress is missing. I'd found it lying forgotten under a pile of other dresses in the back corner of her closet.

When I'm done strapping the sequined white heels on my feet, I tap on the window. Mermaid opens the door and slides in next to me. At her command, the overhead lights brighten. We've spent hours experi-menting with my makeup and accessories, and now she moves with precision. Soon, she's rubbing gobs of tinted creams onto my skin, then patting on powder. Next, the eyeliner pencil comes out, followed by the fake lashes and tinted drops that will turn my hazel irises a soft, baby blue.

Sitting back in the seat, Mermaid gives me a critical look. At least I assume it's critical. I can't see her eyes, but her generous pink lips press together tightly.

"You need to be ready for anything," she says for about the thousandth time.

I swallow. "I'll try."

"Don't try. Do. We can't afford any mistakes." Her voice is sharp, brooking no argument, and I wonder again why Sequoia demanded I play this central part in the plan. Mermaid would be so much better. Even now, I feel like my heart's about to explode out of my chest and sweat is already puddling under my armpits. Mermaid doesn't have a single golden hair out of place.

She was made for big, dramatic heists like this. I'm just trying not to crumble to pieces.

"Do you... ever feel afraid?" I ask, the whispered words dropping unbidden from my lips.

She leans in to inspect my face.

"Fear is an indulgence," she says. Her hand goes into her bag again, and this time she brings out the short blond wig. After gathering my own brown hair into a knot at the base of my neck, she puts the wig on me and adjusts it until the pointed bangs curve down each side of my face.

She straps a wide, flat belt across my hips and then takes the final accessory from her bag. The curtain of beads hums softly as they clink against each other. She lays it across my head, sticking the pins deep into my hair so that it stays on. The beads drip down over my head, tickling the tips of my shoulders, and obscuring my vision.

I hate the veil of beads. Mermaid has made me wear a holographic version of this piece in our practice simulations, and they always get in my way, blocking my vision and causing me to stumble.

"It's the only way to hide your face," Mermaid reminds me as if she can sense my dread. This is also a familiar refrain. "Everyone will be taking pics and vids at the event. If you get caught in the background and the Stream's facial recognition software tags you, then you're done."

I nod reluctantly and the beads swing in front of

my face, making their music. She's right, of course, and without all her precautions and the unrelenting practice she put us through, we wouldn't have a chance.

I move to leave the car, but Mermaid puts her hands on my shoulders to still me. "You look... fine," she says after a moment. I wonder if she wishes she were in my place. I certainly do.

"Thanks for your help," I say and give her a smile.

Her hands tighten on my shoulders. "No mistakes," she says again, this time whispering it under her breath like a mantra.

"No mistakes," I agree.

Mermaid lets go of my shoulders and opens the door.

"We're ready," she says to the others outside.

It feels like just a moment later when Mermaid's car slides into the receiving line at the library. Sequoia and I now sit side-by-side in the back seat while the others squeeze together up front. The library is just so big, rising like a haughty queen, strings of glittering lights washing over its green roof and brick façade. A proud statue sits at each corner of the roof. I'm not sure what they are, but they look beautiful and old. In Grandma Rosario's time, this used to be a real library, the kind that offered rows and rows physical books filled with delicate paper pages.

Now it's gotten some upgrades. The windows alight with holographic images, showing off the many items on auction today. It's all just so much.

I close my eyes.

On his blog, *The Henchman's Survival Guide,* Tickles the Elf shared his own personal mantra that he'd tell himself before each big mission. I whisper it now under my breath, "I can't control which cape tries to stop me. I can't control whether I am victorious or defeated. I can only commit to the heist."

I pull in a long, deep breath and try to force my heart to slow. Now I think of another mantra, freshly learned. *Fear is an indulgence.* Sitting in the front seat now, even The Professor seems small, cowed by the feat ahead of us. The bright lights flooding into our car find every crag in his face, making him seem impossibly old.

Next to me, Sequoia fidgets. He keeps running a hand through his wavy orange hair. Our car reaches the front of the line. Mermaid turns in her seat and pins Sequoia and me with an intense stare.

"Stick to the plan," she says.

I nod like a puppet on a string.

"Unless it all goes gutter, then run like hell," Gold jokes. His smile is just a little too big, his hands busy fussing with the buttons of his lab coat. He, Mermaid, and The Professor all duck down in their seats as a man in a powder blue tuxedo opens my door for me. I honestly can't tell if he's a breather or a robo. His face is smooth and serene. Probs a robo. I take his hand, step out of the car, and stumble in my heels.

A perfect start to what will likely be the biggest mistake of my life.

CHAPTER 13

Running for the presidency is not currently on my agenda.
Next question. ~ Mayor Ash Anders, Press Conference

~

As I step out of the car, I can't help but gape at the large, beautiful library swathed in lights and the equally glam people flowing toward the front door. And then Sequoia is beside me, reassuringly solid and big. Just before our car moves out of the receiving line, a small cam drone detaches from the rear bumper and rises into the night. Its soft hum reminds me that Leo is watching, recording. I try to force my face into a calm expression.

Sequoia hesitates then takes my arm in his. I realize I haven't moved from the curb and the next car is waiting to disgorge its guests. With a gentle tug, Sequoia pulls me forward. I glance up to give him a grateful smile and am surprised at how handsome he looks in his fancy tux. The piping on his collar glows a soft white and a stag gallops across his holographic pocket square.

I lean against him to help steady my balance. I haven't worn heels since Lysee dragged me to one of the ear-shattering clubs she favors the first year I lived in Biggie LC. That night had resulted in a twisted ankle, a throbbing headache, and near suffocation on male cologne, so I'd never repeated it.

Steady on, ankles I think to them as we shuffle toward the entrance. My dress is restrictive, a mass of ruffled red with a plunging neckline and petaled sleeves. The beads from my headpiece swing in front of my face, and I focus on looking past them as I squeeze my small purse to my side with my other hand.

"You look... uh..." Sequoia stutters.

"Scared? Pukey? Like I've clearly made poor decisions in my life?" I offer.

"Ridic," he admits. "I like you better as a brunette."

"I feel like a caterpillar pretending to be a butterfly," I tell him. As we move closer toward the door, the other butterflies surround us. Each person is more radiant, more silly, more desperately trying to grab attention than the one before. A woman swishes past us in a dress made entirely of feathers that shift colors. Even her hair looks like feathers. A man with a square chin and checkered suit strides by, tiny gold chains swaying from the many hoops in his ears. I briefly meet the gaze of a woman with huge eyes–clearly enhanced—with lashes so long I wonder that they don't tangle with each blink.

"Butterflies are weak," Sequoia says.

"But caterpillars are slimy."

He laughs. "Caterpillars aren't slimy."

"I guess I haven't actually seen many caterpillars," I admit. The insect population collapsed decades ago, and now man-made chems are used to pollinate almost all the indoor industrial farms.

We stop in front of the door. Sequoia's arm tightens around mine. I feel the heat coming off him, see a sheen of sweat on his brow.

Guess he's never kidnapped a major political figure before, either, I think. The adrenaline is making me a little punchy.

"I'm nervous," he whispers to me.

"Same," I admit.

And then he looks down at me with a soft smile. "I suppose we should go in anyway."

I swallow. My throat seems to be shrinking. "I suppose."

I turn on my Band and he does the same. No more sneaking around, at least not for us.

"Ready," I say, trying to mean it, at least for the sake of the cam recording our entire interaction.

"There's just one thing," he murmurs and brings a hand toward me. In the wash of light from the windows, I can see every freckle, every tawny hair on the back of his hand.

What's he going to do? I think wildly. I watch his hand drift down and gently tap my belt. The flex screen wakes, light pulsating for a moment. Then it shifts into the pre-programmed vid of snow gently falling against a dark sky. Sequoia procured this special piece for me. I can't imagine how many Loons it cost.

"Now we're ready," he says. I wonder for the hundredth time why Sequoia chose me to be on his arm. Mermaid was obvi the better pick. She would have matched, even exceeded the beauty of many of the women around us. I'm also certain she could float in heels instead of staggering along like a lummox.

Sequoia gently pulls me forward through the door, our cam drone following just behind. We enter a security room where a female-like robo in a pristine white suit and book-patterned tie greets us. Sequoia gives his name and mine. No point in using pseudonyms. The robo asks me to hold back the curtain of beads while a second cam drone buzzes overhead, recording our faces and matching them against gov records.

We are officially committed now.

The robo smiles. "Welcome to the auction," she says. "Please, one personal camera drone per person. We ask that you not record other guests without their permission or request selfies. Here is your paddle." She pulls one from a pile sitting on the table. "Please place your thumb on the sensor pad to connect it to your profile. If you should like to bid on an item, simply hold up your paddle and tap the sensor pad again. This will initiate your bid. We hope you have a wonderful time and thank you for supporting the Boys and Girls Outside Group.

The door on the other side of the room slides open.

And here we are, walking into a grand open room filled with light, music, and richies. My heels click on the polished marble floor and lights shine through the latticework of glass and trusses from the ceiling above. The tinkle of soft music bounces around the walls and crowds of people flutter throughout the room.

This crowd makes me itchy. They really shouldn't let so many people gather in one place. Then I remember that we aren't in Biggie LC anymore. In Chicago, they don't have to worry about Evil Santa's lunatic elves snatching citizens away in red felt bags or Shadow slipping out of the darkness to wreak havoc.

The beads of my headpiece clink as my gaze swivels from side to side. There must be a few Captains here, the men, women, and nonbinaries who control our biggest industries and gladly take the majority of the money they generate.

Bright holo-screens splash the walls showcasing the items to be auctioned, including the top item of the night, some ruby ring from the British monarchy. Ever since the U.K. inexplicably voted themselves off the global stage they've slowly slid into irrelevance and destitution. Their kings and queens have been hawking the family jewels one by one for decades.

Another screen shows depressing stats about VR addiction.

"Over 62% of teenagers spend four or more hours in virtual reality every day," a narrator claims. "24% spend more than eight hours in virtual reality a day on average, and every year over 6,000 teens die of VR exhaustion, a condition now recognized by the World Health Organization."

I wonder how many hours my brother, Alby spends in VR. Too long. I shudder and force my mind off him. I need to gain my bearings. This room is similar to what Sequoia built for our VR practice simulation but it feels so much bigger in person. The music is louder, the lights brighter. The smell of perfume and aftershave and body mist are almost a physical cloud.

All around us, people move into small clumps while short, bullet-shaped robos with arms roll through the crowd offering up trays of hor d'oeuvres and flutes of champagne. Each robo wears a sleek bowtie and glows with subdued patterns, polka-dots, zebra stripes, autumn leaves, and more.

I snatch up a glass of champagne, just for something to hold. We've got a little time to kill, and I'm feeling my caterpillar nature more acutely than ever.

"What do we do at these things?" I mutter to Sequoia.

"You wander around, drink champagne, see who's here, and try to talk to someone slightly more important than you," he responds grimly.

"Well, everyone is more important than me, so I guess I have a lot of new friends to make."

Sequoia is quiet a moment and then he says roughly, "You might find that most people won't prefer to be friends with you."

And now that he says it, I immediately understand. Even as the people around us laugh and murmur, their eyes dart from face to face searching for a bigger fish to corner. When Sequoia and I pass, their eyes glance down at their Bands, searching the proximity column of their Streams for our identities. If my Stream were public, with its dismal follower count and gutter citizenship score, I have no doubt that many would scream in horror. Some of these dandies might even faint.

Fortunately, Sequoia put up serious currency so I could temporarily privatize my Stream. While it's totally plausible for Sequoia to be here, rubbing elbows and fat currency wallets in this crowd, it'd be more than a little suspicious that a nobody from Biggie LC made it onto the guest list, especially after The Professor makes his big debut.

Instead of reacting with sheer horror, the people who glance at their Bands merely frown in puzzlement when they see that my Stream is blocked. Hopefully, they'll think that I'm some eccentric artist going off Stream, a growing trend in certain wealthy circles. Most ignore me, their eyes searching their Streams for the next worthy catch. When they see Sequoia's profile, the line between their brows disappears. His Stream score isn't impressive either, but his last name is. A man with platinum silver hair and wearing a staggeringly orange suit jacket approaches and shakes Sequoia's hand. He gives me a polite greeting, but his eyes never leave Sequoia's face as he begins babbling about an idea for a new show, something about a puppy beauty pageant combined with a puppy-kid team obstacle course. On and on he goes, laughing and occasionally clapping Sequoia's shoulder. The man wants to know if Sequoia could possibly mention this idea to his father. Just a test run and they'll see. The outlay of capital will be so small in comparison to the profits.

I glance up at Sequoia. His expression is tight. I can practically see the tension in his shoulders. He nods along, trying to politely interject, but the silver-haired man must have gills because he never even pauses for a breath.

"Well, sir, I believe that is an absolutely fab idea," I finally announce, interrupting his monologue. "Oh, don't you think so?" I bat my eyes at Sequoia. "Puppies and children. How adorbs!" I give our new friend a full wattage smile.

Next to me, Sequoia's beleaguered expression shifts. "Why, I believe you're right," he says. "It is a superbly, uh, unique concept. I will most certainly present it to my father. If you could just provide me with your contact info…"

The man falls all over himself to connect to Sequoia's Stream and then tries to go on about his idea.

"The tunnel has to be big enough for a puppy and a small child," he explains.

"Dear, I think we must tell your father at once," I say to Sequoia over his babble. "We don't want anyone else to grab this diamond out from under us."

"Yes, right again," Sequoia declares. "Off we go. Ta!"

He swings me around so fast I nearly fall off my heels. I have to keep from laughing as we plow through the crowd. We slow down next to a wall near the front of the main stage. There's a pocket of space here, enough for me to finally catch my breath.

"Does that happen to you a lot?" I ask him.

"You learn not to go out in public unless you have to," he says. "At a high-class event like this most people aren't so rude. He was probably a desperate person's date."

Now he frowns. "Was it a good idea to connect to his Stream?"

"You're supposed to go to fancy-schmancy things like this," I remind him. "Nobody is going to blink twice. You just gotta be careful when..." I trail off. Over Sequoia's shoulder, my gaze lands on a small group of people standing only a few meters away. I notice the security personnel first, a few breathers in silver-plated suits and three security robos that look like thick metal coat racks. In their midst stands a man with black hair and tan skin. He wears a dark green suit, reserved but clearly expensive.

"The mayor," I breathe.

Ash Anders holds a tight smile on his face as a short, round man grasps his hand and wags it forcefully. The short man's wife is all dripping smiles and jiggling boobs, one practically popping from her yellow dress as she pushes her husband aside to daintily kiss the mayor on each cheek.

"We probs shouldn't gape," I whisper under my breath and force my eyes away.

I'm just about to pretend laugh at a non-existent joke when I feel Sequoia stiffen next to me. His arm locks in mine, practically dragging me into his body. I follow his gaze. A man approaches us, and the crowd parts for him as if he were a wrecking ball, a saint, or the devil.

The man is Sequoia, or at least a slightly wider, older version of him with manicured nails and a more sophisticated haircut. As the giant comes closer, I notice one other stunning difference. His freckles are almost entirely gone, as if he had them scrubbed right from his skin. More likely he lasered them off.

"Hello, Father," Sequoia says formerly as the man stops in front of us. His voice has taken on a reedy quality. "May I present my friend, A... Aliyana," he stammers, barely remembering my cover name.

Quickly, I paste a jerky smile on my face and hold out my hand to the PAGS Regional Director of Media Sector 7.

"Charmed," I say.

Steward-Ryland Briggs is actually a few inches shorter than his son, but he seems like an immovable mountain. When he takes my hand, he engulfs it, and though our shake is gentle, I feel the hum of power within him.

"I see your Stream is blocked, Aliyana. You hiding something or just trying to inflate your ego with a little mystery?" His smile is an echo of a laugh.

Just protecting myself from the upcoming crime I plan to commit, I think, but I keep my smile in place. "Actually, I prefer to live my life offline as much as possible," I say out loud.

Briggs's eyes glint. "That, my dear, is a very poor life

strategy. Where did you find this creature?"

That question is tossed casually to his son. Sequoia's face is very, very red, and his arm is locked so tightly into mine that we might be fusing together.

"We, uh, we work together," he says. His eyes flick down. His voice is soft.

Briggs looks me over again. "You're cute enough but you aren't getting any of his Loons. It's all in a trust. He can't land you on a show either." His voice is jovial but his blue eyes are ice. He may stalk boardrooms and his troops may wear suits, but I can see, plain as day, that this man is a killer. And something tells me that he relishes the conquest.

I laugh, high and tinkling, the way Lysee does when boys and girls approach her at the clubs. "I don't want him for his Loons and connections," I say and add some sauce to my voice. "What we do together don't cost a thing."

Briggs grunts. "She's got kick. I can appreciate that. But lust never lasts. And sooner or later she'll try to pry open your bank account." He shakes his head and even seems a little sad as he looks at his son. "I approved your tickets out of curiosity and perhaps the foolhardy hope that you had returned to the city permanently. My offer expires at the end of the night. This is your last chance."

Sequoia's head sinks lower and lower as his father turns on his heels and glides away. I see the telltale indents beneath the skin under his temple. I've heard of ocular nerve implants but have never seen anyone with them. No wonder Sequoia's father never looked at his Band.

Besides me, my friend seems to be deflating. His

elbow loosens against mine and his shoulders sag.

"What offer?" I ask.

"He gave me thirty days to come back, to formally apologize, and then he would reinstate me with the company," Sequoia says, his voice weary.

"Reinstate you? You worked for PAGS?"

"I was a glorified errand boy. Father believes in working your way to the top. And abject humiliation."

"I noticed," I say dryly. A robo wheels by. I beckon it closer, put my empty glass on its tray, and grab two full champagne flutes.

"Well, you aren't an errand boy today," I tell Sequoia, offering him one of the glasses. I lean in close and lower my voice. "Today you are an evil henchman, and we're going to bring this place to its knees."

Sequoia's head comes up. Those sensitive blue eyes search my face. I adore all his freckles and his shaggy, curly hair. My friend smiles at me. I hold up my glass. He clinks it with his and we both down the bubbly drink.

Just then, music flares from the hidden speakers. The lights dim and the holographic vids switch to pulsating pastel ribbons. A glittering woman with a truly impressive crown of molded pink hair bobbles on stage and breathily opens the event. She giggles through a few tepid jokes and thanks a long list of names, some of whom I've heard in passing on Lysee's gossip Streams.

"Now?" Sequoia whispers to me.

"Not yet." I keep my eyes on the stage, politely clapping with the rest of the audience while my mind goes through the plan again and again.

"We are *so* pleased to have a special guest here tonight," the woman croons from the stage. "He has been *instrumental* in supporting the Boys and Girls Outside

Group. Truly he needs no introduction. Please offer a warm welcome to our mayor!"

The woman skips off stage, and Ash Anders saunters to the center of the stage surrounded by a swell of applause and more than a few female sighs. He takes a moment, surveying the crowd. His brown eyes sweep across me and I force myself not to shrink back. He probs can't see anyone with the stage lights shining on him.

His posture is casual, his chin up like he was born to be on this stage, right here right now. I've done plenty of research on our target, and I know he wasn't always the golden boy. He went wild in college, just when his mother was steadily climbing the political rungs. According to stories at the time, he drank like a fish and mixed his booze with synthesized drugs. It's a miracle he didn't permanently scramble his brain. There were stories of fights with his frat brothers, scuffles with cops, failing grades, but his mom always shielded him from any serious consequences. And then his girlfriend overdosed and Ash Anders disappeared from the gossip Streams for years. The few scant reports I found put him in a carousel of lux rehab facilities.

And then, one day six years ago, his name appeared on the ballot for a Chicago City Council seat. He ran as an Independent, gave pretty speeches, and visited hospitals and civic groups. He did all the right things, but he mostly won on name recognition. Two years ago, he ran for mayor against the stodgy frontrunner practically crowned by his mother. He gave speeches about change and hope and breaking the holds of the Captains of Industry; of re-creating a sense of community and offering our unemployed population a path of dignity.

It was all pointless tripe in my opinion. Nice words to soothe aching souls. But enough people believed his happy fairytale. He won. The rumors say Sage Anders was furious.

"I happen to think that we owe each other something," Ash Anders begins, his voice clear and strong. He puts a hand in his pocket. "We owe each other something as neighbors, as citizens of the United States, as human beings. If you listen to anthropologists, they'll tell you that we're tribal creatures. For most of our existence, we were just naked apes clutching stone tools. We had to stick together to survive."

The Gossip Streams say Ash Anders doesn't drink. Doesn't even swallow a Sweet Dream before bed. He just works and works and works. His staff is fiercely loyal but rumors swirl about his famous temper.

"I believe our bond is deeper than just survival," Anders continues. He begins to slowly stroll across the stage. "Because only together can we create. Only together can we build cities and industries and farm enough to feed our population. We can always do more, do greater when we work together, when we lift each other up. Right now, outside of these walls, our fellow neighbors, our fellow Americans, our fellow humans are suffering. There aren't enough jobs and too many Streams. Too many shows. Too many VR games. Too much distraction. The flame of industriousness that lives in every soul has been diminished. Our children are losing their grip on reality."

He pauses again. The entire room is quiet, everyone straining to hear, though Anders's voice flows from speakers in the walls. Even I find myself captivated by his words.

"We have created a virtual reality that is a better, more exciting, more fulfilling place to live than our own world. And so our children are severing their bond with society and with each other and choosing to hide in that fake world. That, my friends, is a true indictment on us, on the world we are offering them."

I find myself nodding. All the politicians have always seemed the same to me, all except for Halnora Button. But his words ring true. Can he truly mean it, or is he just saying what we all want to hear?

"This auction is a start," Anders continues. "We must help the children already lost to the fake world. We must try to pull them back and replant their minds, hearts, and souls here. But I believe we must save all of our children, and the only way to do that is to make this world, our world, the better choice. My friends, we are running low on hope and we must bring that back."

I find myself clapping hard, our collective applause drowning out the rest of his words as he begins laying out policies he is trying to implement in Chicago.

"I didn't believe the rumors," a woman behind me whispers to her partner, "but now I do."

The other woman's voice is a little loud and slurred when she answers. "Oh, this is def a presidential speech. He's going to run against dear old Momsy, and you know what, Handlah? I'll be sending him a nice big donation with my compliments. Just don't tell my husband!" The women giggle.

"Enough policy talk," Ash Anders says on stage with a wry smile. "This is a party, after all. This organization has a lot of amazing and rare objects up for auction, but beware, I have my eye on the original Poe manuscript and the rumors that I'll do anything to win aren't exaggerated." His smile widens.

The crowd laughs but I don't. During the mayoral race, news leaked a week before the election that Anders's opponent participated in a secret Stream group that shared 3D-print schematics for child-like robos. Within an hour of the story breaking, Anders's campaign was plastering every Steam with brutal attack ads. Even I heard about them in Biggie LC.

The twinkling woman totters back on stage. "Alright, alright," she sings, "we're about to begin. Make sure you've synced your paddle. Let me introduce our most esteemed auctioneer..."

I lean over to Sequoia. "See you in ten mins," I whisper to him.

"Shining luck," he whispers back. I feel like my stomach is filled with a thousand live wires.

Louder, I say, "Dear, I'm going to hit the restroom. All the champagne." I smile, unlink my arm, and gently push through the crowd. On stage, the auctioneer introduces a gobbly statue created by a human-robo collaboration.

Commit to the heist, commit to the heist, commit to the heist, I mentally chant to myself.

Just before I leave the main ballroom, I pluck a crumbly crab cake from an appetizer tray offered by a service robo.

Here we go.

CHAPTER 14

I am proud to present the Grand Museum's latest acquisition, an incredibly rare and valuable ancient Japanese tea set. No, I don't anticipate any security issues at the event. ~ Mayor Grimbal Wisenberg, interview with Reena Masterson at Grand Museum private event

~

I slip through a back door and move down a long hallway. The lights are dim in this part of the building. Service robos whoosh around me. Some tuck empty trays under their arm while others sail toward the ballroom holding their trays aloft laden with ever more flutes of champagne or slivers of real farmed salmon laid across crackers and dabbed with caviar, also locally farmed, at least according to proud holo-display messages scrolling across the robos' chest plates.

"Ms., please return to the ballroom," each robo says politely to me after noting my presence.

"Just looking for a restroom," I slur back and giggle. Hopefully, the robos aren't programmed to report suspicious behavior to the event's security team. If they do, our timeline will be dramatically shortened. We've practiced that particular scenario, but it's always tight. We'll manage. *We have to.*

I count the hallways silently in my head as I pass them and turn right down the fourth one. The churn of robo wheels and the clattering of dishes quiets away. I am alone, except for dim overhead lights that wake with my passage. The only sounds are the tinkling of the beads swaying over my face and the soft whir of the single cam drone that hovers in front of me. I imagine Leo on the other end of the lens, probably shaking his head and cursing us all. If we get caught, he'll surely have some uncomfortable questions to answer.

"Big breakthroughs often carry great risk," I say to the cam and offer a smile. It's an old line of The Professor's, one he often repeats before big missions. I slip out of my heels and sigh with relief. I wish I could just drop them in the hallway, but it's not exactly brills to leave your DNA in an off-limits corridor. I hook the heels with my finger and proceed forward.

The hallway seems so much longer than the simulation Sequoia built, but it's probs just in my head. It also doesn't help that I've got a curtain of annoying beads swinging in front of my eyes with each step. I pass closed doors, some made of actual wood, lovingly retouched. According to Mermaid, these doors guard real, physical books that residents of Chicago can still check out with special permission.

My ears strain for the sound of an approaching security person, but I hear nothing. And then, up ahead, I set eyes on my first foe. A security robo stands guard in front of an emergency exit. The original sign, white with red letters, still hangs above the door.

The robo senses me when I get within 10 meters. Its strange little head pivots, cams focused on my face. I know it's trying to identify me as it submits a security alert.

The clock has officially started.

"This is a restricted area. Please return to the ballroom," the robo says.

"Is that the bathroom?" I ask and take a wobbly step forward. I squint at the serial number etched on the robo's chest plate, trying to make out its model number.

"Bathrooms are located in the ballroom. Please return," the robo says. "This is a restricted area. A security member has been called to escort you."

"Oh, blight!" I cry and then giggle. "The restrooms are in the ballroom? I didn't even see them. Here I am wandering all over the place and my bladder's fit to explode." As I speak, I stumble forward, step by step.

Right on cue, the robo turns its coatrack body toward me, laser ports still capped but pointed in my direction. *There it is!* I make out the tiny digits of its serial number. The first three are V-42.

Inwardly, I sigh. Mermaid poured through all the available specs on the various models made by Talos. After Talos acquired its last security firm competitor a decade ago, it became the only major defense contractor still standing. At least it was shining easy to figure who was supplying this shindig with security.

The real challenge was planning for the different possible robo models the event planners could hire. Sequoia was confident they'd spring for a Valkyrie model, something in the V-40 to V-44 range, but even within that scope, the robos have significantly different capabilities, protocols, and identified weaknesses. We'd created plans for each and every one of them, but the V-42 is good. *Very good.*

"Sorry, sorry. Don't shoot!" I laugh at the Valkyrie and hold up my hands. This robo doesn't look a thing like an ancient female warrior, but I know it's deadly enough if I get too close.

"Do not approach. I repeat, do not approach. I am authorized to use force if I perceive a threat," the robo states.

"Whoa, whoa, I'm not a threat. K! I'm leaving. I don't need this," I huff. "Just give me a sec. Oh!" I look down at the crushed crab cake in my hand. "I forgot I had this. You guys don't eat crab cakes, do you? Otherwise, I'd share."

I pop the piece of food in my mouth. "You know, you've been very rude to me," I slur through the crab cake. "You shouldn't threaten people. In fact, who's your manager? Let me..." I take another step forward.

"DO NOT APPROACH! I AM AUTHORIZED TO USE FORCE," the robo says in a booming voice.

I begin to choke. My eyes bulge. I open and close my mouth. Flap my hands near my face.

The robo watches me, its cam ports shifting.

After the Burning Cars Riots three decades ago, Talos responded by creating the nearly indestructible Valkyrie robos. This coat hanger in front of me can't be taken down with a laz pistol, torch gun, or even a bomb. The newest models can even handle an EMP burst.

My only hope of beating it is, ironically, empathy.

My eyes water. I open my mouth again, trying to gasp for air and then stumble to my knees.

"Are you in distress?" The robo asks.

I nod like a lobotomy and start crawling toward the robo. If this were an older, V-40 model, it would stun me into oblivion. But, starting with the V-41 models, Talos added a basic suite of lifesaving protocols to their fleet of Valkyries and—most importantly—a rule structure that allows them to abandon their post if they perceive a life-threatening emergency.

This Valkyrie 42 model–bless its programming–wheels behind me. Its flexible arms come around me, meaning to lift me up and start performing the Heimlich, one of 49 lifesaving interventions it can offer. Instead, I jump to my feet and turn around. My hands fumble with my belt.

Come on! Come on! The shigit beads bump against my face.

Then the belt is off. I slap the belt across the robo's primary cam port. "Belt, full power, white," I cry, spitting crab cake everywhere. The belt responds to my vocal command, its screen going white, pouring 1,000 watts right into my savior's cam port.

The robo's arms immediately drop away from my body.

"Camera offline," it says. "Camera offline. Camera offline."

With no ability to assess the situation, the V-42 immediately shuts down all functioning. Talos added that little safeguard just 12 years ago after the Detroit "Work Again" protests. The protestors shot up flares, maybe to confuse the robos, maybe to ruin the shots from the news drone cams, or maybe just to grab attention in our Gogg zombie world. Whatever the reason, all that light messed with the Valkyries' sighting systems, and they ended up spraying the mostly peaceful crowd with high-level stun lasers. Even hit a few kids.

I tighten the belt around the robo so it won't slip off, and then I wipe my gooey, crumb-covered lips with the back of my hand. I know the robo sent a security alert as soon as I approached. It'll send another one now noting its condition and requesting a replacement. Anyone on the other side of those alerts who wasn't already suspicious certainly will be now. Our clock is speeding up.

I take one step toward the exit door and hear running feet far down the hallway.

"Ms.?" a female voice calls. "Ms., stay away from that door."

Buddha's eye boogers! The service robos in the main hall must have sent through a security alert. I've just run out of time. I glance over my shoulder and catch a glimpse of a woman in a silver coat racing toward me.

"I gotta go, the bathroom," I slur at her.

"That's not a bathroom," she says, a touch of irritation in her voice. Her hand relaxes from its position on the handle of the laz pistol at her hip. Then she sees the security robo standing silent a few meters from the door. Her expression clouds with confusion.

I lurch for the door, slamming myself into the big metal bar. It compresses, but the door doesn't budge. My brain screams. Sweat soaks down my back. *No, no, no!* And then, like a flash of providence, or just the hundreds of training simulations Mermaid put me through, I remember.

The manual lock.

Mermaid made me practice flipping it over and over again in the stimulation, and I'd still forgotten it in the panic of the moment.

My fingers grasp the lock and twist it. I shove my weight against the door, pressing the bar, and this time it swings open. I practically fall outside into the warm night.

"Guard, guard," I pant.

A figure waiting on the other side of the door steps swiftly around me, leans into the open doorway, and shoots. I hear a croak of surprise, then the sound of a body smacking the ground.

Mermaid holds her laz pistol steady, like a statue, waiting to see if any additional guards follow.

"Oooh," Gold winces as he steps around Mermaid and helps me up. "That didn't sound like a pleasant fall."

"Any problems?" Mermaid asks. Her blue lab coat fits snugly and her bowtie flashes blue sparks.

"Mostly smooth," I say. "Took a little longer than anticipated."

Gold flicks a crumb off my chin and lets me go. My legs are shaky. In fact, my entire body feels like it's been doused in cold sweat.

"Happy birthday," Gold says, offering me a bulky purse I snagged from Lysee's closet. It's flashing yellow sequins clash with my dress, but given how fast the fads spin these days, it might actually be in style. Anyway, it was the only big purse I could find on short notice.

I nod at Gold and shove my arm through the strap of the purse, hooking it on my shoulder. My shaking fingers grip the zipper. It seems determined not to move until I finally yank hard and it gives way. The purse gapes open and I reach into a small side pocket and pull out a tiny earbud. Even before I press the bud into my ear canal, I hear a voice squawking on the other end.

"Update. Update!" The Professor shouts.

"We're in," Mermaid hisses. "Maintain radio silence."

"What is the situation?" The Professor barks. I glance out the door and spot the barest outline of a black car parked at the corner. We all agreed it was best for our vil to stay out of sight. Our plan is too risky, the threat of capture too great, and with his famous face, he'd be a sure target the moment we revealed ourselves.

"Hello!" a happy voice calls at the door. Kitty sails in, a wide smile on her silicon lips. She somehow still manages to look sexy in her powder pink lab coat and glowing white bowtie. Two cam drones follow her through the door, and I drag it closed after them. Leo has one more cam, which he must be keeping in the car with The Professor.

"You understand your assignment?" I ask Kitty.

"Yes, oh yes. My new programming is a little buggy, but I believe I can comply." Her cats eyes lower. "I certainly want to comply," she says in a husky voice.

"No, none of that right now," I hiss. Once a sex bot always a sexbot.

Ahead of me, Mermaid hooks her arms under the arms of the unconscious security guard and drags her into a nearby office. The guard almost certainly has a tracking device on her, and they'll send a team soon enough when she doesn't check in, but no sense in leaving her sprawled in the hallway to make it easy for them.

"Iron, go," Mermaid says as soon as she closes the office door. I nod and force my wobbly legs to propel me past them and down the hall. My ears strain for the sound of running steps, or worse, the soft hum of robo wheels coming toward us.

Nothing.

"If they send robos, we're done," Gold breathes just behind me.

Like I needed the reminder. The robo guarding the

door would have sent out a security alert about a guest approaching the door. The key is whether the robo's algorithm categorized me as a low-grade or serious threat. Did my drunk routine fool it? And did the human guard manage to send off a high-level security alert before Mermaid pegged her? If she did, we'll have the entire security apparatus pounding toward us in a couple of secs. Not to mention that Ash Anders's security team will whisk him away before we even make it back to the ballroom.

Every stage of our plan depends on perfect execution and more than a little luck. I drag in a deep breath. All I can do is proceed as normal and remind myself of something Tickles the Elf wrote on his blog last week —*Don't ever count on the other side being incompetent, but you'll be surprised at how often they are.*

Again we pass the quiet doors where the old books linger. Mermaid, Gold, and Kitty peel off down different hallways to prepare for their parts. I continue forward until I make it to the main hallway, where the service robos continue to whiz back and forth.

I sigh in relief. They wouldn't be following normal protocol if the security contractor had released a serious threat alert. We're still in business but our time is borrowed. As soon as they find our unconscious security guard, the game will be up. I swing out into the larger hallway, scattering a bunch of robos. "Please return to the ballroom," they squawk at me.

"Yeah, yeah," I slur drunkenly even as my stride picks up speed. I barely remember to shove my feet back into my heels before re-entering the ballroom. I move through the entrance, followed by a stream of service robos.

My bladder contracts. Out of nowhere, I realize I need to pee. Ironic, considering how I just spent the last ten mins pretending to look for a bathroom. No time for toilets now. I move into the crowd. On stage, the auctioneer rambles off numbers as the holo-screens display a small tree in a beautiful pot. I wonder what makes the tree so special, but I suppose I'll never find out. Quietly, I slip through the mass of bodies, keeping close to the walls. Every so often I bend down, grumbling about my heels.

And then, after ages and ages, I am again at Sequoia's side. In the overhead lights, I see sweat beading his forehead. He glances down at me and then back up to the auction. His warm hand closes around mine, and he takes the earbud tucked in my palm. When it's affixed in his ear, he turns toward me, and I step in close to his body.

We've done this little dance a million times in our virtual reality simulations, but it's different in real life, with his body pressed against mine, the heat pouring off him. His eyes are on my face. I wonder what he's thinking, if he could possibly feel as sick with adrenaline and fear, so itchy in his own skin, as I do right now.

"Bear claw donuts, bear claw donuts," I whisper in his ear while he reaches into my open purse and pulls out first one stun laz pistol and then a second. He laughs softly at my non-existent joke as he lifts each pistol between our bodies and tucks them inside his jacket pockets. If anyone glances at us, it would look like we're sharing an intimate little joke.

"Bear claw donuts," I say again and smile widely as Sequoia slips a pair of specially tinted glasses into the inner pocket of his suit jacket.

"You're making me hungry," he says and I hear the echo of his voice through my earpiece.

"You think Ash Anders like donuts?" Gold jokes through the com line. "Maybe we can all go out and grab a bite when we get back to Biggie LC."

"What are you talking about?" The Professor's voice is sharp in my ear. He's the only one who can afford not to whisper.

"You ready, Professor?" I hiss, keeping my body tucked into Sequoia's big frame.

"I suppose, my dear. I've had so little time to prepare, but I shall rise to the moment."

I can't help but smile for real. He may be raging pissed at our switch-er-roo, but this heist will make him, once again, into the biggest vil in Biggie LC. Well, he'll at least match Shadow.

No matter how this heist ends, The Professor will be a legend. He couldn't ask for more.

"Gold?" I ask.

"The AV robos have been incredibly accommodating," he replies. "Must be my charm."

"Wait for my mark," I say.

I glance up at Sequoia again. Our eyes meet. I suddenly want to hold onto him and never let go. But Mermaid already stunned the guard. There's no going back now. I give Sequoia a sharp nod, and then he's gone, melting into the crowd. The bidding for the tree is getting furious now. I reach into my bag, and my fingers wrap around a chunk of cool plastic.

I edge closer to the stage.

"Sold," the auctioneer hollers, "to number 142."

In one quick motion, I set the small triangular object onto the stage and give it a little push. The Pod slides a few centimeters onto the stage, near the auctioneer's foot. He doesn't notice.

"What was that?" an older woman asks just behind me.

"What was what?" another voice chirps.

"Now," I croak and then whirl into the crowd.

The Pod brightens to life, shooting a wide, flat holoscreen from its tip. And there's The Professor's face, filling the screen, the crazy silver hair, the cracked goggles, the glowing bowtie pulsating at his neck.

The crowd gasps.

"Greetings," his voice booms over the speaker system. "My, you all look so fine tonight."

Inwardly, I sigh. Gold successfully patched into the room's speaker system. Mermaid predicted the room wouldn't be guarded. She must have been right. *Lucky again,* I think, but for how long?

"Please, stay calm," The Professor says. "There is no need for anyone to get hurt. I am simply here to acquire The Queen Consort's Ring. That luscious ruby is a necessary component in a rather exciting invention I am currently constructing."

At this point, Gold jumps on stage. His golden lab coat glints in the overhead lights, and his goggles give him a strange, not-quite-human look. He holds a stun laser in each hand. Two cam drones buzz next to him like dogs on floating leashes.

"Where's the ring?" Gold growls at the shocked auctioneer.

The tall, lanky man seems about ready to swallow his tongue. "… what?" he stammers dumbly and looks out at the stunned audience as if they could help him.

The crowd is mostly silent, aghast, though I hear

a soft murmur, and far in the back a man laughs. A woman next to me presses her empty champagne flute into her ample breasts. For a moment I enjoy their shock, all these Captains and richies so soft and protected in their big, beautiful buildings. Now they'll know what it's like to be dragged into the low, ratings-obsessed world they've always controlled behind the scenes.

"While I have your attention," The Professor continues, "might I add my personal endorsement to this worthy cause. I agree that our young people are far too focused on the fantasy worlds hidden inside a pair of Goggs. Personally, I believe we should engage them more in the hard sciences. Perhaps then, this critical field of study would get the respect it deserves..."

As The Professor drones on, the crowd begins to break down. Some continue to watch in confusion, while others stream quickly toward the exits. An undercover security guard in a wispy white dress approaches the stage, pulling a laz pistol from her purse. A shot fires from the crowd followed by screams, and the woman in the white dress topples to the ground like a rock.

I glance over my shoulder. Mermaid stands in the back corner of the room, gun already panning for more threats. She's positioned perfectly to protect Gold from any encroaching security guards... well, at least from human guards. As if on cue, a team of at least 20 Valkyrie security robos roll through the back door and begin fanning out as they move toward the stage.

"The ring!" Gold cries and grabs the auctioneer by the lapels of his yellow suit. A spark of annoyance flashes through me. Gold is still glamming for the cams, even now. Mermaid shoots three times in quick succession and three human guards on both sides of the stage go down. She dashes through the crowd to take up a new position as several Valkyries turn and begin scanning the crowd.

"Place your weapons on the ground and put your hands up in the air," the rest of the Valkyries call as one. "This is your only warning."

In answer, Gold grins, aims his laz pistol, and shoots at the robo closest to the stage. The laser discharge absorbs harmlessly into the robo's breastplate. In unison, the robos raise their laz ports and unleash a volley of shots at the stage.

CHAPTER 15

No point in looking backward. Look at my future,
and you'll see some amazing things. Guaranteed.
~ Gold, Interview with J Bennett

~

Panic. Sheer panic all around me as the crowd begins to stampede. The warning laz shots from the robos sail cleanly over our heads, but men, women, and nonbinaries scream in horror as they shove toward the main exit. One woman slips, and the crush of people half drag her along. Another man, crystalized Goggs dangling from one ear, tries to move against the crowd and is quickly swallowed up.

I duck my head and use my elbows to shove my way toward the wall. A nonbinary huddles nearby, hands over zir head, trembling. I glance toward the stage. Gold holds the auctioneer in front of him as a shield. The Valkyries pause their volley to recalibrate. I know from the extensive research Mermaid pulled on all the Valkyrie models that the robos are programmed to minimize risk to innocent bystanders as much as possible. But they will stun hostages if they determine that's the only way to get to the threat.

Gold only grabbed himself a short reprieve, and not much of one at that. The human security guards are not as cautious as the robos. One shoots at the stage, hitting the delicate tree. It tips over as its multi-colored leaves curl into brown husks. Mermaid shoots that guard and then another one elbowing toward the stage. She dives under a banquet table to escape return fire from a Valkyrie to her left.

"Kitty, now!" I holler.

She gives me a happy salute from the service entrance, and her eyes pulse as she sends out the command. On the floor, the small flare pods I scattered around the ballroom like cookie crumbs brighten to life. Their lids pop off and they each catapult a charge into the air. Many in the crowd pause and watch the streaks of light arch up elegantly like strands of twinkling pearls.

These types of light charges are mostly used on the Fourth of July and are meant to climb high into the sky. Instead, they hit the ceiling of the library and burst, each exploding into hundreds of individual glowing orbs. Contained within the ballroom, the brightness is eye-searingly intense. I'm already digging into my bag. My fingers land on the specially tinted goggles Sequoia printed for me. I tear the horrid curtain of beads off my head and shove the glasses on my face. The room immediately comes into focus.

The crowd becomes even more unstable. Now they lurch drunkenly in various directions, tears streaming from their closed eyes. They trip over the service robos, bump against the Valkyries, and slam into walls. I see the little round man who earlier shook the mayor's hand with such glee barrel into Sequoia, almost knocking my friend over. Cries fill the air mixing with a symphony of crashing champagne flutes.

One sound, however, stops.

The Valkyries cease their forward progression toward the stage. All the new, man-made stars drifting down across the room confuse their sensors, making it impossible for them to safely distinguish the threats from the civilians.

I say a little prayer of thanks to Buddha. Talos's latest and greatest Valkyrie model, the V-44, is impervious to light-based attacks, a known weakness in their earlier models. If that first Valkyrie I met at the back door had been a V-44, we would have had to call off the heist. Fortunately for us, the V-44s cost major Loons even just to rent for a night. We'd bet everything on the hunch that the security contractor for this little soiree would choose an earlier, cheaper Valkyrie model that still contained the flaws. After all, who would use an intense light attack indoors?

"Run! Run for your lives!" Kitty screams, rushing from the service door, her tail swishing in agitation. She makes a decent show of lurching around, upping the general chaos even more as she begins deliberately knocking into the Valkyries, shoving them over, turning them around, and smearing caviar on their cam ports. It won't really slow them down much when our light attack is over, but any little distraction helps.

The strobing light beads gently drift from the ceiling. They won't last long, and as soon as enough of them blink out the Valkyries will resume their shooting. It's time to close our trap. I press a hand against the wall and gaze through the chaos.

"I don't see him," Sequoia calls in my earpiece.

"Neither do I," Gold says from the stage. He still has a tight grip on the now-weeping auctioneer.

"Got 'em!" I cry. Not 15 meters away, I see the

mayor's human security team surrounding him like a shell. They shuffle slowly against the crowd, moving toward me.

"They're going for the door at the western wall," I say.

"On my way," Sequoia says.

"I'll start picking 'em off," I tell him and pull my laz pistol from my bag. No lasso this night, thank you, Buddha! Just as I raise the weap, a woman in a shining sequin dress stumbles past me, makeup-stained tears pouring down her cheeks in dark rivulets. She limps, the precariously tall heel broken on her left shoe. Her pink hair, done up in a single large bun dotted with numerous bows, sags on one side of her head.

It's Tatianna Wentworth, President of the Big Little City Council. I had no idea she was even here.

Tatianna Wentworth is not scared. She doesn't scream or run or panic like the others. She is pissed. She staggers, hollering curses, shoving bodies out of her way. I watch delightedly as she storms right into a wall and falls on her ass. I consider giving her a laz stun for good measure, but we'll need to negotiate our new show run with her if we pull off this crazy thing.

Reluctantly, I drag my eyes away from her and resettle my attention on the mayor's security team. They're getting closer to the door. I raise my pistol, sight, and shoot the security guard closest to me. The shot knocks him on his back, but he sits up. As he struggles to his feet, I hit him again.

"Jackets on the mayor's security detail have some kind of shielding," I say. "Up the power."

"Check," Sequoia responds as I tap a pad on the side of my gun, setting it to maximum stun.

I shoot again. Another guard goes down and she stays down. One of the guards shoots in my direction but I've already moved, using a few straggling guests as cover. More shots come my way, but they're far off the mark. The security team can't see anything in the glaring lights. Just in front of me, a handsome man in a maroon tux dashes into a service robo and spills to the ground.

I step over him and squeeze off a couple more shots. My hands shake. The guard team is moving faster. Two of my shots miss, but the third tags another guard. Only three guards left. The team lurches, changing tactics. Now they're moving back toward the crowd, probably going for a secondary escape route.

"I'm in place," Sequoia says in my ear.

The room is growing darker beneath my tinted glasses. The flares are beginning to die. We're running out of time. I squeeze off another salvo of shots. This time, I get lucky. Two guards go down.

"One left," I say triumphantly. It's working. Our plan is actually working. We're going to pull this off. I can see Ash Anders now. His face is drawn but set. The remaining security guard grabs him and shoves him behind her body as she moves him as quickly as possible away from my vicinity.

Just behind the mayor, I see Sequoia, his own tinted goggles in place, waiting. The trap is closing. Sequoia is our final surprise. No one will see him coming. All he has to do is grab the mayor and hustle him out the door.

"I got her," I say as I aim at the final security guard.

Then I hear a laser gun discharge behind me.

Could the Valkyries be coming back online? Impossible. It's too soon. There are still enough light beads in the air to keep them quiet.

I swivel around. A good portion of the crowd has made it out of the room, but fifty or so blinded guests still stagger around in various stages of shock. The Valkyries remain standing in the middle of the room, like intimidating contemporary art. And then I see him. A man in a subdued black tuxedo, hand shielding his eyes, points a wavering pistol at the stage.

Human security!

"Arsenic," I cry.

"Where'd she—" Gold starts. The guard sprays sloppy laz shots across the stage. One hits the auctioneer. The man goes down, dragging Gold with him. I swing my gun and shoot desperately at the undercover security guard.

Miss.

Gold rolls away, jumps to his feet, and sprints toward the side of the stage where he can slip into the backstage area. The security guard is still firing, his shots splattering across the stage like raindrops. Gold is two steps away from the end of the stage.

Almost there. Almost there.

A shot hits him square in the back and he crashes forward like a virus wiped his programming in an instant.

"No!" I screech.

The security guard leaps on stage, gun in hand. He takes one confident step toward Gold and then goes tumbling down. I look over my shoulder. Sequoia is just behind me, gun raised, mouth set in a grim line.

"I missed," I whisper as shock sends cold streams down my bones.

"Where's Arsenic?" Sequoia says. I note that he's got

a glob of caviar smeared across his pristine shirt. Somehow this is unbearably funny, except all I want to do is cry.

"Here. I'm here." Mermaid's voice is a croak. I wonder in a faraway, hollow place if she's been injured too. But no. As I glance around, I find her, that simple blue lab coat so different from the frills and bows on the few remaining people in the room. She stands near the back of the room, right next to the exit Ash Anders and his security guard were going for.

Ash Anders! The thought of the mayor is like a deluge of ice water, snapping me back into the present, focusing my thoughts with sharp, urgent clarity. He was going for the door Mermaid now stands near. I look around, but I don't see him. He couldn't have gotten past Mermaid. Did they see her and swerve away?

It doesn't matter, I realize as the reality of the situation crashes onto me. Ash Anders is gone and so are our hopes for completing this heist. Our flares are dimming enough for people to grope toward the exits, and the room is emptying out. In another min, the Valkyries will boot back up and our laz pistols won't be able to put them down.

"What's going on? Update," The Professor says in my ear.

"Is he dead?" Sequoia asks softly as he gazes at Gold's unmoving body on the stage.

I look to Mermaid. She always knows what to do. Except she's silent. Her gun shakes in her hand. During all our preparation, all our practice scenarios in the virtual simulation, she was always clear on what we needed to do if one of us was compromised.

"Leave them," she'd said. "If anyone is injured or

killed, they become a liability and we can't afford that. Focus on the mission. Our only hope of escape is the mayor."

That was Mermaid's philosophy, but Mermaid isn't offering any opinions now. Did that security guard have his weapon set to stun or kill?

Doesn't matter.

"Nitrogen, get Gold," I command. "We missed the Ruby. Let's tail it."

"Who's dead?" The Professor barks.

No one answers him. Sequoia rushes across the ballroom, shoving past the silent Valkyries. Mermaid is moving too, making for her designated exit. She seems slow, her normally fluid gait stilted and unsure. When Sequoia makes it to the stage, Mermaid pauses. So do I. Together, we watch as Sequoia scoops up Gold as if the smaller henchman weighed nothing. Even from here I can see how loose Gold's body is, how his head lolls over Sequoia's arm.

No time. Can't think about that now.

"Get to your exits," I growl. In case the heist went south, we each have our own escape route to lower the chances we'll all be caught. Kitty is a blur of pink, rushing through a back door. Mermaid jerks into motion, moving to the service hallway. I barrel toward a small door near the stage that leads to an old staircase.

Just as I yank open the door, I hear a rising hum. The Valkyries are waking. One fires a laser. Then another. I tear the tinted goggles from my face and kick my shoes off my feet before plunging down the stairs into the belly of the library.

We failed but I'm more worried about Gold. Is he dead or just unconscious? *This was all my idea,* I think.

I'm the one who wanted to go big. Be bold.

All for a paycheck.

What have I become?

I stumble off the last stair into the basement. For some reason the lights are on, revealing shelves filled with neat rows of metal boxes.

I hear the shuffle of footsteps. They seem close.

"At the car!" Sequoia's huffing voice explodes through my earbud, and I start, almost banging into the shelf. I tap my comm off and strain to listen. More hurried footsteps. Someone is definitely down here with me.

"Where is the damn exit?" someone whispers nearby.

"It's okay, Quinla," a calm voice answers. "The security robos will keep them contained. They were only after the ring, anyway."

I recognize that voice. I've been listening to it as part of my research for the last three days. I gulp in a deep breath and dash past two shelves, throwing myself up against the third. I hear them, moving cautiously just on the other side. I don't have time to think, only to react.

In one smooth movement, I twist around the shelf, laz pistol ready, and squeeze off a single shot. The security guard croaks and drops heavily to the floor. Her laz pistol slides beneath the shelf and she doesn't move.

I point my gun at Ash Anders. Our eyes meet. His gaze is steady, intense.

"Mr. Mayor, I'd like to formally invite you to an exclusive tour of my boss's lab," I say and force a smile on my lips. Behind me, I hear the soft, steady buzz of Leo's cam drone, recording what will surely become one of the most iconic moments of semi-reality history.

CHAPTER 16

PAGS provides a vital service to this country and to this world. Everyone deserves an escape now and then. ~ President Sage Anders, Interview with National Public Radio

~

Ash Anders stares at me for one long second. I wonder if he'll scream or beg or try to run. Ash Anders does none of these things. Instead, with a surprising flash of speed, he drops down and scrambles for something at his ankle. I see the glint of plastic–a small pistol tucked in a holster against his leg.

"Nah-ah," I say, taking a quick step forward so that I'm just out of arm's reach. I keep my pistol pointed and wrap my finger around the trigger. "I'll shoot," I tell him. "It'd be a pain to drag your ass to the getaway car, but I will."

My hand shakes with adrenaline, but I'm standing so close to him I can't miss.

Ash Anders has the small pistol in his hand, but he's still crouched. There's no way he could move to aim it without giving me enough time to get off a shot. He's in an impossible situation and must know it.

Still, he pauses.

"Toss the weap," I bark at him.

After one more moment of reflection, he says, "Dragging would be so undignified" and calmly drops his pistol. He straightens up and smooths his jacket. "You've a stun laz then?" His eyes dart down at his unconscious guard.

"Yes. She'll be fine. They all will." I appreciate that he cares about his employees.

The Mayor of Chicago looks me over. "You're with The Professor, that looney vil from Big Little City?"

"Iron, at your service," I say pleasantly. "Let's take a walk. How about you turn around and move forward slowly."

"Let me guess, no sudden moves."

"I would appreciate it. As I said, dragging your unconscious ass would be a hassle."

"And undignified," he adds. He's clearly noticed the cam drone drifting overhead, recording all of this. He begins walking.

I suck in heavy breaths as my heart hammers in my chest. My hands feel slick with sweat and a part of me wonders if this is all a dream. Maybe I got hit with a laz shot in the main ballroom, but then I blink and see the back of Ash Anders's expensive green suit as he moves slowly in front of me.

"Make the second left," I tell him.

"You are setting an incredibly dangerous precedent," Anders says as he complies with my directions.

"Well, you wouldn't believe how cutthroat the competition for ratings is in our little town," I reply.

"You might be surprised," he says lightly, but there's something dark in his voice. A sharp point of fear stabs into my stomach. It's starting to hit me, what we're doing. Who we're kidnapping. All the consequences that will cascade from this.

"Next right," I say gruffly.

"You know," he says in that same light, dangerous tone, "I think I'll personally escort you and all your costumed little friends to the New Path Rehabilitation Camp. We've been testing some highly promising new protocols there. You'll have a truly excellent stay."

Instead of answering him, I tap my comm back on. Immediately a swarm of voices pounds into my eardrums.

"Is he breathing?"

"I don't see her."

"We can't wait much longer."

"I hear sirens."

I clear my throat and say as loudly as I can, "I need a pickup. I have the ruby."

All the voices stop.

"What?" Sequoia squawks after a beat.

"You heard me," I say. "Get the car to my exit. We'll be there in one min."

Every single bit of me wants to ask about Gold, but I can't afford to lose focus. Not now, when I can see the exit door ahead. I swallow. My brain feels like it's overheating. I can practically hear Gold whispering in my ear. *Don't waste this lens time, Wholesome.*

"Keep moving," I bark at Ash Anders. He walks to the door then pauses and turns around. Again, his eyes grill into me.

"What a foolish little game you're playing," he says, a note of disgust in his voice.

"Yes, I suppose it is," I reply sadly, "but we are truly desperate. Now, if you'd be so kind as to remove your Band and turn it off, we'll be making our getaway."

He doesn't move. Instead, he stares at me. I wonder

if he's going to try something, if I'll have to shoot him. That will complicate our escape immensely, plus the ground is hard. I really don't want to be the reason the president's son gets a major concussion.

"Your heist was decent," he says. "You took advantage of the element of surprise. You diverted attention away from me. Utilized a flaw in the security robos. I assume you got lucky a few times, but you obviously planned and executed this well." He pauses to let his next words sink in. "Things will be different from here on out. The authorities have been called. They're probably already here. They will track you. Every cam will be searching for my face. They'll blanket the skies with drones. You'll never be able to escape."

I force what I hope is a brave smile on my face. "Well, Mr. Mayor, I was hoping you would help us with that."

Now he smiles. "You thought wrong."

"Turn off your Band and hand it over." I wave my pistol at him.

"We're here," Sequoia says into my ear.

"I could put in a good word for you at your sentencing if you turn yourselves in now," Ash Anders says.

I shake my head. I admire his quiet courage. If he wasn't a politician, I might even respect him.

"We've come too far for that now," I say.

He nods. "Worth a try."

"Your Band."

He turns it off and unlatches it from his wrist slowly, obvi playing for time. I'm surprised to see he wears a Crane model Band. It's slim and sleek, plated in white gold and etched with some swirly Latin phrase. Cranes are old. I haven't seen one in years. I'm sure he's retrofitted it to put in chips with higher processing speeds and greater bandwidth. Still, it's a surprise that he's not showing off a fancy Falcon or Wyvern or the new Raptor that all the Captains like to flash.

"Toss it over," I instruct.

He drops his Band straight down so that I'll need to get within reach of him to pick it up and lower my gun in the process. *Nice little trick.*

"Your jacket, too," I say, just in case he has any surprises hidden in there.

Ash Anders raises an eyebrow but complies, just as slowly. He wears a spotless white button-up dress shirt beneath. Well-made but understated, just like the rest of him. He drops the jacket on top of the Band.

"I do hope you'll allow me to keep my pants," he says.

"Turn out your pockets."

He does and reveals a cartridge of breath mints, caffeine drops, and a small, curved seashell.

"Put them on the floor," I order. Personal trackers can be made to look like everyday objects. Some of the capes and sidekicks have been known to use them. The only reason the Glory League found the Fat Tubist after he was captured by Femme Feline was the tracker kazoo in his pocket.

Ash Anders pops a breath mint in his mouth before he tosses the container and caffeine drops onto his coat. "Not this," he says of the shell and slips it back in his pocket.

"No, drop that too," I sputter.

He hits me with a look. "It's just a shell."

"Then you won't mind putting it on the floor."

"No."

I almost shoot him. We're right at the door anyway.

It wouldn't be too hard to load him into the car. But we need him conscious and there's something else. Ash Anders already believes we'll be caught. He has good reason to think so. There's no way we can make it out of the city on our own. If he's so confident, why would he risk a stun laz to keep a tracker on his person, and why would it be such a random object?

Unless it's not a tracker. Unless it's some kind of personal token.

"We're coming out," I say into my earbud. "Ruby first. Be ready."

"Check," Sequoia says.

I point my gun at the mayor. "Open the door and get into the car. If you try anything, you'll get a stun laz."

Ash Anders smiles at me. "You sound a little nervous."

"I am nervous."

"Good." His smile widens. Glamour's Stream listed him as the fifth hottest politician last year. They weren't wrong. He pushes open the door. Mermaid's car waits for us outside, the back door hanging open.

Ash Anders looks around. I tighten my grip on my gun. He ducks smoothly into the car. I grab up his coat and Band and follow him in, shoving him roughly and slamming the door behind me.

"Drive," I croak.

The car is at capacity. Even with Kitty in travel mode in the trunk, it's still a tight squeeze. The Professor and Mermaid have the front seats, with Gold buckled between them. He slumps sideways, his head resting on Mermaid's shoulder. My stomach clenches. Gold is always so animated, never seeming to be able to contain all the energy inside of him. Now he is utterly quiet.

We roll away from the library, its walls still splashed with glittery holograms of the objects up for auction. Dazed guests stand outside in clumps.

"Hello, Mr. Mayor," Sequoia says, finally, as he tries to adjust his big body to give our captive more room. "I hope you're doing well."

"Not my best night," Ash Anders replies

I meet Sequoia's eyes. He looks thoroughly panicked. I try to give him a reassuring smile, but I'm sure my own face betrays my nerves.

"How's Gold?" I ask.

"Unconscious," The Professor answers. His voice is soft, none of the usual flights of fancy in his voice. "Breathing is steady. Strong pulse. I believe it was a heavy stun hit."

"Of course he was stunned," Ash Anders says from between us. "My security team always tries to convince me to give them lethal authorization, but I don't allow it. Not with civilians present."

"How kind of you," I say.

"It has nothing to do with kindness, Ms. Henchman," he replies. "Robos are predictable. People are not. I won't have dead innocents on my watch."

Overhead, I hear the heavy *whomp, whomp* of an approaching helicopter. Many of the cars around us gently glide to the curb and their lights die. The transportation department must have disabled all the city-owned rental cars. Sirens wail in the distance. The security net is tightening around us.

Ash Anders leans back in his seat, seemingly unperturbed. He knows there's no way we can possibly escape the city, not if we had months to plan this heist and a couple million more crypto Loons. The best we can hope for is to hide out for a few hours until the authorities track us down.

The Professor turns around to face the mayor and I suck in a heavy breath. Here we are, at the final, most brazen part of our plan.

It's not going to work, I realize. Now that I've seen Ash Anders up close, gotten a sense of his pride, I know we are as doomed as the glaciers.

"Mr. Mayor, may I introduce myself. I am The Professor," my boss begins, a slight edge of uncertainty in his voice. Even he seems a little undone by the audacity of what we're doing.

"I know who you are," Ash Anders snaps. "Is this the part where you reveal your big plan?"

"Indeed," The Professor says, "but to clarify, this is the part where I reveal our plan, because, Mr. Mayor, I would sincerely appreciate your assistance in coordinating our escape."

Ash Anders is quiet for a moment and we all listen to the heavy approach of sirens. Then the Mayor of Chicago laughs. I see the flash of his white teeth as we pass under a streetlight.

When he recovers, he says, "I know what my next line is. I'm supposed to ask, 'Why in the world would I ever help you?'"

Now The Professor smiles. "Because, Mr. Mayor, I believe I can help you become President of the United States."

Ash Anders doesn't laugh at that.

CHAPTER 17

Nope, never practiced. The laugh is utterly natural.
You just have to let it happen. Don't overthink it. ~ The
Professor, Interview with Reena Masterson

~

We sneak the car into a temp lot where city-owned cars wait to be ordered. Ash Anders leans back into the seat while The Professor explains the value of media attention.

"People don't listen to the news. They don't watch your debates. They'll never remember the budget you spent all your political capital to pass," The Professor says. "But what they do listen to is the gossip Streams. What they do watch is my show."

My boss pauses. Ash Anders gazes out the window, his eyes far away.

"You're just another politician making pretty promises," my boss says. "I can turn you into a Persona, into a hero."

The Professor continues, explaining the plan just as Mermaid, Sequoia, Gold, and I laid it out for him just a few hours earlier. He points out every benefit to Anders, adds flourish to the details, and finally offers the kicker. "Mr. Mayor, your name is already famous, but when this is all over, everyone, every *voter* will know you."

No one speaks. I can hear Sequoia breathing. Around

us, the sirens grow louder.

Ash Anders won't agree. What happens next? Do we try to hide or let him go and flee? Turn ourselves in and beg for the mercy of the court?

"Very well." Ash Anders says the words so quietly, so suddenly that for a moment I wonder if I imagined them.

"Are you sure?" The Professor says, a hint of suspicion in his voice.

Anders nods. "I don't like you. Any of you. I don't like what you've done or why you've done it, but you have a goal and I have a goal. Those two things align for the moment. I won't turn away an opportunity just because it's crass." He looks at me while he says this.

"So you are a politician after all," I say.

"I suppose I am."

"Excellent, excellent!" The Professor cries and claps his hands together. "Let us commence with the final stage of our escape, now, shall we? Mr. Mayor, if you would be so kind."

I hand Ash Anders his Band. He turns it on and begins making calls, first to his chief of staff, then to the chief of police who apparently connects him to some military general. We all wait in silence, listening as he gives the same six-digit code followed by smooth, fluid orders while the men, women, and none-binaries on the other end of each holo-call nearly burst with questions, doubts, and fury.

"I assure you, I am under absolutely no distress," Anders says again to the military general, a note of irritation finally entering his voice. "I gave you the code, didn't I?" The general squawks back. His voice is so loud that even with the sound shied feature engaged in Anders's Band, I swear I hear something about artillery at the ready. "That is patently unnecessary, General," Anders snaps. "Tell Mother I am handling the situation. Look, you have my Band location. Track me for all I care but stand down. I've discovered a sudden desire to take a working vacation in the lovely town of Big Little City, so there you have it."

The General sputters some more. Ash Anders hangs up on him, calls his chief of staff again, and begins speaking as soon as she picks up. "You pulled the guest list and security cam footage from the event? Excellent. I understand your concern. Oh, yes, this is certainly a terrible idea, but we've taken risks before." Ash Anders nods, listening. "That's your opinion. Keep all my meetings on the books, but the hospital visit will need to be rescheduled. Not one word about my whereabouts. If I see any leaks to the media, I'll get rid of the whole team starting with you. And feed the cat."

He hangs up and turns to The Professor. "That should about cover it."

The car reeks with our sweat. And then, just like that, the sirens go quiet. The steady *whump, whump, whump* of the helicopters fades and the heavy spotlight goes dark.

"Roads are clear," Ash Anders says. "Off we go."

"You were really able to erase the guest list and security footage from the auction?" Sequoia asks.

Anders smiles at him. "They are now in my possession, but they certainly aren't erased. And that took quite a few favors, just in case you were interested."

"Much appreciated," Sequoia mutters.

It's as good as we're going to get and more than I had hoped for. Even the most novice detective will realize that there must have been some inside people to help The Professor pull off this caper. No one will find it suspicious that Sequoia was at the event, but I'm a nobody without a single Loon to my name who also happens to be a resident of Biggie LC. My name on the guest list would be an obvi giveaway. That annoying curtain of beads paired with my platinum wig will hopefully disguise my identity if anyone caught me in the background of their selfie vids. The rest of the caper was washed out by the light attack, so we should be safe.

Until Ash Anders gets what he wants and betrays us, I think grimly.

"Let's get to the lair," The Professor says. Our car pulls out of the lot and we move toward the highway. It could be a trap, of course. Ash Anders may have sent our GPS coordinates to his chief of staff through his Band. The police chief could have a blockade waiting for us. But we've already risked everything. No way we can go back now. Our salvation depends on how much Ash Anders wants good optics.

A few cars now share the road with us. The driving blackout has been lifted. As our car picks up speed, I keep glancing at Gold's sagging body. Mermaid might as well be unconscious too. She stares out the front windshield, her eyes far away.

"We will record a grand hostage video," The Professor says. In the dim light of his glowing bowtie, I can see the stretch of his smile.

"Naturally, I would like to review and approve the script," Ash Anders replies. This is not a request.

"Of course, of course!" The Professor is now a gracious host. "I assure you all will meet with your expectations. You shall act quite brave in the video, hurl whatever insults you please. We'll broadcast it throughout town and on our show's official Stream. It will get picked up everywhere."

Ash Anders nods. He turns to me. "Alice Hannover," he says softly.

I shouldn't be shocked that he already knows my name, but I feel the breath evaporate in my lungs. The way Ash Anders looks at me, it's like he's imprinting my face onto his memory. He's been known to hold a grudge. After Anders became Mayor of Chicago, the father of his old girlfriend—the man who threw his own daughter out of the house when he found out she was an addict—suddenly found his contracts drying up, one by one. The banks called in his loans and now he's living in some cargo container, just another faceless subsister.

Ash Anders doesn't forget.

Neither do I. "You were out of position," I say to Mermaid. "You were supposed to provide cover for Gold."

She glances at me then back out the windshield. "I thought you'd gotten the mayor. I was moving toward my exit."

"I never had him."

"I misheard." Her voice is steady. "It was loud."

"Strange," I say.

"It's fine," Sequoia speaks up. "Gold's only stunned. He'll come around in another hour or so."

"It was only shining luck," I say. "That could have been a kill laz."

"We all knew the risks," Mermaid whispers, almost to herself.

"Let us not focus on what could have been," The

Professor says. He can barely keep the grin off his face. "This night has been a triumph. Tomorrow, the whole country, no, the whole world will be talking of our heist."

I slump back into my seat. Ash Anders is looking at me, but I turn my face toward the window and watch the road slip by.

On the way back, The Professor keeps up a mostly one-sided convo, idly planning the hostage vid we will shoot the next day. Ash Anders asks small, safe questions that Sequoia answers. Eventually, the talking dies away and we each retreat into our own reflections while Anders fires off messages to his staff and takes another call from the Chicago Chief of Police and repeats his code again.

I close my eyes as exhaustion ripples through me. Was this all worth it? I remember Alby's video, the sun on his pale face. I hope so, but I'm becoming less sure.

All is quiet until we cross over into Biggie LC.

"Something's wrong," Mermaid says, her voice flat. She almost sounds weary.

"What?" The Professor snaps.

The soft glow of her bowtie highlights Mermaid's high cheekbones. "The cams haven't moved for the last ten mins. They're on auto."

Two small cam drones sit in the car with us, the other two cling to the outside. One drone sits on the dashboard and the other hangs in the back corner. There's little room to maneuver, but now that Mermaid mentions it I haven't heard the soft buzz of the lens adjusting or seen the cams rotate in the last few mins.

"Maybe Leo went to bed," Sequoia says.

"Right in the middle of our biggest heist?" I'm already shaking my head. No, Leo will be waiting for us in the lair. I can almost see the tight expression in his amber eyes. He'll be raging pissed at the risks we took tonight, but he'll also recognize the sheer ratings potential we've handed him. I bet he's already working on teasers with tonight's footage to drop on our show Stream, and of course, there's the hostage vid to begin planning.

I stare at the quiet cam, passively recording. Leo wouldn't go to bed. He wouldn't put the cam on auto. Fear lances through my stomach and suddenly the exhaustion weighing me down like an unpowered exoskeleton evaporates.

"What did you do?" I growl at Ash Anders.

He holds up his hands. "Nothing. Not yet."

"He couldn't know where Leo is," Sequoia tells me gently. "If he wanted to stop us, he could send our GPS coordinates to the authorities at any time."

It's true, but the emotions inside of me slosh angrily, desperate for an outlet. I drop back into my seat, my shoulder bumping Ash Anders.

"It could be Beacon," Mermaid says.

We all digest that terrifying possibility as our car slowly cruises the quiet backroads of Biggie LC. The Professor orders the car to pull over two blocks away from the mansion. Someone has to go check out the situation.

Mermaid is our best fighter but she volunteers to guard Ash Anders. It's a surprising decision. Babysitting our hostage won't get her any screen time. Then again, our producer isn't filming, so maybe this is a canny move on her part. As I consider the possibility of

Beacon waiting to ambush us, I wish I'd requested hostage-watching duty.

Just as I'm about to open my car door, Gold sighs. His head lolls on Mermaid's shoulder and she touches his leg.

"Gold?" she whispers.

"I think…" his voice is soft, webbed with dreams. "… I fell."

"We caught you," Mermaid says.

"Good." He puts his hand on top of hers and is quiet.

"He's coming round," The Professor states, sounding relieved. For all his excitement and gloating over the past few hours, I've noticed his eyes darting to Gold again and again and the way he's been gnawing his lip. It can't be easy asking others to put their bodies on the line for you.

The Professor looks away from Gold and turns to me. "You two had better go, assess the lair."

I nod.

"Be careful," my boss says quietly.

If Beacon is lying in wait, we won't be coming back. It's the reason our boss isn't going with us. No sense in giving up our vil after we just pulled off such a lobotomy heist. I open the car door and step out. The night seems chillier. Dawn is still a few hours away.

"Shining luck," Ash Anders says, a little smile playing on his face.

Without a word, I close the door. The sky spits down a light drizzle. I take a breath and then Sequoia is by my side, a weak smile on his face.

"Here we go again," he murmurs.

"Record yourselves with your Bands," Mermaid calls out the window. "And put on your goggles so we won't have to blur your faces."

Oh, right. I sheepishly open the car door again and dig around the pile of my discarded clothes on the floor until I find my green-tinted goggles. I slip them over my eyes then trace the pattern to turn on my Band. The screen alights and resolves into the pudgy, unshaven face of my Totem.

"What's happening? Why was I turned off? Why are you dressed all glam?" Bob tosses these questions at me and burps. He doesn't allow me to answer. "Your Iron Stream has 500,432 followers and 82,342 pings. You've got another interview request from Reena Masterson and sixteen requests from other outlets still pending. Oh, and your Alice Stream has one ping. Ollie wants to know when you can study."

"Quiet," I hiss at him. I'll have plenty of time to study for the chem midterm in the hospital or the Biggie LC jail – both equally likely destinations if Beacon is indeed waiting for us.

Sequoia puts his goggles into place and turns on his Band. "Good evening, Chauncy," a beautiful female sprite says from his screen. "What can I do for you?"

"Just record me," I mumble to Bob. "Don't post."

"Hi, Evangeline," Sequoia says. "I'd like you to start recording until instructed to stop."

"Whatever," Bob says.

"Of course," Evangeline chirps.

As we walk to the mansion, the rain seeps into my dress, gradually flattening the ruffles. I can practically hear Tickles the Elf whispering for me to start some jaunty banter with Sequoia. This is primo lens opportunity right here, but all I can do is watch a reel of Beacon's best fights play in my head.

There was that epic fight on top of the BLC Express against The Professor that put her name on the map. Then the time she took on the entire Beast Horde at the end of Season Six and put Cerberus in traction. I see her in my mind tearing through Cleopatra's serving men, pummeling Evil Santa's lunatic elves through Iconic Square, and tossing Lotus Ninja across an entire warehouse with her Aura Arcs.

Hell, just last month, she survived a gritty punchfest with Zombie Lord and then crushed half the League of Darkness with Shine by her side. They say Lady Silver still has a limp from that fight.

"How are your feet?" Sequoia's voice pulls me from my spiraling dread.

I look down at my bare feet. They feel numb with cold. "Fine," I say and shiver. I tuck myself closer into Sequoia's big body. The rain flattens his wavy orange hair and it dangles into his goggles.

"What will you do if Beacon's in the lair?" I ask.

He's quiet for a moment and then a big, warm jacket drapes over my shoulders. It's a little musty from all his nervous sweating, but I appreciate the warm shield from the rain.

"I'm going to fight her," Sequoia says. "We have to. It's our job."

"I was thinking about running away and screaming," I admit and pull the jacket tighter around my body.

"Well, maybe your screams will distract her and I'll get in a hit or two before she knocks me out." He gives me a wan smile, but it's not really a joke. Sequoia is an excellent fighter, but Beacon is the best. She is a master of practically every fighting style, and with her Light Blade in hand, she's practically untouchable.

No one has ever been able to beat Beacon, and Sequoia and I certainly won't succeed where hundreds of vils and henchmen have failed before.

The mansion looms ahead of us. I pull my stun laser from my purse. Sequoia has his at the ready. When we approach the front door, I shrug out of his jacket and he leaves it on the porch. My dress is heavy with rain and tight across my body. It won't do me any favors in a fight, but maybe if I get tangled in my own ruffles I'll make one of those "Hilarious Henchmen Fails" listicles I see popping up in my Stream every week.

The lights blink on in the foyer as we enter the mansion. My heart clobbers painfully in my chest as I swing around, casing the room with my stun laz. I cover Sequoia as he pulls away the trick bookshelf and puts in the secret code to bring up the hidden elevator.

We squeeze into the small elevator and it descends. Next to me, Sequoia is jumpy with nerves. I see Leo in my mind. Did Beacon hurt him? I try to imagine Leo fighting or running, desperate to escape her clutches, but I can't see it.

Leo is too much of a pragmatist. He'd know better than to try to fight Beacon. No reason to take a pointless punishment. I can almost see him holding out his wrists, resigned as she clamped her energy cuffs around them.

Sequoia steps out of the elevator first, panning the open training area with his gun. I put my back to his and gaze around the connected lab area. The lights flicker on at our movements, sweeping the shadows away.

The room seems untouched. There's the ancient chalkboard, still filled with our plans for the bank heist. Sequoia's rack of beakers sits on a cluttered tabletop. There's no one here. I take one step forward and then remember one of Tickles's most strident warnings.

Quickly, I look up, panning my gun across the ceiling. So many henchmen forget to look up, and they pay the price. Hummingbird was particularly good at hovering above her enemies and dropping down on them when they least expected it.

Sequoia looks at me.

"Go to Leo's office," I tell him. "I'll check on Shine."

He nods. We move to the hallway and then split in different directions. It only takes me a few strides to reach Shine's cell. The door is still closed but it now sports a wide hole, like someone used a fire gun to melt out a big circle.

It was a messy job. Low budget. No glam at all. But the hole is big enough.

"Empty," Sequoia calls from down the hall. "No Leo. All his editing equipment is still here though."

I take three slow steps forward and crouch next to the hole in the door of Shine's cell. I already know what I'm going to find but I have to check just to be sure. It feels foolish to keep my gun ready, but I do it anywhere as I stick my head through the hole and peer into the cell.

"Leo's gone," Sequoia says behind me.

I sit back on my knees and lower my gun. "So is our prisoner."

Sequoia looks confused. "What do we do?"

I set my expression. The cams are still rolling, after all. Now is not the time to look weak.

I look up at Sequoia and push back all the worry and doubt flooding through me. "We get Leo back. That's what we do," I tell him with as much confidence as I can muster. "But first, we find a new lair."

CHAPTER 18

Of course I'm a natural blonde. ~ Beacon, Ask Me
Anything forum on personal Stream

~

"Our show got swiped."

These words drag me from a tangled, fitful sleep. "Uh?" I moan. I force my eyes open and stare at a decorative sconce on my wall. Except I don't own any decorative sconces. I wouldn't waste expensive material cartridges to print something so useless.

"Did you hear what I said? Is that big lout still sleeping?"

I push myself up into a sitting position and immediately realize that everything is wrong. This isn't my soft, multi-colored blanket wrapped around my legs. These aren't my peach pajamas I'm wearing. I'm not even in a bed.

Where am I? What happened? And who do these deliciously comfortable peach pajamas belong to?

And then it comes to me. The compromised lair, which also meant a compromised apartment. Fleeting memories wake in my tired brain.

A quick hustle out of the mansion with Leo's editing equipment cradled in Sequoia's arms.

A short, testy discussion with The Professor inside Mermaid's car.

Ash Anders's bemused smile.

The drive over here—to Sequoia's house—just as dawn's light cracked the hold of darkness.

I remember Sequoia offering Ash Anders his bedroom. The Professor took the guest room. It's not like he could go back to his penthouse in our building either. And then Sequoia insisted I take the couch.

I look down and see my big friend sprawled on the floor, snoring away as bright sunlight from the window pours over him. He'd meant to print an air mattress for himself on his Anders 3100 3D printer, but I guess he didn't want to wait the hour it'd take. I could barely keep my eyes open while Sequoia printed me these PJs and blanket. I must have conked out before he even printed himself a blanket.

"I said OUR SHOW GOT SWIPED!"

"I heard you," I snap at Gold who stands just inside the living room, both hands pressing on either side of the opening to the hallway. "Looks like you're talking in complete sentences again. Shining job."

He'd barely been able to string two words together last night when Sequoia half dragged him to the couch in the office. Mermaid had insisted on putting him to bed.

"Yes, my courageous injury was quite severe, but I have fully recovered to heist another day," Gold proclaims. I notice that he's reapplied his gold lipstick and painted gold bars down his face, which disappear and then reappear from the edges of his golden goggles.

"Wait, we got swiped?" I cry. His words are finally sinking in. I try to stand and almost fall off the couch as the blankets tangle in my legs.

"What?" Sequoia blinks awake. He looks around,

confused, his eyes still clouded with sleep.

"Tatiana Wentworth was not pleased when I called her this morning," Gold says. "She swiped us."

I flop back on the couch with a groan. All of it was for nothing. If I had any food in my stomach, I think I'd vomit.

"She thought we came all the way to Chicago to steal that old ring." Gold gives me a wide grin. "I told her we didn't get the ring. We kidnapped Ash Anders instead."

"Who'd we kidnap?" Sequoia asks with a yawn.

Gold frowns at him. "You're really ruining my moment here."

"Wait, wait, wait..." I swing my hand in front of me, trying to sort all the new info slamming into my brain. "How'd you get Tatianna Wentworth's personal Stream number, and why were you even gabbing with her in the first place?"

"We needed a representative to negotiate on behalf of the show now that poor, dear Leo is indisposed," Gold explains. "I humbly volunteered my services."

"Big surprise," I grumble.

"I don't think I printed the air mattress," Sequoia says. His hair is adorably flattened on one side.

"And The Professor had her private deets, of course," Gold continues, ignoring Sequoia. "As you oh-so-shrilly pointed out the other day, she *is* our main sponsor."

"*Was* our main sponsor," I correct. "You just said she swiped us."

"She did," Gold confirms, "but when I told her that the Mayor of Chicago was our special guest, she rebooted nice and quick." He pauses for dramatic effect. "She tripled our show's budget and gave us a guaranteed second season."

"Holy Buddha!" I shove off the blanket and jump to my feet. Before I know it, I'm squeezing Gold in a hug, and then I'm dragging Sequoia up and wrapping my arms around his wide chest.

"We did it!" I cry. I'm pretty damn sure I could fly right now. After all the fear, all the worry, all the chaos of last night, our show survived after all.

"Course we came through," Gold says as if our drooling, despo plan was always a sure thing. He wriggles out of my grasp and his brows furrow above his goggles. "But we've got a lot of work to do. There's a hostage vid to record, a new lair to find, our producer to rescue, and an ep to put out."

The reminder of Leo douses my enthusiasm. I release Sequoia and step back. He still seems a bit dazed but he smiles down at me. I pat him on the shoulder. Gold is right, we do have a lot to do. But it's worth taking a moment to appreciate all that we've accomplished and all we could have lost.

"I'm glad you're hardy," I tell Gold sincerely. I notice a bruise on his cheek from where he fell and hit the stage. Still, his smile is as wide as ever.

"Aw, Wholesome, don't get sentimental on me now," Gold says. He glances away. "The cams aren't even rolling."

I wonder if he can possibly know how much he frightened me last night; how even Mermaid seemed worried for him.

"Now, enough resting and laurels and all that," Gold says. "We've got a brills hostage vid to make."

*

An hour later, Sequoia's home is busy with moving

bodies and voices. I fiddle with the buttons on my lab coat and discreetly sniff my armpit to see how ripe my uniform has gotten. Two cam drones swoop drunkenly around the main room as Kitty watches them with a wide smile on her face.

"Slower, darling" Gold instructs her. "We want nice, even shots."

We'd dug up a simple vid recording program in her software that allows her to connect and control up to four individual cam drones. I shudder to imagine how Mayor Wisenberg might have used that particular feature. In our case, at least, clothes will be staying on.

As Gold, our self-appointed producer, works with Kitty, it becomes apparent that the sex bot's recording program is more than a little clunky. A cam bangs the ceiling and spirals down, almost crashing into the floor until it sputters back into a smooth-ish orbit. Kitty also seems intent on only getting super close-up shots. Ew.

Mermaid is unusually quiet, standing near the window in a clean blue lab coat. She didn't stay the night, instead driving off to her own secret lair as soon as she'd put Gold to bed. Sequoia tries to keep out of the way, but it almost seems to make things worse. His body is so big that there's no corner he can squeeze into. He's already gotten tagged by a cam drone twice, accidentally knocking one into the wall when he turned around too quickly.

The Professor paces in the hallway, his voice lilting up and down as he growls out his lines. I move into the hallway and watch him quietly for a moment, admiring the energy and passion of his preparation.

"Don't forget to limp," I tell him.

"Ah, Iron." He turns and smiles at me. "What a memorial hostage vid this shall be. And it's all due to your quick thinking."

"I got lucky."

The Professor wags a finger at me good-naturedly and proclaims, "Luck gives you opportunities. Wit and skill allow you to take advantage of them." He pauses and his voice loses its bombast. "Do not doubt your iron will."

I can't help but smile back at him. "Then you're not mad about the slight change of plans yesterday?"

"Furious, but no scientist worth his PhD can argue with results, can they?"

"I suppose not." I'm relieved he isn't pissed at me, and it's not just because he signs the paychecks. I've always been fond of Gerald, but over the past weeks, I've come to realize I care about him and about what he thinks about me.

Don't get attached. That's one of Tickles's most important rules. Villains routinely swipe their henchmen or "kill" them off to gush ratings. Gerald isn't a father figure. He's my boss, and I need to remember that I'm always expendable unless I prove otherwise.

Speaking of which...

"I uh... I had some ideas to glam up the hostage vid," I say softly to Gerald... no, to The Professor. He leans in closer to me.

"Do tell, my dear."

A few mins later, Gold leans into the hallway. "We're almost ready," he reports. "Professor, how about you stand here." Gold motions to a spot near the window. "That will give you some good light. I'll need the henchmen to huddle here. Mr. Anders will be right between us. Mr. Mayor?"

From the kitchen, our hostage raises an impatient finger. "The firefighter union chief is crying about robo integration again and I've still got to swipe my security company," he says, distractedly.

It's been business as usual for Ash Anders since he came charging out of the master bedroom an hour ago looking like he got little, if any, sleep. His collar is unbuttoned, his hair just the smallest bit ruffled, but otherwise he's dialed up to full power player. So far, he's spent his stay with us stalking around whatever room isn't occupied, yelling into his Band, listening and nodding, and directing his staff on the schedule of the day. His stamina is impressive and annoying. He's gotten more done in the last 30 minutes than I think I've accomplished in my entire life.

"Mr. Anders, if you'd please," Gold says. "We have to get this hostage vid up before anyone figures out you've been kidnapped. We don't want the gossip Streams to beat us to our own story!"

Those gossip Streams are busy enough gushing about our heist. Shaky vids from the evening are everywhere showing Gold on stage badgering the auctioneer and the march of the Valkyrie security robos. One or two swing around to catch Mermaid firing her laz pistol and knocking down security guards in quick succession. The vids always cut out after a flash of light washes across the scene. I see myself in one vid, a blur of red ruffles and bright beads swinging over my face, scurrying with the panicked crowd. Nothing suspicious.

"Fine," the mayor says. "Where do you want me?"

"I want you to sit on the couch between me and Arsenic looking meek and scared. Iron and Nitrogen, you stand on either side of the couch and try to project at least a sliver of intimidation."

"Meek isn't going to work," Ash Anders proclaims. "I'll do defiant and I'll be standing, not sitting."

Gold looks pained by the stubbornness of his subject. Ash Anders has already refused to be tied up or even encased in a block of dry ice.

It takes some shuffling but eventually Ash Anders stands tall and proud in front of the couch, arms crossed over his chest, face set in a steely expression. The unbuttoned collar is a nice touch, I realize. He looks a little unvarnished, but his expression shows that he isn't cowed.

Kitty stands on the other side of the room as she controls the drones. "You all look so glam," she gushes. "And so very handsome." Her voice drops into husky tones.

"Interesting robo," Ash Anders comments.

"She's a reformed sex bot," I inform him.

"Oh."

"Alright, here we go. Billion-Loon expressions," Gold hollers. "Kitty, start rolling. Professor, when you're ready."

Our boss glares into the cam. "You dismissed my ideas. You denied my grant applications. You laughed behind my back," he says, his voice low and dangerous. "You thought I was just some lunatic, settling scores with heroes in Big Little City, but this town cannot contain me. I am THE PROFESSOR." His voice rises up in righteous indignation. "See how you laugh NOW!"

He bellows on while I try to stare menacingly at Ash Anders. Our hostage is stoic as The Professor rants.

"Villainy isn't confined to a single city or single state. It can strike anywhere. Anyone," The Professor says, voice dropping to a low growl. Clearly, Gerald relishes every single sec of this, and he's good at it, too. I feel a chill travel through my bones as his gravelly voice projects throughout the room. "So, Chicago, if you want to see your precious mayor again, I demand $10 billion in unmarked bills, delivered to me in Warehouse Six by... Sage Anders herself!"

"Don't do it!" Ash Anders cries fiercely. Gold grabs him and throws a light jab into his face. Anders stumbles but doesn't fall. The blow was hard enough to leave a mark on his cheek.

"I'll see you in my petri dish, Ms. President," The Professor says and unleashes his iconic laughter. I hold my spot, keeping my expression tight until Gold finally claps his hands and strolls to the center of the room.

"Excellent! Excellent!" Gold says. "Did I hit you too hard, Mr. Mayor?"

"What the hell was that?" Ash Anders says, practically spitting on The Professor. "We didn't discuss bringing my mother into this."

I secretly congratulate myself on the suggestion I'd given The Professor. It seems the rumors are true. Ash has more than a little animosity toward Momsy. Throwing her into the equation will surely up the ante of our vid, and—bonus—it clearly hit a nerve with Ash Anders. I don't miss the loss of his self-satisfied, know-it-all smile one bit.

"Not to worry." The Professor waves away the mayor's anger. "She won't come, obviously. That was simply a dramatic flair. They'll probably send Mayor Wisenberg." He gives Ash Anders a friendly look that says, *You understand, right?*

Anders looks at me. Can he see my fingerprints on the plan? I give him a shrug. The Professor is right. Ash Anders should understand. As far as I'm concerned, semi-reality and politics are basically shades of the same color.

"I don't even think we need another take," Gold is saying. "I'll just edit the vid, throw in some effects, and then we'll figure out how to take over all the screens in the city and run this in an hour or so."

"Call Crystalise at the City Council. She'll walk you through it," The Professor says, a wide smile on his face. This hostage vid will travel across all the gossip Streams, splash on the news Streams, and squarely place The Professor back on his throne as the top vil in Biggie LC.

"You shouldn't have brought her into this," Ash Anders growls again. His eyes are full of storm clouds. He stalks out of the room. "Get Lindselai," he barks at his Band and slams the door to the master bedroom. He's been calling her all night and all day. I still haven't figured out if she's his chief of staff, his press secretary, or maybe his girlfriend.

"How about I whip up some breakfast for everyone?" Sequoia suggests. As soon as he says the words, I realize that my stomach is an open pit of hunger.

"I'll help," I volunteer, shamefully positioning myself for first dibs on whatever grub Sequoia's got.

Gold has already retreated to the office where we've set up Leo's editing equipment. I have no doubt his enthusiastic offer to help edit our hostage vid is just an excuse to make sure he grabs as much lens time as possible. Then again, I'm already conniving how to get more than my fair share of food. I suppose we all strive where our passions lie.

Gold has also offered to edit our next ep. Too bad Leo's vid files are all biometrically locked. That's a major prob. No Leo means no ep delivered to the PAGS Sector 8 Regional office in two days when it's due. Tatianna Wentworth likely won't be so forgiving of our Chicago field trip if we don't have any dramatic footage to show for it.

But that's a knot to untangle after breakfast.

"Well, my dear, I suppose that leaves us to work on the problem of a new lair," The Professor says to Mermaid. "Our newly available budget should be quite helpful in this endeavor."

The tall, blonde henchman seems to shake away her thoughts and forces a smile on her lips. "Of course, Professor," she says. This side adventure will probably get her some good lens time as well. As Tickles the Elf says, "The lens is always focused on the boss."

Realizing I've been out-maneuvered once again by my savvier coworkers with a helping hand from my traitorous stomach, I slink to the kitchen after Sequoia. One cam drone buzzes after me, dinging a wall as it swoops through the opening.

Sequoia's immaculate kitchen contains a decorative stove and pots and pans stacked neatly in little cubbies below the counter. A holographic border wraps around the top of the walls showcasing plants that slowly grow and ripen. I expect Sequoia to pull some fancy snack bars or pre-made boxed meals from one of the cabinets. I doubt he has to live on cardboard-tasting gov nutra-packs like I do. Still, I'm shocked when he places a pan on the stove.

Stoves are usually only for show, though sometimes rich people spend tons of Loons on specialty cook robos that are programmed to use them. Sequoia doesn't keep a full-service robo in his home, just a cleaning bot that's currently hibernating in a closet to keep out of the way.

"Everyone likes scrambled eggs, right?" he asks.

"Real eggs?" I blurt out.

Sequoia glances at me, his freckled face quizzical. Then, quietly, he asks, "You've never eaten real eggs before?"

I despise the pity in his voice. He probably grew up eating fresh eggs every day.

"Course I have," I hiss. My father would take Alby and me out to breakfast on our birthday each year. I remember how he'd proclaim loud enough for everyone to hear, "real eggs and buttermilk pancakes for Twinly One and Twinly Two." That was when he had a job. When we lived in a house just a little smaller than this one. That was before he left to look for work and found an entirely new life instead; one that didn't include us.

"I'm sorry, I didn't..." Sequoia begins.

"I'm worried about Leo," I say, abruptly.

"The Professor says that no one knows who Leo is, so he's not a valuable hostage," Sequoia responds as he places the pan on the stove. He pulls open the door to his fridge, dips inside, and pulls out a bumpy container. The face of his fairy Totem, Evangeline, appears on a screen above the stove. "Doing some cooking?" she asks kindly.

"Yes, eggs please," he says.

"You got it, Chauncy." She winks at him and the stove hums to life. Sequoia cracks an egg on the side of the pan. I watch the goopy thing fall into the pan, the bright orange yolk swimming in a puddle of translucent white. It's so strange to think it came from the body of an actual animal.

How much do eggs even cost? With dust storms across the Midwest, drought parching the west, and super hurricanes in the south, raising livestock is risky and expensive. Most of the largest farms keep their animals permanently sheltered in climate-controlled grow houses.

I push those thoughts away and refocus on Leo. The Professor isn't exactly right. Leo *is* a valuable hostage. He reviewed our paperwork when we applied for the show and knows all our identities. A cape wouldn't have much reason to badger him for a ratings boost, but there's plenty of reason to try and make him talk off screen.

"Leo could unmask any of us," I point out. "Even The Professor."

I can smell the eggs. Sequoia has cracked a dozen, and now he mixes them around with a big wooden spoon.

"But torturing a producer..." Sequoia shakes his head. "It's just not done."

I realize that the holo-plants on the walls are fruit trees. Just above Sequoia's head, an orange tree slowly blossoms with its round, brightly colored fruits.

"Things are changing," I tell him. "Personas aren't following the unsaid rules anymore. Shadow isn't."

The eggs are growing firm in the pan. Sequoia mixes them again and large chunks rise from the goo.

"The Professor thinks it was Beacon who released Shine," he says.

Now I'm the one shaking my head. It wasn't her, I'm sure of that. "Beacon wouldn't have made such a mess of the door," I tell him. That hole was sloppy. Beacon is nothing if not elegant. Her Light Blade could have carved the entire door out. "And Beacon would have waited for us to return," I add. "She wouldn't have wasted an opp to take down The Professor or at least a few of his henchmen. It had to be someone else."

Sequoia shrugs. "Well, I guess Shine will surface soon enough and release an ep of what happened. Then we'll know."

The scent of the eggs fills the kitchen and my stomach aches for food. It's strange watching Sequoia cook. It's such a rich person thing to do. Sure, the Streams are filled with cooking shows, everything from cupcake competitions to tutorials on how to create mouth-watering meals using only synthetic protein gel, but no one I know actually cooks. Well, except my mother, but heating up oats for breakfast and then rice and some veggies for dinner is the extent of her culinary skill.

"I find it relaxing," Sequoia says as if he can read my skepticism. "Cooking. My mom taught me. We had robos, but she said cooking your own food made it taste better and she was right." There's pride in his voice.

I check my Band. One egg costs the same as four gov nutra-packs. What a drooling waste of money.

I lean against the counter and cross my arms over my chest. "Will your father really kick you out of the company?"

Sequoia gives me a thin smile. "He knows I was trying out to be a henchman for The Professor. It was a terrible embarrassment to him. I suppose he'll figure out I was involved in the kidnapping last night." He grabs up two small, silver obelisks, turns them upside down and shakes them over the fluffy pile of scrambled eggs in the pan. Salt and pepper fall on them like snow.

"Will your dad unmask you?" I ask, curious.

Sequoia stares at the eggs. "No," he says softly. "That would tarnish our family's reputation, make us vulnerable. He'd never let that happen."

I remember the intensity of his father's gaze last night, the way people shrunk away from him as he moved through the crowd. It strikes me, suddenly but with pure conviction, that Sequoia may actually be the bravest of us all.

"I have a younger sister, Geneva-Rose" Sequoia says. "Dad will probs bring her into the company. She's spoiled and, well, not very canny. She won't do well." He opens the fridge and pulls out... What are those? I look at the red fruits nestled in the small container in his hand. Strawberries. Of course the guy has real strawberries just sitting around in his fridge for an afternoon snack.

"I don't have many," he says. "Wasn't expecting company, but I'll chop them up."

"You were saying?"

He pulls a knife from a block I had assumed was purely decorative. Overhead, I watch grapes ripen on holographic vines. Sequoia chops the strawberries slowly, carefully.

"I'm still not exactly sure if he only cast me out from working under his division of PAGS or from our entire family." More chopping. His head is down but I see the red flush rising in his cheeks. "I haven't deemed it wise to ask for clarification."

I push off the counter and put a hand on his arm, suddenly ashamed of my jealousy and resentment. "I'm on my own, too," I say quietly.

The knife pauses and he looks at me. There's something in his eyes, something that makes me uncomfortable.

I take my hand away and step back. "You have to learn to be strong," I say to him. "If people see your weakness, they'll take advantage of you. They'll... they'll take all your strawberries." I pluck the last one from the container and pop it in my mouth.

Now his smile is weak, uncertain. "Thanks for the advice."

"That's what friends are for," I mumble around my mouthful of sweet fruit. I turn and tail it out of the kitchen before he gives me another one of those longing gazes. Outside the kitchen, I look up and down the hallway wondering where I should go. If Leo were here, he'd probs tell me to spend time posting on my Iron Stream. After all, according to Bob, I've got over 121,000 hate messages to answer. *Hmmmm,* maybe I can help The Professor and Mermaid look for a new lair, preferably somewhere within walking distance of Culprits Coffee. That place has the best bear claw donuts and soon enough I'll actually be able to afford some.

"Iron, a moment of your time," a voice calls from down the hallway. I follow it into the office. Gold leans back in his chair behind a sleek desk, arms clasped behind his head. A Pod on the desk casts four separate screens in front of him, two stacked on each other. Sequoia's Anders 3100 3D printer fills a good portion of the room. It's not nearly as advanced as Adan's printer, but it's still one of the nicest 3Ds I've ever seen. And it printed those amaze peach PJs for me last night, so I am eternally grateful to that machine.

"Ta, Wholesome," Gold says. I hate that little nickname, but I'm not about to show it.

"You called, Mr. Producer?" I ask, sarcasm heavy in my voice.

One screen follows Sequoia as he walks into the living room and offers a plate of scrambled eggs and strawberries to Mermaid and then to The Professor. Another screen shows Ash Anders pacing tightly in the master bedroom, barking commands into his Band. Those are obvi the live feeds from our cam drones.

The third screen displays a frozen screenshot of The Professor's ransom video, while the fourth screen replays my convo with Sequoia in the kitchen. The volume is on mute. I watch Sequoia break the eggs again. He keeps glancing over at me as I lean back against the counter and stare at the growing holo-plants above us.

Gold watches the screen too. "This scene needs a lot of work," he says and shakes his head sadly as if I have disappointed him. "You're flat, Wholesome. I'm going to need you to dial up the sexual tension by a magnitude of..." he pauses to think, "about 300 percent."

"Sexual tension? With Sequoia?" I laugh.

"Sex sells," he says. "We need more of it."

"*You're* the one going for the romance angle with Arsenic," I point out.

A small frown flickers across his face, then he's all smiles and charm again. "That plot point is taking a little longer to come to fruition than initially anticipated," he admits.

"She's not interested."

"She is not currently aware of how interested she

shall shortly be."

"What?"

"Nitrogen is hotter than a New York heatwave for you," Gold says. "Why don't you give him a little..." He puckers his golden lips and makes a wet smacking noise for emphasis. "The viewers like him. He's a puppy. You... well, you tricked and imprisoned the world's most fav sidekick. The entire teen population of the planet wants to throw you into the middle of Z Town."

"But I'm... I'm plucky," I manage.

"That pause there? That pause is your problem." Gold gives me a solemn look. "You need a storyline. Something to draw in the viewers. So give that boy some rubbing and maybe you'll get a little of his charm on you."

"I can't," I spit out.

Gold sighs as if I am testing all the patience he possesses within his wiry body. "Wholesome, just bat your eyes. Give him a little pat for the cams. You need this. The show needs this."

My feet begin to move and I pace in a tight circle. "I can't," I say again. "He's a nice person."

"Course he is. That's why everyone hearts him. A nice henchman. The viewers are eating it up."

"No." I shake my head. "That's not what I mean. He's good. He's actually a good person."

Gold must hear the strain in my voice because the smile finally slides off his face. Now he's just confused. "What has that got to do with anything?"

"He's kind and gentle," I explain and drag in a heavy breath, "and I hurt good people, k?" I tap my chest. "My heart is dry as dirt in California."

It's true. There is nothing good inside of me. I hate

my father for leaving our family. I despise my mother for wilting away after he left, for retreating into Buddhist-Minimalism as if giving away all of our possessions would somehow balance the despair inside of her. Alby was the only good thing in my life, and I destroyed him with my ambition and my hope.

The darkness in me is why I'm drawn to other broken people. Like Matthew. Like Lysee. Even poor Ollie. I sense that brokenness somehow deep inside in Leo, and it's why he seems to pull me toward him no matter how hard I fight it. I've even programmed my Totem—a person's one true friend—to treat me like garbage.

I'm bad. I'm rotten. The only use I can think of for my life is to try and fix this world for the other people. The good people.

I expect a sarcastic response from Gold or even amusement at this show of weakness.

"I understand," he says.

We can't see each other's eyes with our goggles on, but I recognize a fellow threadbare soul. I remember that Gold grew up in a kid drop-off depot in some nothing town. The gov calls them "Child Development Centers," but it's just a place for parents to toss their unwanted kids. I've heard they're terrbs, filled with wild children, monitored by glitchy care robos and a few underpaid breathers.

You can't make it out of that kind of place without a few scars.

"Sequoia deserves better," I finally say.

Gold chews his lip. "Some viewers do like you," he admits finally. "They admire your gumption. But you still need a storyline. Alright, we'll go with unrequited puppy love. Just keep being awkward and standoffish. I'll make it work. And stop talking about your families. I've got to cut all personally identifying info out and I haven't figured out how to do that yet."

"I'm not awkward and standoffish," I mutter.

"Then awkwardness has an identical twin and it's you." Gold smiles at his own joke. "Now get outta here. I've got to finish our amaze hostage vid. This thing is solid platinum. I've got to get it out by…"

His words falter as all four holo-screens flicker and then cut out.

"Who is it?" I ask as my Band hums and projects a black holo-screen on my forearm.

"Someone who's trying to steal my thunder," Gold grumbles.

Some producer in Biggie LC has paid a hefty sum to the City Council to hijack all the Pods, Bands, and screens in town to broadcast some big announcement. This happens a lot. In fact, just two weeks ago, The Professor did the same thing to announce his return.

The screen brightens and two resplendent figures stand proudly in front of the cam. One of them is Shine, glam in his orange-and-gold suit. The other is…

"Buddha's spleen!" I hiss.

"Hmmmm, that ain't Beacon," Gold says, leaning forward toward the holo-screen. "Looks like Shine got himself a new partner and she ain't half bad looking."

"Greetings, citizens of Big Little City," Shine says. "As you can see, I have extricated myself from the clutches of The Professor."

"With the help of his daring new sidekick, Dreamer!" chirps the woman next to him. She bats her eyelashes and juts out a hip. Her purple-and-white costume manages to be both ostentatious and skimpy.

Lysee was always talented at that particular combo. I stare at my roommate as she preens for the cam and wonder why I feel so surprised.

CHAPTER 19

Stressful? Yes. And after nine kidnappings, I can say that with authority. But at least there are no boring days in Big Little City! ~ Reena Masterson, Documentary: The City of Heroes

~

On the holo-screen, Shine details how stoic he was under The Professor's relentless torture. Lysee stands by his side, lips pursed, arms crossed over her chest. Though a stylish purple mask covers most of her face and artfully curves around her pink lips, I have no doubt it's her. I recognize the shape of her face, those round, bright eyes staring back at me, and the way she presses back her shoulders to accentuate her cleavage.

As Shine continues to detail his harrowing captivity, I silently fume. I captured Shine fair and square! K, maybe not fairly at all, but it was still a legit nab. And now Lysee has stolen away my prize.

It seems so obvi now. Lysee knew we were holding Shine prisoner. She had stumbled into the lobby of the mansion while I was tying up Shine. No doubt Matthew gave her a tour of The Professor's lair at some point in the past, complete with showing her the trick book-shelf and elevator code.

On screen, Shine heaps praise on Beacon. "I can't tell you how grateful I am for all you've taught me," he says. Next to him, Lysee nods. Her leotard doesn't leave much to the imagination and I wonder how she'll possibly fight crime in those thigh-high purple boots with stiletto heels. Her mask glitters with sequins and her purple hair is a beautiful mix of complex braids and thick curls. She is gorg and glam and an utter traitor!

I can imagine how it all went down, Lysee sneaking into the lair while we were risking our necks in Chicago. She probs stood in front of Shine's door bargaining for her new position with a fire cutter in hand.

A stew of bitterness bubbles in my stomach. I should have seen this coming. Lysee was so despo to get in front of the lens. And then there was all that babble about following her destiny the other night.

All's fair in the Fame Game, Tickles says on his blog.

And yet, it still hurts.

"He's obvi spinning off," Gold says as he leans back in his chair once again. I'd almost forgotten my fellow henchman was in the room. "Beacon would never take him back after he tried to poach The Professor."

"She's not going to be happy about this," I find myself saying automatically.

Gold laughs. "Beacon is going to piss her costume."

But what can she really do? I remember what Adan told me. The City Council is trying to swipe Beacon. She's self-funding her show, digging in with her fingertips. In the old days, when she was at the top of the ratings, she could have easily squeezed Shine, turning sponsors against him, making sure no juicy villain storylines found their way to him.

Now?

Maybe Shine has a chance if he can get a sponsor. Will Tatianna Wentworth still work with him after his capture?

"But now it is time for me to forge my own path, be my own light in the darkness," Shine is saying on the screen.

"Spinning off," Gold says with a satisfied nod. "Wonder how far he'll get."

Me too.

"And finally, I have a special message for The Professor," Shine says.

"Ooooh, we've got a new rival." Gold chuckles. His hands tighten on the armrests of the chair. "This could be very good for us."

Shine looks directly into the cam. His face is hidden by his gold-and-orange mask, but those green eyes are as familiar as ever. "Professor, you thought you could break me, but you made me stronger. You thought you could humble me, but I am more dedicated to the mission of justice than ever."

"Oye," Gold groans, "he's overplaying his hand."

"No, he's playing it perfectly," I say reluctantly. Shine looks strong and noble. His square jaw and bright eyes will make girls, guys, and nonbinaries swoon all across the world. I can't help but admire his gall, calling out The Professor, trying to poach Beacon's greatest rivalry away from her.

"Professor, take this warning," Shine says, his voice low and gritty. "I'm coming for you. I'll knock down your henchmen one by one and then I'll give you the recognition you've always wanted. I'll make sure you're the most famous prisoner in the Big Little City Prison."

"Watch out!" Lysee adds. When she moves her head, her hair sparkles with silver hues.

"Professor, we have something that belongs to you." Shine smiles and pauses, letting that mystery sink in with the viewers. "If you want your producer back, I'll give you a chance to retrieve him shortly."

He glances back at Lysee, gives her the slightest nod, and together they chant, "Let justice shine!"

The screen fades out, but my anger continues to burn.

***

The Professor calls us to an assembly in Sequoia's living room to convo this new development. I foolishly assume we will discuss ways to bargain for Leo.

"Should we reshoot the hostage vid and include a response to Shine?" The Professor asks.

Gold shakes his head. "Shine is an upstart. He's beneath you. Your only focus is on Beacon. She's your mortal enemy. Don't let a pretty boy in a shiny costume ride your lab coat to fame."

"He's not just a pretty boy," Mermaid points out. "Shine has a strong following. This spinoff will make waves."

"We're about to drown that news," Gold says. He perches on the edge of the couch.

"Gold is right," Ash Anders speaks up. The Mayor of Chicago stands in the doorway of the living room, having evidently decided to drop in on this meeting. Now he looks at The Professor. "Don't split your focus. By giving Shine attention you only make him more powerful. Focus on your true opponent."

The Professor nods.

"Perhaps we should engage Shine," I mention. "He has Leo, after all."

"We can get by without him," Gold says with a

shrug. I haven't failed to notice how the lenses of the drone cams seem perpetually turned on him. Kitty is controlling them, but no doubt he added a few special commands to her program. He who controls the cams controls the story.

I suddenly recognize what a weapon we've given to Gold. If he turns against any one of us, he can edit us right out of the show. I've got to be even more careful around him than I already am, and we def need to get Leo back.

"Leo is the only one who can access all the footage from the Chicago heist," I point out. "We've got to submit the ep in two days."

"Look, we all want to recover our valiant producer," Gold says, his words dripping with false sincerity, "and that footage is handy, but if need be, we can make do without it."

I open my mouth to argue but Gold continues. "We've got all the footage of our secret planning, and we can use a mix of the Band recordings from guests at the auction along with some cut-out narratives from the rest of us to fill in the full picture. Even the mayor can grudgingly tell his side of the story." Gold grins at me. "Viewers will call it *avant-garde*."

The Professor frowns. "We do need to retrieve our producer, but I don't believe he is in significant danger. There is no call to abuse production staff. It isn't done."

I hold in my groan. That might've been true in the old days during The Professor's original show where everything was *wink-wink*, but nothing is off-limits anymore. Shadow proved that when he blew up my restaurant and hacked police officers to death with his molten ax. The old rules of decorum are gone as the glaciers.

"If we ignore Shine, maybe he'll just let Leo go," Sequoia says. He stands next to me against the wall. "Does he even have a headquarters?"

Good question. How long has Adan been planning his spinoff? Surely he hasn't had time to set up his own headquarters yet. Does that mean he'd take Leo to his house? No, Adan isn't that lobotomy. He knows I know where it is. Maybe he's staying with a friend or he's using one of the empty, dilapidated buildings in what we politely call "The Old Neighborhood" and less politely deem the "Villain Spawning Ground." More than one vil has gotten their start in an empty factory or vacant storefront in that area of town. Capes, too. Lobo hibernated in a creepy old dress shop filled with disfigured mannequins until his ratings jumped enough for him to rent a real headquarters.

I tune back into the convo. The others are discussing when to release our hostage vid.

"We lose impact if we post it right after Shine," Gold is saying. He's on his feet now.

"The heist is already all over the news," Mermaid points out. "Everyone knows The Professor crashed the auction. It's only a matter of time until someone figures out that we kidnapped the mayor. We need to take control of this story. I say we release it now."

"Yes, release it now," Ash Anders says. "I would prefer to be back into Chicago sooner rather than later, and we still need to discuss my dramatic escape."

"In good time," The Professor assures him.

This is how we convinced Anders to become our willing kidnapping victim. It's why the Chicago PD isn't tracking his Band and why the gossip Streams have only run shaky vids from guests at the auction and no recordings from the library's security cams that could clearly identify us. The Professor promised Anders a dramatic kidnapping followed by a courageous and death-defying escape that will turn him into a celebrated hero overnight. That's a kind of publicity no politician can buy, no matter how many crypto Loons he has.

As the group continues to argue, my Band bleeps angrily at me. Bob's scruffy face appears on the project holo-screen. "Hey," he says, "I got something to tell you."

"Shhhh," I hiss and slip into the hallway, away from the babble of voices. I look down at my Totem. "You're supposed to be on mute."

"Yeah." He grins at me, "but I can override that for high priority messages and appointments."

"I got a high priority message?" Did Alby contact me again? Or what if something's happened to him, and my mom is calling with the bad news? What if he took too many Mellows or he had one of those VR seizures the news Streams are always warning about?

"Nope, not a message. You've got school."

I stare at Bob's round face and beady eyes. "School?"

"Midterms," he clarifies.

"Midterms?" I croak out the word as the realization dawns on me. "Midterms! Buddha's knuckle warts!"

I'd forgotten.

Utterly...

Totally...

Forgotten. What, with kidnapping the Mayor of Chicago and then having our evil lair infiltrated, midterms totally slipped my mind. I stand in the hallway like a drooling lobotomy as my mind painfully adjusts, and then I look at the time again.

Blight! My legs move. I careen back into the living room. "I have to go!" I huff. "It's an emergency."

The Professor frowns. I give him a pleading look and he finally nods. "Get back as soon as you can."

I nod. Sequoia looks at me with questions in his eyes, but I don't have time to explain.

"Release the hostage vid tonight," I say, "just after the sun goes down. That'll put it in the nightly and morning news cycles. Everyone will already be talking about it by morning." I move to the door.

"Iron," The Professor calls softly.

I turn to my boss. He gives me a polite smile. "Perhaps you wouldn't wish to remove yourself from this dwelling in your current wardrobe?"

I look down at my scarlet lab coat, and my fingertips brush the goggles securely placed over my eyes. "Oh, right," I mumble. With a short huff of a sigh, I unbutton my lab coat and pull the goggles off my face. I've already unmasked in front of my fellow henchmen and Ash Anders saw my face in the basement of the Chicago Library. Still, I feel almost naked without my goggles. Sequoia steps up to take my costume from me, and I give him a grateful smile. Beneath my lab coat, I'm only wearing a pale gray tank top and black exercise pants that Sequoia printed on his Anders 3100. This outfit rings in with a zero fashion rating, but it'll have to do. At least it's comfy

Ironic. The 3D-printing company Ash Anders's mother built into a behemoth is the very reason I have clothes on my back. It probably printed the plates I ate my breakfast from and the decorative sconces on the wall.

"Thanks," I whisper to Sequoia and push through the open doorway. If I had any money in my crypto purse, I'd order a car, but my balance is still in the negative.

My first paycheck is due tomorrow. Too bad it's the producer's job to hand them out. I force my mind to the present. Midterms first, then paychecks, then rescuing Leo. Wait, no. Midterms first, then rescuing Leo, then paychecks. Yes, that's the right order. My legs move. I start with a fast walk then speed up to a trot.

My apartment is only three kilometers from Shield University, but Sequoia's house is double that distance. Chem starts in 50 minutes, an easy walk from my apartment and a very not-easy run from Sequoia's house.

The day is cool, and if I weren't running for my academic life, I might take some time to appreciate the new leaves unfurling from the trees or the bright sun streaming through a cloudless sky, or the fact that radiation levels have been nice and low this entire week.

Instead, I run, sweat, and huff. By the time I make it to the university, my legs and lungs burn.

"Three mins until class starts," Bob points out helpfully. "Wow, you really sweat a lot. Are you sure you don't have some sort of glandular condition?"

"Clap it!" I hiss at him. I break out into a full-on sprint, rushing up the slowly churning stairs and skid into the third-floor hallway. My feet pound the tiled floor. Thankfully, the door to the chem classroom slides open when it picks up the signal from my Band. Exactly one minute to spare.

I suck in heaving breaths as I step inside. A trickle of sweat rolls down my back. At my table, Ollie brightens and waves. Seated next to him, Adan gives me a breezy smile.

CHAPTER 20

Never allow a lull. Add in backstory, build relationships, scheme a little. ~ Tickles the Elf, The Henchman's Survival Guide

~

"Adan has returned," Ollie helpfully informs me as I drop like a stone into my seat, still panting from the run.

"Would you look at that," I manage. And then I do look at *that*. Adan is glam as ever, his black hair artfully waved, that strong jaw set like he could plow down doors with it.

"Ta," he says, all breezy. He wears a fitted black t-shirt covered in silver zippers, some strategically un-zipped to show tantalizing bits of flesh and chiseled muscle. Zippers, of course, are the new fad of the week. I wouldn't be surprised if that was the first thing Adan looked up when Lysee sprung him from our cell.

"You look a little tired," Adan says. "Got a lot on your mind?"

"Just the midterm," I lie. I haven't thought about the test once in the past week. That doesn't bode well for my grade. Course, that might be the least of my worries.

Adan knows my identity and now he's free to crow about it to anyone and everyone. *But I know his secret identity, too* I remind myself. I stare at him, trying to somehow read his mind. *What's he going to do about it?*

Then, with a start, I remember that he has Leo. Here I am thinking about my own rep when the arrogant troll nugget sitting next to me is holding my producer captive.

"Alice, perhaps you wouldn't feel so worried about the midterms if you'd studied with me," Ollie says. He wears red suspenders over a rainbow shirt. I'm sure some K-pop phenom pulled off that look spectacularly in his latest music vid, but it's not doing Ollie any favors. "You said you would contact me, but I never received a communication from you. Is your Band functioning properly?"

Adan's mouth drops open in feigned shock. "She blew you off?" he asks Ollie. "Alice, that's not very kind."

My neck begins to burn. "I uh, I was busy with, uh, personal matters. I'm sorry, Ollie. I should have..."

At that moment our Bands hum and switch over to test mode.

"The test is beginning," the human teaching assistant says as he strolls past our table. He holds his hands behind his back, long fingers tapping. "No speaking please, and do not attempt to look at your tablemate's screen."

Wouldn't help anyway. The university made each of us download their special testing software on our Bands. The holo-screen projecting from my Band looks clear only when I stare at it head-on. A person looking sideways at it would see only a blurry mess. Not that anyone would be lobotomy enough to copy my answers.

On my screen, Professor Hersherwitz gallops toward me and then stands on his hind hooves. "Alice, it's been a pleasure exploring the cosmos big and small with you these past weeks," he says. His shape changes, turning round and sponge-like. "Let's see what you've absorbed." The spongy blue unicorn morphs into a million tiny atoms. "Shining luck!" they cheer and then zip off the screen in a roiling blue cloud. I get the feeling I already used every drop of my luck during the heist in Chicago.

When the first question pops up, my suspicions are confirmed. The test is a nightmare. The questions seem to fly out of my head as soon as I read them. The answers are nowhere to be found in my puny brain. There are rumors that some Captains of Industry are grafting data interfaces right into their gray matter. I wistfully wonder how much it costs.

On screen, little electrons zip around the nucleus of two different atoms. I need to figure out what type of chemical bond they have. Instead, I feel Adan next to me, his very presence stealing away my focus even though he's currently frowning at his own screen.

I move to a different question. I'm given a pile of electrons, neutrons, and protons and must construct the three isotopes of hydrogen. My brain feels so fuzzy. I move one proton to the middle of the screen with my forefinger and leave it hanging there, alone and unprotected.

Like Leo. I see his face in my mind, his pale brown eyes staring mournfully at me. I picture his wavy brown hair, the nose that's a little too pointed, and the mole just under his left eye. Worry nibbles holes into my stomach.

Do I actually miss Leo? A producer? A person whose

job it is to twist us like towels until all our fears, faults, and weaknesses bleed out for the lens?

Yes. I do miss him and I'm afraid for him, and that makes me angry. I don't want to like Leo. Hell, I can't afford to since he's technically my boss, but I need to know why his eyes are so troubled, why the only thing hanging on his wall is a blurry pic of half-starved children from Tanzania.

As the timer in the corner of my screen counts down, I rush through the last questions of the test. Adan scowls, his hands flapping as he rearranges something on his screen. On his other side, I notice Ollie fidgeting and drumming on the table with his fingertips. He must already be done with the test. I really should have studied with him.

"Time's up," Professor Hersherwitz says, his blue horse face suddenly filling my screen. "Your knowledge is just radiant." A sun rises behind him, lighting up the screen. "We will tabulate your score and post it to your account this evening. Until then, don't stew too much on your grade!" He morphs into a beaker filled with a bubbling compound.

They could grade the test instantly, but the administrators don't want students exploding into puddles of tears or burning anger on campus.

"Good job, everyone," the teaching assistant says and flicks back his artfully cut black bangs, which immediately fall over his eyes again. "If anyone has questions about the test, please feel free to ping me during my office hours."

I wonder if anyone will actually take him up on his offer. As soon as our grades are posted, we'll be able to go back through the test and get a full explanation of each answer. It's built into every testing software the university uses.

Next to me, Adan sits back in his chair, an easy smile on his face. I wonder how he did. It's not like he could have studied in his cell, and he's been out less than a day.

"You look nervous," he tells me. "Didn't do so well?"

"Shine has spun off!" Ollie blurts out. The kid is fit to explode. His pale blue eyes are wide and both hands tap complex rhythms on the table. "And The Professor has attempted a heist in Chicago, clearly outside the boundaries of Big Little City. Technically, he is not the first villain to ever conduct a crime outside the city limits. The Map Collector once buried Shooting Star's golden staff four kilometers over the border, but that was not located in another township.

"It was a bold move if you ask me," I say.

"Bold or desperate?" Adan asks.

"But the repercussions could be enormous," Ollie says. "How will the City Council respond? Who will have jurisdiction over their crime?"

"What happens if they get caught?" Adan asks, that stupid smile on his face again. "I hear Chicago's working on some new and improved drooly camps."

"Well, The Professor's henchmen are clever," I stammer. "Who says they'll get caught? After all, Iron did manage to kidnap Shine."

Adan sucks in a breath. "He was tricked."

Ollie nods. "Iron pretended to be injured and Shine tried to help her. She wasn't wearing her goggles, so he didn't know she was a henchman."

Thankfully Leo had blurred my face for the ep. What a drooling mistake to forget to slip on my goggles.

"Plus, Shine escaped," Adan says. "So clearly he outwitted The Professor."

"Shine had help," I point out. "He would have never gotten out on his own."

"Exactly, yes, we must discuss Dreamer," Ollie jumps in. He leans over the table, forcing Shine to sit back in his seat. "Who is she? What are her capabilities? Does she know any martial arts fighting styles? Does she use any weapons?"

I feel a smug smile of my own dawning on my lips. I happen to know the answers to all those questions.

Capabilities: Recycling and reprinting her entire wardrobe each month

Martial arts specialties: None

Weapons: Batting her eyelashes, hugs, and spewing outrageous optimism.

"I'm sure she's eminently qualified and will make an excellent sidekick for Shine," I say. "That is, assuming he gets sponsored. I'm sure Beacon won't stand in his way after he stabbed her in the back."

"Perhaps Shine has his own resources," Adan murmurs. "Like any great hero, he has a plan, I'm sure."

Ollie's head twists back and forth as we speak. "Certainly, certainly. Shine must contend with the fact that Beacon will not be pleased with his behavior. There is much to discuss. My fellowship and I have been updating the wikis as fast as we can, but there is still much to do. Perhaps you two would like to assist?"

I stare at Ollie. Wiki? Fellowship? Doesn't he know we have a hostage vid to send out tonight?

No, he doesn't, I remind myself. "I, uh, I have another midterm today and I have to study for two tomorrow," I murmur.

"Same here," Adan says quickly. "I need to study."

"Then tomorrow, after our classes." Ollie looks at us.

Adan grimaces but then his face smooths. Even without a cam drone in the room, he still knows how to tame his expression. "Let me get back to you on that," he says to Ollie. "Alice, I have a question about the test, maybe I can walk you to your next class?"

My fake smile matches his. "Yeah, Ollie, I think I might need some downtime after all this studying. Let's raincheck our hero chat date. Plus, you know I don't like capes anyway. Just a pompous bunch of asses in my opinion."

Ollie frowns. "They keep our city safe," he says. "But alright, I will follow up with you both this afternoon. We shouldn't wait too long to discuss this. Things are changing very quickly." He shakes his head, stands, and walks out of the room.

How right you are, I think.

Adan watches him go. "He's an interesting character."

"He's the only one of us who isn't a character," I point out. I look around. Most of the other students have already filtered out of the room. A few linger, probs discussing the test, but they're far enough away to be out of earshot. Even so, I keep my voice low.

"Kidnapping our producer was a dirty move. Production staff is off limits."

Adan's smile grows sharp. "One dirty trick deserves another, and there are no limits now. Not after what Shadow did. The ante is upped. You nabbed the Mayor of Chicago."

I jerk to my feet and turn my face away so he won't

get the satisfaction of seeing my shock. How the hell did he know that?

"Did Leo tell you?" I ask. It stings to think he would have given away such a crucial plot point of our show to our enemy.

"I saw it on his screen when we picked him up, just after Lysee sprung me," Adan admits. "He had earbuds in, recording your ep. He didn't even hear us coming."

I'd wondered why he hadn't managed to get off a call for help.

"Tatiana Wentworth confirmed it," Adan adds.

I turn to face him. "She agreed to sponsor your spin-off?"

A flicker of worry crosses his face but then it's gone, shoved behind his casual mask. "She's considering it. When I rescue Ash Anders, she'll be begging to fund me."

"So you're going to rescue Ash Anders are you?" I try to sound teasing but inside my stomach knots.

Adan laughs. I can't tell if it's fake or real and I wonder if even he knows. "It was a gutsy move," he admits. "Risky as hell, but what a reward. Every gossip Stream is already gushing about the heist and they don't even know you have Anders. What do you think the president's going to do when she finds out? That is, if she doesn't already know."

I swallow. I've thought about Sage Anders of course, but she's such an inscrutable figure. I have no idea how she's going to respond. Hopefully, Ash will keep his mother from sending the Navy SEALs after us, though I wonder if he's even told her about our little scheme. Those two aren't exactly on chummy terms, and the reason Ash agreed to this whole thing in the first place was to beat her in the next election.

If she rescues him that would look great for her re-election campaign, I realize with horror. I glance toward the windows, wondering if some sniper is gazing at me through a scope somewhere off in the distance.

"You're right," I admit to Adan. "We were desperate. Tatianna was pissed that I captured you. She was going to swipe us. We had to do something iconic."

"Well, you did." There's warmth in Adan's voice.

"I was so terrified," I whisper. I don't know why I'm admitting this weakness to him. Adan nods and his green eyes almost seem kind. This thing between us is so strange. We're enemies but we understand each other. I despise him but I trust him. He's selfish and vain, but then there was that vid of him with the two younger girls—his sisters. He's fake and real at the same time.

"We need to come to an understanding," Adan says.

I nod. The last students trickle out of the classroom. I have 20 mins until my next class. Plenty of time for a high stakes poker match I feel utterly unequal to.

"We both know each others' identity. Either one of us could destroy the prospects of the other." Adan starts.

"But then they would condemn themselves," I finish his thought. "Mutually assured destruction."

Adan props an elbow on the table. "I propose that we both swear not to unmask the other or use our knowledge against the other."

I let out a breath. "Deal."

We stare at each other.

"How'd you do on the test?" he finally asks.

"Bombed it. You?"

"Same."

He laughs. So do I.

"Is Leo safe?" I try to be casual about the question but Adan isn't laughing anymore. One eyebrow arches.

"Yes. Safe and secure."

"What do you want for him?"

Adan doesn't answer the question. He doesn't have to.

"Ash Anders," I say.

"We can do a hostage trade."

I'm already shaking my head. "The Professor will never go for that. Ash Anders is too valuable. He wants to use him to flush out Beacon."

"The Professor won't have a show if he can't put out an ep," Adan says. He leans back casually in his chair.

"We have a contingency plan," I say and try to sound convincing. Gold's ideas are a sad patchwork at best. Our viewers would be majorly disappointed if we can't deliver great vid of our kidnapping heist. There's something else to consider. If we can't give Ash Anders the heroic escape he was promised, he won't hesitate to toss each of us into a drooly camp for years.

"Why are you even going after Beacon?" Adan asks. "I already told you, she's on her last days. Convince The Professor to set up a rivalry with me. We could be epic foes."

I glare at him. "Beacon made you. It sounds like you don't even care that she's being forced out."

That slaps the smile right off Adan's face. He presses his lips together and his voice is rough when he speaks. "Of course I care. I owe her a lot. But this is the Fame Game. She's the one who taught me how to play it. We all get swiped in the end, even the masters."

He sounds regretful but is it all an act? I hate this. I can't tell truth from fiction and I'm not even sure if they're that much different at this point.

"I'll deliver your message to my boss," I tell Adan through gritted teach.

"When will your hostage vid go out?" Adan leans forward in his chair.

"Tonight."

"I want an answer by midnight," he says. "We can arrange a hostage exchange, but I'd prefer a dramatic confrontation with The Professor and a rescue. I'm willing to allow The Professor to escape as long as I come away with Ash Anders."

"How kind of you," I murmur knowing immediately that his plan is a no-go. Ash Anders will not tolerate being rescued. The Professor promised him a dramatic escape. Gold and Mermaid are already planning how to make that happen.

"Talk it over with your boss and we can arrange the specifics once he agrees," Adan says.

I stare at the zippers on his shirt trying to think my way out of this.

"And what if he says no?" I ask. "What will happen to Leo?"

Adan studies my face. What does he see there? Whatever it is makes him square his jaw. "If The Professor says no, then perhaps you and I can make an arrangement of our own. All I need is a location and I can do the rest."

"You want me to betray my boss? Lose my job?"

"There could be a better one waiting for you."

This convo just became far more dangerous than it already was.

"What do you mean?" I ask.

Adan gives me a sly look and his voice drops to a soft whisper. "Lysee's got good lens presence but otherwise she's worthless. No skills. No brains. Just every self-help catchphrase that's ever existed."

His green eyes appraise me, unabashed.

I laugh. Nothing about him surprises me anymore. "You'd swipe Lysee just like that?" I ask. "After she saved you and your career?"

Adan shrugs. If he recognizes my distaste it doesn't bother him. "I had to take her on. She was my only way out, but anything can happen at the beginning of a new series. Characters come and go. I'll certainly give her great lens time in my first ep and during our inevitable breakup."

"How gallant you are, Mr. Hero," I spit out.

"I can't be a hero if my sidekick holds me back." Adan's brow furrows and I realize he looks tired. This close, I can see he's wearing some kind of powder on his face, but the dark pockets under his eyes still faintly show through.

"You wouldn't hurt Leo," I say, trying to sound sure.

Adan stands up. He's only half a head taller than me but his body is big and muscled. He is a presence. "I don't have to hurt him," he says. "If Leo doesn't deliver your next ep on time, PAGS will fire him. Again."

"Again?"

Adan smiles. "It's good to have connections in the City Council. Sometimes a personnel file accidentally gets forwarded to the wrong Stream."

I look down at the table. I don't know what to say. It feels like Adan is ten moves ahead, carefully maneuvering me toward a cliff. I keep my expression neutral and raise my eyes until I meet Adan's gaze. I give him a little smile that I hope is enigmatic, offering hope without a promise while the fires of fury rage inside me.

"You'll have your answer tonight," I tell him sweetly.

"Excellent," Adan says. "It's always lovely doing business with you, Alice. Think about my offer."

"I'm not sure I'm ready to switch sides."

Adan laughs at that. "Here's a little secret." He leans toward me, so close I can smell his expensive after-shave. "The capes, the vils, the sidekicks and henchmen —we're all on the same side. The side of ourselves."

Our eyes lock. His face moves closer to mine.

My Band buzzes and a blindingly bright holo-screen jumps up between us. Adan steps back.

Bob's face fills the holo-screen. For once my Totem looks serious. What now?

"The Supreme Court released its decision in the Castillo v PAGS case," Bob says.

"What was the decision?" Adan asks sharply. The case is just as important to him as it is to me. Why does he seem so nervous? There's only one way the court could have decided.

"The court overturned the appeal and sided with PAGS," Bob says.

Adan curses, and I... do nothing. My mind is still. Empty.

I don't understand.

"Are you sure?" I whisper to Bob.

"Sorry, darling," my Totem says.

Gradually it begins to sink in. Rusted hooks sliding down my soul. This means PAGS can't be held liable for injuries, even deaths that occur on its semi-reality shows even if their producers knowingly created or condoned excessively dangerous situations. As long as contestants sign the waivers, PAGS can do anything

And they will.

"There's a lot of analysis about the decision coming out," Bob says. "Want me to start putting a file together?"

"No," I croak. Everything that happened to me and Alby, that endless trek in the desert, the heatstroke, his broken brain, all of it was for nothing. PAGS will get to hurt other children. They'll get to hurt Gold, and Mermaid, and Sequoia.

A sob hiccups out of my chest.

Strong arms wrap around me and I rest my face against Adan's warm skin. The zippers on his shirt dig into my cheek but I don't care. I lean into his warmth, into his solid, reassuring body.

"What does it mean?" I gasp as the first hot tears burn down my cheeks.

Adan is quiet for a moment and then he says. "It means everything just got a lot more dangerous."

CHAPTER 21

*Spirits are high, the stars are gorgeous, and we
dream of Martian dust beneath our boots. ~*
Phoenix Shuttle Commander Thane-Ambrose
Garcia, Live Q&A on NASA Stream

~

I hardly remember rushing through my social
stratification midterm. All the questions and answers
bounce through my brain like errant ping pong balls.
I am gutted. The Castillo v PAGS decision has scooped
out all the dwindling hope I had left in humanity.

The day is gorg as I slowly walk back to Sequoia's
house. The weather Streams predict rain tomorrow
and warn of a dry, dusty summer, but today the sun
shines low on the horizon in a cloudless sky. A few birds
trill in the distance. It's all so jarring, the beauty around
me, the sunlight shining even as darkness gathers in my
heart.

I pass Palinksy's, my old gym. Through the plate-
glass windows, beautiful people pantomime kicks and
punches, each of them no doubt dreaming of lens time,
sponsors, and the fickle love of a faceless crowd. Even
with this Supreme Court decision, they'll still strive.
Hell, they may appreciate a looser leash. For the past
two decades, it was always understood that vils and
capes never tried to actually maim each other. We all

use stun weapons and keep swords blunted. When a sidekick or cape is defeated, they're typically tied up and imprisoned in the villain's lair. Never killed. Even torture usually involves only moderate shocks and body punches.

The only deaths in town are contractual ones. A cape may "die" on screen if their show gets swiped, and there are plenty of sidekick and henchmen "deaths" to keep storylines humming. In those cases, the deceased character usually slinks out of town, ready to try their luck in a new media sector.

Injuries are unavoidable, of course, like when Beacon's boot thrusters malfunctioned and she fell off the roof during her huge tangle with Evil Santa last year, but bumps and bruises can heal. This decision means PAGS can unleash vils and capes to seek blood without the threat of lawsuits or even criminal liability.

And they will. If I've learned anything from my three years in Biggie LC, it's that PAGS will always push a little bit farther, a little bit harder... until someone tumbles off a cliff instead of a roof.

PIC – Pain Is Currency.

Someone is going to get killed for real. It could be me. Or The Professor. Or Sequoia. My heart nearly explodes in fury and horror at the thought of my gentle, loyal friend lying on the pavement in a puddle of blood because some antsy sidekick wanted to bump their ratings.

Suddenly, I hate all those beautiful people in Palinksy's. How many of them would be willing to kill to claim their own show? I don't want to know the answer.

I walk, and walk, and walk until I find myself in Iconic Square. Around me, half-filled tourist trolleys roll down the streets, their conductors gushing about whatever big fight took place on this or that corner. A few tourists take selfie holograms in front of The Hero statue, but the sidewalks are oddly quiet and mostly empty. I only see two gorg townies jogging down the street, probs hoping to get mugged and rescued by a hero.

The town seems half alive, or half dead, depending on how you look at it, and I know the reason why. Shadow. He's scaring away the touries. Even most of the townies don't want to linger outside too long.

Is this the future of Big Little City? Are we destined to become a ghost town, haunted by Shadow or whatever murderous vils follow him?

I make it back to Sequoia's house just as the sun is setting on the horizon. I find my lab coat folded neatly on the couch, my bowtie and goggles placed on top. I pull the coat on over my clothes and add the accessories, even though I don't see any cam drones buzzing about. Technically, I have another hour until my official henchman shift starts, but with everything going on, I'm not sure the old schedule applies.

I don't know what to do with myself. If I were at home, I'd probs collapse in bed and try to shut off my angry brain by watching the progress of the Phoenix settlement ship or maybe a recording of the live Q&As the shuttle commander, Thane-Ambrose Garcia hosts every week. Instead, I send a short, pointless message to Alby—*Hope the sun is shining where you are. Love Twinly Two*—while I wander through the quiet house. The office door is closed. I try the master bedroom.

Inside, the Mayor of Chicago lounges on the bed, listening intently to a meeting on his Band. I notice the seashell in his hand, his thumb absently stroking its ridged edges. His brown eyes flick up to meet mine and he shoos me out of the room.

I consider informing him that *he's* the hostage, but now he's barking at someone about road closures for some upcoming event and I slink out of the room. Maybe I'll just crash on the couch for a while and hope no one notices me.

"Coffee?" a voice asks from the doorway of the kitchen. "You look like you could use it."

Mermaid stands at the counter, a mug in hand. I breathe in the warm, delicious scent of coffee grounds. Coffee is a habit I've never been able to afford, but now I gratefully nod, and she pours another cup from some gizmo on Sequoia's countertop.

Mermaid looks as gorg as ever. Her blonde-and-blue hair is piled on her head in attractive ringlets, and she wears a shiny white sports dress beneath her unbuttoned blue lab coat. Matching white bands encircle her thighs and calves, and a single silver zipper cuts diagonally across her dress.

Mermaid hands me the mug and I wrap my hands around the warm ceramic.

"Where is everyone?" I ask.

"Nitrogen and Kitty went with The Professor to scout a few lairs."

I raise an eyebrow. That's prime lens opportunity. Even if they aren't successful, their search is sure to at least generate a montage in our next ep... assuming we have a producer to put it together. I wonder why Mermaid would pass on such a chance to grab lens time.

"Gold is putting the finishing touches on the hostage vid. Ash and I stuck around to provide input."

Ah, now I understand. No doubt, Gold and Mermaid will both feature heavily in the vid, which will be playing across every news and gossip Stream tonight. I also don't miss the fact that Mermaid called our hostage, *Ash.* Could she be brewing something other than coffee?

I find that I hardly care.

"You look a little gutter," Mermaid says.

I consider offering up some lame-o excuse, but I don't even have the energy for guile. "Midterms were today. I didn't do well," I tell her, and then add, as if it weren't obvious, "I'm trying to get my bachelor's."

Mermaid shrugs. "Schooling doesn't matter." She brings the mug to her lips. "There are no job skills the robos won't eventually learn. The only thing that matters is ability."

I laugh into my mug. The sad thing is that I can't disagree with her. Mermaid has proven her point well enough by dominating all three of The Professor's tryouts and by taking charge of our little henchman group. During the tryouts, there were plenty of rumors that this wasn't her first semi-reality appearance. I even heard that she made it to one of the last rounds in a season of *Z Town.*

Going the distance in *Z Town* requires enduring the most primitive living conditions and dishing out loads of betrayal while also fleeing and fighting a growing horde of robo zombies. Last year, a contestant lasted two months by hiding under a pile of leaves and gobbling frogs that hopped her way.

"You make it seem like life is just a game," I tell

Mermaid.

She gives me a look as if I am an utter lobotomy. "What else could it be?"

The incredulity in her voice sparks something inside of me. Out of the pit of darkness, anger rises to the surface. I lean back against the counter, propping my elbows behind me.

"Gold seems to have fully recovered," I say.

Mermaid takes a casual sip of coffee. "Yes."

"It was shining luck he only got hit by a stun laz," I plod on. "When he went down, I was terrified. I thought for sure he was roasted."

Mermaid carefully sets her mug in the sink. Sequoia's house robo will clean it later. Then she turns to me. I wish I could see her eyes beneath her cloudy blue goggles. "We all knew the risks going in," she says carefully.

"It's a shame you were out of position," I say. "I'm sure you would have been able to stun that security guard before he could tag Gold."

Mermaid doesn't turn away. "It was a chaotic situation. Easy to get turned around. I made a mistake."

We both know that Mermaid doesn't make mistakes.

"What were you doing by the exit?" I ask. Was she trying to make a run for it, leaving the rest of us to take the fall? No, I don't think so. We had the situation in hand. Mermaid wouldn't tail it, at least not empty-handed.

"I keep thinking back," I muse to myself. "It all happened so fast, and there was so much going on, but I could have sworn Ash Anders and his team were heading for that same door."

Mermaid was going for him. I'm sure of it. Did she merely want to take him down to gain the glory for our next ep, or was she planning to nab him for herself? Stealing the Mayor of Chicago right under The Professor's nose may have been enough to spin off into her own villain show. Then there's the possibility she might have meant to warn Ash Anders, maybe even turn coat and fight against us. Such a heroic act could have given her a platform to spin off as a hero.

"I told you, I got confused. I made a mistake." Mermaid's voice is calm.

Whatever she was planning didn't come to fruition. I still remember how she'd stood, frozen and uncertain, staring at Gold's unmoving body on the stage. She'd thought he was dead, too. And in that hesitation, Ash Anders's remaining security guard changed the route and pushed him toward the basement exit where I would stumble upon them mins later.

"Fortunately, it was only a stun laser," Mermaid says, "and we got Ash Anders. As soon as we release the hostage vid, our ratings will gush. We're all in a brills position."

I stare at her and realize I'll never know what her true intentions were that night. With our ratings set to rocket, she's on our side... at least for now.

Mermaid tilts her head just a little, and hint of a smile tugs at her lips. "Alice, I like you," she says. "If you weren't a threat to my popularity on this show, I think maybe we could be friends."

I almost choke on my coffee. "You want to be friends, with me?"

"No. That's the point. I can't have friends. Friends are a liability."

"That's a sad way to live," I tell her.

"It's also a successful way to live. My mother taught me that when we moved to S3."

Media Sector Three. That's in the northwest of the country where PAGS films all of its children-focused programming, including an endless array of child competitions.

"Your mom was a lens pusher?" I ask. She wouldn't be the first parent to drag her kids all the way to S3 to try to gain fame for her progeny.

"She was a realist," Mermaid corrects. "That's how I got *my* education." She takes a step closer to me. She's a head taller, forcing me to look up. "Life is a game whether you accept it or not," she says softly. "The game is played in front of the lens and behind it. If you aren't playing, that just means you're losing."

I stare at her. "Why are you telling me this?"

"Because you've got potential, and I want you to know that there are no hard feelings. What I may have been planning, what I may be planning, and what I may do in the future is just the game. It's not personal."

Her words disgust me, but I also feel resigned. Mermaid is a creature of the lens. At least she's honest about it. I wonder what it must have been like for her as a small child, trying to break through in Media Sector 3. I imagine a life filled with endless practice sessions. Every week a new, nerve-wracking audition, and her mother hissing criticism in her ear after each one.

Mermaid turns and crosses toward the door.

"Do you resent your mom for putting you through all that?" I ask.

Mermaid pauses. "Of course not. My mother made me strong."

"What about the Castillo v PAGS decision today? Aren't you nervous?"

Now she smiles in a soft, sad way. "At least now we all see the playing field clearly."

"DONE!" Gold roars. A door down the hallway bursts open, and he saunters out, his golden lips peeled back in a proud smile. "DONE, DONE, DONE!" He shakes his hips and does a sleek little dance in the doorway of the kitchen. "I have created a hostage vid so brills the sun is gonna need shades."

He grins at us and then seems to finally take in the scene in front of him. "Whoa, were you doing girl talk? Hold on, hold on, let me get a cam in here. Iron, wipe that scowl then go back to what you were doing. Repeat the whole convo. Any claws come out? Because I was thinking we need some tension in the group. Maybe a henchmen feud. You two would be perfect. The cunning beauty versus the..." he looks at me, clearly digging for a descriptor.

"Wait, which one is the cunning beauty?" I ask sarcastically.

Gold ignores my question. "Let's brainstorm this. We'll need something to start the conflict."

"Nitrogen," Mermaid says. "I'll seduce him and Iron gets jealous."

Gold frowns. "I see what you're saying, but it seems, I don't know, not exactly believable. I mean, you hearting Nitrogen?"

Mermaid shrugs. "He could be handsome if he tried, and he's a strong fighter. We could make a good match."

Gold's big, easy smile is nowhere to be seen. In fact, his shoulders seem suddenly tense. "It's just that..." he begins, but Mermaid cuts him off.

"We don't tell Nitrogen a thing. He'll be confused, flustered by my attention. Viewers will love that."

I stare between the two of them as they toss around Sequoia's heart like it was a toy. "You're both awful!" I cry and push past Gold to leave the kitchen.

"It's just the game, Wholesome," he calls after me.

"That's what I was trying to tell her," Mermaid says.

I have nowhere to go inside the house, so I stumble outside, letting the cooling evening air soothe the flames in my mind. Everything Mermaid said echoes in my head, and I think I'm starting to believe her.

Life *is* a game. Mermaid is playing it. So is Gold and even The Professor. Adan is def playing the game, and he's holding Leo in the balance.

Leo.

We've got to save him and not only to rescue our next ep. I hate to admit it, but I want Leo back on our team. I want to see his calm face, hear his smooth voice spiced with hints of amusement. I want to see his eyes and try to guess at all the hard memories hidden behind them.

A realization crashes into my mind. If I want to save Leo, I've got to step onto the board and start playing the Fame Game. I exhale a long, long breath as a new molten certainty settles across me. It's time I stop reacting to what everyone else is scheming and start making my own moves.

***

An hour later, we gather in Sequoia's living room. The Professor grins with unsuppressed glee. Gold paces, chewing the golden lipstick off his lips. Ash Anders lounges on the couch next to Kitty, scrolling through messages on his Band.

"It should be any..." Gold begins and then my Band vibrates.

"Here it comes," Sequoia says.

A holo-screen projects from my Band, splashing up my forearm. Sequoia's Pod throws a much larger holo-screen on the wall. All the screens begin playing the same vid. The Professor peers from the screen, looking grimly satisfied. We henchmen stand behind him in our colorful lab coats guarding a nobly unbowed Ash Anders.

"You dismissed my ideas. You denied my grant applications. You laughed behind my back," The Professor begins. As he continues the spiel we recorded this morning, the cam flicks from The Professor to a close-up of Gold's face, then Mermaid's, and then lingers on Ash Anders. It pans back, to take in the whole room.

I stare at my own hard expression and clenched fists. In some strange way, I feel like I'm watching a different person, someone cold and cruel. A henchman. We are all silent as the short vid plays out, ending with The Professor's demand for President Sage Anders to deliver $10 billion in unmarked bills in order to reacquire her son.

Overall, I have to admit Gold did a decent job with the hostage vid. He relied too heavily on startling close-up shots, and the background music was overly aggressive, but I appreciate the slight echo he added to The Professor's voice and the filter he used that leeched most of the color out of the scene. No surprise that Gold and Mermaid were heavily featured in the vid, including several close-ups of their faces looking sufficiently menacing.

Leo would have been more artful about it, I think. Gold's hostage vid was bold but predictable. Still, not bad.

The Professor is obvi happy with it. "Excellent! Excellent!" he crows. "That will certainly give the world something to think about! No one shall discount The Professor anymore."

"You shouldn't have brought up my mother," Ash Anders says. He came off well in the vid, looking defiant and courageous. "Now, let's discuss my brilliant escape."

The Professor frowns.

"Mr. Mayor, the cams are rolling," Gold tells him beseechingly and points to the two cam drones floating above us, capturing our reaction to our own hostage video. "We don't want the fans to know you aren't really a hostage, so I'll have to edit out that last part. How about you look nervous and angry? Maybe say something like, 'You'll never get away with this, Professor!'"

Ash Anders gives Gold a look of distaste. "I'll look suitably angry *after* we discuss my escape."

"I do have some thoughts on that," The Professor says, "but I'd rather discuss them with you privately. So, if you'd please, Mr. Anders, I would like to continue with a short bit of gloating for the ep. I expect we shall receive an official response soon enough."

Ash Anders crosses his arms over his chest. "Fine. Finish your scene. Then we talk."

He smirks at The Professor. "Nice little vid, Professor, but you won't be getting your $10 billion anytime soon. Seeing as I am not a lobbyist with pockets full of Loons, my mother will hardly care I'm in your custody."

Ouch! Leave it to Ash Anders to take a political dig at Momsey during his captivity.

The Professor laughs in delight. "You talk a big game for a prisoner."

"Well, I hear you don't currently have such a great track record of hanging onto your prisoners," Ash Anders shoots back, a little grin on his face. He still wears the green suit. His jacket is rumpled, and his jaw sports dark scruff that gives him a handsome, unvarnished look.

The Professor frowns dramatically and points his cane at Anders. "It just so happens that my last *guest* was going to help me test out a very special and experimental machine I'm building. Since he so rudely escaped, I'm on the lookout for another test subject."

I glance up at the two cam drones hovering at opposite ends of the room. I need to time my words just right. "Professor, what an excellent hostage vid," I pipe up. "The world will tremble at your name, but we have another problem."

I haven't told anyone about Adan's ultimatum or about the big bold plan I've crafted over the last hour while walking circles in Sequoia's backyard. I want their reactions to be authentic. All eyes in the room turn to me. I open my mouth to deliver my hook when my Band buzzes.

Again.

I glance down as the holo-screen washes up my arm, then I look to Sequoia's Pod, which has also automatically activated. Another town-wide message? That would make three in a single day. It's unheard of, but, then again, these are highly unusual times.

We all look to the holo-screen on the wall. It flickers white for another moment and then resolves into a face that launches sparks up dread up my spine. Beacon stares back at me from beneath her iconic golden helmet. Her loose blonde hair tumbles around her shoulders. I can see the upper part of her costume, all twisting shades of red and gold with the glowing lighthouse emblem stamped in white on her chest. Behind her, I see the pale purple walls of her study. She must be at her headquarters.

"Professor, your depravity knows no end," she says, her husky voice so familiar and damning. Her violet eyes seem to stare right at me. I want to gape—Beacon is talking to us!—but the cams are rolling, so I force myself to seem calm.

"This time you've gone too far," Beacon continues. Despite her position of disfavor with the City Council, she must still have some allies tucked away at PAGS. She knew The Professor's vid was coming. There's no other way she could have gotten on the air so soon afterward.

"I admit that it was never my intention for you to tumble into that solar furnace all those years ago," Beacon is saying now, "but, Buddha help me, I wish you'd stayed there."

Now she looks angry, her lips pressed tightly together. "And yet, here we are. Professor, I have a new deal for you. I can't get you the $10 billion you asked for, but I can give you something else you want." She pauses and lifts her chin just a millimeter. She looks so proud, so beautiful as she speaks.

"I can give you me."

"What?" The Professor cries, ever the performer,

leaning heavily on his cane.

Beacon looks steadily into the cam. "I'll trade myself for Ash Anders." Beacon swallows. A look of regret wash over her face, which is impressive considering her face is mostly covered by a mask.

"Meet me in Iconic Square tomorrow at noon to make the exchange." She gives the cam one more fierce look, and then the vid feed cuts out and the holo-screen disappears.

We all stare in silence at the now-empty wall. My heart beats wildly in my chest. A prisoner exchange with Beacon!

"It's obvi a trap." Mermaid is the first to speak.

"Of course it's a trap," The Professor says and raises his index finger as if to bestow upon us an important lesson, "but it is also an opportunity. No doubt Beacon has some sort of plan, but she must also be present at the exchange. That gives us a chance."

"What about my escape?" Ash Anders explodes. Gold grimaces. He'll need to do a lot of editing on these scenes.

"Perhaps we can arrange that as part of tomorrow's exchange," The Professor tells him and then looks pained. "It would be helpful to have our erstwhile producer back with us to record such a momentous occasion."

Beacon's appearance has thrown my thoughts asunder, but even I can recognize a good lens opportunity when it rolls out the red carpet for me.

"I think I can help with that," I pipe up. I step closer to The Professor and slap an amused little smile on my face. My boss gives an assessing look. He knows I'm preening for the lens. Will he let me continue or slap me down?

"Yes, my little element?" The Professor asks.

I let my gaze sweep the room. In this moment the lens is all mine. "I've made contact with Shine," I tell the room. Beacon's vid changes things, but I think my plan can still work. *Adapt, adapt, adapt,* Tickles preaches.

"Shine wants to make a deal," I say and give the quiet laugh I've been practicing before bed each night. "But I have a better idea. I say we give him a little surprise that will make him regret ever leaving his cell."

CHAPTER 22

Injury and death are always a possibility, but the greater risk is doing nothing. ~ Beacon, S12, E3

~

I wake up to the gentle buzz of my Band and the heavy aroma of coffee. Sunlight streams from the front windows of Sequoia's living room, and I wince at the brightness. My brain is groggy, wallowing in wispy dreams. Then, in a moment, reality strikes, blowing away the remnants of those dreams.

Castillo v PAGS.

Beacon.

Leo.

Flashes of memory hit me. We'd stayed up nearly all night, the others planning the big prisoner exchange in Iconic Square this afternoon while Sequoia and I cemented our mini side adventure. Even Ash Anders had gotten into the swing of things, tossing out bold suggestions for his big escape. I remember The Professor stepping into the hallway to begin making calls.

Now my stomach tightens as I realize what I have to do today. It's not just that my plan is risky, it's also a little... evil. Will I be able to cross those lines? Should I?

Adan's the one who nabbed Leo, I remind myself. *And Lysee went behind my back. They're both playing the game.* These thoughts are true, but they're hardly comforting. Instead, they make my stomach twist more. *We need Leo back.* This thought, at least, doesn't feel slimy. Leo is the only one who can unlock the footage of the Chicago heist. We also need him to capture our dramatic hostage swap with Beacon this afternoon.

I sit up on the couch and notice a thin figure standing in front of the windows, gazing out into the world. The Professor is in full costume. Did he ever go to bed last night? In the kitchen, I hear Sequoia humming softly to himself. A glance at my Band tells me that I have only about half an hour before the two of us need to set off on our quest. I push myself off the couch, sway a little, then find my feet. Before I head to the bathroom, I step up beside The Professor. He clutches his hands behind his back. The sunlight turns his steely gray hair almost white, like a halo around his head.

"Today I meet Beacon once again," he says, his eyes still riveted outside. "I have my plan and she has hers." I notice his bowtie no longer shifts colors. Its charge must be dead.

I look over my shoulder. No cam drones hover in the air.

The Professor shakes his head sorrowfully. "Back in the day, we'd plan a battle like this for months. My producer would have lunch with Beacon's producer. They'd catch up and then plot out our eps together. There was still room for improvisation, mind you," The Professor says as if this is important, "but the outcome was already planned. No one got hurt that way."

Outside, a rental scooter zips by carrying a teenage girl, her skirt pleated with zippers and her scarlet hair streaming behind her.

"But the crush of ratings got heavier and heavier,"

The Professor speaks. "Heroes and villains began to quarrel about who got the best storylines. Some of the personalities didn't follow their cues. The sidekicks and the henchmen started to steal lens time. Then Bright spun off. That was the first major defection." The Professor's voice is deep and smooth. "These days, we linger in our lonesome camps, everyone trying to outwit the other," he continues. "Only the City Council knows all the threads. They watch the cams, they maneuver the producers. We play their game now."

The Professor looks tired, but there's also something else in his expression.

"You love it anyway, don't you?" I ask.

He turns to me, his eyes almost colorless in the pale sunlight. "I think perhaps I am getting too old for this game, that retirement was the wiser option." Now a wry smile pulls at his thin lips. "But it is exciting, is it not, Iron?"

His plan for today is bold. And very dangerous. Especially now, in the post-Castillo v PAGS world. Yet, I can't help nodding.

"Yes, it is exciting," I admit. No matter what happens, viewers will remember this day.

"Coffee," Sequoia says behind us.

"Excellent!" The Professor nods. "I do hope you used adequate heat to extract as much volatile flavor compounds from the coffee beans as possible."

"Oh yes, it's plenty hot." Sequoia grins and holds out a steaming mug in each hand.

"Actually, I need to get ready," I tell him, suddenly aware of my mussed hair, sticky eyes, and serious morning breath. "We've got to go soon."

The Professor takes his mug and turns again to the

window. "Go on, then," he says warmly to me. "I would very much appreciate the presence of our fearless producer at this afternoon's festivities."

I tidy myself up in the bathroom as quickly as possible. As my hands quickly weave my dark hair into a braid, I stare at my face in the mirror. I see the same brown eyes and blunt nose, but inside I feel different. I'm not just Alice Hannover anymore. Iron lives inside me, too, and I'm going to need her strength and cunning today if I'm going to beat Shine and get Leo back.

But why do I feel so weak, so uncertain? Why does every move I make in this dark game feel like I'm losing myself a little more? I tie the white bow to the bottom of my braid and turn away from the mirror.

In the office, I find Gold asleep at the desk, head cradled in his arms and goggles tossed to the floor. We've all been letting our guard down about protecting our identities, all of us except Mermaid. She still slips away each night to her own place and has never removed her goggles.

"How long was he up?" I ask Kitty who stands guard next to him.

"He fell asleep three two hours and twenty-six minutes ago after stitching together a stupidly aweso scene of our plan to defeat Beacon," Kitty answers with a big smile.

"Just make sure he doesn't oversleep," I tell her. "The Professor will need all the help he can get." *Especially if Sequoia and I can't make it to the Square in time,* I think to myself.

"Oh yes," Kitty says. Her pointed ears swivel on her head. "I have strict orders to wake him up at 9 AM or if he starts having nightmares."

Nightmares? I glance down at Gold again. In sleep, his face is soft and young, his lips their natural color. No golden lipstick yet. He almost looks innocent. I don't know much about his past, only that his parents abandoned him in one of those kid drop-off depots. I'd probs have nightmares about them too if I'd grown up there. Then again, I have nightmares of my own.

Gently, I reach over Gold and tug Sequoia's Goggs from his hand. Gold frowns, and his eyes flick open. I can practically see the dreams still dancing in front of him.

"Go back to sleep," I tell him.

I'm not sure that he hears me, but his eyes sink closed and he sighs softly into his arms. My heart trembles. Will he get hurt again today? What if it isn't a stun laz this time? What if it's a full laz shot that roasts him from the inside out?

I realize that I care about Gold, despite his scheming and his antics. Mermaid, too, though I know she'll betray us again if the opportunity is good enough. Over the past few weeks, it feels as if my old life has faded into the background and this new henchman life has come to the forefront.

"Watch over him today," I tell Kitty.

"Of course. I will watch over you all," she says, smiling again. Her whiskers glow in the sunlight from the window.

Clutching the Goggs, I leave the office with my thoughts whirling. What's happening to me? Why do I feel like Mermaid, Gold, and even Kitty are becoming almost like a family to me? This is all fake, all just a drooling show, right?

I pass the open doorway to the master bedroom.

Inside, Ash Anders sits on the floor, back straight, eyes closed, hands resting lightly on each knee. His coat hangs on the bedpost and the dress shirt he wears is rumpled and stained in the armpits. Sequoia offered to print him a new shirt, even a new suit, but Anders refused.

"That's canny," I say softly as I step in the room. "Wearing the same clothes. It makes you look weathered."

Ash Anders doesn't open his eyes. I notice that he holds the pale pink seashell in his left hand. "People would notice if I were wearing a different outfit when I escape," he says. "They would say my captivity must have been comfortable."

"We can't have that."

"Are you leaving to grandly rescue your producer?" he asks.

"Yes. Right now." I wonder if I should say goodbye or wish him luck on his impending escape from our clutches. It's been strange getting to know him over the past day. Despite the fact that he's spent most of his waking hours testily lecturing to someone on his Band, it almost seems as if he really cares about his city and its inhabitants.

"You're not very cam savvy, you know," he says.

I lean against the doorway. "I'm getting better."

He opens his eyes and appraises me with a penetrating stare. "You have good ideas. Good instinct for plot, but you never seem to have that spark on cam. You don't like being in front of the lens."

"If that were true, I wouldn't be a very good henchman, would I?" I say the words sarcastically, but I feel like his eyes can see right through my pretense.

275

J Bennett

"I've been wondering about you," he says. "The others I understand. Arsenic wants power and control. Gold wants love and adoration." Ash's voice is soft but weighted with surety. "Nitrogen wants a family."

"And what about me?" I ask. "What do I want?"

Ash Anders smiles. "You're a paradox."

"A paradox?" I have to leave, but my feet stay planted in the doorway of the bedroom.

"I think you want to change the world," Ash Anders says. "Like me."

I cross my arms over my chest and force out what I hope is a casual laugh "Why would you say that?"

"The classes you're taking at the university. The things you've posted on your personal Stream."

I frown. "You've been spying on me."

"I like to know who I'm working with," Anders replies casually. "My new security firm has performed thorough evaluations of all of you."

"And yet I'm a paradox."

"I can't quite figure out how this henchman thing fits into your plans," he admits.

I don't owe Ash Anders an explanation, especially since he's paid people to dig around into my past. And yet he seems genuinely curious.

"The money," I say roughly.

Anders shakes his head. "That's not it. Your Universal Basic Income could cover a room in a smaller town. If you shared the room, you could even afford gov nutra-packs with a little left over for a pair of Goggs."

"That's not a life," I hiss.

"It is a life for roughly 19.4% of the population. But you..." he wags a finger at me. "You're fighting for something." He smiles at me. "A hidden mission?"

I don't like this inquisition.

"It's about Alby, isn't it? About what happened during *The Ends of the Earth*."

I grab the doorframe to hold myself up. It feels like he reached inside and pulled the secret right out of my living, beating heart.

I should have been prepared. After all, the semi-reality show credit is permanently attached to my Stream, though I deleted all my own personal mentions of the show and those foolishly optimistic vids I posted during our training.

I imagine some bored, low-ranking security intern digging up season six of *Ends of the Earth* from Media Sector 3. That person would have no idea that I begged and begged Alby to try out with me; that I promised him we would win and use the prize money to move out of our cramped cargo container and into a beautiful house with a yard and separate bedrooms. Then our mother would smile.

Instead, that intern would have seen a young, brother-and-sister team, fraternal twins, trekking throughout parched California, searching for clues and resources on a carefully designated course. They would have heard the show's host sneakily admit that the big twist this season was that our maps were incomplete. One by one, the teams got lost, wandering off course, far from the caches of supplies they needed, those precious bottles of water.

I can almost feel the heat beating down on me during the day and the cold leeching into my bones as soon as the sun sunk beneath the horizon. On that final day, the unrepentant sun practically burned through my eyelids as Alby and I slogged through the endless, cracked land of Death Valley. I wonder what the intern thought when I finally fell despite Alby's determination. Did the intern feel anything when Alby picked me up and kept walking and walking until he collapsed into seizures? Our last scene shows the producers finally sending an ambulance chopper to cart us to a medical facility. They never follow up, never tell viewers that Alby was in the hospital for two months, that his organs nearly failed and he suffered brain damage that couldn't be fixed.

That is the price of semi-reality. PIC – Pain Is Currency, and we paid so much to the cams. More than we had to give.

I force myself to meet Ash Anders's eyes and I see pity. I look away.

"I've got to go," I say roughly.

"Wait." Ash Anders unfolds his legs and stands. Even in his rumpled outfit, he looks strong and in command. *Like a president,* I think.

"I'm sorry for what happened to you," he says.

I grimace.

"You want to change the system. That's why you're here. I don't know how this show fits into your plan but it does." Anders takes a step toward me. "Ironically, we're on the same side."

I snort a laugh. "You want to go up against PAGS?"

"That's a dangerous thing to say." He picks his coat up from the bedpost and tosses his arm through the first sleeve. "I wanted to let you know that I have magnanimously decided not to criminally prosecute you and your associates as soon as I complete my daring escape to great fanfare."

I shake a finger at him. "A vil is never supposed to reveal their true plan to their enemies."

"Despite what you think, Alice," he says, pointedly using my real name, "I am not a villain, and we are not enemies."

I don't know what to say to that or to anything Ash Anders has revealed. Can it really be true? Is he against PAGS? The conglomerate practically bought the Oval Office for his mother.

Anders slips his other arm through the jacket, and I watch him drop the seashell into the left pocket of his pants.

"It was a gift," he says.

"What?"

"The shell. It was a gift from Val."

Valerie-Rhyn. I know that name from the research I performed on Anders before our kidnapping. Val was his college girlfriend. She and Ash overdosed together on some rocky beach in Washington. Ash survived. Valerie-Rhyn did not. That was when he finally got clean.

"We all have our own reasons to fight for a better world," Ash Anders says.

My chest is tight. I nod like we're agreeing to something. A secret pact of some sort, but I don't know what it is. Only that it feels big, more important than all the chaos swirling around us. And then I push those feelings away. I need to concentrate on the here and now, on surviving the next few hours.

"I've got to go," I say in a tight voice.

Ash Anders gives me a killer smile, the same one I've seen a thousand times on top gossip Stream stories when I was researching him.

"Shining luck, Wholesome," he says softly.

Sequoia is fretting in the living room. His green

lab coat stretches over his big chest, and the torn sleeves make his shoulders look huge. He would look menacing, big hands and rocky muscles, if he didn't give me a relieved smile when I entered the room.

"The rental car is here," he says.

"Had to get the Goggs," I tell him, holding them up. I don't have the processing space for my convo with Ash Anders right now and all the painful memories stirred up in my mind. We've got a mission to complete and a savvy cape to outwit.

"Let's go," I say to Sequoia. I turn on the Goggs and hear the soft buzz of the cam drones in the office coming online.

The Professor still stands next to the window. A wisp of steam rises from the pale yellow coffee mug in his hand. As we head to the door, he turns to us. "Please do bring back our producer," he says, "but don't be late to the Square. Infamy awaits us today!"

***

Our rental car takes us to the middle of Iconic Square. Yesterday, the Square was half dead, but things change quickly here in Biggie LC. Even this early in the morning, townies and tourists mill around the sidewalks in droves. Some line up to take selfies in front of The Hero statue. Today, she looks even more like Beacon than usual, with her flowing locks and proud stance. Though her arm drapes around the shoulders of a small child, the statue seems fierce, even menacing. Then again, it's probably just my imagination. I try not to remember how Shine described the pain of Beacon's Aura Arcs.

As we pull off the road, a tourist trolley rumbles by, filled to capacity. This is a vil trolley, decorated with the faces of Evil Santa, Cleopatra, and members of the Dark League. Will The Professor's face be plastered on the side of those trolleys someday soon?

"It's busy," Sequoia observes, glancing out the window. He's been fidgeting next to me the whole ride over. I think even his freckles are shivering.

"They're here for the showdown between Beacon and The Professor," I say.

"Really? Don't they know it's going to be dangerous?"

I glance at Sequoia and remind myself that despite all his recent progress he's still city soft.

"That's the point. Some will try to steal lens time. Others just want to be part of something, anything." I look across the square. On the opposite side of the street, half a block down, one building slumps at an odd angle. Its windows have been boarded up, the glass shards swept away, but the pitted, broken sign still tilts drunkenly over the entrance.

The Redemption Café.

Sequoia follows my gaze. "What happened there?"

"Shadow blew it up," I whisper as I watch several touries pose in front of the building while their personal cam drones take pics and vids. One woman pretends she's fleeing in fear. Maybe they wonder what it was like to be there the night Shadow slipped into the building and terrorized the diners with a holo-clock that slowly counted down from ten minutes.

I could tell them. The memory of Shadow's grease-covered face flashes through my mind. His eyes, tinted unnaturally red, seemed to cut right through me. I remember the rotten yellow ribcage tattooed over his skinny chest and the mutilated face that sat in place of his heart.

Looking into his eyes, I saw only darkness and depravity. It's been nearly three weeks since he attacked a tourist trolley, murdering five touries and two police officers. Police Chief Memphis McDonald is still in serious condition in the hospital, but it looks like he'll live. The authorities still haven't found Shadow. I swallow. It's only a matter of time before he strikes again, and now with the Castillo vs. PAGS case decided, the last vestiges of restraint are gone.

How far will he go next time? How many more people will die?

"We should probably do the stickup," Sequoia says, shaking me from my icy memories.

He's right. I force myself to focus on the task at hand. This job should be simple, but I can't let myself get too cocky. *A confident henchman is a defeated henchman,* Tickles wrote on his blog yesterday.

I turn to Sequoia. "This'll be good for you," I tell him. "Just remember, be aggressive. Be mean."

"Mean, aggressive," he whispers. I glance out the windshield. We'll need to move fast to escape the notice of all the people milling about. Fortunately, most of them are either staring at their Bands or grinning for selfies. I put my hand on Sequoia's arm and wait. A minute later, the coast is mostly clear.

"Now!" I hiss.

Sequoia goes first, flinging open the door of the car and walking purposefully into the shop just in front of us. I slip Sequoia's Goggs over my eyes and quickly follow, cradling the small cam drone in my arms.

"Welcome to the... oh," says the proprietor of the shop. I glance around the small space. No other customers in the shop. I let out a small, relieved breath.

Colorful bottles line the shelves. My Goggs helpfully magnify their labels as my eyes focus on them. I see arthritis medication, generic carcinoma blockers, sexual enhancers.

"Don't move!" Sequoia barks and flourishes his stun laz as I manually lock the front door.

"We are being robbed," says the person behind the counter.

"Yeah, you are," Sequoia says. "So don't do anything dim."

"I understand," the proprietor says. "I have significant experience with burglaries. In fact, this pharmacy has been robbed exactly 26 times in the history of our business, though I have only been present for eight of those robberies. I was not allowed to work here until four years ago."

The person behind the counter is Ollie, of course. This is why I make a point of standing behind Sequoia, my face turned away. With the Goggs over my eyes, I can't wear my tinted goggles to help protect my identity.

Without prompting, Ollie unlatches his Band, lays it on the counter, screen down, and gives it a small push so that it slides out of his reach. Hunched behind Sequoia's back, I subvocalize a command. *Rise.* The cam drone in my arms hums to life, its blades spinning on both wings. As it lifts up slowly into the air the video feed washes across my Goggs.

Quarter window, I command and the video feed shrinks into a box that slides to the right side of the frame.

"You are Nitrogen," Ollie says, "a henchman for The

Professor. And behind you is Iron, also a henchman for The Professor."

"Uh," Sequoia stutters.

"I was most impressed with your recent kidnapping of Ash Anders," Ollie says. He keeps his hands raised in the air. "Your hostage video was interesting. Very reliant on close-ups. I assume this is due to the fact that your producer is currently the prisoner of Shine."

"Uh," Sequoia says.

The drone hits the ceiling and flutters to the ground. On my Goggs, the video whirls and shakes.

"Blight," I hiss.

"Operating drones requires practice," Ollie informs me.

"What's going on?" a voice calls from a door behind the counter.

"We are being robbed by Nitrogen and Iron, two of the The Professor's henchmen," Ollie explains to the voice. "I am handling it quite well."

There's a pause and the door behind the counter swings open. Sequoia crouches and points his laz pistol at the tall, thin man who emerges. I crouch with him, and the drone wobbles as it lifts back off the ground.

"Hello, hello," the man says, "or ta, as the kids say." Like his son, the pharmacist unlatches his expensive Band, slides it down the counter, and then raises his hands. "No need for violence, I assure you. We are happy to assist with whatever pharmaceuticals you need."

"I am not happy to assist," Ollie corrects his father. "I do not believe we should support villainous activity. I was just now attempting to stall them."

His father chuckles easily, as if he has a lot of practice ignoring his son's oddness. I zoom in the cam and see that telltale glaze in the older man's eyes. Just like the last time I visited, he's clearly popped or vaped a few Mellows.

"Fortunately, I'm in charge," he says to Sequoia. "We actually have quite a bit of experience working with the more villainous element of the city."

"We have been robbed 26 times," Ollie says. "I already told them that, though this would make 27."

I elbow Sequoia.

"Uh, no funny business," he stammers.

"Of course not," Ollie's dad says. He possesses his son's pale blue eyes, blond hair, and beaky nose. "I am happy to assist you with your needs. After all, injuries don't pick sides." He laughs at his little joke. "Last month, the Vengeful Knight broke in here demanding several medications for zir sister, Scarlet Paladin, who I believe was injured in a fight with Lobo. I was able to provide some excellent blood clotters and generic stem cell injects, though of course genomically personalized stem cells are always recommended."

I elbow Sequoia again.

"Uh, clap it," Sequoia says and then barks out our drug request.

"Patch form," I cough out.

"Yes, as a patch," Sequoia says. "Please."

"Oh, excellent choice," Ollie's father says. "Yes, those are quite a popular robbery target. Might I make a professional recommendation?"

"What?" Sequoia asks.

"Go with two patches," the pharmacist suggests. "Application can be a bit tricky if you haven't done it before."

"Sure, sure." Sequoia wipes his forehead with his

other hand.

The pharmacist's voice is calm and soothing as ever. "I just need to turn around here and pull them off the shelf." He moves slowly, keeping his hands in full view. I suppose 26 robberies will teach you not to get twitchy.

"I will box them up," Ollie says and ducks behind the counter.

"What's he doing?" Sequoia asks, stepping toward the counter.

"As I explained, I am procuring a box," Ollie's voice replies, slightly muffled. "Here is the box." He pops back up holding a small paper carton.

The pharmacist, meanwhile, carefully unlocks a cabinet and rifles through a bin. All the psychoactives are behind the counter. It would be easy enough to build a protective window in front of the counter that could resist laz shots and blunt force, but the City Council would never approve that remodel request. Capes are supposed to foil robberies, not commonsense security precautions.

"Ah, here we go," the pharmacist says. "I am reaching into my supply bin and lifting out two patches," he says. It seems that Ollie's father has developed his own defenses made of smiles, soft words, and slow movements he clearly narrates.

As his father fulfills our prescription order, Ollie leans over the counter. Polka dots cluster his shirt. According to Lysee, the polka dot trend has been dead as steering wheels for weeks.

"Is this part of your plan to defeat Beacon this afternoon?" he asks.

Sequoia swallows. "I can't tell you that."

"Your martial arts skills were highly impressive

during The Professor's tryouts. I believe you must be at least a black belt in judo. Is that accurate?"

"Actually, second level black belt," Sequoia clarifies. "I've also trained in muay tai for several years."

Ollie nods. "That is exactly as I thought. Several others in my fellowship suggested your background might include aikido"

Sequoia is already shaking his head. "A lot of people get judo and aikido confused. They're both based in grappling, but…"

I clear my throat loudly.

"I mean, that's hardly relevant right now," Sequoia manages. He shifts his weight. I can see sweat prickling on the back of his neck. "What do you mean 'fellowship'?"

Ollie taps his fingers on the counter. "I am part of a fellowship of observers who manage and continually update a wiki of all hero and villain activity in Big Little City."

"Yes, Ollie is fascinated with our town's Personas," his father says, turning back around to the counter and placing our order in the box. "It gives him something to do, and I suppose it's social interaction of a kind."

"It is social interaction," Ollie confirms. "I have many discussions with the fellowship. For example, we are currently debating whether or not Lobo has a new sidekick. A little-known criminal stickup man has recently been seen assisting him on missions, but it seems that Lobo does not appreciate his presence."

I wonder if the stickup man in question happens to have a glowing star on his t-shirt. Three weeks ago I ran into my old coworker, DeAngelo. Well, technically, he tried to rob me, but once I got that all sorted out with a sharp throat punch, he explained his grand scheme to turn his little stickup gig into a sidekick position with Lobo. Maybe he's managed to pull off his drooling plan for fame after all.

Abruptly someone pounds on the door behind us. Sequoia flinches. Thankfully he still has the safety clicked on his pistol, or I'm pretty sure he would have dropped the pharmacist like a ton of bricks.

"Godwin," a plaintive female voice calls through the door. "My Throttle is out."

"Why hello, Ms. Banner, or ta as the kids say," Ollie's dad calls loudly. "We have some unexpected visitors at the moment. If you don't mind waiting outside for a bit, I promise I'll be with you soon."

Silence on the other side of the door.

Is it a trap? Did Ollie's dad somehow manage to tip off the authorities before he came out from the back room, or did Ollie hit a panic switch under the counter?

"Alright but tell them to hurry up!" the voice outside squawks.

"Will do!" Ollie's dad says. He looks at us apologetically. "Ms. Banner really shouldn't be taking so much Throttle, not with her blood pressure, but the poor dear can't get enough of it. Who am I to judge?"

Though Throttle isn't usually his crutch of choice, Matthew assures me that it offers a reliable buzz that keeps your energy up all day if you don't mind your heart pounding in your ears or seeing weird sparkles in certain surfaces. Course, if you take too much, you end up running half-naked down the street convinced your shadow has come alive and is trying to eat you. A vil named Wizard Blue got heavy into Throttle a few years back. It made him an interesting Persona to follow for a while until he started inexplicably smashing robo pets with his Celtic staff. His show got swiped after he took a swing at a real cat that belonged to a City Council member.

"Hurry up," I bark, keeping my voice low. "This is a robbery, not a tea party."

"Yes, yes, I understand your impatience," Ollie's dad says. He closes the lid of the unmarked box and pushes it across the counter. I try to bring the cam drone close to get a view of the box, but it hits the edge of the counter and spirals to the ground.

"Oh my," says Ollie's father.

"Their producer was recently kidnapped by Shine," Ollie says.

"Yes, I see. What a shame," the pharmacist murmurs. As the cam drone wobbles back up, the pharmacist explains how to use our new medication.

"Normally, I would request a prescription for a dosage this high," he continues, "but I have decided to waive that requirement in this situation." He gives us both a pleased smile.

"Fine," Sequoia says. I dart from behind him and snatch the box, keeping my face turned away from Ollie.

Ollie's dad continues. "As a pharmacist, I must say that it is against the law to administer any psychotropic drugs to another individual without their permission. The subject will start to feel the effects within one to five minutes, depending on their size, metabolic rate, and application site. Its effects are quite strong and will last for up to six hours."

"Thanks for your help," Sequoia says politely. I hide my groan. Henchmen are most certainly not supposed to thank their robbery victims.

Sequoia must realize his slip-up, because he barks out, "If this turns out to be some sort of trick..."

"Oh no. Tricking villains is not a good long-term business strategy," the pharmacist says. "Shining luck with your mission."

"I shall not wish you shining luck," Ollie says. "In fact, I hope you fail and that justice will prevail."

"Well, that's uh, that's your right, I guess," Sequoia says.

I unlock the door and it swishes open.

"It's about time!" an older woman squawks. Her hair shines metallic green and she holds a small creature in her arms. Luminescent eyes stare out from a mass of poofy pink fur. It must be one of those make-your-own robo pets. At least I hope so. Some of the genetically spliced animals they're making these days are majorly creepy.

"Which one are you?" she asks me.

"Outta the way," I snap tucking my face into my arm. I shove her aside with my elbow.

Sequoia is behind me now and we quickly throw ourselves into our rental car. I bark the GPS coordinates. The car hums to life and starts moving away from Iconic Square while seatbelts slide across our bodies and click into place. I lean back against the seat and sigh.

"What an interesting experience," Sequoia muses beside me. "Not at all the way I imagined robbing a store would be, but it went well, wouldn't you say?"

I decide to be kind and not inform him that he is probs the least intimidating henchman on the planet. I don't think he could scare a baby rabbit.

"We got what we came for," I say instead, holding the box in my lap. That's all that really matters. I smile wryly to myself. "Time to head home."

CHAPTER 23

Plan for everything, including betrayal. Especially betrayal.
~ Tickles the Elf, The Henchman's Survival Guide

~

The car drops us off a kilometer from The Professor's mansion. After I contacted Adan through his personal Stream last night, I thought it odd that he chose the site of his captivity for our prisoner exchange. But, after pondering a bit, I realize the cleverness of it.

If all goes according to *his* plan, he'll walk out of The Professor's lair with Ash Anders in tow. It'll be an epic ego smack for The Professor and a delight to Shine's viewers. Course, no matter what happens today, Shine won't be strutting away with Ash Anders.

As Sequoia and I walk to the mansion, the sun beats down on us. The air is warming fast. It's one of those freak spring days that feels like summer. I glance at my Band. The drug store robbery took longer than anticipated, but we've still got two hours until the scheduled prisoner swap and three hours until Beacon will give herself up in Iconic Square.

Sequoia and I move into the woods surrounding The Professor's mansion. He wears the Goggs now, and the cam drone flies beside us, moving more or less in a straight line as it records our trek. I touch my tinted goggles and set my face into a grim look of determination.

From here on out, I play a battle of wits against Adan.

What will he do? I ask myself for the millionth time. Will he actually believe I somehow managed to sneak Ash Anders away from the rest of my team as I told him in my message? That I truly intend to make the trade for Leo as promised?

No, he's too canny for that.

Adan may look like just another glam, empty-headed striver, but he hasn't survived for over three years as Shine by being a drooling lobotomy. When he was named at Beacon's latest sidekick it was big enough news that even I paid attention. I remember watching those tryout eps just before I moved to Biggie LC. Adan faked a romance with a hulking nonbinary during the tryouts, and the two of them teamed up to survive several of Beacon's tests. The last tryout was particularly brutal, a free-for-all fight in the Villain Spawning Grounds with various blunt weapons allowed. Adan was already positioned as one of the top contenders, so it was no surprise that three other competitors teamed up to take him out. He managed to beat them back —showing off his impressive fighting skills in the process—but he came away with a shattered nose, several broken ribs, and probs a concussion for good measure. I remember thinking he was done as I watched him stagger into an alley, blood pouring from his nose. It was only a matter of time until someone else found him and finished the job.

Fortunately for Adan, the one who *did* find him was his love-struck nonbinary. Ze protected him for much of the rest of the fighting. When the competition was almost over, Adan and the non were walking through a dimly lit building. Something hit the cam following them—there's endless speculation about what it was. When the next cam found them, the non was unconscious and so was the last remaining competitor, a female with raven hair. Adan alone stood victorious, clutching a rusted, blood-splattered chain. To this day, he claims the raven-haired girl knocked out his friend, but she had been slight and swift, choosing to hide for most of the competition. It's possible she waited until the end to launch her attack, but somehow I doubt it.

BGR. Betrayal Gets Ratings.

"What do you think so far?" Sequoia whispers, pulling me back into the present.

I look around, straining my ears to listen. "No danger yet."

"No, not about this mission, about, well, about being a henchman. What do you think?"

I turn and raise an eyebrow at the question.

He shrugs. "Tickles the Elf says too much silence smothers ratings. Whenever there's a lull in the action, fill it with meaningful conversation, particularly if you can add in some non-identifying personal backstory."

"You've been reading *The Henchman's Survival Guide*," I say and nod my approval. I think about his question. I know what I *should* say—that this job is thrills; that I couldn't be happier working for The Professor. But Tickles also says being authentic is one of the best ways to grab fans and hearts.

"I hate it," I admit.

"All of it?" Sequoia sounds surprised.

I nod. "In the past week my shoulder's been dislocated, I've risked my life and my freedom, Gold could have gotten killed, and we lost our lair. So, not exactly a playground."

"Hmmm." Sequoia's brow furrows.

"What?"

"It's just that… well, you seem good at it."

I make a noise in the back of my throat. "Gold is good at this. Arsenic is great at this. The Professor is the best in the biz. I'm just trying not to drown." I glance at him. "What about you?"

He smiles. "It's been amaze. The adventure. The fear. The risk. And…" He glances away, as if pretending to monitor our surroundings. "… I like being part of a team."

"Your other team members would stab you in the back if it would help them get an extra min of lens time," I inform him.

"I know you don't trust them, but we've been through the fire together," he says. "That has to count for something."

I almost laugh. The poor kid is serious. "You're too trusting," I tell him. "You'll be disappointed."

"I trust you and I haven't been disappointed yet."

"That's because I'm soft," I mutter.

"I think being trustworthy is a strength, not a weakness."

I don't say anything to that. I've tried to toughen up Sequoia, but he'll eventually have to learn the hard way. I just hope it won't cost him, or me too dear when he does.

"The mansion is just up ahead. No more character building," I whisper as I move around a tree covered with budding green leaves.

Is Shine already here? I wonder. Whoever takes the

field first can lay the trap. I wish we'd gotten here a little earlier, but we're still an hour and a half ahead of the exchange time. Even so, just to be safe, we approach the house from the back.

A little shed sits on the edge of the property. Its lock is biometrically programmed, but it has a code backup. I type in the digits The Professor gave me—Matthew's birthday—the same code to his lair. Sentimental but sloppy. Carefully, Sequoia and I pull out the ladder and I lean it up against the house.

"Be on the lookout for cam drones," I hiss at Sequoia. That will be a telltale sign of Shine's presence. He nods and starts up the ladder. I know he's trying to be quiet, but the ladder groans under his big body. I'm up next. I do my best to look fierce as I climb. Using a trick that Tickles suggests on his blog, I imagine what the edited video of this scene will look like when it airs. In my mind, powerful music swells. The screen shows a closeup of my hand grasping the side of the ladder, my boot pressing against a rung, and the sun washing across my face.

Sequoia holds out a hand to help me transition from the ladder to the roof. It'll make me look weak to accept his help, but I don't want to hurt my friend's feelings, so I take his hand. He pulls me up easily, as if I weighed nothing. We pull the ladder onto the roof.

My skin is damp with sweat and beads of moisture shine on Sequoia's freckled skin. I pull an earbud from my pocket and fit the comm into my ear. Sequoia does the same.

"Let me know the moment you see anyone approaching the house," I tell him.

"They could already be inside," Sequoia replies, his

voice echoing through the comm.

I nod. This is the risk I'm going to have to take.

"Wait for my word before coming down," I say. "No matter what you see on the cam." I'm going to have to play this so carefully. Adan thinks I'm coming alone, and we can't tip him off, not until the very last moment. Surprise is our only weapon against him, our only chance.

Sequoia raises his eyes and our gazes lock. He still hasn't learned to mind his face and his nerves are plain to see. I hold out my hand. Here we go again into the fire, but knowing Sequoia has my back makes me feel safe. Perhaps he's right. Maybe trusting someone isn't a weakness after all, as long as you trust the right person.

Instead of taking my hand, Sequoia pulls me into a warm, sweaty embrace.

"Be careful," he whispers in my ear.

"They won't kill me," I say back.

"But with Castillo v PAGS..."

"I'm more valuable alive than dead," I assure him. *At least I think I am.* He lets me go and I walk over to the broken skylight. Shine crashed his way through this light and into the penthouse three weeks ago. Now a thin translucent film covers the gaping hole. *Guess the landlord hasn't had time to repair the damage,* I think ruefully. I kick through the film with my boot, giving myself an opening.

I unwind the lasso at my hip, swing it, and playfully toss the loop over Sequoia. "Got me," he says with a little smile as he adjusts the rope around his waist.

"Just as long as you have me," I banter back. His smile grows wider and I realize we're having two different convos. *You're too good for me,* I think to him and wonder why he hasn't figured that out yet. No time to poke at that particular landmine, so I ignore his hopeful smile and toss the rest of the rope through the window. No jumping straight through the skylight this time around. My poor ankles still haven't entirely forgiven me for that lobotomy move three weeks ago. Instead, I grab onto the rope and lower myself down. The lasso doesn't reach all the way to the floor of Matthew's penthouse, but it goes far enough that I can drop down without splintering my shins. As I glance around Matthew's living room, the lasso drops down. I catch it and quickly wind it back up and attach it to my belt.

Sequoia's head appears over the entrance of the skylight.

"Shining luck," he whispers. I nod.

From here I go alone.

The cam drone buzzes after me as I move through Matthew's living room. Even though sunlight streams through the windows, the place feels cold and empty. My gaze stumbles on a human figure looming in the corner, and I almost cry out in alarm.

The figure is grotesque. One arm is gone. Fins jut out from its head. It wears a torn, black shirt, and its eyes stare sightlessly at me.

Snake eyes.

Betty!

I struggle to recognize Matthew's companion robo. She looks so different from the last time I saw her just a few days ago. Those jutting fins have replaced her hair, and the tattoos stitched across her skin are now more extensive. The patterns are erratic, flowers blooming into skulls and fractions. I even see chemistry equations scrolling down her neck and shoulder, right to the empty socket where her left arm should be.

Betty's unicorn horn is gone, leaving behind a jagged hole in her forehead that shows her carbon fiber plating. Her lifeless eyes shine in the sunlight. She's been powered down or allowed to run out of juice. The older models like Betty need to be recharged every few weeks.

"What is that?" Sequoia asks in my ear. He can see the robo through the cam drone floating next to me.

"Nothing for you to worry about," I reply. It is, however, something for *me* to worry about. I know exactly what this means. Matthew isn't spiraling anymore. He's fully immersed in the black waters of his depression. Using time I don't have, I search the penthouse. In the master bedroom, Matthew's bed is unmade. Another bad sign. My bestie is always fastidiously clean.

The penthouse is empty. No surprise. Matthew doesn't actually like living here. But where would he go? Not out. When he gets like this, he prefers to hole up. He'd go to someplace small, dark, and familiar.

And then I know where he is.

I take the elevator to the second floor and walk down the hall to my apartment. I can't help looking at Leo's gray door.

Have they been treating him well? Is he scared? I try to imagine Leo scared of anything but I can't. He always seems so unflappable, so removed from the push and pull of emotions all around him. I admire that about him even though it drives me crazy. Usually, because it's my emotions he's manipulating.

I face my yellow door.

Would Adan think to lay a trap here? Lysee could have easily told him where I live. There's no way he could be

J Bennett

sure I'd come back, but it might be worth the chance that I would need supplies. It's a risk to go inside, but my plan requires me to, and so does my friendship with Matthew.

"I think a friend of mine might be in my apartment," I tell Sequoia so that he doesn't come barreling down from the roof to protect me if I confront someone inside. "This friend, he knows my identity and he's kind of in a bad place, so just... just let me deal with him."

After a short pause, Sequoia responds. "K." Just that one word, but I know there's a lot behind it. I'll have to finally tell him about Matthew later. I pull in a deep breath and step close enough to my door for my Band to sync with the lock. The door swishes open.

Matthew sits on our old, sagging couch, watching facts scroll down a holo-screen in front of him. He doesn't look up as I cross the room and sit down next to him.

"Ta," I say.

After a moment, he blinks. "You hate that word."

"So do you."

His face looks pale, sickly, but it's probably only the wash of the light from the screen.

"I found Betty upstairs," I tell him.

"She ran out of power," Matthew says carefully. He's on something. Mels? He usually doesn't like how those make his mind fuzzy. My throat tightens.

"Betty didn't have an arm."

Matthew finally turns to look at me. His neck seems so thin for that big head, for all the chaotic thoughts and worries that weigh him down. "She's not real," he says.

The words are a blow. I can almost feel the darkness

300

inside of him, a darkness I recognize all too well. If only I could lance those old wounds, drain away his pain, but how do you heal something you can't see or touch, something that bleeds invisible blood?

"Of course Betty is real," I insist. "Not human, but she's real. She's been adapting to your feedback for over 15 years. Her programming is unique." Matthew loves Betty, but he also enjoys hurting the things he loves when he gets like this.

"Are you real?" He smiles but it's a wounding expression. "I think not. There's a part of you that's real, but it's shrinking." He tilts his head. "Can you feel it? The shrinking?"

I bite my lip. Matthew is further gone than I imagined. He needs help. My help, but I'm also running out of time. Shine could arrive at any moment.

"When was the last time you've eaten?" I ask. "I think I've got some nutra-packs around here somewhere."

Matthew laughs. His black hair is greasy and unkempt. "Shrinking, shrinking."

I stand up and move into the kitchen. My thoughts race as I fill a glass with filtered water and grab a handful of nutra-packs from the cabinet. Lysee's metabolism turbocharge shakes are in there too. I feel a sudden stab of regret, seeing her fancy shakes lined up side-by-side with my nutra-packs in quiet harmony.

The shakes make me realize that Lysee probs abandoned the apartment, too, after she sprung Shine from our cell. That means Matthew's been alone in the house for days. *And then Betty ran out of power*. Even she abandoned him.

My heart cracks for my friend, for the darkness that

grips his mind and his soul. I will help. As soon as I get through this drooling day, I'll come back here. We'll talk for hours, throw an all-night dance party, paint each other's fingernails. Whatever it takes to get Matthew to smile again.

I bring the food and water into the living room and resume my place on the couch. The facts continue to scroll. There's something about food production in Argentina, the score of the World Series in 1969, the name of the first baby genetically modified to be immune to the flu.

"Matthew, you need to charge Betty and boot up her therapeutic protocols," I tell him. "I'll help you with that as soon as I can."

"But you're busy now," he says. "Lysee's busy too." He laughs. "You two were friends. The real you. The real her. And now you're both shrinking." He ignores the nutra-pack I hold out to him. "We were friends too."

"We're still friends," I insist. "And this thing between me and Lysee, it's just... it's just the Fame Game." Even as the words come out of my mouth, I realize how weak they sound.

"You're turning into something else," he says. "Someone else. From Alice to Iron."

"What are you on?"

He laughs again. "You don't have to kidnap a mayor to be a villain."

"Stop it." I stand up. This is what happens when Matthew gives up. He gets mean. He wields his broken heart like a weapon.

"You've been ignoring your friends," he accuses in a soft, dangerous tone. "Me. Lysee."

Alby, I add silently. He's finally been reaching out,

and I've only responded to each of his messages with short replies. We haven't spoken in two weeks. *Even Ollie.* I'd promised to study with him and had forgotten. I've been losing my grip on school too.

What if Matthew is right? What if my real life *has* been shrinking?

"This is how it goes," Matthew says. "It switches. You begin to believe the unreality and distrust the truth."

He needs to stop talking. His words are twisting my soul, and I can't afford to be distracted. Not now when I need all my wits about me.

"That was you," I hiss. "You're the one who lost touch with reality. I'm fine." I storm to Lysee's room. The little cam drone follows me.

"You're not a villain," Sequoia says softly in my ear. I can't imagine what he's made of this conversation.

"I know," I whisper, but the truth is I'm not so sure. I suck in a deep breath and shove all my doubts away. I'm still on a mission. I glance around Lysee's room. It looks like someone triggered a miniature tornado in here. Clothes lay splayed across her bed and floor as if she packed in a hurry. Bottles of makeup, jars of shimmery powders, and stick-on jewels litter the top of her dresser. I hunt around her possessions and finally find something that will work for my plan. I snatch it and sit on Lysee's bed, atop her rumpled pink comforter. As I prepare to prep my new talisman for action, my hands pause.

Am I really doing this? I stare at the object in my hand. A week ago, I would have never even considered doing something so devious… so villainous. *But Lysee betrayed me first,* I remind myself. The thought is cold comfort. I hesitate, teetering on the brink.

But we're running out of time. This is the plan. This is what I need to do to play the game. *If you're not playing the game, then you're losing.* Mermaid's words echo in my mind. Hastily, I prepare the item.

When I return to the living room, Matthew hasn't moved. Black bangs fall into his eyes. His well-cut blue-and-rose jacket is creased with wrinkles. Even the black polish on his nails shows flakes.

"I have to go now," I tell him, "but I'll be in touch soon. There's a couple of things going down, but once that's over, we'll talk. I'll help you get through this."

"Are you sure I'm the one who needs help?" Matthew asks.

"Please power Betty up, and whatever you're taking... stop taking it."

I hate to leave him like this, but I'd be lying if I didn't say a part of me is angry, too. Matthew is too fragile. Too weak. We've all been through hardship, but some of us don't have the luxury of melting down. Some of us have to push our emotions away and fight.

"Give my father my best," Matthew says. "I'm sure he'll finally defeat Beacon this time. I mean, the villain has to win eventually, right?"

I walk out the door, followed by Matthew's soft, cracking laughter.

CHAPTER 24

No one can ever truly replace our fallen comrades, but evil doesn't rest and neither can we. That's why, and an extensive and exciting tryout process, we're honored to reveal the new Fire and the new Seed. The Elementals are whole again! ~ Rain, Elementals S4, E6

~

I rush down the stairs putting distance between myself and the seething anger behind the yellow door of my apartment.

A soft, quivering voice speaks into my ear. "That was Energy," Sequoia says.

"Yes." I make it down the stairs and into the lobby. "We can't use any of the footage of him, but Leo already knows that. He'll edit it out." *If we save him.*

Sequoia says nothing else, but the quiet feels heavy between us. I never told him that I knew his childhood hero. Sequoia dreamed of being Energy, The Professor's confidant, sidekick, and son. And this whole time I've known that Energy grew up into a wounded and bitter adult. *Matthew is kind, too,* I remind myself. His heart seems to swing between love and hatred with equal ferocity and little in between.

I'll help him, I vow to myself again. *Later.*

In the sitting room, I pull aside the fake bookshelf and tap Matthew's birthday into the panel. The elevator doors open. As soon as the elevator brings me down to the lair, Sequoia speaks again.

"I see movement. A car coming down the road."

"Understood." My heart begins to clobber in my chest.

What are they planning? I've asked that question endlessly trying to figure out every possible angle and strategy. *Stop,* I tell myself. The only thing I can do now is deploy my own plan and hope it's enough. I stalk across the padded mats where Mermaid and I sparred just a few days ago. I remember her words of encouragement. She said my combat skills were getting better, but I'm still nowhere near good enough to take on Adan one-on-one. *That's what Sequoia's for,* I remind myself. If I can take Lysee out of the equation and Sequoia surprises Shine, maybe the two of us can take him out, or at least distract him long enough to let Leo escape. It's a shaky plan at best, foolhardy at worst.

I sigh and stare at the old chalkboard in the corner that still holds the convoluted plans for the bank heist that never happened.

"Dreamer just got out of the car. She has Leo," Sequoia says.

I glance at my Band. She's an hour early. Probably hoping to catch me off guard.

"Where's Shine?" I ask.

"I don't see him."

Buddha's gizzard! "Keep your eyes sharp," I tell him. "They're up to something."

Will they think to glance at the roof? Lysee probably won't, but I bet Adan will. Sequoia can stay out of sight as long as he lays flat against the roof on the side opposite the entrance. Although, if Adan circles the whole property, will Sequoia be able to move fast enough to remain hidden?

My hands are slick as I set down the Pod and turn it on with a voice command. "Play vid file Ash Anders One on loop."

A 3D hologram of Chicago's mayor appears, hands tied behind his back, blindfold knotted around his eyes, and tape over his mouth. Ash Anders hadn't been amused at my request to record him in this state, especially when I demanded 20 mins of footage, but he complied. Now the figure grimaces, turns his head, and sways a little. I study the hologram carefully. No flickers. The lighting matches well enough.

Still, it seems glaringly false to me.

Will it fool them? Probably not, but I won't make it obvious. I step sideways, putting distance between myself and the hologram so there's no risk of me accidentally chopping through Ash Anders's arm with an enthusiastic hand gesture.

The elevator opens. I take a deep breath readying myself. Once I cross this line, I know I'll never be able to go back. My heart quakes.

Can I really do this?

Leo shuffles out first, his steps restricted by ankle cuffs. His wrists are cuffed too, but this state hasn't dampened the touch of amusement in his amber eyes. His brown hair is lank, his shirt wrinkled, but otherwise, he looks undamaged.

Relief washes through me, but I keep my expression tight and measured.

"You've struck a poor deal," Leo says. "I don't suppose I can talk you out of it?"

"Clap it," Lysee snaps and gives him a little shove,

which makes him stumble. She clomps forward in her tall boots. The jewels in her hair wink in the lights. Truly, she looks stunning in her glittering purple-and-white costume, with its plunging neckline and throbbing LED lights.

"You're early," she snaps. Her purple lips purse under her mask.

"So are you," I point out.

"Well, I guess... I guess we should get this over with, then."

"Where's Shine?" I ask.

"Don't worry about that." Lysee holds a laz pistol in her hand and points it at me. Three cam drones buzz around us. Two of hers. One of mine.

"We agreed no guns," I say, though I'm not surprised she brought one.

"This is just insurance, in case you try any of your little tricks," Lysee says waving the gun with her words. I pray the safety is on. My roommate looks nervous.

"No tricks," I say. "I've brought what you asked."

Leo's eyes flick to the mayor then to me. He doesn't say anything.

"Yeah, that was good. Canny," Lysee says. "Mr. Anders, have no fear. It is Dreamer. I'm here to rescue you. All will be well shortly."

Ash Anders doesn't respond.

"I told him not to move," I say quickly. "Isn't that right, Mr. Mayor?"

Again, no response. "See? He's a good little friend," I say and put acid in my voice. "Unlike someone else I might mention."

Here we go.

Lysee purses her lips. "It... it wasn't personal," she

sputters. "I had an opportunity and I took it. You should be happy for me."

"Happy for you?" I explode. "You stole my hostage! That was the only damn reason The Professor let me on his team. If anyone found out my roommate released Shine and stole our producer, I would be swiped!"

The cams are drinking this in. Leo arches an eyebrow. I guess Lysee never mentioned we were roommates, but soon the whole world will know.

"Well, that was your own fault," Lysee snaps. "You could have gotten me a henchman spot anytime you wanted, but you didn't.... cause, cause, I bet you didn't want to share the spotlight."

I pause.

Just a moment.

I have to do this. *For Leo. For our show. For my future.*

And then, with hands clenched so hard my fingernails dig into my palms, I cross the line of our friendship, never to return.

"I couldn't have gotten you in with The Professor even if I tried," I sneer at her. "You have no talent. No skills. No lens presence. The only reason Shine took you on as his sidekick is because you were his only ticket to escape." I let out a small breath and then add in a poisoned whisper, "And I assume you slept with him too."

Lysee gasps. Her Band sends up a shocked giraffe emoji, its jaw dropping the entire length of its long neck. Even through the layers of makeup, I can see her cheeks flush with anger.

"You're... you're just jealous!" she splutters. "You've always been jel, and the only reason you ever made it as a henchman is because you stole my lasso and my goggles, and... and... my necklace!"

"What, this?" I touch the golden chain dangling around my neck that holds a large, gaudy butterfly charm. Its electronic wings shiver to life at my touch, beating softly against the collar of my lab coat.

"That's mine!" Lysee shouts. She points her gun at me again.

"Fine, have it, you bitch!" I pull the necklace over my head and hurl it at her.

She makes to catch it, then wisely rethinks and lets the necklace hit her in the knee before bouncing on the floor.

"It's hideous anyway," I add, "just like that ridic costume!"

"It IS NOT!" Lysee bends down, grabs the necklace, and puts it over her head, taking an extra moment to adjust it so the charm lays fetchingly against her cleavage.

"You know what, I don't even want to talk to you," I say. "Let's just do the prisoner swap."

For one tiny moment, Lysee's lips tremble. "I was hoping you'd understand," she says quietly.

I look at her. I know I should say something cruel, something biting to further fuel the rivalry I'm building between us, but I can't. My heart aches too much. I drop my posturing. "I do understand," I say. *And I hope you'll understand what I've done, too.*

Lysee points the gun at me. "Maybe it's better this way," she says. "I have to stun you anyway."

"What? We had a deal."

"Yeah, but I can't have you following me." Lysee offers a weak smile. "Shine was... was... said that was important." She laughs abruptly and sways. "You know, Shine said you wouldn't be drooling enough to trade the mayor for Leo. Not after Beacon offered herself on a sli... slipser platter, but here you are."

"Shine isn't here," I say as the truth downloads. "He's going to Iconic Square."

Lysee nods, the gun waving with the motion of her head. "Which means I'll get the mayor, all by m'self."

Leo meets my eyes. He nods softly toward Lysee. Her attention is off him, and he's taken slow, careful steps behind her. I shake my head just a little and he remains still.

"Wow, I'm so glad that worked out for you," I tell my roommate.

"I'm gonna really embarrass you, here" she crows. The gun tilts in her hand. Even if she pulled the trigger, the shot wouldn't come anywhere close to hitting me. "I'm getting the mayor, and all you get is Leo. Though he's nice... not glam... but whatsa' word for it? One of 'em old words. Handsome. He's veeeery had'som. I can see why... why you've got a thing for him. But now I hafta... hafta stun you both. Shine said that... would be best." The gun droops in her hand.

"Mr. Mayor," Lysee says, "you can come over here now. You're rescued. Res-cused." She takes staggering steps toward him. "Mr. Mayor?"

I step out of the way. Lysee reaches up to put a hand on Ash Anders's shoulder, and her fingers slide through the hologram. She really should have read *The Henchman's Survival Guide* like I recommended when we were both trying out for The Professor's show. Then she would know that you always double-check that the hostage you're rescuing isn't a robo or hologram before making the exchange. It's a classic henchman mistake.

"What?" Lysee whimpers. "Mr. Mayor?" She turns

to me, her purple-tinted eyes glazed and uncertain. "What'sa wrong with him?" She wobbles. The gun clatters to the ground. She tilts sideways, her ankles and knees buckling. I'm ready to catch her.

"Tired," she murmurs.

"I'm sorry," I say to her.

"Me too," she whispers as her eyes flutter shut. Carefully I lower her to the floor.

"It was the necklace, wasn't it?" Leo says behind me.

The butterfly charm lays across Lysee's chest, the Sweet Dreams patch attached to its back seeping powerful barbiturates into her bloodstream. I'm thankful again that my own henchman costume includes a fully buttoned lab coat.

"She might not have noticed you were wearing her necklace," Leo says.

"Of course she would," I answer him.

"She might not have put it on."

I hold Lysee's hand in mine. "That's why I had to break her heart," I whisper.

"You being roommates will make for a nice B storyline. Is it true or did you work out that little gimmick with her beforehand?"

"Does it matter?"

Leo studies me with his amber eyes, and he nods to himself. "She was the one who came into the lobby when you captured Shine. You are roommates." He awkwardly kneels down, takes Lysee's hand from mine and presses her finger against the biometric lock on his wrist cuffs. They *bleep* and release. "I don't suppose she'll forgive you anytime soon," he says, repeating the procedure with his ankle cuffs.

I look down at my peacefully sleeping roommate.

"I don't suppose she will," I agree, and suddenly my heart seems as heavy and cold as an anvil in my chest.

"It's a good vendetta story," Leo says. If he notices my drift into a bottomless pit of self-disgust, he doesn't show it. "You must have had a plan for Shine," he adds.

Right on cue, Sequoia speaks in my ear. "We have company."

I shoot to my feet. "Shine?" He must have been monitoring the cams during our prisoner exchange nearby. I tense and look toward the elevator door.

"Not exactly," Sequoia says.

CHAPTER 25

I'm sad to say Iron's got a serious flaw though—a good heart. Nitrogen too. But not to worry, I'll get them into shape. We can't have softies on this team, though it does make them easy to walk over. I wouldn't do that, of course, but Arsenic. She's fierce. Those two better watch out for her. The Professor, too. ~ Gold, Interview with J Bennett

~

When Sequoia explains who's coming to pay us a visit, I consider it for a moment then say, "Leave him to me."

I turn to Leo. "The Professor meets with Beacon in Iconic Square at noon. We have most of your gear there but pick up anything else you need."

He studies me carefully. "What are you going to do to our visitor?"

"Teach him a lesson."

Leo nods. "I don't have my Goggs. I won't be able to put a cam on you."

"It's not worth it, anyway," I tell him truthfully. I doubt our next ep will have room for this confrontation with everything else that's going on. I look up to the cam drone hovering over my shoulder, controlled by Sequoia.

"I don't want you recording this," I tell him. Sequoia doesn't respond over the com, but the drone floats to his lab table and sets down.

Leo stands and gives his cuffs a little kick. He looks at me, and I remember how Lysee blurted out my secret crush on him. Well, she and I won't be having any late-night confessionals over glasses of cheap, synth-wine anymore.

I look away and Leo turns, taking purposeful strides to his office. I glance down at Lysee again. Her closed eyelids shimmer with purple sparkles. The plan had seemed so solid in my head last night, but now it only feels wrong.

I crouch down, touch my fingers to my lips and transfer a sad kiss to her forehead. "I'm sorry," I whisper, knowing those words aren't enough.

After a min of consideration, I decide to leave Lysee where she is. Some producer or freelancer is operating her cams. They'll send someone, possibly Shine to retrieve her quickly enough.

"Nitrogen, keep on the lookout for anyone else," I tell my friend as I move to the elevator.

I make it to the lobby and just barely manage to push the bookshelf back into place when the front door to The Professor's mansion swings open. The skinny freeter slinks in, his cape almost catching in the door. My gaze sweeps across his poorly printed costume, those silly white diamonds marching down his black sleeves and pants.

He sees me and stumbles to a halt. Behind the black mask, his eyes widen, but then he proudly poses.

"I command you to cease whatever evil plan you are implementing," he says. "Diamond Shield is here to stop you."

I sigh as it all clicks into place. It's not the sound of

his voice—the freeter has gotten his hands on a basic voice modulator—but the words themselves that give his identity away. I'd assumed that Ollie or his dad contacted the freeter after we'd left the pharmacy, or maybe it'd been that drooling lady with her robo pet. But who would tip off this freeter? He has no name recognition. No sponsors. No money to pay out to a tipster.

Now I understand.

I pull the unmarked box of Sweet Dreams from the pocket of my lab coat and turn it over. I don't see anything on the outside of the box. That'd be too obvi. I pop open the lid, and then I notice the faint outline of a clear film stuck to an inside wall. A few tiny wires wiggle through the microfilm like veins, sending out our location.

A tracker.

I look from the box to him. His eyes meet mine and dance away. Blue familiar eyes. Ollie's eyes. His words. His unrelenting quest for a phantom justice.

I realize what I have to do. My cracked heart rebels. Then again, what's one more fracture to that battered organ after what I've already done to Matthew and Lysee?

"I don't want to hurt you," I say, keeping my voice low.

"Then give yourself up to the authorities."

I sigh. "This isn't real. You know that, right? I'm just playing a part in a story."

"You kidnapped the Mayor of Chicago. That was real," the freeter points out.

I wish I could take Ollie aside, explain how the mayor let us escape the city, how he carefully edited his own hostage vid, but Ollie wouldn't listen. Not unless I unmasked myself, and I can't take that risk. Ollie wouldn't understand that either.

I carefully unhook the lasso from my belt. "Please, just walk away," I whisper. Because if he doesn't, I'll have to teach him a lesson. Ollie isn't trained. He isn't sponsored. He doesn't even wear basic protective armor. He's a danger to others and especially to himself. And now that we're living in a post-Castillo v PAGS world, the risks are even higher.

"A true hero can never turn away from the face of evil." He pulls a baton from his own belt.

If Ollie keeps trying to fight crime on his own he could get hurt. Or killed.

Unless I stop him.

I swing my lasso a few times and then toss it at him. It's only a feint. I'm not nearly good enough to snag a moving target. Ollie dives dramatically out of the way, and I rush toward him.

As he rolls back to his feet, I'm ready. I grab his shoulders and slam my knee into his abdomen, then strike him across the face with my forearm. He stumbles and falls, dazed. This is the beauty of Krav Maga. It's fast, vicious, and designed to immediately take the fight out of your enemy.

Ollie struggles to sit up, but I take one step forward and press my heel into his chest, forcing him back to the ground. I kneel on him, my kneecap pressed into his neck.

I lean in close and hold the box of Sweet Dreams in front of his face. "Clever, Ollie," I hiss at him, "but not clever enough."

His eyes widen when I use his name.

"It was so nice of your pops to suggest two patches instead of one," I tease him as I pull the second patch out of the box.

"No," Ollie cries. He bucks beneath me, but I grind my knee deeper into his neck, and he gags. I peel the backing off the patch, lift my knee just a little, and slap the patch on Ollie's exposed neck. His fingers dig into my thigh, but I hardly feel it.

I press my knee back down across his neck to keep him still.

I lean close again, putting my lips right to his ear. "You're weak, pathetic," I hiss at him. "You can't even beat a lowly henchman. You're no hero."

My heart twists as tears prickle in his eyes, but I have to do this. I have to shatter his drooling dream. It's the only way to protect him.

"I could unmask you right now and broadcast your face to the world," I say. That would be the ultimate humiliation. A total defeat. "But the truth is, I don't think anybody would care."

His eyes are slipping closed, his fingers relaxing on my thigh, but he murmurs, "I won't... won't give..." The last words die on his lips. I feel his body go slack beneath me. His hands fall away from my leg, but I hold my position just a little longer, just in case. Ollie's not a big person, so the patch should work pretty quickly, but you never know.

After about 20 secs, I press my fingers to his pulse and feel it slowing down. He can't fake that, so I ease off him and stand up.

"I'm sorry," I say. I know I hurt him, far more seriously than a few bruises to his face and chest. But I had to. Funny, that's the same excuse I used to defend what I did to Lysee.

You don't have to kidnap a mayor to be a villain.

Matthew's words echo in my mind. I shake my head as if I could ever dislodge them or the memory of my best friend's accusing stare. How have I managed to betray three of my closest friends in less than an hour?

My eyes burn with tears, and I angrily scrub them away. A throat clears delicately behind me. I turn around and see Leo standing just in front of the elevator He carries a bag on his shoulder bulging with equipment.

He glances at the freeter. "That seemed personal," he observes.

"Did it?" I ask, trying for non-committal.

Leo's eyes drill into me asking questions I'm not about to answer.

"We have to go," I tell him. We've got less than an hour before The Professor's showdown with Beacon.

"One more thing," Leo says and walks up the stairs. He returns in two mins, and I'm grateful for the short reprieve to pull myself together. Leo must have grabbed something from his apartment, but he doesn't carry any extra bags filled with clothes or personal possessions.

When Leo and I leave the mansion, Sequoia waits for us outside. The ladder is gone, politely returned to the storage shed. The cam drone, which followed us out of the house, drops into Sequoia's arms and he pulls off his Goggs. He looks down at his boots and won't meet my eyes. No one speaks of the freeter.

My heart is filled with shards of pain and guilt. My soul feels threadbare. But the day is not over yet. Beacon awaits, and despite her promise of a peaceful prisoner exchange, I know she won't hand herself over willingly. It'll be a fight.

I swallow, pushing all my emotions deep, deep down inside of me and look at my two companions.

"Iconic Square," I say to them.

CHAPTER 26

Take the beating. That's your job. ~ Tickles the
Elf, The Henchman's Survival Guide

~

The drive to Iconic Square features pleasant, sun-soaked views of the town and loads of tension. My whole body feels raw and empty from all the betrayal I dished out back at the mansion. Sequoia won't look at me. In a monotone voice, I explain The Professor's plan to Leo, trying to pretend I can't feel his body next to mine or that Lysee didn't blurt out my secret, pointless crush.

"So that's the general idea," I finish. "It's loose. We'll need to adapt as the thing plays out."

"And Beacon will certainly have her own plan," Leo says, but he's nodding. "Not bad. If The Professor plays it right, it could be big, very big."

"As long as Beacon doesn't outsmart us," I say.

Leo's mouth quirks in half a smile. "Setbacks are all part of the story. Sometimes the hero has to struggle so they can show what they're made of."

"But we're not the heroes," Sequoia mutters.

"A villain is the hero of their own story," Leo replies softly. The convo sinks into a weary death and we're silent the rest of the way to Iconic Square.

Plastic barricades line the Square and Big Little City

police officers stand in front of them. In a stoic vid posted to her Stream this morning, Beacon asked the City Council and Big Little City Police Department to allow the exchange to take place without any interference.

Surprise, surprise, the City Council was all too happy to comply and let this fireworks show play out.

Our car approaches the barricades. The officers try to hold grim expressions, but I can see the twitch of excitement on their faces. Crowds huddle behind the barriers, taking selfies, peering out into the square, and gabbing with friends through their Bands. Overhead, the air hums with the whir of cam drones.

Our car drives right up to the barriers and Leo instructs the car to roll down its windows. I suck in a heavy breath as a cop peers inside at us, taking in our lab coats, goggles, and bowties. The officer is young and handsome, all dashing blue eyes and an overly enhanced chin. His navy-colored uniform with all its brass buttons seems a size too small and struggles to stretch over his muscled frame.

"You're The Professor's henchmen," he says and shakes his head. "You make me sick!" He slams a fist disgustedly on the hood of our car. I have to force myself not to roll my eyes behind my goggles. What a lens stealing little striver. Nice try, lens grabber, but there's no way this measly interaction is making our ep, not after my prisoner exchange with Lysee and our upcoming battle with Beacon.

"You gonna let us in or what?" I growl at him and throw in a taunting smirk for good measure. Might as well play along or he'll stand here preening all day.

"I outta arrest you right now," he snarls.

"Do it or let us in," I say right back. "We're on a tight clock."

He grimaces for three long seconds, then angrily shoves the barricades aside. "You're going down," he spits out as our car rolls past. "Beacon won't let you get away with this."

"Get better lines," I call through the window and blow him a kiss as our car moves forward.

Leo dutifully records it all using Sequoia's Goggs and our lone cam drone. "Your cam presence has improved since I've been away," he notes.

I fall back against my seat. "Thanks," I mutter, but I hardly consider it a compliment.

Iconic Square is eerily empty. The tourist trolleys sit quietly on the side of the road, no speakers blaring or Bands pointing out the windows. "Closed" signs glow brightly in every storefront window.

Our car pulls over. I check my Band again. "Ten mins." We've cut it close. Leo pushes the Goggs onto his forehead and opens the car door.

"I'll set up over there," he says, pointing to Culprits Coffee Shop, which includes an outdoor patio filled with tables and wide umbrellas. "I'm close enough that I can re-establish my connection with any of my cam drones already out here. Wish I had my Goggs, though."

"Gold's probs using them," I say. I glance at Culprits Coffee and remember all the happy, bear-claw-donut-filled times I've had there. That feels like another life. Another person. I force my thoughts back to the present. Culprits has seen some serious damage in past fights, just like most buildings in the square.

"If something goes wrong, get out fast," I tell Leo.

He gives me a tight smile. "I know how to handle

trouble." He puts his hands on his hips and pins me with one of those deep looks that could mean anything. "You'll need to react fast out there."

"I know." I've been trying not to think about what comes next. Soon enough, we'll face Beacon, who's beat every villain our town has ever spawned.

"You have good instincts, Iron. Use them." His voice softens. "And you both be careful."

"I can take care of myself," Sequoia snaps as he steps out of the car and immediately begins walking toward the center of the square. I linger back, suddenly overwhelmed with the fear of what we could face. Beacon won't really give herself up. She's got a plan, just like we've got a plan, and surely someone's going to get hurt, or worse.

"Strong as Iron," Leo says next to me, and there's something in his voice. It might be admiration.

I don't feel strong. I've never felt strong. But I'm learning to be a better actor. I give Leo a nod and follow Sequoia.

The day is warm, but a soft breeze makes it comfortable. A few wispy clouds stretch across the sky, and I see heavy gray clouds in the distance. A storm is coming.

"Are you angry?" I ask Sequoia as I jog to catch up to him.

He keeps his gaze forward. "What do I have to be angry about?"

It could be the cruel way I treated Lysee, but that was all part of our plan. No, I think his tight jaw and clenched fists have something to do with what Lysee said about my feelings for Leo.

"It's just that you've been—" I begin.

"Iron, we need to focus on the mission."

Leo's cam drone follows us. It's right for Sequoia to use my henchman name, but it still stings. We walk the rest of the way in silence while I feel prickles on the back of my neck. It feels like an army of ghosts is watching us. I keep catching flickers of movement, shifting shadows, at the corner of my eye, but it must just be my adrenaline-soaked imagination.

In the center of the Square, the statue of The Hero rises in front of us, almost blinding in the sunlight. It looks so much like Beacon, big and towering, kissed by the sun. At the base of the statue, The Professor waits impatiently, arms crossed in front of his chest, frowning. He taps his foot as his wild hair waves in the breeze.

Ash Anders looks stoically out across the square. His hands are nominally tied in front of him, but he doesn't wear a gag or blindfold. He also seems to have convinced The Professor against any type of leg shackles. Mermaid and Gold stand on either side of him, faces like stone. Kitty is here, too, a smile plastered on her synthetic lips. Our three remaining cam drones buzz around the ensemble, soaking in the tension.

Gold sees us first, along with the cam drone following us. "Finally!" he says. "Kitty, release control of the cams."

The three cam drones drop unceremoniously from the air only to swoop back up just before hitting the ground. I can't imagine Leo appreciated that abrupt handoff, but he got control of them just in time.

"Wonderful! Now I can help guard the prisoner," Kitty chirps. She practically skips over to Ash Anders, her tail swishing with each step. "Someone's been a bad boy," she says to him in a husky voice. "Don't you dare even try to escape."

"Welcome, welcome, my elements," The Professor says. "You've successfully recovered my producer?"

"We did," I confirm.

"Well done." Our boss nods. "You don't happen to have my original prisoner handy, do you?"

I shake my head. "Shine didn't show."

The Professor squints across the square, then glances at his Band. One min till noon. "I suppose we'll have to make do with the one we have." He gives a menacing grin to Ash Anders.

We wait. Sequoia and I take our spots behind Ash Anders so that we effectively surround him without blocking the cams. My eyes keep flicking to my Band to check the time. I notice the others doing the same. The numbers flip.

Noon.

The Professor steps out from the shadow of The Hero.

"Ooooh, Beacon," he taunts, his voice carrying across the empty Square. "I have your present wrapped up all nice and tidy. Why don't you come out and fetch him?"

He turns to Ash Anders and pulls a highly modified laz pistol from his lab coat. Colorful wires and blinking lights cover the gun. A strange tube sticks out of the side. "On your knees," The Professor barks at our prisoner. "If Beacon doesn't show, I might as well see if my atom fuser prototype works."

Anders doesn't move. He looks romantically bedraggled, his expression haughty and proud.

"I said kneel!" The Professor bellows and stamps his foot for good measure.

Ash Anders yawns.

Gold gives him a kick to the back of his knees. Anders makes a good show of stumbling forward and hitting his knees on the grass. Gold puts a heavy hand on the mayor's shoulder.

"I admire your courage, Mr. Mayor," he says, "but the boss says go down, so you better stay there." Gold's voice is tight with emotion. The gravity of this moment is even getting to him.

I'm no better off. Adrenaline pumps through my body, and my stomach churns with fear, excitement, and serious nausea.

"Now, let's see," The Professor says, sauntering around Ash Anders, banging his cane with each step. He fiddles with his gun. "I'm not sure I remember the right setting, and this *is* a prototype after all, so the results might be a little unpredictable." He grins.

I plaster a careless smile on my face and give a little laugh that sounds squeaky in my ears. I feel Sequoia looming next to me. I hope he's minding his face and looking appropriately sinister. We won't get a second shot at this scene, so it needs to be perfect for our ep.

The Professor presses a sensor pad on his gun, and it glows a bright green. A small gear begins to turn on the side of the weap.

"Looks like Beacon was too afraid to face me," The Professor announces. "Quite the right move. Unfortunately, Mayor Anders, that means you've got no hope of rescue." His words are smooth and perfectly articulated. If he's afraid of what's to come, I can't see it. Instead, he seems to fully embody his role. He *is* The Professor. I almost believe he'll zap Ash Anders any moment.

The Professor gazes down at his hostage and sneers.

"Any last words?"

Ash Anders takes a deep breath. "As a matter of fact..."

"Stop," a voice calls, echoing through the stillness of the day.

It's a familiar voice. A voice that has uplifted generations, a voice that could spell our doom. A slim figure walks to the edge of the bank's roof just across from the statue. Even from a distance, Beacon makes a powerful impression. Her armored costume gleams in the sunlight, and her streaming golden hair wafts in the breeze. She looks like some ancient Greek goddess, ready to strike vengeance against all who oppose her.

She jumps off the roof and executes a flawless front flip, her propulsion boots slowing her descent so that she lands softly on her feet. Four cam drones float around her, recording from every angle.

"I am here," she says simply.

"Well, well, well," The Professor gloats. "I'm not surprised your foolish morality got the better of you. Did you come alone and unarmed as promised?"

Beacon holds out her arms and spins, revealing that her Light Blade and Aura Arcs don't hang from the belt around her waist.

"Then you are a damn fool!" The Professor cackles at her. "Did you really think I would just let my darling little mayor walk away? Not a chance! Now I have *two* guinea pigs for my lab."

I glance at Ash Anders out of the corner of my eye. Gold pretends to watch the exchange between Beacon and The Professor with consuming interest. With a quick flip of his lab coat, he clearly reveals the laz pistol in his belt. Ash Anders quickly shimmies out of the rope bindings, just the way Mermaid showed him. Now, he carefully puts one foot beneath him.

My attention snaps back to the confrontation. Beacon laughs, showcasing perfect white teeth. "Oh, Professor, where are all those IQ points you always brag about? Of course I knew you'd double-cross me. You didn't think I'd really come alone, did you?"

A confident laugh rumbles above us, and we gaze around, trying to spot its source. Then I see him, a resplendent figure standing on the roof of the Grand Museum. Shine's costume glows orange, like fire, and he holds Beacon's Light Blade in one hand, her Aura Arcs in the other.

"I don't believe I ever thanked you for your hospitality, Professor," Shine calls. "Perhaps you'd let me repay the favor."

Even as I gape dramatically for the cams, I can't help but be impressed. Somehow Adan made a deal with Beacon. He must have realized that this confrontation with The Professor, the inevitable rescue of Ash Anders, would ensure Beacon's continued reign as our city's top hero. He found a way back into her good graces so he could ride the ratings wave. I wonder what he did, what he said to convince her to take him back. I probs don't want to know.

Ash Anders makes his move. He leaps to his feet, grabs Gold's gun, and shoots at The Professor.

"No!" Mermaid cries, leaping in front of the shot. She takes the hit and crumples to the ground, arms splayed. The gun was on the lowest laz setting, but you'd never know it by how still Mermaid lays on the ground.

"Why you!" The Professor hollers.

Ash Anders shoots at him, which was def not in the

plan we agreed to, but Sequoia is already moving, grabbing The Professor and tossing him behind the statue.

Flustered and screaming curses, The Professor points his gun at Beacon and pulls the trigger. The weap rattles, wheezes, then several of the gears fall off, as planned. There was no way Ash Anders would allow The Professor to point a real weapon in his face.

"Blight!" The Professor hollers as the mayor sprints away. "Get him!" our boss hollers, then he whirls toward Beacon. "And... and get her too!" He hurls the gun to the ground and stomps on it.

I sprint after Ash Anders. In my peripheral, I see Shine leap from the roof of the museum.

"It's over, Professor. Time to go on a long, long sabbatical," Beacon is saying while she stalks toward him.

The Professor releases his infamous laugh. "Oh, my dear, every good scientist knows that not every experiment will be a success. That's why one should always devise a backup plan." The Professor sticks two fingers in his mouth and whistles.

Ash Anders pauses and so do I, even though I know what's coming. In the hush, a tall, beautiful woman steps from behind the city tour booth. Her hair is black as night and falls all the way down to her hips. An intricate golden crown sits upon her head. Her lips are ruby red, and black liner rims her eyes ending in sharp points at the corner of each eye. Four bare-chest, glistening men surround her.

"Cleopatra!" Beacon hisses, her expression crumbling into rage. Her reaction is so good, I can't tell if it's real or fake.

Cleopatra touches the thick golden band around her neck, and it shivers to life, red eyes opening, forked tongue poking out of its mouth. The robo snake slides down her arm and then shifts into a short blade.

"It's time we face each other at last," Cleopatra says. She takes one step forward and a howl cuts through the afternoon. Everyone knows what that means. I look around frantically and Lobo bounds out from between the taco shop and drone rental store. A tattered wolf pelt hangs off his back. His shaggy hair, beard, and filed teeth make him look truly fearsome. No wonder this dark and conflicted hero appeals to so many viewers. Lobo leaps dramatically onto a lamppost, assisted by magnetic gloves and boots, and lets out a second curdling howl.

Another figure emerges from behind the taco shop, a handsome, muscled black man wearing a sleeveless shirt stamped with a shooting star across his chest. I recognize my old coworker, DeAngelo. The last time I saw him, he was only a nameless stickup guy with dreams of riding Lobo's wolf pelt to fame and glory. Looks like he's managed to pull off that lobotomy plan.

I would be impressed if my mind wasn't spinning with the implications of what's happening.

"So you've brought a few friends," The Professor says, his expression malevolent. Then he smiles. "Well, it just so happens that I've called in a few old favors as well."

He grabs a corked test tube from an inner pocket in his lab coat and throws it to the ground. The glass shatters, releasing a billow of black smoke that rises in a column, darkening the face of The Hero statue.

At this signal, figures begin emerging from nooks and crannies all around the square. Lizard Man, Pinn, and The Scream, all from the Dark League, step out of the alleyway next to the mayor's mansion. The Vengeful Knight rides zir robo horse right out of the Buddhist temple. Nurse Pippi bounds from the wreckage of the Redemption Café, clutching an impossibly large needle in each hand. A few more painted, glowing figures slink into the Square, carrying an odd assortment of weapons.

The Professor's grin grows. "I believe you're outnumbered," he says softly to Beacon.

Beacon looks around at the approaching villains, but she doesn't seem upset or even perturbed. Then she settles her gaze back on The Professor. "No matter how hard you try, no matter how many you set against me, you cannot stop the light!"

The dark plume from The Professor's signal is dissipating allowing the sun to break through. It lights up Beacon in a dazzle of gold. At that moment, three sky skimmers scream overhead and circle us.

The Dragon Riders are back for round two.

On the other side of the square, near where Nurse Pippi emerged, a figure flutters down from a decorative tree. Hummingbird, the reformed vil, shimmers in an array of dazzling colors. The Museum doors open, and I recognize Gust and Rain from the Elementals, along with two new members wearing the costumes of Flame and Seed. Someone darts out behind the ice cream cart just ahead of me, blocking my path to Ash Anders. I recognize him. Even The Kid is here, his duster jacket sweeping behind him, his eyes hidden behind his hopelessly outdated sunglasses.

I gaze around the Square, now filled with beautiful and fearsome people wearing beautiful and fearsome costumes, each one holding a weapon and gazing around to pick a target.

I look to my boss for instructions. The Professor's face is serene. He understands what this is.

He and Beacon have accomplished something that's only happened once before in the entire history of our town, something that will ensure a ratings bonanza like no other for the ones who make it out.

"BRAWL!" DeAngelo hollers. I barely manage to unhook my lasso before utter chaos descends.

CHAPTER 27

If you're ever in a brawl, Rule One: Survive. Rule Two: Find the cape with the highest ratings and punch 'em in the face.
~ Tickles the Elf, The Henchman's Survival Guide

~

Voices rise. Weapons cut through the air. Bodies hurtle toward each other.

The first and only brawl to rock this city happened over ten years ago and pitted Beacon against Ebony Hex, a twisted, evil version of herself. The property damage to the Square was extensive, but the ratings gushed and held for months. New stars emerged from the wreckage, while others were left bleeding in the dust, their injuries so severe their shows got swiped.

And that was before the Castillo v PAGS decision.

As these thoughts scroll through my mind, I catch sight of Ash Anders disappearing through the crowd of tangled bodies. Already, the whoops of battle are turning into grunts of pain.

Panic seizes me, ripping electrical sparks up and down my spine. My feet are planted to the ground.

What do I do?

Where do I go?

But I know the answer. The Professor. My boss needs to make it out of this thing in one piece. Otherwise, he'll never get to enjoy the swell of ratings from this glorious boondoggle he's created. If he goes down, so does our show.

I have to get to him. Protect him. And avoid any ghastly injuries myself.

Bodies lurch and grapple around me. Cleopatra's high priestess—a beautiful blonde in a white armor-plated dress—delivers a fierce blow to Seed, the newly minted Elemental, as he vainly tries to work the computerized cuffs on his costume. He goes down, blood exploding from his mouth. Cam drones buzz above us, dancing around each other and swinging down to catch a certain fight. Two crash into each other and spiral down together, almost landing on top of Cleopatra who is trying to make her way to Beacon, who herself is fighting toward Ash Anders. The Vengeful Knight's robo horse gallops just in front of me, sparks pouring from a deep gash in its side, its rider nowhere to be seen.

Fortunately, my low status as a henchman makes me an unworthy target for most. Everyone will be looking to take down someone bigger, more popular than themselves. I just need to be careful not to get caught in any crossfire.

I deftly move around the fighting pairs, struggling to make it back to The Hero statue. Sweat pours down my body and my heart drums in my ears. Something hurtles at me, and I throw myself to the ground. I recognize Lizard's boomerang tail as it sails overhead and spins toward Lobo, who deftly leaps out of the way. On its way back, the tail crashes into a parked tourist trolley, ironically right into an image of Lizard pasted on the side of the trolley.

I leap to my feet, hunching low, looking out for threats. Through the maze of bodies, I catch sight of

The Professor up ahead. Just as I straighten up, a body slams into me. I hit the ground hard and my teeth clap together. For a moment, I lay dazed, gasping for breath, but I see movement next to me and force myself to sit up.

DeAngelo shakily pulls himself to his feet. Did he tackled me on purpose, or was he thrown into me from another fight? Whatever the answer, DeAngelo seems to make up his mind and lurches toward me. He isn't wearing the spangled tights and shiny cape that was part of our embarrassing uniforms at the Redemption Café when we worked together. Now he looks suitably intimidating in the ripped jeans, tight shirt that show off his well-developed muscles, and glittering star mask covering his face. DeAngelo takes a swing at me. I fall back to the ground and watch his knuckles skim the air just over my face. I roll to the side, scramble to my knees, and lash out a leg to sweep his ankles.

DeAngelo tumbles down hard, the air punching out of his lungs. He flops onto his back, wheezing. I could finish him, but as I glance ahead, I see The Professor is in trouble. Sequoia grapples with one of the Dragon Riders, while Mermaid and Gold stand back-to-back as three members of the Glory League surround them. I don't even remember seeing those sparkle-doused capes join the fight.

The Professor is unprotected, shooting his spasmodic ice ray at a Glory League member in a short silver dress who approaches warily.

"PROFESSOR!" Shine bellows, and now I see the orange glow of his costume as he tears through the crowd, making his way toward my boss.

"Raincheck," I say to DeAngelo and bound away

from him.

Shine shoves past the Glory League hero in the silver dress, who cradles a frosted arm against her chest. The Professor shoots his ice ray, and its charge splatters frozen crystals across Shine's breastplate, not stopping him for a single moment. The Professor curses as he realizes that his weap is useless against Shine's fancy suit. My boss scurries around The Hero, grabbing up a small case hidden in the shadow of the statue.

Enclosed in the case is his jet pack, but the thing will take a min to unfold and rev up.

Sequoia finally manages to pummel the Dragon Rider into the ground, but then DeAngelo staggers into his path, ready for another fight.

As Shine swings around the statue, Kitty pops up in front of him.

"Hi," she says brightly. "Want to play tag?" She winks at him, and her voice grows soft and whispery, "I bet you can't catch me."

Shine pulls back his arm and delivers a blow so vicious I can hear the impact on his titanium gloved fist against Kitty's face. Her cheek crumbles inward, her eye dislocating. She sways.

"Ouch," she says mildly. "I do not appreciate this level of roughhousing. Safe word. Safe word." Then she topples to the ground. Shine grins and steps over her body. His shadow falls across The Professor, who desperately unfolds his jet pack with shaking hands. There's no way he'll have time to slip on the pack and power it up.

"You're mine!" Shine growls.

I leap desperately at Shine. He sees me at the last moment and raises his arms to catch me. We tumble to the ground together, rolling across the grass. He hits the base of the statue and grunts, but I doubt he feels the impact.

He's up quickly. I stay down and swing my leg at his feet. This same move worked beautifully on DeAngelo, but Shine dances away and gives me a brutal kick to the kidneys. My breath explodes out of my lungs and colors dazzle in front of my eyes. He kicks at me again, and I grab his foot, desperately curling myself around it to soften the blow. This throws him off balance, and he hops awkwardly. I yank down hard, and his knee hits the ground.

I swing for an uppercut, but he bats my arm away and I feel his elbow drive into my shoulder blade, slamming me into the ground. I cry out as pain radiates across my back. Even if Shine weren't encased in an impenetrable suit, I'd be no match for him. Adan is the superior fighter by far, and I've no more tricks up my sleeve today. Shine smiles as I roll onto my elbows and knees. I'll never know what final blow he has planned, because The Scream from The Dark League leaps onto Shine's back, screeching like a banshee. Her enhanced vocal adapter turns the sound in a wailing cry that nearly bursts my eardrums.

I gasp in a painful breath and flop onto my back. Overhead, I watch as something—possibly Lizard's tail —hits one of the Dragon Riders square in the chest. He tumbles off his sky skimmer and plummets to the ground. That fall would kill a normal human, but his reinforced costume will save his life, though probs not the structural integrity of all his bones. I wince, knowing that his career—whichever Dragon Rider he was—is probs over.

Then I hear a high whine growing louder and louder. I look up and see the riderless sky skimmer tumbling through the air, headed right at us. Next to me, Shine rips Scream off his back and bodily tosses her into the base of The Hero statue.

"Shine!" I croak. He follows my gaze to the incoming sky skimmer. I wobble to my feet, already knowing I'll be too slow to dive out of the way. Unlike the Dragon Riders, I'm not wearing an impenetrable carbon fiber costume. I'm going to die. Def going to… Suddenly I'm in Shine's arm. He tucks me into his body as he leaps away from the statue. We both watch as the sky skimmer slams into The Hero, shattering half her face and shearing off her sword arm, before slamming into the ground.

Thick, oily smoke curls around us. Through the haze, I see Sequoia dragging DeAngelo away from the flames. I don't know where Gold and Mermaid are, or my boss. I look up at Shine. Adan's bright green eyes stare down at me in concern from beneath his mask.

"You alright?" he asks softly. My ears are ringing from The Scream so that I can barely hear him, but I nod dully.

Then I see a figure rising into the air through the smoke of the downed sky skimmer. Wearing his jet pack, The Professor bobbles into the air, apparently unharmed. His face is tinged with soot, but he must be hardy because he lets out his signature villain laugh.

I pull in a painful breath and then carefully push myself out of Shine's arms. I plaster what I hope is a gloating smile on my face, though I can barely keep up the pretense.

"Looks like you won't get what you came here for," I

say to Shine. Our eyes meet again, and I give him silent permission to slip back into his role as my enemy.

"Then I'll just have to make do with you," Shine says. "A sorry substitute, but maybe I'll take those goggles as a personal trophy."

"Just try it," I growl. Slowly, painfully, I force myself to my feet. I hope I look noble for the cams as I bring my arms up and put a foot back, positioning myself to fight. Shine grins, and just when he moves into his fighting stance, I turn and sprint toward the densest part of the crowd as fast as my legs will carry me.

That's one big bennie of being a villain. I don't have to be noble. I don't have to stand and fight, no matter the cost. I can cut and run, save my bruised ass to plot another day.

I take five glorious steps toward my victorious escape when something coils around my waist. I look down and recognize what it is.

"Buddha's gallbladder juice," I hiss as Shine's Torch Whip sends an electric shock through me. My muscles contract. My limbs flail. I gag on my own spit and darkness beats black feathers over my vision. And then I'm lying crumpled on the ground. The battlefield shifts in and out of focus above me and my fingers twitch outside my control.

"That was setting three," Shine says as he steps up next to me. He reaches down and grabs the collar of my lab coat. My head lolls forward as he jerks me to my knees. I concentrate and lift my head so that I can meet his eyes. I know I'm defeated, so what happens now is critically important.

Go out big, Tickles says. It's my only hope. The majority of henchmen are disposable, but if The Professor's viewers heart me enough, they'll pressure him to break me out of the town's prison. Maybe Leo can even turn my rescue into the main plot of the next ep.

But only if the viewers think I'm worth the trouble. My brain is ringing and sputtering, but I know I must look brave now.

"The Professor got away," I taunt Shine, forcing my eyes to focus on his face. "I doubt Beacon will be pleased that you failed to capture him again." I try to laugh, but it comes out as a wheeze.

Shine gives me a tight-lipped smile. "I bet you know where his temporary lab is." He pulls, and the whip tightens around my waist. "Want to see what the highest shock setting does?"

"Iron!" Sequoia bellows somewhere behind me, but he sounds far away.

"Your little boyfriend won't be able to help you," Shine sneers.

My vision blurs and refocuses as I look past Shine. Something catches my attention, a figure slinking on the edge of the battle. He wears a tattered black leather jacket.

My heart freezes in my chest and every last molecule of oxygen evaporates from my lungs.

"Shadow," I whisper.

Shine laughs. "You don't think I'm going to fall for that."

I watch Shadow stroll around the battle, a wide smile on his face. A few others have seen him, and they fall back in fear. Shadow leisurely pulls his Molten Ax from the sheath across his back. Even from here, I can see its tip begin to glow with heat.

"No," I whisper. Shadow isn't like the rest. He won't

stop at a broken nose or busted lip. Shadow lives only for destruction and chaos.

Adan must see something in my expression, or maybe he feels how my body begins to tremble because he turns his head and follows my gaze. And then he drops me, his whip uncurling from my waist. I watch the flash of his orange-and-gold costume disappear into the fight as he plunges toward Shadow.

Shadow. Just as I remember him. His face smeared in black grease. Those throbbing red eyes glowing even in the midday sun. And the huge ax clutched in his boney hand.

He strolls with purpose.

Nearby, I catch sight of Beacon. She is a whirl of glinting arms and golden curls as she dispatches Cleopatra's last manservant with a beautiful roundhouse kick. The two others already lay at her feet and the high priestess is nowhere to be seen. Cleopatra clutches her short sword, ready for the fight that's been building between them for years.

Neither of them sees Shadow.

Not until he laughs. The sound seems amplified, coming from all corners of the Square. It rattles inside of me, echoing off my nightmares. And then he hurls his ax.

I think the weap must be aimed at Beacon, but the trajectory seems off.

And then I understand.

A few meters behind Beacon is the man she's been valiantly protecting throughout the entire fight. Ash Anders is on his hands and knees, hair disheveled, green coat torn. His gaze is intent on the ground, his hands brushing through the grass. As the Molten Ax hurtles toward him, he smiles, reaches into the grass, and grasps the pink seashell in his hand.

"ASH!" I cry.

"LOOK OUT!" Shine's voice overlaps mine. He shoves desperately toward the mayor, but he's too far away.

Ash Anders looks up, stares uncomprehendingly at the ax whirling at him, and then a flash of gold and scarlet blocks him from my vision.

In the hushed silence, we hear the cry that softens into a gurgle. We see Beacon stagger and then fall. Shadow's Molten Ax is embedded in her chest, but that can't be possible. Beacon's armor is nearly impenetrable. It's the very best money can buy.

And yet I'm close enough to see the ruby gush spilling over her costume as her hand flutters weakly at the ax handle. Shine stumbles toward her and falls to his knees next to her. He leans over her, his hand touching the handle of the ax and then shying away.

Ash Anders hasn't moved. His face is white.

The fighting has almost entirely stopped. Most of those still on their feet stand quiet and uncertain.

I watch as Beacon's hand slips off the ax handle and lays still on the ground.

No.

This can't be happening. Beacon is perfect. Immortal. In a world wracked with darkness and uncertainty, she has always been the light.

The Professor lands near Beacon, drops the jet pack off his back, and joins Shine to hover over her. A murmur breaks out among the heroes and vils. The cam drones are turning away from the others and swarming over Beacon like gnats.

"GET AWAY!" Shine screams at them, but they only cluster tighter. The Professor leans over Beacon, but after a moment, he sits back on his knees and shakes his head.

"No!" Cleopatra staggers forward. Her face is distraught. "No, No, No!" she keens. She rushes for Beacon. Shine stands up, catches her.

"NO, NO, NO!" she cries, her voice cracking. She tears herself out of his grip and stares at Beacon.

Numbly, I glance around, but Shadow has disappeared.

Cleopatra howls in agony, and it feels like her scream is loud enough to break open the sky.

CHAPTER 28

Dawn will always conquer the long night.
~ Beacon, S4, E12

~

That night the clouds roll in and unleash a heavy, drenching rain. The wind screams around us as we make our pilgrimage to The Hero statue. For two hours, the Big Little City Police only allow sponsored vils and capes into the Square so that we can commune with our fallen comrade and dutifully record our lamentations. At midnight they will pull away the barriers and open the Square to all. Already the crowds are gathering; pale, anxious faces set aglow by the screens of their Bands.

But for now, it is only us. The rain chills my skin as I stand at the base of the statue. She is a broken thing, her face cracked in half, that strong, protective arm, gone. The child grinning up at her seems vulnerable now, easy prey.

So many capes and vils come to the vigil. Most from the earlier brawl manage to make it, their arms in splints, noses puffy, and eyes black. One of Cleopatra's manservants sits in a wheelchair, but he stubbornly wheels forward to nudge a spot close to the statue's base. There are many others who weren't at this afternoon's fight, faces from shows swiped long ago. I recognize The Fat Tubist, The Map Collector, Wild Infinity, Vine, Feline Fatale, and more. Even Evil Santa makes his appearance surrounded by a gaggle of his Lunatic Elves, including Tickles who has served as my online mentor. When I see my henchman hero up close, Tickles looks pudgy and old, his jowls sagging and heavy lines stitched around his mouth. He's made no secret of his affinity for Mellows, and he's got that telltale glaze in his eyes.

The capes and vils lay tokens at the base of the statue. They murmur greetings to former allies and foes, and always their eyes dart around the Square. Even as torment rages through me, I catch myself scanning the darkness. Shadow is still out there, and a gathering of so many capes and vils in one place would be a rich target for him.

Just in front of the statue, Reena Masterson speaks softly to a cam drone and pulls capes and vils aside for hushed interviews. The air is filled with cam drones. Every Persona with a current show will certainly include a scene of themselves paying homage at the statue, most likely followed by a lengthy reflection on the day's events and Beacon's impact on the city from the comfort of their lair or headquarters. Leo has already requested such an interview with The Professor, and I know at least two of the cam drones hovering above us belong to our show.

RTS – Ride the Storm. No matter how terrible.

The bouquets and wreaths the others place against the statue are glorious. Many include real flowers. The Professor's token is simple by comparison, but he worked on it all night. A little track rings his wreath and a small magnetic train chugs round and round. The colors of the train and the tiny letters painted on its side are familiar. It's the BLC Express, the site of The Professor's first major battle with Beacon. That victory made Beacon a name in this town. Now that little train will always stay on the track, will always be safe.

I feel a small, wry smile curve my lips as I remember what Adan told me. Beacon was never supposed to be on that train. She found out about The Professor's plans and stood against him, grabbing all the fame that was originally meant for some other cape.

And from that day on, Beacon was... everything. She was the town's protector. She was beautiful and righteous and always had smiles for the children and tourists. Just a flash of scarlet and gold could send villains shrinking in fear.

She was unbeatable. Unbreakable. Immortal.

Until she wasn't.

Until now.

As I look at the mangled statue, I feel shattered too. And so afraid.

Shine stands in front of the statue, chin up, shoulders back, as he accepts condolences from our town's most fearsome villains and greatest heroes alike. His costume sets the raindrops and puddles around him aglow, and in this moment he truly looks like a hero. When The Professor shakes his hand, I stay behind him with my fellow henchmen. Lysee stands at Shine's side, shivering in her thin costume. Her purple hair hangs in dripping rivulets around her face. I manage to meet her eyes once and she quickly turns her face away. And then The Professor is marching away from Shine and from the statue. I have no choice but to follow.

Our vigil is over.

*

When we arrive back at Sequoia's house, The Professor retreats to the master bedroom and slams the door. Leo's cam drone hovers in front of it, drinking in the poignant moment. In the living room, Mermaid drops onto the couch. Gold briefly disappears into the kitchen and returns with an ice pack, which he places gently on her swollen ankle. They speak together in hushed voices. Apparently they both turned in strong performances during today's brawl, starting with Mermaid's brave dive in front of The Professor to absorb Ash Anders's laz shot. She was able to rouse herself just in time for the big fight and took on several members of the Glory League, coming out with only a sprained ankle and broken finger.

Gold claimed he tagged Lobo with his laz pistol and survived a tussle with Hummingbird. He looks mostly unscathed, though I notice a long scratch down his cheek, and several gold beads are missing from his dreads.

I turn away from the living room and head to the guest bedroom. As I pass the office, I see Sequoia sitting inside, Kitty's head cradled gently in his lap. The left side of his face is bruised, his lip is cut and swollen. I remember catching glimpses of him slugging it out with one of the Dragon Riders, desperately trying to protect The Professor.

I lean against the doorway wishing I could offer him an ice pack as a token of peace. Somehow I doubt he'd accept it. Sequoia has peeled away the synthetic skin from Kitty's face and is working to reconnect her eye into its socket.

"I hope you can get her up and running," I say, and he

starts at my voice. "I've actually grown fond of her."

Sequoia looks down at Kitty. His wet lab coat is crumpled in the corner of the room, his goggles tossed carelessly on top of it. It feels like forever since I've seen his full face, all those scattered freckles and stormy blue eyes.

"Yes, me too," he finally says. I can see the pain inside of him, the pain I caused, and no ice pack will fix that. I don't know how to convince him I'm not worth the trouble or heartache.

So instead, I just say, "Shining luck," and it comes out as a hoarse whisper. He doesn't respond.

In the guest bedroom, I close the door behind me and pull off my wet lab coat. Every movement causes pain. I've re-injured my shoulder and my ribs are bruised. I unclip the bowtie from my neck and un-buckle my belt. Slowly, hissing in pain, I peel off my shirt and pants and then step out of my underwear. I stand naked in front of the bed, a few cold drops of water running down my back from my braided hair.

My bruised, swollen body aches for sleep, but when I tuck myself under the covers all I can see is Shadow's face, that hideous grin, his ax hurtling through the air, and Beacon's hand slipping down into the grass.

I throw the covers back. I can't sleep. Won't sleep. Not until I'm so tired I can slip into a dreamless coma. But I can't stay in this stifling house either, not with Sequoia's hurt and Leo's cams both suffocating me. Goosebumps ride up my skin as I hook the wet bra around my chest and pull my soaked t-shirt back on. I struggle with my wet pants but finally manage to tug them on. I leave the lab coat, bowtie, belt, and goggles on the floor where they fell. When I go back out into the night, I am simply Alice Hannover. By now, the rain has lessened to a soft, cold drizzle. The moon offers a pale, diffuse glow behind the clouds.

I don't have any particular destination in mind, but I'm not surprised when my feet take me back to Iconic Square, back to The Hero statue, now crowded with thousands of townies and tourists, with more pouring in every min.

They fill the square, swamping the statue. Tears stream down their faces. They clutch replica Light Blades and Aura Arcs. Many wear t-shirts stamped with the lighthouse emblem. Others are dressed as Beacon, in cheaply printed costumes and tinny helmets. A tall, black woman next to me throws back her head and wails like it was her own sister torn so brutally from life. I can't get close to the statue anymore, but I don't mind. I just need to be here. To absorb and reflect the pain.

It strikes me, how much Beacon meant to this city and its people. Sure, we might be a semi-reality town, but the emotions around me are real and raw. For the first time since I moved here, I feel connected to my fellow townies. I see the true part of them in the tears on their cheeks.

I may have despised everything Beacon stood for, but her loss is like an open wound inside of me. She was part of the fabric of this place.

Big Little City. My city.

I stand in the chill, shivering for a long, long time knowing that eventually, I'll need to turn around and go home. No, not home. To Sequoia's house. My Band buzzes. I look down. A new message from Alby. This time it's just a single emoji. A little lighthouse.

Growing up, we used to watch the shows that came out of Biggie LC. Alby was always a fan of the villains, but I cheered on the heroes.

Love you, Twinly One, I send back to him.

Just as I make up my mind to leave, a voice speaks near my ear.

"Alice. Hello. Wow. There are a lot of people here. It isn't safe. Not with Shadow still at large."

I turn to the figure who has walked up next to me. Ollie sports the black eye I gave him.

"Hello," I manage.

"Beacon is dead," he says and shakes his head in that strange manner that I'm starting to recognize shows his anxiety. "This is unprecedented. And it serves as definitive proof that Shadow is not sponsored. He must be a rogue agent."

"Then why haven't the police caught him?" I ask numbly.

Ollie nods at me. "My fellowship and I have considered this question thoroughly, and we believe he might be receiving assistance from someone with resources. Someone with the means to shelter and protect him."

This is a new idea. I turn to him. "Who? Why?"

"I am not sure yet, but I am investigating the matter fully."

I grimace. "That sounds dangerous."

"Someone has to stop him." Ollie glances at me for just a moment and then his head bobs down, but I see the conviction in his eyes. I've failed. I tried to scare, hurt, and humiliate him into giving up his lobotomy crusade to be a hero. But, if anything, he seems more dedicated, more fervent.

He will keep fighting, and perhaps the next wreath will fall on his grave.

I feel so helpless. So empty. All I can do is wrap my arms around Ollie and pull him into a hug. His body stiffens and he stands awkwardly.

"Please try to be safe," I tell him.

"Ah, I see," he says, backing away as soon as I let him go. "Then, we are friends?"

I shiver in the cold. "Of course we're friends."

Ollie looks past me. "I wasn't certain. Your behavior is... confusing. And inconsistent."

"We're friends," I insist.

He nods once. His face is pale in the glow of the streetlights. "Then I will give you the same warning. Be safe. If you need help, please contact me. I will protect you from harm." He thinks on this statement. "I will try to protect you from harm," he amends.

I smile at him. The light mist of rain hides my tears. "Thank you," I whisper.

He nods. "I must return to the pharmacy. Requests for anti-anxiety medications have been significantly above average today. My father is keeping the store open all night." He begins fighting his way back through the crowd then pauses, turns back, and says, "Ta, Alice. I shall see you in class when school resumes."

I hold up a limp hand. My throat is so tight I can't speak. When Ollie is gone, I turn and begin working my way out of the crowd. Just as I finally break through the swell of weeping, shivering masses, some recording sniveling vids of themselves, I spot a familiar figure. He stands alone, back from the edge of the crowd, observing all the people.

Adan is soaked to the bone. He must have been out

here for hours. His face is pale, his lips almost colorless, and he shivers. When I walk up to him, he glances down, notes my presence, and then resumes his vigil. He wears the shirt covered in zippers again. This is the first time I've ever seen him repeat an article of clothing.

"They really love her," I say. The words feel drooling and inadequate.

"She was impossible to work with," he says quietly. "She planned everything so meticulously, all the scenes of her eps, her interviews. She even gave me lines to say sometimes." He chuckles, a soft note with no power in it. "She would go ballistic if I tried to grab too much lens time, if she thought I was preening in an interview. She was always paranoid I would spin off."

"And you did."

"And I did," he agrees. "When I found out that PAGS dropped her, I knew I would be dead as steering wheels if I stayed." He smiles, but the expression is all pain. "But then she and The Professor came up with the brawl. It was brills. She would get Ash Anders and even take down Cleopatra, for the time being, of course. She had to pull some serious strings, but she got Cleo on board too."

"The brawl was planned?" I suddenly feel so drooling slow. Of course it was. I had known The Professor's end, all the pings and messages and calls he made to the other vils last night. But how could Beacon have mustered all her allies unless she was in on the scheme too?

"Course." Adan looks at me with a little pity. "Something like that doesn't come together organically." He gazes at the crowd. "She would have been back on top after the fight. Saving the Mayor of Chicago would have been Iconic. And all the heroes would have owed her a favor for letting them get in on the action. PAGS would have had no choice but to sponsor her again."

"It's like the BLC Express," I say. Beacon made her own story, her own destiny no matter what PAGS wanted. I shake my head, impressed.

And then Adan begins to cry. He does it softly at first, his breath sending tendrils of steam into the air. Tears glisten at the corners of his green eyes, matching the raindrops already quivering on his cheeks.

"She could be kind," he whispers. "When it mattered. When the cams were off, she could be kind. And she believed in it, you know? Really believed."

"Believed in what?" I ask softly.

His crying isn't quiet anymore. He tries to speak, but only hiccupping sobs escape. I open my arms. Adan folds into me as if seeking shelter. His shoulders are so broad I can barely get my arms all the way around him. In this moment I wish I were big as the billowing clouds overhead so I could wrap Adan in my embrace, so I could warm him up, so I could protect him from the pain.

He gathers himself quickly. The sobs quiet, but his body still trembles. "She believed in being a hero," he finally says, his voice cracking. "It wasn't just about the ratings or the money. She wanted to give people hope."

This is when I make a decision—one I should have made long ago.

Adan pulls out of my arms and turns his face away. Our moment is over.

"Sorry," he says.

I look over at the statue, giving him space to collect himself. The temp is dropping fast, but more people keep coming.

"What happens now?" I ask softly.

Adan straightens his spine and pushes his shoulders back. "Now we find a new hero," he says. His voice is still torn, but it sounds strong. "And we destroy Shadow."

"Shining luck," I tell him and I mean it. But I won't be part of that mission. Without another word, I shove my hands into my pockets, turn, and walk out of the Square. I need to see The Professor. I need to tell him that I'm not strong enough to play the Fame Game. I can't bear all this loss and pain, all the betrayal I've already dealt to my friends.

I have no heart to be a henchman and I never did. It's time to quit, no matter the consequences.

CHAPTER 29

You're a henchman. You will lose. ~ Tickles the
Elf, The Henchman's Survival Guide

~

When I return to Sequoia's home, I find my friend
asleep on the couch, softly snoring. No surprise that he
left the guest room open for me and took the couch.
I douse the light from my Band, and my heart cracks
a little at the thought of leaving him. Will we still be
friends when I'm no longer part of the henchman team?

He doesn't want to be your friend anymore, anyway, a
nasty thought whispers in my mind. That's right. I'd almost forgotten the hurt in his eyes this afternoon, the
coldness in his voice.

Worry drips through me as if the chilling rain found
a way into the hollows of my bones. Sequoia will need
to toughen up now that I won't be around to look
out for him. How will he survive with Gold and Mermaid scheming around him, grabbing all his lens time?
Would they push him out? No, more likely they'll use
him to forward their own ends.

I look at Sequoia's sleeping face, all those freckles,
that big warm heart filling him up. I need to find a way
to repair our friendship so I can keep teaching him,
keep guarding him against Gold's and Mermaid's worst
instincts.

I cross the living room meaning to head straight to bed in the guest room. I'll speak with The Professor in the morning. But as I tiptoe down the hallway, I see a soft spill of light flickering from beneath the door of the master bedroom. Should I talk to the boss now? Probs not, but I find myself at the door, fist raised to knock. It's better to just get it over with, or I might chicken out tomorrow morning when I consider the empty depths of my bank account.

My fist raps softly on the door.

No response. I'm just about to turn and slink to the guest bedroom when a voice says, "Come in."

I turn the knob and enter the room. The Professor sits on the big bed on top of the covers. His goggles are gone, but he still wears his damp lab coat and even his scuffed black boots. Light flickers across his face, and I see a Pod sitting on the floor projecting a holo-screen on the wall.

The screen shows a closeup of The Professor's face. He wears a wicked grin and a huge pair of goggles that blink with spastic colors. The cam pans downward. A small, slender boy with black hair and identical goggles says something, and The Professor laughs and ruffles his hair. There is no volume to the video so I can't hear his words.

Matthew. The boy is Matthew. No, not Matthew. Energy, The Professor's child sidekick. On screen, The Professor frowns and turns his head. The cam pulls back. I recognize the old antiques sitting in large cases on pedestals. They're in the Grand Museum. The Professor clutches some old relic, one of those laptops, under his arm. Now the cam swings to the entrance of the museum. A figure stands, silhouetted in the doorway. Back to The Professor. He says something and pulls a strange, disc-like contraption from inside his lab coat.

The figure steps out of the light. It's Beacon. Her costume is generations old, a pale yellow crossed with pinkish slashes, so different from the rich scarlet and gold hues of her most current costume. That lighthouse emblem on her chest is as recognizable as ever, though.

"I'd almost forgotten about this ep," I say to The Professor.

"It wasn't one of our more noteworthy clashes," he agrees. On screen, The Professor throws the disc, and it begins to pour clouds of gas as it whirls through the air. Beacon clutches at her eyes and falls to her knees.

"That gas was harmless," The Professor says and chuckles, "but Beacon came up with the idea of it blinding her."

"That's right," I say, remembering now. "She was 'blind' for a few months. The docs told her it could be permanent." It'd been big news at the time, splashed across all the gossip Streams. By then, I was old enough to know those stories were mostly fake, so I hadn't paid much attention.

On screen, Beacon waves away another person who stands uncertainly in the doorway of the museum. I think it might be Bright, her sidekick who eventually turned into Cleopatra. Now, Beacon unties the pink sash from her waist. She wraps it around her eyes and beckons The Professor forward.

"It was her idea for the brawl today," The Professor says. "Brilliant of course. In the past, our teams would spend months haggling over the details, but she contacted me directly." He shakes his head with a shadow of a smile. "Don't even know how she got access to my private Stream, but she did and she knew about Ash Anders even before we released the hostage video."

I look at my boss's face. His eyes are red. So is the tip of his nose. The lines of his face seem carved more deeply in his skin. There is no maniacal laughter inside of him. No gloating. No evil schemes hatching. I see only pain. A friend lost. And maybe I see a little fear as well.

"It was a grand fight, wasn't it?" The Professor looks to me, a strain of desperation in his voice.

"Yes, it was."

"Everything was going perfectly. We agreed that I would get away, but she would rescue Mr. Anders. And I believe she had some ongoing negotiations with Cleopatra about a different storyline." His voice meanders off. "It was all going so well..."

On screen, The Professor points a gun at Beacon and shoots. She falls to the floor, clutching her shoulder. The Professor shoots again and she curls in on herself. And then suddenly, her sidekick—yes, it is Bright—cartwheels through the museum entrance, over Beacon's shivering body on the floor. Bright wears a pair of goggles. A henchman's goggles, I realize, and now she kicks the gun out of The Professor's hand.

"I remember how this one ends," I say. "You and Bright tussle. She's about to beat you, but then Energy throws you his ray gun and you stun her. You think you've won and start gloating..."

"But then Beacon stands up. She's weak, shaking, but she holds the laptop in her hands," The Professor says, his voice raw and catching in his throat. "She threatens to smash it."

"A stalemate," I say.

"Yes. She trades me the laptop for Bright." The Professor closes his eyes, "and she's holding her Light Blade in one hand. I decide the fight isn't worth it, so Energy hops in my arms, and I use my copter blades to rise up and crash through the skylight to freedom."

I find myself smiling. In Beacon's episode, the last scene of the ep showed her standing over Bright, heaving in breaths as blood trickled from beneath the sash tied around her eyes. It was beautiful, epic, and perfectly planned—just like everything Beacon did.

"She was amaze," I say.

"Yes. A worthy opponent in every way and a good friend." The Professor's eyes are glazed, and they look past me to the screen where the action continues to unfold. "It should have been grand. The fight today. A pinnacle for us both."

He looks so lost. So sad. Like he doesn't recognize the world any longer.

"Goodnight, Professor," I say softly.

"If only it were, my element. My girl of the iron will," he says.

My will is anything but iron, which is why I turn away with my own words unsaid. I will give him my notice tomorrow when the sun finally washes away this terrible night.

After I close the door to The Professor's room I only make it two steps toward my own when a voice speaks up.

"Where did you sneak off to?"

I turn. Leo leans against the doorway of the office. Of course he would be here. His apartment is compromised, just like my own. Shine's escape feels so long ago and so small.

"I went back to The Hero. As myself. I wanted to do that alone."

"A shame. If you'd kept on your costume, that might have been good footage," he says. "I could have caught your sensitive side. Viewers like that about you."

"That's all you can think about? The show?" I'm too tired to even feel angry. All I dredge up is disappointment.

"The viewers appreciate that you're complex."

Leo's changed into new clothes, a simple green shirt and jeans. Sequoia must have printed them on his 3D. He's also grabbed a shower. He looks clean, fresh, and handsome, but that doesn't mean anything. It can't mean anything.

I wrinkle my nose. "I hate what you do."

"But you don't hate me. That's an improvement." He gives me a small smile.

Heat kindles in my chest and it humiliates me. I imagine running my hand through Leo's honey-brown hair, kissing the smooth skin of his jaw. How can I even be thinking these things after everything that's happened today? When Beacon is dead and legions of her fans are shivering in the rain just three kilometers away?

"I have something for you," Leo says and retreats into the office. I move across the hallway toward his door. Inside, three holo-screens hover above his desk, each filled with multiple tiles. Cam angles, I realize. There's a frozen shot of The Professor laughing. Another of Ash Anders pointing a gun at The Professor. I even see one of myself chasing Anders, my braid suspended in the air, mid-stride. One still image in the far corner draws my eyes. In it, Beacon stands on the rooftop of the bank. She looks strong and beautiful.

"I think you'll appreciate this." Leo turns to me, his brown eyes peering into mine. It takes me a moment to look down at the object in his hand. When I first moved to Biggie LC, I'd never seen a check before except in the old historicals. Everyone pays by direct cryptocurrency transfer these days, usually with Loons. Not in Biggie LC. Everyone, from the waitress at the diner to henchmen and sidekicks, is required to cash real checks at the bank for paper dollars. It gives vils a clear target to hit, something real to steal from townies.

"Your first paycheck," Leo says, since I've been staring at him mutely.

"Uh, thanks." I take the square of paper stamped with printed letters and numbers. Those numbers are important. This will be enough to get me through my current semester at school and renew Alby's therapy program for another month.

I laugh. "I tried out for the show because I needed money to get my degree so I could actually start helping people," I tell him. "But all I've managed to do is hurt the people I care about most." It doesn't matter what I say to Leo now. I don't need to impress him or play a part.

Leo is quiet for a few moments, and my weak laugh hangs between us. Finally, he says, "Helping people is dangerous work." He looks over his shoulder. I follow his gaze. There, sitting on the desk is the blurry pic of the skinny children.

So that's what Leo went back to his apartment for after I freed him from Lysee's grasp.

"What were you doing there? In Tanzania?" I ask.

Leo smiles and his eyes are so sad. "You could say I

was trying to help people."

I shiver, but I hardly feel the wetness of my clothes. I hear only the ice in his voice.

"Tell me," I say because I have nothing to lose.

Leo glances at me, and I notice that his face is drawn. It strikes me that he must have spent the whole night stitching together our next ep, which is due tomorrow... no, technically today. Normally, it would have been enough to showcase our kidnapping of Ash Anders and call it a day, but with Beacon's death echoing across the entire world, everyone will be rushing to push out their own eps of the brawl.

Leo would have had to capture everything—Anders's kidnapping, Shine's escape, my showdown with Lysee, the brawl, and finally the impromptu memorial —all in a single ep. I wonder if he negotiated with the City Council to make it a double ep. I'm sure they'd be glad to give him the extra Stream time.

He must have been working all afternoon and all night on the eps. How long did he edit and cut the scene of Beacon's death for maximum shock value and trauma? How many mins and hours did he take to carefully sculpt our devastation at the memorial? He's spent the whole night stewing in those images of death, all that genuine fear and pain. They've worn him down. I can see it. And I can see something else.

Leo is sad.

"I used to produce news," he says softly. "Real news. Not gossip. We reported on stories across the world."

"Even in Tanzania?" I ask.

"Yes." Leo turns and walks to the desk. He picks up the framed picture and holds it gently in his hand as if it were the most delicate thing in the world. "This was taken four years ago. The Arabian Vanguard was trying to cleanse the rebel insurgency with bombing campaigns. They claimed it was a massive success, but we heard rumors they were bombing civilians, desperate to show they were accomplishing something. We tried to get the story out." He tucks the photo closer to his chest as if it somehow needs protecting.

"We were a small crew. Me, a reporter, a cameraperson, and a freelance photographer who kept crowding in on our story." His face softens and he looks down at the picture. "This was the last photo she ever took. The village was hit during a raid." He looks at me. "I was off in the woods taking a piss. That's the only reason I survived."

"Lucky piss," I say.

"Was it?" He gently places the photo back on the desk, and this is when I know I've been right about Leo all along. He is broken. Just like me. That's what I recognized in his eyes the first moment I met him. The agony of the survivor. This is why I've been drawn to him.

He doesn't say it, but I know he loved that photographer. He's so handsome and poised that I bet she loved him back. Maybe they dreamed of saving the world together, or at least that little village full of skinny children.

"After that happened, they started sending robos and drones to report in war zones," Leo is saying. "Not that they even report much international news anymore. Poor ratings." He gives me a crooked smile that is so sad my heart nearly shatters.

All I want to do is take a step forward, tilt my face, and kiss away all his pain, but some instinct warns me off. He's still hurting, still grieving.

He loved her. Not me.

And so I look down at my feet and mumble, "I'm sorry."

"Me too."

"What was her name?" I ask, "The photographer."

His voice is so quiet I'm not even sure he knows he says the words out loud. "Ella-Ann."

Ella-Ann. I feel like I can almost see her, a spark in Leo's eye, the sad twitch of his smile. I wonder if she was beautiful. I bet she was.

I mumble a few more pointless words and then duck out of the office, away from that tragic photograph and all those frozen shots of our fight, including that singular image of Beacon so alive. I look at the door to the guest bedroom but I can't go in.

I can't stay here. All of me is trembling and cracked.

My feet move. I pass The Professor's door where the faint light still flickers beneath and then cross through the living room where Sequoia sleeps in peaceful bliss. The air is cold outside, but the rain has stopped. The clouds are parting, and a sliver of moon sits low on the horizon.

By the time I make it to the fancy, well-manicured neighborhood, my teeth chatter and my hands ache with cold. I knock on Adan's door knowing he would never be drooling enough to come back to his house. Even if he was here, he wouldn't be awake at this hour or inclined to open his door to some lobotomy person with the audacity to knock instead of ping him through his Band like a normal human being.

But he is home, and he is awake, and he does open his door, because suddenly he's standing in front of me shivering in his damp clothes just as I'm shivering in mine.

"You were dim to come back," I hiss at him. "I could have set traps. I could have told someone where you lived. The Professor."

"I trust you, Alice," he says simply. I thrust myself into his arms. He leans down to kiss away my hurt and I kiss away his.

We cling to each other as we stumble into his house, filling the other's despair, using our bodies so that our minds and souls can rest. We move through his living room, and there's a desperation in the way I tear that ridic zipper shirt off his muscled torso, how I put my mouth on his damp, cold skin. He said that he trusted me, and even as this is happening, I realize that I trust him, too. I couldn't do this otherwise.

I feel his need as he peels away my t-shirt, and his shivering fingers fumble with the zipper of my jeans. We totter into the bedroom, past a pleasant greeting from Martha, his house robo. He tosses me onto the big, soft bed, and then his body is pressing against mine, his hungry mouth on me.

Leo's face flashes through my mind, but I push it away. Leo doesn't want me, and even if he did, I couldn't do this with him. Not this way. Not with my fingers clawing at him with an almost panicked desire for release.

Adan and I use each other, our eyes agreeing without words. His hands press against the bruises he put across my body. I cry out, but I don't want him to stop. And then he's inside me, filling me, and I wrap my legs around him trying to press him in further, deeper. After he pulls away, the tips of his hair now dark with sweat, we move more slowly, languidly as we explore each other's bodies. I don't want to let go of him. I need the feel of his hot skin, the touch of his lips, the physical connection. There's some lobotomy part of me that believes as long as we're connected nothing can hurt us. Nothing else exists except the two of us in this bed.

But eventually my body begins to feel numb and heavy, and I lay with my head on his chest, listening to his heartbeat. We are quiet, and he gently strokes the small of my back, now careful to avoid my bruises.

Here. Forever here. Where shadows do not linger.

My Band buzzes on my wrist, pulling me from my drowse.

"No news," Adan says. "I don't want to see anything."

I turn the screen of my Band toward me and read the message Bob has sent. "You'll want to see this," I tell him.

With a little work, I sync my Band to the Pod in his room. Sitting up in bed, we watch the Phoenix shuttle hurtle down through the atmosphere of Mars. This is the most treacherous part of the journey, the phase where two previous shuttles burned to ashes.

I grip Adan's shoulder as we watch the shuttle miss its landing site and tumble roughly across the barren landscape. The shuttle comes to a halt in a plume of dust, and we wait six agonizing minutes until finally the voice of Thane-Ambrose Garcia, the shuttle's commander, crackles over the grainy satellite image.

"Houston, we got a little shook up and we have a few minor injuries, but The Phoenix has landed."

My heart squeezes painfully in my chest. Something is blooming inside of me. Something dangerous. It feels like hope, and it terrifies me.

Our first interstellar pioneers are on Martian soil,

ready to create a human colony on another planet.

A new start. A new day.

I can't help myself. I yelp with joy and feel tears prick to corners of my eyes.

"I didn't know you could do that," Adan says

"Cry? Of course I can cry," I tell him.

"No." He looks at me with a wide grin on his face. "I didn't know you could smile."

CHAPTER 30

The criminal known as Shadow is a threat to everything
that makes this city great. You have my word, he
will be captured and brought to justice. ~ Mayor
Grimbal Wisenberg, Press Conference

~

The desert finds me in my dreams. Burning sand crackles under my feet while the sun reigns in the sky overhead, its eye never turning away. In the dream, I am not a spindly teenager, and my brother, Alby doesn't stagger next to me, panting out futile reassurances. Instead, I am Beacon, except my costume is made of metal instead of a flexible, adaptable polymer complete with a highly intuitive temperature control interface.

The metal costume heats, and I begin to cook inside. It sears my skin. Burns. But I can't take it off and reveal my identity to the world. And so I walk through the endless, rocky dunes. My tongue swells. My eyes are dulled by the cascade of white light. One little cam drone buzzes overhead recording my pain. Around the world, audiences watch in delight. They wait for me to die.

I shudder awake. For a moment, I don't know where I am. I expect to find gritty sand beneath my cheek, but I feel only the softness of an adaptable gel pillow.

J Bennett

"Shhhh," a voice says somewhere in the darkness, and an arm hugs me in close to a warm body.

My muscles tense, and then I remember. Shine. Adan.

"Bad dream?" he asks. I turn in his arms. I can only see the outline of his face in the darkness, liquid eyes, frown lines puckering his forehead.

"No," I lie.

"Sure seemed like it." His voice contains no cobwebs of sleep. Those eyes are bright and awake, staring at my face.

My heartbeat is slowing, my eyes growing heavy. My body aches for more sleep, and I feel myself slipping back down. Fuzzy thoughts drift through my mind like delicate bubbles. But even as sleep struggles to claim me again, I know what we did was a mistake. I shouldn't be here. Especially with him. Yet, I snuggle closer into his body where it feels safe. Where he will protect me from my nightmares.

"I still despise you," I lie, the words sticky on my tongue as my eyes sink close.

I feel laughter rumble through his chest. His lips press lightly on my temple. "I know. Go back to sleep."

And I do.

***

When I blink awake next, sunlight pours into my room.

Blight! I've got school. I rocket up into a sitting position, and then I remember.

Beacon is dead.

I'm at Adan's house, in his bed. Classes were canceled today.

The Phoenix.

I smile then remember something else. Soft words spoken in the night. A gentle kiss at my temple. The feeling of safety. I look over, but the other side of the bed is empty and already neatly made. What does it mean? Where do we go from here? Instead of dealing with those questions, I shake my Band, and Bob peers out at me with a skeptical expression.

"What?"

"How is the Phoenix doing?"

Bob yawns and takes his sweet time compiling a file filled with vids, articles, and recordings from the crew. "Long story short, the settlers made it to Martian Biosphere 6. There are reports of eight broken bones, eleven sprains, and two concussions from the landing, but other than that, everyone's okay. Thane-Ambrose Garcia is set to hold a press conference in three hours. The settlers have already started harvesting the garden and have even made a loaf of bread. Want to see the recipe they used?"

I shake my head. It's enough to know that they're safe and beginning their new lives on a foreign planet, something that has seemed just beyond our grasp for so long.

Such risk. Such courage.

Now it's time I show a little courage of my own. I slip out of bed and notice that my clothes are folded neatly on top of Adan's fancy dresser. When I pull on my shirt, I can tell it's been cleaned. The armpits smell like unicorns and angel smiles.

I'm guessing that Martha, Adan's house robo, had something to do with this. Not that I'm complaining. Clean clothes beat dragging still-damp, stinky jeans over my legs. I visit the bathroom and when I look in

J Bennett

the mirror I laugh at the bruises on my body and my messy hair. I can't do anything about the bruises, but I run my fingers through my hair, breaking the worst knots.

And then it's time to face Adan. The thought of sneaking out is tempting, but I'll see him in chemistry class eventually, so best not to leave things any more awkward than they already are. And there's something else. Adan was kind to me. I keep wanting him to be an arrogant, empty striver, but he's not. He has a heart, and I suspect that heart's bigger than I've ever given him credit for.

I find him in his too-perfect living room, pacing as he speaks softly into his Band. His dark head is bowed, his face serious. He's in uniform, his costume dazzling this close, but he doesn't wear his helmet. Sweetheart sits on his shoulder, proudly displaying her gorgeous silver chest and indigo wing feathers. Adan glances up at me and then back down to his Band.

"I need to go. Can I ping you back shortly?"

"We have a lot to do," the voice on the other end of the chat says. The words are barely perceptible. Adan's lux Wyvern Band clearly includes audio focus capabilities. Yet even that soft murmur sounds familiar.

"I know. I'll call back soon." Adan ends the call and looks to me. "I was expecting you to sneak out."

I walk into the room and sit on the edge of his fancy couch. "I almost did, but..."

"Did you want breakfast? Well, I guess it would be lunch. Martha can make you something."

I shake my head. "I didn't mean to interrupt you."

"It's fine. I need a break anyway. Things have been... moving fast." He sits down on the other end of the couch. Sweetheart walks to his other shoulder and trills a soft, perfectly pitched note. He strokes her head.

Of course Adan would be busy. Beacon's death will create a huge power vacuum. Biggie LC will need a new top hero. Everyone will be fighting for that role—The Crusader, the remaining Dragon Riders, Lobo... and Adan.

I know I shouldn't be surprised by how quickly he's trying to step into the boots of his mentor. That's just the Fame Game. *You see an opportunity, you grab it,* Tickles the Elf says on his blog. *And you don't let it go. Sometimes you only get one chance for glory.*

Now, the biggest prize of all is up for grabs. The fight will be ruthless.

I stand up. "I'm not hungry," I say coldly. I remember the suffocating crowds circling the statue of The Hero last night and Adan's tears. He really did love her. I believe that, but it won't stop him from taking her place.

"You sure?" Adan's eyes are questioning.

"I just wanted to say goodbye before I left, and thanks for last night." I feel myself blushing. "I was in a bad place."

"We both were," Adan says.

I look into his green eyes, and my emotions tumble inside me. Adan's eyes, but Shine's glowing costume. How can I admire, even care for one and hate the other?

"Alice..." he begins.

"Shining luck on taking Beacon's place."

"There's more at play than just that," Adan says. He sounds tired.

"I'll see you in chem." I turn and walk through the pristine kitchen. Martha greets me, but I ignore her offer of food and slip through the back door.

**

First, I walk to The Professor's mansion. Matthew isn't in his penthouse, though Betty still rests in the corner. With some struggle and more than a few unladylike grunts, I manage to drag her to the charging port inside a hallway closet. At least when Matthew returns she'll be ready for him.

I send him yet another vid message begging him to ping me back so we can meet. I'm sure he'll ignore this one too.

My apartment is similarly empty. I've sent almost as many messages to Lysee as I have to Matthew, and she hasn't responded. When I open the kitchen cabinet to grab a nutra-pack, I see that all her special shakes and powders are gone. The bathroom looks so different without her paste-on jewels, glowing lipsticks, and shimmery skin powders lined up like soldiers along the sink. I don't really need to, but I step inside her room. The bed, dresser, and nightstand are still there, but the clothes, jewelry, Pod, personal cam drone, and massive skin rejuvenating system are all gone.

I stand in front of her dresser and look into the mirror, which automatically reshapes my proportions so I look like a skinny, doe-eyed model. A holo-note blinks on in the corner.

Be a hero today, it says.

I sit on the couch and send another apology vid to Lysee. "I will always be your friend," I say, my voice shaking, "even if you no longer want to be mine." I even add a little emoji of a squirrel holding a heart at the end of the message so she'll see how despo I am to make things right.

I don't really have anywhere to go, so I wander to

Iconic Square, wondering if I can deposit the paycheck in my pocket. Thankfully, it seems that Martha took it out before washing my pants and then replaced it again. Even before I get close to the center of the Square, I can see the crowd. There must be tens of thousands of mourners now filling up the entire Square. All of them are here to say goodbye to Beacon.

It hits me then. Beacon was a hero. A real, true hero. She touched lives. She gave people hope.

Biggie LC, my town, my home, doesn't feel the same without her.

Bob pings my Band with a flagged story. "I thought you might like to see this," he says.

I play the vid. Ash Anders, now neatly groomed and finally in a new suit, black with scarlet slashes—a clear homage to Beacon—stands at a podium and announces the creation of a new commission in partnership with the mayors of eight major cities to look at PAG's practices to see if there might be another way to hold them legally accountable for the injuries and deaths their shows promote.

Ash Anders looks into the cam, directly at me, it seems. "We must take back our reality," he bellows and pounds his fist on the podium.

A new message dings on my Band. The Professor requests my presence for a meeting in three hours. I feel myself smiling grimly. I need to tell him I'm quitting the show. I've been delaying all day, but I can't hold off any longer.

I leave the edge of the Square and start toward our temporary hideout. Time to bow out of the Fame Game once and for all.

CHAPTER 31

Justice is a beacon shining in the night, banishing the shadows. ~ Beacon, S1, E2

~

That evening I regretfully button up my scarlet lab coat and stick my feet into my boots. I throw my hair into a messy braid tied with a white bow and hook my lasso on my belt. Finally, I slip Lysee's cracked, smoky goggles over my eyes. This will be my last time in this uniform.

All afternoon, The Professor has been locked away in Sequoia's master bedroom, his voice rising and falling. From my position standing outside the door waiting for an audience, I could hear his footsteps ceaselessly pacing. And then an hour ago he burst out of the room, waving me away and chanting, "No time! No time!"

A rental car promptly pulled up outside and whisked him away without any further explanation. Even Gold doesn't seem to know what's happening, though he's reported lots of whispers in his network of contacts. The capes and vils are moving, testing the waters, making their plans.

Leo def knows something. His face is a sea of calm while Mermaid and Gold frown and whisper to each other. I have been making plans as well. After whatever this meeting is, I will announce to The Professor that I am leaving the show. I'll be gracious about it, allowing him and Leo to plan my exit as they see fit. Maybe they'll have me get captured during our next mission, or I'll screw something up and The Professor will fire me in some huge blow-up. Maybe they'll even "kill" me off, though I wonder if that's wise after Beacon's real death.

I haven't figured out how I'll pay for school, but this paycheck will at least get me through the rest of the semester. One more year and I'll have my undergraduate degree. I also won't be able to afford Alby's expensive therapy program or the extra food rations I buy for my mom. I've been thinking about that. Maybe Alby doesn't need his program if I spend more time with him. That means more than a short message or vid every week. I could go out to the cargo encampment, go on hikes with him, really talk.

Other questions and fears percolate in my mind as I walk down the hall toward the living room. I'll need to leave Sequoia's house once I turn in my goggles and glowing bowtie. Lysee hasn't responded to my last apology even with the squirrel and heart emoji. I can't possibly afford the apartment by myself, especially since my landlord is about to become my ex-boss.

I'll figure something out. I always do. I've gotten this far on my own.

At the appointed hour of our meeting, I drop onto the couch next to Sequoia and offer him a small smile. He pretends to look out the window. From the loveseat, Gold catches my eye and raises an eyebrow.

Kitty skips into the room.

"Ta," she sings to us and offers a wide smile. She is

no longer the beautiful feline sex bot she once was. The left side of her face is crumpled inward, the ridge of her eye socket weirdly distorted. When she blinks, the left lid comes down more slowly than the right and doesn't fully cover her eye. At least her interface seems to be back online and cheerful as ever.

"Welcome back, Kitty," I tell her.

"I'm so glad to see you, too," she murmurs and flutters her lashes. The movement is more than a little unappealing, but I find myself smiling. Kitty is something unique now. A little dented. A little ugly. I feel like she's finally part of the team.

The team you'll be abandoning, a thought whispers in my head. Abandoning? No. Leaving. Just leaving. Something sparks through me. It feels like regret, but it can't be. We aren't really a team, a family… are we?

Mermaid walks into the room and stands next to the couch. Gold scoots over on the loveseat and pats the cushion, offering her a spot. She ignores him. Now it's my turn to catch Gold's eye and raise an eyebrow.

Hard to get, he mouths with a wily smile.

At last, Leo comes out of the office where he's been holed up all day. We already know that The Professor is gone.

"Outside," Leo says. "You're taking a trip."

As if on cue, two rental cars pull up outside the house. I look to Leo, a question in my eyes, but his face is a stoic mystery. I wonder if that photographer in Tanzania, Ella-Ann, could crack through his façade and make him smile. I bet she could.

We leave the house and I make a point of slipping in next to Sequoia as soon as he chooses a car. Not that I had any competition. Gold is practically clinging to

Mermaid like a magnet. Kitty stands, smiling, looking from car to car.

"That one," Gold tells her, motioning to our car. Kitty nods and walks to our car, swinging into the seat next to me. One cam drone floats into our car and settles on the dashboard. Another enters the second car. My guess is that the other drones in our fleet are with The Professor on his mysterious mission.

Our car starts, the electric motor almost silent as the seatbelts slide over us and click into place. Seatbelts are practically relics, and most cars don't even have them anymore. In most of the world, car crashes are almost unheard of, but here in Biggie LC you never know what's going to come hurtling across the road or screaming from the sky. That means seatbelts are still a requirement within city borders.

As our car begins moving, Sequoia makes a point to stare silently out the window. I have a lot of friendships to repair, so I might as well get started.

"What do you think's going on?" I ask him.

He shrugs.

I sit back in my seat.

"I think we're going to a picnic," Kitty says. "I hope it's a picnic."

"It's not going to be a picnic," Sequoia retorts. He sounds tired.

I lean over and peer at his hand. "Hmmmmm," I say. He shifts uncomfortably.

"Hmmmmmmmmmmm," I murmur again.

Kitty leans over and stares at Sequoia's hand. "Yes, he certainly does have big hands, doesn't he?" she tries to wink at me with her broken eyelid.

"Uh... sure, but that's not... that's not the curious

thing," I say, trying to recover.

"Oh? What is it?"

I smile at her, glad to have an unwitting partner in crime. "Well, you see that freckle on his knuckle?"

"Which one? He has many."

"On his index finger."

"Yes. I see it."

"I'm pretty sure it moved."

"Oh!" Kitty exclaims and then she frowns. "I don't believe freckles can move."

"See, that's what I thought too," I tell her, "but I'm pretty sure he didn't have a freckle on the knuckle of his index finger before."

"Stop it," Sequoia grumbles.

"I mean, that's pretty strange, right?" I ask. Out of the corner of my eye, I notice the lens on the cam drone in our car shift out of its auto-recording state.

"I'm reviewing my database of human conditions and illnesses," Kitty announces, "but I don't see any indications that freckles can move."

"Wow! So you're telling me that this is an all-new condition? Nitrogen, you're one-of-a-kind," I tell him.

"It didn't move," he grumbles.

"Are you sure?" I ask him. "Do you catalog all your freckles?"

"Yes, is there a database we can access?" Kitty asks. She leans over me and peers at Sequoia.

"Oh. Oh!" I cry and point his neck. "One of his freckles moved. I saw it. I swear!"

"They don't move!" Sequoia says finally turning to me.

"Of course not. That would be ridic," I say and smile.

"Then... then... why..." he splutters.

"Because now you're talking to me," I say, "and if I have to lie about moving freckles or pretend my appendix burst or that I personally know Bigfoot just to get your attention, I'll do it."

"Bigfoot is not real," Kitty pronounces and then lowers her voice, "unless we want to use our imaginations in a fun, fun way."

Ok, so robo wing-woman maybe wasn't such a brills idea.

"You're mad at me and I think I know why," I say, plowing ahead before Sequoia can freeze me out again. "And if I'm right, then I'm really sorry if I gave you the wrong idea."

"You... uh... it doesn't matter," Sequoia says as his cheeks flush. He glances at the cam. He's noticed the movement of the lens, too. Good. His cam instincts are getting better.

I wish I could tell him the truth. That's he too good for me. That I can't be trusted to hold his big, beautiful heart in my hands. All my jagged edges would cut it to pieces. But the cam and the world don't get to know that. Neither does Leo.

"I don't want to lose our friendship," I whisper to Sequoia. "It means a lot to me." I swallow. "But if you'd rather..."

"I'll be your friend," Kitty says to him in her sultry voice.

I let out a small laugh. "See, you've got a replacement Iron waiting in the wings."

"I don't want a replacement Iron," Sequoia says and sighs. "I was just hoping... but I guess..."

"Friendship is all I can offer, and maybe some help with good lines," I say.

Sequoia looks at me, all those freckles like a universe of stars mapped on his skin. His brow furrows as if he's struggling with some inner turmoil. Finally, he says, "A good henchman adapts to every situation, even when things don't turn out the way they want."

I recognize the quote from *The Henchman's Survival Guide.*

Sequoia continues. "If all you can offer is friendship, then I'd be a fool to turn it down."

I lean into his shoulder and smile. "I guess you don't need to work on your lines after all."

He nods and smiles, but the sadness still clings to him. It will take more time, more effort to get things back to the way they were between us, but I'll do whatever it takes.

"I accept your friendship as well," Kitty cries and wraps us both in a hug.

***

Our car brings us to Iconic Square and slows as it millimeters through the churning crowds of mourners. Many of them wear Beacon's helmet or different versions of her costume. It feels like Beacon is all around us, a thousand ghosts haunting the city she once protected so fiercely.

Eventually, we pull up in front of the Grand Museum behind a line of other cars. I turn in my seat and glance behind. More cars line up in back of us. Sequoia and Kitty open the doors and step out. Sequoia offers me his hand, and I take it gratefully.

Gold, Mermaid, and Leo step out of the second car, and our henchman team, plus producer convene on the sidewalk outside the museum. I immediately spot one of the Glitter Girls, a relatively new girl hero group, walking into the museum, her sequined skirt winking in the sunshine.

Next to me, Sequoia tenses, and I see Gold reach inside his lab coat for his gun.

"This is a parlay," Leo says. "No fighting."

We look at each other. A parlay? Yet another rare occurrence in Biggie LC. There hasn't been a cape-vil parlay in years.

Together, we enter the museum and follow a lighted path through a variety of rooms and displays. We walk past the wing for rare jewels, always good vil bait, then the wing for ancient relics, another vil hotspot. Several people stand in this room, many of them wearing expensive Goggs.

"And this is where I leave you," Leo says. "No producers in the main shots."

I look ahead to the next opening. So, something big is about to go down, or at least something worth recording.

"No fighting," Leo reminds us again. "Stay quiet, be good, and listen."

"I won't throw the first punch, that's all I'm promising," Gold says. There are clearly too many capes and sidekicks around here for his liking.

I give Leo one last questioning look to see if he'll reveal any more details, but he just makes a shooing motion with his hands. Our group moves forward into the next room, which is the museum's main atrium, dedicated to the history of Big Little City. The room is filled with holographic avatars of the sponsored heroes and villains who have prowled and protected our streets since the city's creation.

Between the vil and cape holograms, cases guard

their helmets, weapons, boots, and sigils. There's the Destroyer's real bionic arm. A 3D-printed replica of it used to hang over Table One at the Redemption Café where I worked. There's Evil Santa's hat and the tattered remains of Rudolph 16. I even see The Professor's notorious solar furnace sitting in the middle of a display dedicated to him, next to a pair of Energy's goggles and one of my boss's many mechanical ray guns. In the center of the room, atop a brand new pedestal, sits Beacon's glowing golden helmet. The lighthouse insignia on the helmet throbs with light.

People cluster uncomfortably in small groups, giving a wide berth to the pedestal. I recognize many faces and many costumes. Most of the vils from the Dark League are here. So is the youngest elemental, Gust. Two of the three Glitter Girls. I even see DeAngelo standing in the corner, his face still puffy from the recent battle.

All of these people were trying to tear each other to pieces just yesterday, and now we stand in small, tense groups, muttering to each other and casting baleful looks around while a cloud of cam drones hover above. Others walk in behind us, including Socket and Crank in their oil-slicked, jangling outfits and Hummingbird, her translucent mechanical wings folded against her back.

"This is strange," Gold says.

"It's been five years since Beacon brokered the second parlay in the history of Big Little City," Sequoia whispers to me. "That was only because a massive dust storm almost leveled the town and no one could record outside for over a week."

I nod. That happened a few years before I moved

here, but I remember the newscasts and how Beacon stood inside City Hall asking the vils and capes to put down their weapons and pick up shovels. Many of them did, using the filtration systems and extra strength offered by their expensive suits to help dig out the town so the shows could go on. The forecasts are predicting bad dust storms this summer. What'll happen then with no Beacon to bring the entire city together?

"So who called this parlay?" Mermaid asks. She gazes around the room but doesn't look perturbed like many of the others. I wonder what opportunities she sees in this gathering.

An elevated stage presides over the front of the room. This is where Mayor Wisenberg and other city officials gleefully unveil new treasures to be added to the museum. It's also where so many vils have dropped through the skylight, risen up from a trap door in the floor, or sent their minions scurrying on stage to grab the vil bait. Inevitably some cape would magically appear to stop them.

How many fights have taken place in this room? More than I can count. Probably half the vils and capes standing around us have committed or averted a heist here.

I catch movement and watch a brightly clad figure quietly make her way to the front of the room, near the stage.

Lysee.

I recognize her purple hair and the shape of her face beneath Shine's mask.

Wait... *Shine's mask*? Why is Lysee wearing Shine's mask? In fact, she's wearing a feminized version of Shine's costume, complete with a newly revealing neckline.

I take a step forward, intent on elbowing my way through the crowd to her, when spotlights flicker on, brightening the stage. The murmur of voices in the room dies down. Whatever machinations have been happening behind the scenes, we're about to find out what they are. I glance around, wondering if this is all some elaborate trap, but then why would both vils and capes be here?

A row of figures walks from behind a curtain onto the platform. I recognize Lobo and Titan, the leader of the Dark League. There's Rain, leader of the Elementals, Paladin from the Glory League with his arm in a sling, and most surprising of all, Evil Santa in his blood-red coat. Evil Santa was supposedly killed last year when he refused to let Beacon save him from falling down that industrial chimney.

Two more figures move through the curtain and make their way to the center of the platform. The others on stage fan out on both sides of them.

One of the figures standing in the center of the platform is The Professor.

The other is Shine.

Except Shine isn't wearing his old costume. Gone is the orange-and-yellow suit and the glowing lantern insignia in his chest plate. Instead, he wears a costume of flashing gold that seems to glow from within. Slashes of scarlet cut down the costume's arms and legs.

It's Beacon's costume. Sort of. Those are her colors, her helmet, her boots, but I notice now that the shades of the costume are slightly darker. The design is also shifted to more masculine lines that show off Adan's muscles and wide shoulders. The emblem on Adan's chest, though, is unmistakable. He wears the light-house insignia—the call of Beacon.

The effect is staggering. I hear gasps in the crowd and even wrought cries. Some are playing for the cams, but I suspect others are not.

"Impressive," Mermaid says next to me. "No one will be able to fight his claim as the next Beacon after this."

"Thank you for coming," says Shine, "and thank you for abiding by the parlay." He speaks slowly, his deep voice moving across the crowd. "Yesterday our town lost its greatest hero. Many of us also lost a friend." He pauses as if to hold back tears. It's a touching, tender moment, and I can't tell if it's real or not. With Adan, maybe it's both at the same time.

"We all have questions," he continues. "What happens now? Will one of us be Shadow's next victim? I suspect some of our more villainous attendees may also be wondering if this is the perfect time to strike Big Little City."

"The thought had crossed my mind," The Professor says. He takes a step forward, leaning heavily on his cane. "But let me just say that as long as Shadow still roams our streets, we are all at risk. He does not pick sides. He does not play by the rules. He hurts heroes, vils, police officers, and civilians alike."

The Professor pauses to let his words sink in.

"Are they... working together?" Sequoia asks, his voice saturated in confusion.

"For 16 years, it's always been heroes versus villains," Shine continues, "but we need to put that playbook aside, at least for now. We face a danger far greater than each other. Shadow is a threat to us all, and more importantly, he is a threat to the city we all call home."

What Shine doesn't say, but what we all know is that Shadow has made our city unsafe for tourists. Without them filling up our restaurants, our sidewalks, our bank, and even this museum, our city would grind to a halt. Their Loons feed our local economy and pay for the subsidies I rely on to make my university tuition and apartment rent affordable. Their presence makes the heists of villains believable, and their rescue turns our capes into heroes. We need people in Iconic Square. Shadow threatens our very way of life.

All around me, heads nod and voices murmur in approval. Lysee gazes up at Shine with clear worship in her eyes. Even I can't help but be swayed by his commanding presence. What he says is true. Shadow *is* a threat to us all. A realization hits me. Even if I quit as a henchman for The Professor, I wouldn't be safe from Shadow. He already blew up the restaurant where I worked when I was only a harmless waitress. What if his next target is Shield University or the pharmacy where Ollie works, or another tourist trolley filled with innocent people?

"What The Professor and I, and all the leaders on this stage propose is a truce," Shine says. "Hero and villain working together until Shadow is found and brought to justice."

"Or killed," Evil Santa bellows.

The mumbling around me is growing louder. Someone claps.

"Whoever takes down Shadow will either be the greatest hero the town has ever known or the most revered villain," Gold says, and he stares hungrily at the stage.

"Assuming they survive," Mermaid adds, but I can practically hear the circuits humming in her head. Even a lowly henchman or sidekick who brought down Shadow could easily use that victory to spin off.

"There is glory in this fight," Shine says as if recognizing the same thought coursing through everyone's minds. "And great ratings too." He earns a soft chuckle for this.

"The life of our city is on the line," The Professor says. "We cannot let Shadow cow us."

"Yeah!" Gold cries, ensuring he'll get a nice close-up on endless eps.

Other voices rise up around us. "Yeah!" "Yeah!" "Yes!"

"We cannot let him destroy our history and tradition!" Shine cries. He raises his fist in the air, and the other villains and heroes on the stage follow suit.

"Yeah!" the crowd cries.

"FOR JUSTICE!"

"Yeah!"

"FOR BIG LITTLE CITY!"

"Yeah!"

"FOR BEACON!"

"YEAH!" the crowd explodes into applause. As the roars of approval and stamping feet roll over me, something in my heart shifts. I've always hated Biggie LC and its population of ruthless strivers. But this is *my* town. These are *my* people. They are *my* family. They are Matthew and Lysee and Gerald, the man behind The Professor. They are Ollie, Adan, DeAngelo, and the sweet old lady who works at Culprit's Café and always reaches for the bear claw donuts before I even ask. My family is Reena Masterson, Lobo, the Elementals, the Dragon

Riders, Evil Santa, Beacon, and all the rest of the lobotomy Personas who drive me to distraction.

Shadow is threatening my people. My family. My town.

And suddenly I'm cheering with the rest. All thoughts of quitting The Professor's show are gone, or at least placed carefully in a temporary storage box. The mission to take down Shadow is bigger than one show, bigger than me. Shadow represents what we lost with the Castillo v. PAGS decision. He represents the new way of violence and destruction—the fake world bleeding over into the real one. He is the desert and the hovering cam drone that watched Alby's soul melt away.

My whole life I've wanted to come up with the ideas others could use to fix our broken world. But in this moment as Sequoia, Gold, Kitty, and Mermaid holler around me; as the Professor stands at Shine's side holding up his fist in solidarity with this incredible new truce, I realize that sometimes ideas aren't enough.

Sometimes you have to get your hands dirty and fix the problems yourself.

"We are all heroes today!" Shine hollers from the stage.

Sometimes you have to kill the shadows.

I raise my voice, giving my cry to the roaring, deafening cheers all around me.

*

THE VILLAINOUS ADVENTURE CONTINUES

Alice is determined to bring down the mysterious killer known as Shadow, but how much is she willing to sacrifice to make that happen? Can she be the hero her city needs, or does it take one villain to defeat another?

I'm hard at work to complete the third and final book in The Henchman's Survival Guide trilogy, HOW TO BECOME A HERO. Be the first to find out when it goes on pre-order by signing up for my mailing list.

Join my mailing list at:
https://www.subscribepage.com/d2x1w3

AUTHOR'S NOTE

Whew! The stakes are getting high for Alice and her compatriots, and it doesn't help that she's sleeping with the enemy (or is Adan really the enemy after all?). The villains and heroes of Biggie LC have forged a fragile peace, but how long will that last as the pressure mounts to keep ratings high and impress an ever-hungry audience?

It was a joy and a struggle to write the second book in The Henchman's Survival Guide series. One of the most challenging aspects of this story was to show Alice's slow (yet inevitable) descent into the dark and desperate Fame Game she's spent her whole life despising.

Alice may be the protagonist, but she's still a henchman. In this book, I wanted to show her darker side. The need to save her show (and her paycheck) forced her to make some pretty painful sacrifices. She pushed Ollie away, ignored Matthew who needed her more than ever, and humiliated and betrayed Lysee. She even hurt Sequoia in the process. At the end of it all, she found herself successful... and alone. The only person she could turn to for understanding was someone who's made sacrifices of his own. Adan. (Where is that steamy relationship going, I wonder?)

The challenge of Alice's character arc in this book was to show her edging over the line to the dark side while making her journey understandable. I have a confession to make. I've always been fascinated with villains, and some of my favorite characters are villains whom you can emphasize with. (Is it weird that I still kind of love Spike from *Buffy*?)

That's not to say Alice is going full villain. My goal is to show that she is just like the rest of us, a conflicted person struggling with difficult decisions. In her heart, Alice wants to do the right thing, but it's easy to start tiptoeing into life's gray areas when times get desperate and options dwindle away.

It's hard to know what any of us would do if we were backed into a corner (and fascinating to think about!). I love these types of questions and putting my characters in tight spots to watch them squirm.

And Alice has a lot more squirming to do.

Let's just say that Book 3 is going to be BIG.

Alice is going to have to decide if her heart is good or evil, if she will keep fighting the system or become a part of it.

Speaking of her heart... Things are getting hot and steamy with Adan, but is he just a friend with benefits or the only person who truly understands Alice? What about enigmatic Leo? His heart has a few dents in it, but something tells me his feelings for Alice are far more complicated than they seem. Then there's Sequoia, the gentle giant. Personally, I am so rooting for this guy, but Alice will need to forgive herself before she ever feels worthy of his love.

That's a lot to consider, and we're just getting started. What will become of The Professor, Alice's fellow henchmen, and Biggie LC? The world just got a lot more dangerous, and we all know Shadow won't go down without a fight.

I'm going to be completely honest. While I'm really excited to start tackling the third and final book in this trilogy, I'm also, well, terrified. I've written the outline, and this book is big. Explosive. Supernova. Big fights will go down. Relationships will crumble. New, unlikely partnerships will form. Blood will spill.

It's going to be a wild ride. And it's going to take a while to write. HOW TO DEFEAT A HERO came out way bigger than I anticipated (over 100,000 words!), and the next one... well, let's just say my fingers are going to be super buff after typing all those words.

So please be patient and soon enough, you'll get to read HOW TO BECOME A HERO.

Your quirky writer friend,

J Bennett

FOLLOW J BENNETT

Newsletter: https://www.subscribepage.com/d2x1w3

Instagram: https://www.instagram.com/jbennett-writes/

Facebook: https://www.facebook.com/jbennett-writes/

Website: https://jbennettwrites.com/

Blog: https://jbennettwrites.com/blog/

ALSO BY J BENNETT

Girl With Broken Wings Series

A gritty and darkly humorous paranormal adventure series about family, loss, redemption, and cool abilities.

Falling (Book 1)

Coping (Novella, 1.5)

Landing (Book 2)

Rising (Book 3)

Recovering (Novella, 3.5)

Leaping (Book 4)

Flying (Book 5)

Girl With Broken Wings Complete Box Set

Made in the USA
San Bernardino, CA
04 November 2019